THE GOOD LIFE

INSPECTOR MATT MINOGUE MYSTERIES

A Stone of the Heart

Unholy Ground

Kaddish in Dublin

All Souls

The Good Life

A Carra King

THE GOOD LIFE
AN INSPECTOR MATT MINOGUE MYSTERY

JOHN BRADY

STEERFORTH PRESS
SOUTH ROYALTON, VERMONT

First published in Canada by HarperCollins Publishers Ltd., 1994
First published in the United States of America by St. Martin's Press, 1995

For information about permission to reproduce
selections from this book, write to:
Steerforth Press L.C., P.O. Box 70,
South Royalton, Vermont 05068

Library of Congress Cataloging-in-Publication Data

Brady, John, 1955–
The good life : an Inspector Matt Minogue mystery / John Brady. — 1st
Steerforth ed.
p.   cm.
ISBN 1-58642-049-6 (alk. paper)
1. Minogue, Matt (Fictitious character) — Fiction.
2. Police — Ireland — Dublin — Fiction. 3. Dublin (Ireland) — Fiction.
4. Drug traffic — Fiction. I. Title.
PR6052.R2626 G66 2002
823'.914—dc21
2002007048

FIRST STEERFORTH EDITION

For my mother, Mary Brady.

The birth of both the species and of the individual are equally parts of the grand sequence of events, which our minds refuse to accept as the result of blind chance.

CHARLES DARWIN

Chapter 1

Gone to hell," Joey Byrne muttered. His wife was staring at the grass by the water's edge.

"What," she said.

He studied the broken glass and the flattened balls of tissue at his feet. He'd found another syringe here last week. The dog pulled against the leash and nosed into the long grass. Byrne let his eyes wander back to the neck of a bottle bobbing in the weeds. At least it hadn't been smashed here on the path. Four, no, five of those condoms today already too. Rings where they were unrolled. Out here by the banks of the canal, here in the middle of the city of Dublin, there were people putting on those things and going at it. Had they no shame?

He sighed and yanked on the leash. The dog lifted its leg. He turned to his wife.

"Come on now, Mary. We'll be off."

His wife of seventy-five rose slowly from the bench. He looked back up the canal. Away from the lock the canal's surface was a mirror. There were no swans this evening. The streetlamps were popping on one by one. God Almighty, he thought, the mess they'd made of Dublin. Poxy yellow lights like a jail, office blocks that belonged in the middle of Arizona. Mary was up at last. She moved stiffly to his side and grabbed his arm. He glanced down at her. The operation last year had aged her ten years. She'd never be back up to par. It had taken them twenty minutes to walk to the canal tonight. He knew because he had timed it.

"God, Joey, I'm stiff as a board."

He bit back the words that sprang to his lips. It wasn't her fault that she needed new hips. But was he himself stuck now, plodding along next to her for the rest of his life? He was seventy-six, by God, but he could leg it out with men half his age. He'd lose that too if he wasn't careful.

"What's the hurry, Joey?"

"Now, Timmy!"

No doubt about it: the Jack Russell was the best. You could throw your hat at the rest of them. There wouldn't be a rat alive within a mile of a Jack Russell's home.

"Joey! Easy there! I'm not as quick as I was."

Her hand tightened on his arm. He thought of the times they had made their way down these footpaths, along this stretch of the canal, in all weathers. Fifty years and more. There'd always been courting couples here but it had never been so sleazy, so dirty. He remembered the white rings of the condoms discarded by the path.

"Honestly. Do you ever see the swans here of a summer's evening anymore? Not on your life, I'm telling you. They're gone too. That's how smart they are. After eight o'clock, even the swans know the writing's on the bloody wall here. If only the other animals . . . Ah, what's the use."

She stopped and took a deep breath.

"Those things," she said. "The rubbers? Is that what you mean?"

He looked down at her. All this smut on the telly: safe sex, et cetera. Was she smiling?

"Do you have to talk like that? Do you?"

She clutched at his arm again. She was breathing hard when they gained the footpath. He looked back down at the water. Mary murmured something between wheezes. There was violet on the canal now. They'd waited until the evening so that the bloody traffic and noise was gone, so as they could take a simple walk down by the canal. Was that asking too much, not to have to put up with chancers coming by looking for a bit of how's-your-father? Drugs. Something stirred in his stomach and burrowed in behind his ribs. He'd seen them the other day too, with their skirts up around their backsides. Standing there smoking, staring back at him; sneering, bold as brass: brassers.

"Where are the Guards when you need them, I'd like to know. I think they've given up, that's what I think. They don't care, do they."

"What Guards?"

The Jack Russell strained at the leash again. He yanked on the strap. The dog stood on its hind legs.

"God and it's still so hot out," she said. She pulled on his arm. She was smiling, he saw.

"Joey. Remember you used to go for a swim here? You and Tom and Ernie and the lads. God be with the days. Do you remember?"

He hated her asking questions like that. He could still make out the mat of weeds and scum on the surface. The bark startled him. Timmy had moved between Mary and him. The terrier had planted his front paws on the stone anchors for the railings and was staring at the canal bank. He drew hard on the leash. The dog braced its legs and barked again.

"Now Timmy! Give over."

He tugged but the dog still pulled back. A rat, he thought. That's all they needed.

"Come on now, boy. Go after them another day. Come on."

A car raced past with a thumping sound pouring out its windows. Joey Byrne pulled the dog away from the railings. He didn't turn to his wife when he spoke.

"Come on, Mary, we'll be off home. Before the bloody vampires are out in force."

∙　　∙　　∙　　∙　　∙

The detective crouched and drew out a pistol.

"Oh, here we go," murmured Kilmartin. "Out comes the shooter. About time too."

The detective was a woman. She was dressed in dark clothes. She had chased the suspect who had shot her partner into a poorly lit alleyway.

"Here, Molly," said Kilmartin. "What do you think of that?"

Detective Thomas Malone cleared his throat.

"She's got all the moves," he said. "I think she's going to come out of it all right."

"Matt?"

"He's up behind that dumpster," said Minogue. The three policemen watched her inch her way along the wall of the alley, the pistol grasped upright in her hands. A police siren sounded in the middle distance.

"He is not," said Kilmartin. "It's too bloody obvious. Isn't it, Molly?"

Malone glanced at Minogue before answering.

{ 3 }

"She's probably better trained than we are," he said. "At going up alleys after drug dealers carrying guns, like."

She sprang away from the wall and took up a shooting stance behind the dumpster. Nothing.

"Told you," said Kilmartin. "He's done a bunk. Long gone."

"Oh, oh," said Minogue. Kilmartin strained to see what his friend and colleague Inspector Matthew Minogue had spied.

"On the ledge," said Malone. "He must have climbed up."

"He did on his arse climb up on any bloody ledge," snapped Kilmartin. "Sure wasn't he shot the once already? A fat lot of climbing . . . Oh, now I see him."

"She was never trained to look up, I think," said Minogue.

"Hoi," Kilmartin called out. "Look out up there — what's her name?"

"Karen," said Malone.

"Karen! Look up, for the love of God!"

A shot rang out. A figure fell from the darkness overhead and landed in the dumpster.

"Smooth bit of work there," said Kilmartin. "Into the bin with the bastard. Nice work, Karen. I thought your goose was cooked."

"It wasn't her plugged him," said Malone. Kilmartin eyed him under a raised eyebrow.

"That a fact now? Well, who was it, if it wasn't Karen herself?"

"There he is coming down the alley now."

"Wait a shagging minute," Kilmartin called out. "That's the partner who got shot, the fella risked his life to save her! What the hell is he doing there?"

"He was only winged," said Minogue. "He's obviously a tough nut. See the arm hanging off him there?"

Kilmartin shook his head.

"Well, seeing is believing, isn't it? I was sure he was a goner. Gave his all for the female rookie on the job. Karen."

"Are you okay?" Karen asked her partner. He hadn't shaved. He was undercover.

"I been better," he said, and grinned. She tapped him on his good shoulder.

"Hope she has the safety on," murmured Kilmartin. Malone picked up his glass.

"What's the story with the gouger in the bin," he said. A squad car came tearing down the alley. Minogue turned away when the ad for Guinness came on. Malone drained his glass and headed for the toilet. Kilmartin's face gleamed in the light of the television.

"What kind of weather is this," he grunted. "Day after day of tropical I-don't-know-what."

The three policemen were temporarily truant from a wedding reception for Detective Garda Seamus Hoey, a colleague of theirs on the Murder Squad. To the consternation of many, Hoey had taken a leave of absence several months ago and flown out to Botswana to be with his fiancée Áine. He had stayed for two months helping to build a medical center in the village where Áine had begun lay missionary work. Amoebic dysentery had floored Áine and Hoey had accompanied her back to Ireland. It had become doubtful whether she'd return to Botswana at all. Hoey had reported to the inspector that Áine had asked him to marry her. Minogue often wondered if Hoey had told Áine that he had halfheartedly tried to kill himself some months previous to his leave of absence.

That letter that Áine — a woman he hardly knew even yet — had written him from Botswana still puzzled Minogue. She had thanked the inspector for "all he had done for Seamus and myself." He took that to mean the bullying he'd done to get Hoey his job back on the Murder Squad.

Kilmartin examined the bottom of his glass. Minogue did not take the hint.

"I thought it was a joke at first," grunted Kilmartin. "Honest to God."

"The wedding?"

"Maybe. No, the messing with the drink, I meant. With the no drink, I should say."

"Not to put too fine a point on it now, but Shea's a recovering alcoholic."

"So the likes of me has to pour that stuff in the bowl into me gullet?"

"I don't know now, James. I rather enjoyed the punch myself."

"'Punch,' is it? Fairy piss. Turned me stomach, so it did."

Minogue looked around the pub. The tables were covered with empty glasses. A girl with yellow and pink hair, a tattoo of a snake on her shoulder, and a black tank top was looking at Kilmartin. The man next to her wore a half-dozen earrings. His head was shaved bald up to a topknot. Kilmartin returned the woman's stare for several moments.

"Welcome to civilization," he muttered. He waved to the barman and called for drinks. He rubbed his hands and fell to looking at the bottles on the shelves.

"Never been to a dry wedding in me life. Honest to God. Can't even spell Methodist. As for getting married in a registry office, well . . . At least Áine gave God a look in."

Minogue raised an eyebrow.

"I meant the few bits of things she said right after signing the forms," said Kilmartin. "The 'God is love' thing. Of course, she's deep enough into the religion and all. Missionary, of course. Stands to reason, doesn't it?"

He lowered his brow and squinted at Minogue.

"But you and I well know she'll have her work cut out for her with Hoey — sure he's a hairy pagan. Your influence, I might add. Oh well, love is blind."

Minogue eyed the chief inspector.

"'God is love,'" he said. "Right?"

"Good man," said Kilmartin. "You're getting the idea. There's hope for you yet."

"And 'Love is blind.' Right?"

"Well, in a manner of speaking."

"Then God is blind. Right?"

Kilmartin gave him a hard look.

"Depend on you to come up with that. You ignorant savage. Hey. That, ah, lump of rock thing you gave Hoey and Áine for a present? Don't get me wrong now. But, well, what the hell is it exactly?"

"It's a stone I took from the beach at Fanore. A friend of Iseult's did the work on it."

Kilmartin stopped rubbing his eyes and looked at Minogue with a pained expression.

"A stone. Okay. But what's it supposed to be?"

"Iseult's friend put the faces on it."

"Oh. Faces. Sorry."

"You're supposed to feel them with your fingers more than just see them."

Kilmartin's expression slid into one of happy disdain.

"Is it for the missus to feck at Hoey in their first scrap maybe? Here, do you know how much I paid for that bloody Waterford glass Hoey has on his mantelpiece from this happy day forward? Well, I'll tell you how much. Eighty-seven quid."

"A beautiful piece it is, James."

"You're not codding, it is. And what do I get? All Hoey had to do was say two simple words, two words normal people use: *cash bar*. Would that have been such a mortaller?"

The barman planted the drinks on the counter and looked to Kilmartin. The chief inspector took out his wallet with a show of great reluctance, eyeing Minogue all the while.

"A bit slow on the draw there, aren't you?"

Minogue shrugged and listened to the weatherwoman relating the prospects of another hot day tomorrow. Kilmartin glared at the barman and held out a tenner.

"Fella beside me's throwing money around here like a man with no arms." The barman grinned.

Kilmartin wiped his forehead with the back of his hand.

"Christ. Fallen among thieves, I have. With you, it's the short arms and the long pockets; with Hoey, it's the bloody Prohibition all over again. Place is gone to hell, that's all I can say."

Minogue swallowed more lager, placed the glass on the counter, and licked his lips.

"It's hard on him, Jim. Hard on Áine too. The drink is a curse."

Kilmartin grasped his pint of ale and gave Minogue a hard look.

"Huh. Married man now, by God, oh yes! 'Áine says this' and 'Áine says that.' Lah-dee-dah. More of the usual. Another good man out in the wind."

Kilmartin took a long draft and patted his stomach. Malone was chatting to a couple sitting at the far end of the bar.

"Will you look at that," muttered the chief inspector. "Molly will probably want the pint I just bought him delivered down the far end of the bloody bar."

"Maybe he doesn't want to be seen in public with two bogmen like us, Jim."

With careful deliberation, Kilmartin placed his glass on the counter and turned to face Minogue. The inspector looked away from the weather forecast and returned Kilmartin's stare.

"You're sailing a bit close to the wind with that one, mister. Yes, you! Oh, and the face on you like a goat pissing on a bed of nettles! Do you think for one minute that *I* want to be seen in public with the likes of a Dublin gurrier like Molly there? Do you think I wanted him on staff *at all?* What damage bloody Tynan didn't finish doing to the squad, you did. You and Sometimes shagging Earley."

Kilmartin grasped his glass, gave an angry flick of his head, and downed more ale. Minogue returned to the weather forecast in time to hear mention of high pressure remaining over Ireland.

John Tynan, the new Garda Commissioner, whose nickname Kilmartin had lately alternated between Monsignor and Iceman, had reorganized the Murder Squad and its parent Technical Bureau. Kilmartin had fought hard to preserve his fiefdom. Tynan had had several conditions for allowing Kilmartin to keep his squad intact. The chief inspector was to cut permanent staff numbers, and he was to set up an interview board for screening and interviewing applicants to the squad. With Seamus Hoey gone for a two-week honeymoon, and with court attendance and casework backlogged, Kilmartin had secured an extra position for this year, a "floater." He and Minogue and Sometimes Earley, an avuncular inspector from B Division rumored to be on the fast track to the top, had interviewed from a short list of applicants for that position.

Detective Garda Thomas Malone had been fourth in line. Minogue ascribed the detour in his nose and the close-cropped hair to what was listed in the file as "Sporting Interests": Tommy Malone was still ranked second in the Garda Boxing Club. A stocky Dubliner with postcard-blue eyes and a laconic manner that Minogue sensed was studied rather than natural, Malone had not been Kilmartin's favorite. Minogue still smiled in recollection of Kilmartin's aggressive questioning during the interview and the results it had brought him. Why was Malone's brother in jail, was Kilmartin's opener. He'd messed up, was Malone's reply. What experience did the candidate think he could bring to the squad? Malone had enumerated the record of service and commendations from his file in a tone that suggested to Minogue that he, Malone, knew that Kilmartin had read it. Kilmartin had pressed him again with the same question, altering it only by adding a *really* and giving Malone a deeper frown. Earley too had almost laughed out loud at the reply. Experience, Malone had replied after a calculated pause. Living with me brother, I suppose. Earley had had difficulty stifling a snigger.

Minogue's and Earley's combined votes had produced a black mood in Chief Inspector Kilmartin. Buying him three glasses of whiskey after the interviews hadn't much lightened it.

Part of Kilmartin's stock-in-trade was nicknames and he wasted no time in setting to work on Malone. "Molly Malone" was too easy, he liked to grumble. Kilmartin's atavistic disdain for Dubliners, their championing of trade unions, and their votes for the Labour Party at the expense of the rurally based populist carpetbagger party he, James Kilmartin, had supported all his life, gave birth to a nickname that Minogue thought had the most bite: "Voh' Lay-bah." Decades in Dublin had honed Kilmartin's mimic abilities and he could manage an accomplished delivery in the classic ponderous, nasal Dublin drawl. Malone seemed to be weathering Kilmartin's sarcasm well.

Kilmartin balanced his glass on his palm.

"Oh well, what the hell," he said at last. "Here's to Hoey. Whatever else you could say about Shea Hoey, he's no gom. He'll soon learn to put the foot down. Did you see where she keeps her own name and everything? What's the point, I'd like to know."

Minogue said nothing. He believed Áine's maiden name, Moriarty, was too good of a name to walk away from. Kilmartin lit a cigarette.

Minogue took another mouthful of lager. The chief inspector began tugging at the loose skin under his chin.

"Eighty-eight quid actually," he murmured. "That Waterford glass bowl I gave Hoey."

Malone made his way back to the two detectives just as the barman laid down another round of drinks. Kilmartin eyed Malone sorting a handful of change. He winked at Minogue as he called out to Malone.

"Hoi," he said. "What poor box did you rob to get that fistful there, Molly?"

Malone's eyebrows inched up but he kept counting.

·   ·   ·   ·   ·

He stepped on his cigarette and stared at the car. It wasn't just the heat, he knew, that made him feel that his chest was full of smoke. His hands were tingling too. The dryness in his mouth had spread to his throat. He might get forty for the leather jacket on the backseat. Probably a tenner for the Walkman. As for the bloody rackets and the bag, he hadn't a clue.

The driver had activated the alarm with the remote on his key ring. Tall type, hairdo, nice clothes. Tennis, et cetera. He'd probably gone to one of those snob schools where they played rugby. Daddy had bought Junior a car for his twenty-first. Not this model though: a GTI cost over fifteen grand. Junior must have gotten a job. Maybe he'd gotten the girl free with the car. How was it that rich people never looked ugly? He'd smelled perfume hanging in the air when he'd walked by the car the first time. He held up his watch and twisted it until he got enough light on it to read it. Five minutes to closing time in the pubs. He'd have to go soon or else forget it. Then he might have to do something stupid in broad daylight tomorrow to get back on track. Otherwise, it'd be shitsville. That had happened last week. He'd messed up by sleeping it out until nearly dinnertime. It had taken him until four o'clock to round up enough money to score. That was a day to forget: out there on the footpath boiling in the frigging sun all day, ready to grab people and throttle them until they dropped money in his hat. It wasn't like he was begging, for Christ's sake. He was an artist. It was art they'd be supporting. Jesus, people paid thousands for some painting to hang on a bloody wall.

He couldn't stop his mind wandering. He imagined a huge drawing of Jim Morrison, a crowd half a dozen thick swarming around him, all oohing and aahing. Purples, yellows — the spotlights, maybe even some lyrics on the top. Put in Jimi Hendrix floating there somewhere too. Bob Marley. A black angel. That was the stuff to get tourists coughing up dough. You never know who'd be walking by on the streets during the summer. Dublin had a name for talent in the music scene. Some big exec from a record company might spot it: hey, we gotta have this guy doing our covers! Or something with a message on it? Save the whales. Just say no. Ah, there were too many iijits out pretending to be real chalkies now. He really should try looking for a steady. If he had a steady number for a job, he could plan. Join a fitness club or something. Get some exercise. Then he could handle it cold turkey. Not that he actually had a habit or needed to worry. It'd be no sweat when the time came. All it took . . .

Something caught in his throat and he began coughing. The bloody city was full of dust and dirt. He looked up through the yellow light at the sky. Buildings going down, new ones being put up all over the place. His coughing began to ease and he looked across at the GTI again. Four cars back was the alley leading into a building site with a half-dozen ways out to other laneways and streets. The handles of the plastic bag holding the brick dug into his fingers. His fingertips had gone numb. He moved the bag to the other hand and swung it in short arcs. Its motion gave him strength. He imagined the car window shattering, a shower of glass in slow motion exploding around him. Ten minutes gone. He let two cars pass and stepped out into the street. He couldn't stop staring at the GTI now. It seemed to move, to float. He put his palm on his chest but his heart thumped harder.

"Deserved it," he murmured.

Mister GTI had been in such a bleeding hurry to get into the pub for last call that he'd parked in a stupid place. He was probably a wheeler-dealer who made money just picking up a phone. Maybe he played the stock market or something. He had holidays in Spain or the States, someplace where all the women have blonde hair and look like models. He looked over the roof of the car at the glass-sheathed building behind it. Christ, he thought, and shuddered. All glass: someone could see out but he couldn't see in. No, he thought then. It was dark outside. The lights in the building were on so you could see in and they couldn't . . . or was it? The glass held only the violet and yellow of the night street. Even the cleaners'd be gone home now.

He stepped out of the shadow. In the window opposite he saw himself sliding, misshapen and jerky, across its surface, the bag beside him. He felt a sudden rage at his own fear and his weakness. He really should try to get someone else in on these jobs, even if it meant splitting the take and having to do more. Was that perfume still hanging in the air? Leaking out of the bloody car. Bastards have everything they want. He swung the bag and turned as the weight pulled his arm up. The bag rose to its full height overhead, came down with a thump on the hatchback window, and fell through.

The car alarm shrieked. He yanked the bag out of the hole and swung again. It hit dead on. The hole in the glass was the size of a television screen now. The perfume coming out of the hole in the clouded window stung high up in his nose. He grabbed the leather jacket and threw it to the ground. His fingers scrabbled at the limit of his arm's reach for the Walkman. He leaned in until his feet came off the pavement. A camera too. Must have been under the coat. The alarm's shrieking seemed to be lighting up the whole street, knifing into his brain. The tennis rackets came out handy enough. He used one to tap out more glass. Headlights turned into the street. He scooped up the jacket, stuffed the Walkman and the camera into it, and held the rackets over the bundle. Someone shouted from far off as he entered the alley. It swallowed most of the alarm's shrieking. He kept going. This bit was a kick in itself. He was proud of how he could still run. The close, thick air rubbed against his face. He was grinning. The alarm began to fade behind him.

·　　·　　·　　·　　·

Minogue was massaging his feet in the kitchen when the beeper went off. He closed his eyes, rubbed his face, and swore before plucking it from his belt and clicking it off. It was half past one.

Kathleen tripped down the top of the stairs, her dress over her arm.

"Is that what I think it is?"

Minogue looked up from the pager.

"Yes, indeed."

He went upstairs and changed while Kathleen filled a plastic bag with a sandwich, a banana, two biscuits, and two tins of soda water. He picked up the beeper, looked again at the dot-matrix display flowing across the face, and plotted his shortest route to the canal. At least he'd travel in style. He reversed his new car, a Citroen with electric everything and the new-car smell as potent as ever, out onto the road. He yawned most of the journey to Donnybrook where he nicked a red light at fifty-five, slowed a little for the bend, and sped up again along Morehampton Road. He was awake and even alert in plenty of time to flout the no-right-turn at Leeson Street bridge. A satisfying rasp of tires came to him over the rush of night air in from the sunroof. He crossed Baggot Street bridge and parked under the trees where a small crowd stood. The yellow plastic cordon tape was up already.

Kilmartin was on him as he stepped out of the car.

"How's James. Long time no see."

Kilmartin yawned and peered in the window behind Minogue.

"Huh," he grunted. "Hard to miss that UFO of yours there. How do you figure out all those fecky-doo buttons on the dash there? Anyway. Looks like Molly beat us to it. Jeepers creepers, why'd we buy those beepers?"

Minogue saw that Malone already had gloves on.

"Howiya, Tommy," he said. "Long here?"

"Five minutes," replied Malone. Kilmartin nodded at the gloved hands.

"You didn't jump in for a swim and look already, did you, Molly?"

"No. I taped it off. Waiting for the lights. It's a woman. I called the Sub Aqua."

Kilmartin turned on his heel and made a slow examination of the street.

"Yeah," said Malone. He nodded at a couple sitting on a bench being interviewed by a Garda. The girl was shivering.

"That pair there. It was the girl saw her first. Green stuff on it, weeds and things."

Tings, thought Minogue. *Gree-an.*

"They better get married after that carry-on," Malone added. "He'd dropped the hand."

"What?" asked Kilmartin.

"He had his hand in her knickers when she saw it."

"Saw what?"

"The body." Malone had left just enough of a pause to suggest humor to Minogue.

"Was that all then?" asked the chief inspector.

"Hard to say. Might've gone the whole hog if she hadn't started screaming —"

"I didn't mean that!" barked Kilmartin. "I meant if she saw or heard anything in the bloody canal!"

Solemn-faced yet, Malone shook his head.

"I just had a few questions with them," he murmured. "Then I let what's-his-face get on with an interview. The uniform from Harcourt Street. Fallon."

Kilmartin looked up and down the banks. Streetlights played on the sluggish waters under the trees, themselves looming, black masses darker than the night sky. Minogue smelled beery breath from the gawkers. He looked at the banks and spotted small pieces of styrofoam, colored and slick things he took to be plastic bags. Kilmartin was talking.

"Why's there not more of her on the surface, I'd like to know." He grasped the railing leading up to the boards that formed the lock's footbridge.

"She drifted maybe," said Malone. "The hair got caught in the lock. Then the undercurrent pulled the feet and the legs in tight?"

Minogue noted Kilmartin's expression. Malone might well be right. A body in water often floated almost upright. Kilmartin was looking from light to light.

"Several lights out of commission," said Minogue. "It shouldn't be so dark here."

"Gurriers no doubt," Kilmartin grunted. "Pegging rocks at the streetlamps. Is this news? Dublin's fair city, my arse. Any sign of our crew yet?"

"Here they are now," said Minogue. Kilmartin looked over the other side of the lock-gate. A cascade of water arched from the brimming canal below his size twelve brogues and splattered far below. He turned back to Minogue and looked over his shoulder at the crowd.

"Get the lights up," he said to Malone. "Video. Pronto."

"Damn," Kilmartin went on. "Wouldn't you know it? I have to water the horse."

Minogue yawned as he made a quick survey of the scene, and then made his way through the crowd. Air thick with the smell of the canal seemed to settle in his lungs. There were about two dozen gawkers now. He searched the faces close to him. An intense light flared suddenly beside him before it shifted down over the water. He turned to find Paddy Dillon, a Cavan man known for wearing his tweed jacket every working day of the year. The cut of Dillon's jacket had become misshapen by his constant storage of batteries, clips, bolts, tapes, and tools. Dillon hefted the camera onto his shoulder.

"How's Paddy."

"Ah, Matt, me oul standby. Steady, boy. Struggling, but steady."

"Close again tonight, Paddy."

"Aye, surely!" Dillon's accent gave his voice a plaintive tone. "Close isn't it, now. It must be the weather we get for throwing in our lot with a united Europe. Oh, yes. I must say now that I can do without this degree of heat. Yes, I can."

Minogue gave Dillon's tweed jacket a lingering glance but Dillon was already absorbed in something else.

"Run up and down the banks first, Paddy. Anybody moves off from the crowd, get a good look, will you? We'll be on the prowl."

Malone led Dillon down the bank.

The quartz light turned the black water khaki. The hair was too blonde to be natural, Minogue thought. Just below the surface, the face and neck looked phosphorescent in the glare. The shoulders were covered. He began to move through the gawkers.

"What's the story here, Chief?" The query came from one of a trio of men in their twenties. All three bore the tired, blurry expressions of men who had been drinking.

"There's somebody under the water," said Minogue. "For an undue period of time, if you take my meaning. Has a Guard taken your names yet?"

"Jases, no! Sure I'm only walking by on me way to get a taxi. What would you, you know?"

Minogue had his notebook out.

"To be sure," he said. "But we have procedures, now. Naturally ye'd want to help."

The questions came automatically. Minogue knew the pub the men cited. He squinted at the three in turn while they spoke. The alarmed righteousness in their voices grated on him less because of its boozy earnestness than because it sounded exactly banal enough to be the truth. Instead of listening closely to the men, the inspector found himself following the canal back inland in his mind's eye. Fed from the River Shannon, it entered the city of Dublin channelled along by terraced houses and blocks of flats, past derelict warehouses and sheds. He thought of the grassy banks out by Crumlin, the skinny kids swimming by the locks years ago. Portobello, the pillars.

One of the men was getting agitated. He had remembered talking to the barman at exactly ten o'clock. Ten, wasn't it, Lar, he kept saying to one of the others. Ten, right? *Ruygh, Lar, waznit?* Kilmartin would goad Malone plenty if he heard a Dublin accent like that. Minogue told him to calm down. He didn't bother to ask him why he appeared so frantic to reassure a Guard.

Here in the south city center, the canal water idled in the shade of trees. The architectural glacier that had begun to grind through Dublin in the early sixties had left the city pitted with office buildings so ugly that they absorbed light and space from the streets they had been driven into. Many of the most ferociously insipid of those buildings had been deposited by the canal. Pockets of older houses still remained by its banks, however, and several times over the years the inspector had noted the glossy red doors and the restored brickwork, the Saabs and the freshly painted railings. Sunday supplement style or not, he commended people for wanting to live here by the canal. Along with the daily ebb and flow of office workers and cars, they had soaring rates of burglary and car theft to contend with for their troubles.

"... and then I switched to the rum and Cokes. That was at last call, right, Lar?"

Minogue eyed Lar, who gave him a tired smile and shrugged.

"So then we were sort of wondering where we'd go, you know? I was all on for getting a burger. Remember, Lar?"

Minogue scratched at his scalp with his pencil and stared out over the man's head into the shadows beyond the lock. He remembered stopping the car by the canal bank some weeks ago to eye a nearly completed block of apartments by Percy Place. Sharp, aggressive corners, he recalled; windows in odd places and green-shaded glass; a lot of industrial-looking metalwork. Within a mile of where he now stood, the canal emptied into the docks where the River Liffey met Dublin Bay. Few craft came inland through those locks any more. Barges that had ferried Guinness and turf were decades disappeared from the canal, and aside from the few pleasure craft, the trickle of passenger traffic on the canal came from sporadic efforts to restore barges enough to get a license to run cruise-and-booze trips between locks.

Episodic cleanups had dredged up disheartening and marvelous tons of scrap from the canal. A youth group had found a 1957 Triumph motorbike in the canal some years ago and restored it to working order. A badly rusted rifle thought to have been thrown in during the Civil War had been placed in the museum. More people decried the degradation of the canal year by year. Something would have to be done. Minogue noted the same words cropping up in the Letters to the Editor: architectural rape, heritage, dastardly. There had been a symposium on the rebirth of the canal system, proposals for strict controls on planning permission, keen talk of demolishing some of the grosser buildings, of a rebirth.

"So there we are," said Lar. "That's how we got here."

Minogue looked from face to face. They looked like schoolboys caught in a prank. One of them was swaying slightly. Someone stifled a belch. The inspector let his eyes linger on the one who appeared most drunk. Then he checked his notes by asking one of the men the same questions about what he had been drinking. He eyed Lar, their erstwhile leader. They weren't planning to drive home, were they? Christ, no — no way! Lar was very emphatic. His cohorts shook their heads a lot and murmured. Minogue checked their addresses and telephone numbers again. He eyed them again and let them go. He watched the lights playing on the surface of the water.

Minogue had walked the canal banks some weeks ago with his daughter, Iseult. It had been after a lunch when she had asked him some very odd questions about when he and Kathleen were courting. He had watched insects humming in the green light over the water while his daughter talked about her work. Lulled into a dreamy state by the lunch and the summer heat, he had fancied the stately passage of a barge as it glided by Pale towns and pastures of two hundred years ago. Over the low roar of traffic he even heard the ladies murmuring to one another under their parasols, the horse's soft clop on the towpath, the occasional calls of the bargee.

Minogue yawned and began to cast around for a ranking uniformed Guard. He caught sight of a sergeant. Callinan had a brother at HQ in the Park. He headed down the bank toward him and shook hands. Callinan, Dónal Callinan, tugged at his ear and shifted his weight. His gaze stayed on the banks while he listened to the inspector.

"Leave us a few lads to secure the site if you please, Dónal. Might as well start the others up along the banks now. We'll have the lights on proper in a few minutes, now."

Callinan nodded and plodded off. Minogue sought out Dillon.

"Parked cars too, Paddy. Both sides of the canal and the opposite side of the street."

Dillon wiped his brow again. Heat or concentration had made his tone querulous.

"Right ye be, Matt. God, it's dasprat hot."

Minogue eyed Dillon's jacket again.

"Give me a Polaroid, Paddy, will you? I want a few things here."

Dillon nodded toward the van. Another technician Minogue could see only in silhouette against the interior light was setting up tripods under the lamps.

Kilmartin coughed next to him.

"There they are," he said. Minogue turned and saw two vans from the Garda Sub Aqua unit reversing up the footpath. Kilmartin continued to adjust the sit of his trousers by standing on one leg and stretching out the other as he pulled at the waist.

"Man alive. Taking a leak behind a tree in the middle of Dublin. It's degrading. It was that bloody punch at Hoey's wedding, I'm telling you."

"Not the few pints and the small ones?"

"Shag off. Get a real job. Away we go, now. Are we right?"

Minogue winked at Malone and followed Kilmartin under the tape.

{ 17 }

Kilmartin sat down heavily on the bench, tore off the plastic gloves, and lit a cigarette.

"The hair's caught all right. Give the frogmen another minute."

The smoke from Kilmartin's cigarette rose and was caught in the glare of the lights.

"Damn," he muttered. "This'll shape up to be a right pain. Between the bloody water and the filth all up and down here . . . Hope to God we nail an admission or bulletproof evidence well away from this kip. We're sunk if we have to rely on site evidence here, man."

Malone stepped up the bank, shielding his eyes from the glare around the lock.

"Hoi, Molly. Any breakthroughs on the case yet?"

Malone's face didn't register the jibe. The gawkers had thinned down to a half-dozen. There were uniformed Guards from Donnybrook and Harcourt Street up and down the banks now. Feeney, a doctor on the coroner's panel, was sitting in his car reading by the interior light, his legs out the door. He had wire-rimmed glasses with a tint and styled hair, something Minogue regarded as flagrant vanity in a man trying to walk away backward from fifty.

"Got ahold of the lockkeeper," said Malone. "Says the lock hasn't been opened since the day before yesterday."

"Unnk," said Kilmartin. He cleared his throat. A frogman surfaced and grasped a rail by the lock. The slick black head gleamed and the goggles flashed as he shook his head.

"Can hardly see a bleeding thing down there," said Malone. "Even with the lights."

He had already relayed the frogman's description to Missing Persons, Minogue knew.

"Well," said Kilmartin. "Have to get her out. Let's decide."

"Open the lock a few inches, I say," said Minogue. "Let her out slow."

"Why not cut the hair?" asked Kilmartin. "And not risk flushing evidence down?"

Minogue didn't know. He wished Hoey were here.

"We could secure her and open the gates a bit," said Malone. "Pull her back then, like."

"'Loike,'" said Kilmartin. He alone smiled. Malone kept looking at the frogman's head.

"All right," said Kilmartin then. "Best idea I've heard yet. Go tell 'em to set it up."

Minogue checked with Callinan. Still no shoes or handbag. Both officers watched Malone take the rope from the diver's hand. Callinan scratched his armpit.

"Yiz are going to pull her out, is it," he said.

"Send yours down to the bridge. See if anything goes through when we open it."

Callinan joined the dozen Guards in shirtsleeves gathered by the lock. They stood shoulder to shoulder with the gawkers who remained, watching as the lockkeeper, a middle-aged man with no neck, white hair, and a black mustache that had strained plenty of drink earlier in the night, readied the boom. The frogmen surfaced and moved to the bank. The stink they drew out of the waters wafted across to Minogue. Kilmartin and Malone stood next to the anchor of the railings where the nylon rope was tied. Malone signaled to the lockkeeper, who pushed at the boom. Water began to spout, then to gush through the gap. The body stirred and drifted against the wood. Over the cascading water Minogue heard a low moan from the bystanders. It stopped abruptly when someone shouted. The shout had come from one of the frogmen. He donned his mask, chewed onto the mouthpiece and slid into the water with the pink safety rope trailing behind. The hair seemed to be sinking. Minogue stepped over to Kilmartin and looked at the rope tied to the body. It had grown slack.

"Bollocks," said Malone. "Have we lost her?"

Kilmartin laid a hand on Malone's arm and snorted.

Clearer as it ascended, the three policemen saw the blonde head appear, then the dark clothing Minogue took to be a blouse. A hand. A Guard hurriedly blessed himself. Malone began pulling on the rope. A blood vessel stood out on his neck. Then he relaxed.

"Close it up again!" Kilmartin called out. "She's free."

CHAPTER 2

Dillon was sitting in the passenger seat of the van taping labels onto videocassettes. Minogue's back ached now. He looked back at the white boiler suits by the water's edge, the torch beams wavering in the weeds.

"Anything yet?" Dillon asked.

"No, Paddy. We've sent the prints off."

"Looks to me that she wasn't long in it."

"Do you think."

"A few hours."

"Is the side of her face clear on the tape you took?"

Dillon nodded.

"Hell of a belt and that's no lie, Matt. She bruised. Died in the water too, I'll bet you."

Minogue returned to where Kilmartin and Malone were crouched. The woman's body had been cradled in the water-stretcher and hoisted onto the bank. The Sub Aqua team had left the water a half hour ago. They sat in their van waiting for Kilmartin to decide. The chief inspector stood up and took a deep breath. He unrolled the gloves, picking at the tips where they clung, and frowned into the lights trained on the water.

"No match to any recent call-ins?"

"No. They've started into Missing Persons."

"Christ. Let's see what Feeney makes of her now. We'll let her go then."

"Do we give the Sub Aqua mob the billy to leave, like?" asked Malone. Minogue saw the chief inspector's lip curl a little. The Sub Aqua squad would never have asked Kilmartin himself.

"Yes, indeedy, Molly. They're done with. Is Feeney ready to sign her over?"

Dr. Feeney stepped out of his car with a clipboard under his arm. He looked down the form.

"Body temperature . . . color . . . well, she's not dead more than six hours. A good look at the tissue on the table will tidy up that, but I'm pretty sure."

Kilmartin raised an eyebrow.

"Anything you can make of the big bruise on the side of her face?"

"She was hit," said Feeney. "I wouldn't be surprised if her cheekbone's fractured. I didn't look at her teeth. Somebody, something big walloped her. The skin's not split."

"Her head rapped off a wall maybe?" asked Malone. Feeney blinked.

"A reasonable guess, er . . ."

"Garda Malone," said Kilmartin. "Molly Malone, loike."

Feeney's grin fell away when he looked from Kilmartin to Malone's face. "Best I can do," he said. "Leave it for the PM now."

The three detectives watched as the body was carried to the van.

"Typed up, for the love of God," said Kilmartin to Callinan. "And photocopies of the lads' books. One of us will phone in the morning."

"Okay," said Callinan. "Yiz have your work cut out for you here by the look of things."

The van door slammed. Kilmartin's gaze lingered on Malone.

"Well, I don't know now," he said to Callinan. "We have one solid lead here."

Callinan scratched under his arm again. "The trade here by the canal, like?"

"It's relating to the perpendicular parking all right," said Kilmartin. "She's definitely not from Dublin."

Callinan stopped scratching and eyed Minogue for a clue. Kilmartin's eyes were wide but he wasn't smiling.

"Didn't spot it? Easy enough, I'd have thought. No? She had her knickers on."

A startled look came to Callinan's face. Malone looked down at his shoes. Kilmartin trudged off toward the lock again. Minogue followed him.

"Jimmy. Give over with the digs."

"What digs?"

"It's not the best time for Tommy to appreciate your, er, sense of humor."
Kilmartin gave his colleague a hard look.

"That a fact now? He acts like he knows it all. The gloves on, the site taped up before we even get there. Calling in the frogmen. Walking around with the phone in his pocket. Cock of the walk."

"So he's keen, Jimmy."

"Keen? He's a gurrier is what he is. Hairstyle cop. Television, et cetera. Where does he think he is, L.A., is it?"

"Just for the record —"

"Record — hah! It's his brother has the record, isn't it? Assault, three convictions — starting from the age of fourteen. B-and-E list the length of the Naas Road. The brother's a druggie —"

"You've done a lot of homework on the brother, I can see."

"A damn sight more than you have, and you handing Molly the frigging job! Ever hear the word genes?"

"Is he his brother's keeper?" Kilmartin snorted and lit a cigarette.

"Oh, very slick one there. Very slick, to be sure. Say a decade of the rosary while you're at it. Have you heard of heredity? How come one's a Guard and the other's a gouger?"

"Give him a chance at least, Jim. A fair trial, then you can hang him." Kilmartin pursed his lips. His eyelids drooped a little.

"There was a time when no one looked twice at the squad, mister. I hired, I sired, I fired. It's your mate, Mr. Refrigerator Tynan, left this bloody bomb behind him, the way he wanted the hiring done. He had me over a barrel, by God."

"Look, Jim. Something has to give here with this. If it's you and Tommy Malone together on this, there'll be —"

"Skin and hair flying. I know, I know. It's the heat. It's his gurrier accent. It's —"

"Let me put him through this one then. Himself and myself. I'll show him the ropes."

Kilmartin studied the lights playing on the water.

"Well?" Minogue asked.

"Well, all right. Better your rope than the one I'd like for him probably. Me and John Murtagh'll hold down the back line then. I'll pull him off the reviews. John can do the desk and feed us what comes in on the hoof from the teams. You and Molly can sweat it out here. Maybe being a Dublin jackeen might help on this one. Oh, yes."

Minogue caught up with Malone.

"It's you and me from here on, Tommy."

"You mean it's your turn to pick a row with me, is that it?"

Minogue stared at him.

"Sorry. It wasn't you at all. It's you-know-who."

"James is from the County Mayo, remember. They were hard hit during the Famine."

"So what's his gig then, the Killer? Is he a shagging cannibal or something?"

"He wants you to prove yourself," said Minogue. "Education by provocation."

Malone frowned.

"Okay," he said.

"Go home, can't you," said Minogue. "I'll close up shop. It'll take a few hours at least for the prints search. First thing in the morning we call a meeting to get everyone on board and go over what we have. Unless we get something coming up in between."

The inspector watched the Sub Aqua van inch down off the footpath above the bank. The driver raised a hand from the window as he drove off.

"We should have a preliminary with a cause of death by dinnertime. A bag or something might turn up in the daylight tomorrow. Might get a call come in from someone worried about her. We really need a name to get going in earnest here."

•   •   •   •   •

It took Minogue a few moments to realize that there was no point looking for his jacket on the seat: he hadn't brought one. Why bother with a jacket if it was going to be another day like yesterday? He remembered the feeling of being incomplete and the sense of freedom when he had backed out of the driveway. It was a quarter to nine. The heat wave hadn't abated. He was dopey. That yellow, metallic tint in the sky he'd noted on his drive through Ranelagh was something he associated with the end of a hot summer's day here in Dublin, not the morning. As he penetrated through to the city center, it seemed to him that the streets and even the buildings had changed colors in a subtle way his eye registered but his brain couldn't confirm. A cement lorry trapped him for several minutes by a building site. Dust in the air seemed to vibrate with the thumping of pneumatic drills. Through an opening in the hoardings he spied foundations of yet another office building. His back was wet when he stepped out of the Citroen in the car park.

"Ah. Éilis. *Lá brea brothollach.*"

She spared him a smile for his recollection of the clichés beaten into generations of students by schoolteachers exacting essays in Irish.

". . . *ag scoilteagh no gcloc le teas,*" she sighed. She retrieved her cigarette from the ashtray and reached for a file next to a snow-dome souvenir of Lourdes on the top shelf behind her.

"Your business by the canal last night. Mary Mullen. She has a record. Had, I meant to say."

Minogue opened the file and slid out the photocopies, a summary from the CRO.

"May your shadow never grow less, Éilis."

He looked at Mary Mullen's face. Four years ago: Mary Frances Mullen, eighteen. Twenty-two and a half when she was killed. She hadn't been at all pleased to have her picture taken. Kilmartin had guessed right. Three arrests in one year for soliciting. Either she had quit then or she had smartened up enough to avoid getting caught again. The first arrest listed her occupation as hairdresser at Casuals, South Great Georges Street. The second and third listed her as unemployed. On her third conviction, Mary Mullen had been committed to the women's wing of Mountjoy prison. There she'd served two months of a three-month sentence. Minogue skipped through the file. Under Associates, he read "Egans?" Mary Mullen had not been cooperative. No admission of pimp, friends, associates. An arresting Guard had annotated in pen: "v. defiant and uncooperative; bad language, etc." What had he expected, Minogue wondered.

Tommy Malone appeared by his desk.

"Here we go, Tommy. Mary Mullen. Last known address was in Crumlin."

"Never saw heat like it," moaned Kilmartin from the doorway. "Saw an ad today for one of those air-conditioner jobs to fit the window. I'm putting me name in for one."

The chief inspector's leather soles scraped and squeaked their way closer. Minogue didn't look up. He finished copying the address and reached for the telephone book.

"Mary Mullen," said the chief inspector.

"Nothing new in from the scene?" Minogue murmured. "Bag?"

Kilmartin shook his head.

"And don't hold your breath on that either. See who's in that file? Egans."

"Gangsters, racketeers, and thugs limited," said Minogue. "Or unlimited, I should say."

"But that file's static for over three years. I phoned Doyler in the whore squad. Left a message to look up any material they have to update us."

Minogue looked up from the file.

"Did you ever get your hair done at a place called Casuals? The bit you have left, I mean."

Kilmartin tugged at the end of his nose.

"Is this one of those knock-knock jokes or something?"

"A hairdresser's."

"Are you blind, man? Short back and sides since Adam was a boy. Yes, siree, as nature intended. Grass doesn't grow on a busy street anyway, mister. Casuals, huh? Sounds like a front office for a bit of you-know-what. Phone-a-whore, et cetera. Modern times, pal. Right there, Molly?"

Minogue glared at the chief inspector. Foe and accomplice both, Kilmartin could well turn out to be right in his guess. No Casuals in the current Dublin area telephone book. No Mullen in St. Lawrence O'Toole Villas in Crumlin either. Minogue clapped the phone book shut.

"Well?"

"Gone since the last book, or else there's no phone in the house."

"Phone Crumlin station. What's his name is the nabob since the Christmas. Mick Fitzpatrick. Yep. Nice fella is Fitz. Temper though. Fitz and Starts we used to call him years ago. Oh, but don't you call him that or he'll rear up on you. Tell him I was asking for him."

Minogue looked at the papers again. Irene Mullen, the mother.

"We'll go out and have a quick look first ourselves," he said. "It's only ten minutes up the road."

Kilmartin laid his jacket on a chair.

"Course you have Tonto here to translate for you."

Minogue closed one eye and squinted at Kilmartin. The chief inspector beamed back. Minogue grabbed his notebook, rapped it once on the desk, and headed for the car park.

．　　．　　．　　．　　．

Everything still seemed too bright and too slow. He could almost hear his eyelids closing and opening. He wasn't hungry, but he knew he should make the effort. He made his way around the bus queues along Abbey Street and slipped down the lane toward the back door of the pool hall. Thirty lousy quid for the leather jacket that O'Connell knew cost two hundred in the shops. Bastard. The look that told him he knew it was the lowest price he could throw at him without making him walk off. The camera was a surprise. He'd said forty and gotten thirty. He'd kept the Walkman but the batteries had run out.

It took him a count of seven before he could see anything beyond the lights over the pool tables. All he could make out were the figures moving, the smoke. James Tierney's closely cropped head appeared in the glare over one table. He leaned in again to cue the shot.

"Howiya, Jammy, how's it going, man?"

James Tierney dropped the cue with a sigh, closed his eyes and then regrouped to line up the cue again.

"Get lost, Leonardo," he murmured.

The cue darted, the white knocked the red hard against the mat and into the corner pocket. By the time the red clicked among the other balls in the pocket, the white was still.

"Ace, Jammy! Brilliant, man! Fucking *ace!*"

Jammy Tierney stood up out of the light. Another man stepped forward. The balls on the table were mirrored in his glasses. Tierney stared at the table and chalked his tip.

"I'm in a game," he said.

"Sorry, Jammy. Sorry, man. I just thought I'd, you know . . ."

"Take a fucking walk."

"Yeah, right. It's okay! Sorry. I'll wait outside like, you know. No problem."

For the next twenty minutes he walked from the front door of the pool hall down the lane to the back. He thought often of sneaking back in and watching somewhere he wouldn't be noticed. He imagined the perfect shot, the ball dropping into the pocket, the money changing hands. If he was Jammy Tierney, he'd be doing better than this dive. He'd be at it night and day until he got to the big time. He stopped by the back door again. What if Jammy was giving him the brush-off and was going to leave by the front? He took a step up toward the open door but stopped when he remembered Jammy's face. He jogged to the front of the building in time to see the guy with the glasses leaving.

The gloom of the pool room seemed to have deepened. Tierney was setting up the balls. A skinny, hippy type was chalking his cue.

"Hey, how did you do, Jammy?"

Tierney jerked his head up.

"What are you doing back here? I thought I told you to get lost, didn't I?"

"I heard you, Jammy. Yeah, and I left. I seen the other fella go, so . . ."

Tierney took a step back and looked him up and down.

"Even in here I can see how wasted you are. The state of you. You're sweating."

"It's a heat wave, man."

"Oh yeah? Look in a mirror, Leonardo. You're a mess."

"Looks aren't everything, Jammy, man. Come on, man. I just came by to talk to you for a minute."

" 'Talk to you'? Sure you're not sussing out the place to see if you can do some dealing to the kids in here? Because if you are, I'll burst you."

"I just wanted to say hello. Is that such a big crime these days?"

"What are you into now, Leonardo? You graduated to the hard stuff?"

"No way!"

"Here, let me see your arms. Yeah, you're with a jacket and it's like the Sahara. C'mere!"

He pushed Tierney's hand away.

"Don't start with me, Jammy."

Tierney laughed.

"Or what? What'll you do, Leonardo? Faint on me?"

"All I wanted was to say hello and that."

He looked back into Tierney's face and took in his scorn. They were the same age. They had been friends since the first day they had started primary school together.

"Did you get a job?"

"I do a bit of this and that. They're going to cut down me rock-and-roll. They found out I was living at home, you know?"

"And you've given up completely on the drawings and stuff, right?"

"No way! Well, not exactly. I go out some days with me stuff."

"I never see you out there. I haven't seen you for months. Anywhere."

"Well, I'm trying to stake out new places, amn't I? I don't like to just do the one spot all the time, you know. That's not how the art business works, Jammy."

"The art business. That's what you're calling chalk drawings on the frigging footpath, is it?"

Tierney folded his arms. The tattoo of the snake and the guitar swelled out from his upper arm.

"It's the summer, man. There are millions of chalkies out there. Jesus! Foreigners even. Every street corner. What am I supposed to do, have a barney right there in the street with every single one of them so's I can have a good spot to show me stuff?"

"Let me guess. You want me to stand there with you and collect money for you."

"I can look after myself, so I can."

"What, then? You came by to talk about the bleeding weather?"

"I want to get on with someone, Jammy. You know."

The shadows dug deeper into Tierney's forehead.

"What," he said.

"You know. Get something going. A future. Show what I can do."

"Show who?"

"The Egans."

Tierney continued to stare at him but his eyes had slipped out of focus.

"The Egans? You are a header. 'The Egans' he says. Like he really means it."

"Don't give me that look, Jammy. Come on! I done stuff!"

"Crack, you mean. Speed."

"You're not even giving me a chance, man."

"Chance at what? Here, let me tell you something. Nothing personal now."

He leaned in close to whisper.

"You're a total waster. Okay? You're out of your box."

"All I'm saying is maybe you can put me in touch with people."

"'People'?"

"Everyone knows you're clean, Jammy. They respect that, man. But the lads in here: you know them, they know you. Fellas come through here every day of the week. Some of them are in the line of what I'm talking about."

"Listen, man. Get this through your head: I'm clean. Like I always been. Like you used to slag me about. I play an odd game here and that's it."

"Don't get me wrong, man! I'm not asking you to get in on something you wouldn't want to. Really, Jammy! I swear. All I'm saying is maybe you could put in a word for me. Only me, like. Not you. I've been thinking, right? I want to settle down, don't I. Get a start and do things right. You know, move in with someone."

"Who's the lucky someone?"

"Mary, maybe."

The scorn left Tierney's face.

"Mary? Mary Mullen?"

"Well, yeah. Maybe you wouldn't understand."

Tierney blinked and looked away to the end of the hall.

"Come on, Jammy! You could get me in the door at least."

"I don't work for the Egans. I mind me own business. So should you. Fucking iijit."

"It's not just them, Jammy! You know people. People coming through here, like."

"Get the message, man."

"I'm good at stuff, Jammy! I am!"

Tierney's eyes bored into his now.

"What the hell are you so good at that the likes of the Egans would want you for? 'Pavement Artist: Leonardo Hickey. Specializing in chalk, and getting high.'"

"I can do cars steady, Jammy. I'm good at it. Regular fence. I do a bit every night now."

"Oh, that's brilliant, man," said Tierney. "Just ace. Oh, yeah. Christ. I'm out of here."

He walked alongside Tierney.

"And I can drive. Aw, man, you know I can do that." Tierney didn't slow his pace.

"You're about ten years too old to be still joyriding. Get smart, Leonardo. Fuck's sake."

He rapped Tierney's shoulder as they stepped out onto the footpath. Tierney whirled around, his face twisted in anger.

"Don't do that, man! Don't fucking touch me!"

"Sorry. It's just that . . . you know."

"It's not like it was! Never!"

"I said I was sorry, didn't I?"

"You never listened to me, did you? Ever. I told you to stay away from that stuff. To look out for yourself, you know. And now look . . . Jesus, you were the best soccer player all the way through school. You could have —"

"I still can, Jammy! You should see me, man!"

Tierney's eyes rested on the far end of the street now.

"Yeah, right, man. Sure. But you're running in the wrong direction."

"What the hell is that supposed to mean? It's easy to judge people, isn't it? Oh, yeah. So easy." Tierney turned to him.

"Look, Leonardo. I don't know if you really listen to anyone. Get this through your head: Nobody trusts a junkie."

"I'm not a fucking junkie, Jammy. Don't call me that."

"Oh, yeah? You could quit cold turkey any time, right? Sure, man. Prove it. Sort yourself out and maybe someone might take you seriously."

"They take Mary seriously and you know what she does —"

Tierney suddenly jabbed him hard in the chest.

"Shut up, man! I can just about put up with you lying about yourself but —"

"I was only saying that she gets to do —"

Tierney grasped his collar and twisted it.

"I don't want to hear it, you lying bastard."

Tierney shoved him away.

"I can do it, Jammy. Whatever it is. Swear to God."

Tierney looked into the startled eyes again.

"What the hell are you talking about? Do what?"

"Whatever it takes, Jammy. I'm good! I've done stuff. Tell them, okay? Will you?"

CHAPTER 3

MINOGUE'S BACK WAS PRICKLY. A cyclist wearing only shorts and runners and a Walkman dawdled by their parked car.

"181," said Malone. Minogue looked at the flowers and the fresh paint. A dozen feet of brown lawn ran from the low pebble-dash wall to the house. Neighbors to one side of 181 had begun what might have looked like a rockery had they not lost interest. A Hi-Ace van squatted on cement blocks at the far end of the street.

Music with a disco beat sounded against the door. Minogue knocked harder. The chain pulled tight as the door opened. A woman with tied-up hair and sharp black lines on her eyebrows peered out. He pegged her for forty, for someone who didn't like that one bit, for someone willing to fight it tooth and nail. She gave him a once-over and looked to Malone behind.

"The windows, is it?"

"No, ma'am. I'm looking for a Mrs. Irene Mullen."

"No. No Irene Mullen here."

She had said it too brashly for Minogue not to notice.

"Aren't yous the Corpo come to fix the windows? I called them a fortnight ago."

Her eyes kept moving from Minogue to Malone and back.

"Do you know a Mrs. Mullen?"

"Who's asking?"

"Sorry. My name is Minogue. I'm a Guard. Matt Minogue."

"That so? Where's your ID."

She barely looked at the photocard. Her eyes narrowed.

"I'm here about Mary Mullen." He fixed her with a glare. "She's the daughter, you know."

"You're wasting your time then, aren't you? She doesn't live here."

"This is her last known address. There was no phone number. We drove out to check."

The sun was on his bald spot now.

"Well, now you know," she said, and closed the door. He strolled back to the car and leaned against it. Two youths emerged from a house up the street. They took their time walking toward the two policemen. Malone watched them, scratching his forearm.

"She's trying to put one by us," he murmured.

The youths stopped by a wall in front of one of the houses, lit cigarettes, and stared at the policemen. A motorbike cruised by, turned around, and stopped. The driver kicked out the stand, switched off the engine, and stood next to the two by the wall.

"I wonder if our timing mightn't be a bit off," said Minogue. "We could come back with a posse, I reckon."

A Post van appeared at the top of the road. Minogue saw the curtains in the upper floor of the house stir. He waved the van down. The driver was a middle-aged man with heavy jowls and a cigarette burning close to his knuckles. Beads of sweat high up on the driver's forehead competed with a face full of large scattered freckles for the inspector's attention. Minogue's eyes kept wandering to the wiry tufts of ginger hair sticking out over the man's ears. He held up his card to the open window.

"Howiya there now. I'm a Guard and I'm looking for someone."

The driver returned his hand to the gear shift.

"Well, good for you, pal. I'm not."

"No — wait, I mean. It's not the way it sounds. There's been a death in the family. I'm trying to locate next of kin for someone."

The driver thumbed his chin. The cigarette stayed in place against his knuckles.

"Yeah?"

Minogue's eye went from the skeptical Dubliner behind the wheel back to the three youths. The man had taken him for a Guard trying to pin a warrant on someone.

"I was looking for a Mullen, Irene Mullen. I don't know about a Mister Mullen, just her. She was here four years ago."

The driver stared down into the wheel well by the passenger seat and then back at Minogue.

"One of her family?"

"I'm afraid so. Do you know her?"

The eyes darted to the house Minogue had just left and he nodded once.

"She said there was no one by that name there."

"Who was it?" His hand moved the gear shift slowly from side to side in neutral.

"I don't know who she is or says she is —"

"I mean the person what's dead."

"Well now, we'd prefer to pass the news on to the next of kin first."

The hand stopped abruptly and the driver's face set into a hard expression.

"Get a bit of cop on, for Christ's sake," he said.

Minogue took a step back from the van.

"Don't you get it? I'm taking a chance here just talking to you. I'm the only one that comes through here now, Chief. You won't even get the Corpo repairmen or the gas and meter fellas without an escort. The people here know me, man. Do you get it? I just deliver letters here like I done this last twenty-three years. I know me onions."

"What are you saying?"

He jerked the ignition off and opened the door.

"Don't they speak English down in Cork?"

"Clare. And I'm here thirty years if you need to be asking."

The driver was nearly a foot shorter than Minogue.

"Let me tell you something, Chief. One year here is longer than thirty of yours."

He shoved his fingers of his left hand in his mouth and whistled. The sound, a skill Minogue assumed was specific only to Dublin corner-boys, was piercing.

"Oi!" the driver called out. "Crunchie! Oi!"

The motorcyclist stood away from his bike and lifted his helmet. His face was a rash of acne. He shook out his hair as he walked over. The Post driver spoke with him and then walked to the door of the house. Crunchie winked at Malone and sat back on his motorbike. Malone nodded once. Minogue joined him by the side of the car. A half-dozen youths, two of them girls, had materialized out of nowhere. Minogue saw faces at some windows, curtains being moved.

{ 33 }

"I think we're all right," said Malone. The postman stepped into the house and closed the door behind him. Crunchie strolled over to the van.

"Oi," he said to someone Minogue couldn't see. "Get away from the bloody van there!" Two teenagers skipped away from behind the van. Crunchie walked around the van and looked at the two policemen.

"What are you looking at," he said to Malone. The detective returned his stare.

"Not much, by the look of things."

"What's that supposed to mean?"

Minogue nudged Malone. The door opened. Minogue took in the fright on the woman's face. She came slowly down to the wall and folded her arms.

"I'd as soon not discuss anything out here now," Minogue said to her. The van driver came down the step and worked his way around her.

"Thanks, Joe," she said. She turned back to Minogue.

"You're not coming into my house. No way. That was a promise I made to myself. Yous weren't there when yous were wanted, years ago."

"Mrs. Mullen?"

"My name isn't Mullen. I have me own name back now. What do you want?"

What Minogue wanted was a phone to check the PM time with Éilis. If this woman was the mother, she'd have to identify the body.

"It's Mary, isn't it," she said, and bit her lip.

"Your daughter?"

She nodded and her jaw quivered.

"Something's happened to her, hasn't it?"

Her voice seemed to be trapped in her throat.

"It's bad, isn't it?"

"I'm very sorry but . . ."

She grasped at her face and turned away. The inspector stepped forward.

"Oh, my God," he heard her gasp. "Oh, my Jesus. Oh, my sweet Jesus."

"Have you people in the house?" Minogue asked. "I think we should maybe go in and sit down for a minute."

"Kevin," she yelled. Her voice was ragged now. "Kevin!" One of the group walked over.

"Get your mother, Kevin. And hurry up with you!"

Malone parked behind an ambulance. Minogue rolled out of his seat and opened the back passenger door. Irene Lawlor made no move to get out. She sat there with the door open, staring down at her hands. Malone looked across the roof at Minogue. Irene Lawlor had said little in the car on the trip over. She had rebuffed most of Minogue's queries with a stare fixed on the roadway by her window. Her companion, a Mrs. Molloy, had big eyes and what looked like goiter. She'd chain-smoked and murmured to Irene Lawlor all the way into the city center. Whatever she'd said had had no noticeable effect. Irene Lawlor's glassy stare remained.

Mrs. Molloy walked around the back of the car and leaned in. Minogue saw the red lines of the car seat impressed on the back of her thighs where her miniskirt had been creased. He stepped back and Mrs. Molloy pulled Irene Lawlor out. She walked in a crouch, as if trying to recover from a punch to the stomach. She entered the hospital, her arms wrapped around her waist.

Murtagh met them inside the front door. He fell into step beside Minogue.

"Any word, John? Bag? Witness?"

Murtagh shook his head.

"They wanted to start the PM in half an hour. Which one's the mother?"

Minogue glanced back at the two women.

"On the left. Can't read her much yet."

Minogue had pieced together some things from the few words Irene Lawlor had let slip, often mere monosyllables that she seemed to wish to, but couldn't summon the will to, prevent the garrulous Mrs. Molloy from detailing. Where did Mary live? Inishowen Gardens, off the South Circular Road. Shared a flat with another girl. When had she last seen Mary? April sometime. Didn't get on so great the last while. Phoned the odd time though. Recently? Couple of weeks back; forgot which day. Had she seemed worried? No. Money troubles maybe? Didn't mention any. Boyfriend? Didn't know. Mary worked in the city center. Some hairdresser's, as far as she knew. As far as she knew: the phrase kept cropping up. Had Mary any contact with her estranged father? Didn't want to have any. He'd gone on the dry a couple of years back. Where was he? Didn't know. Somewhere in Ballybough, she'd heard. Did he contact her? He'd come by the house a half a dozen times before he finally took the hint. Asking to see Mary. Did he say what for? Wanted to make up with her, she supposed. Mary didn't want anything to do with him. He'd gotten Jesus or something because it helped him dry out. Mary had told her a while back, last year maybe, that her father had tried to talk to her a few times on the street. He'd seen her and him driving by in his taxi. She told him to get lost. To drop dead. She hated him. Irene Lawlor hated him too. Did she know or had she maybe heard anything about Mary lately, anything that suggested things were not going well? It was the only time Minogue remembered Irene Lawlor taking her eyes from the passing roadway and looking at him. Mrs. Molloy with her big mouth broke that one up. What sort of trouble, she'd asked, and Irene Lawlor turned back toward the open window.

Minogue took Malone aside.

"You go with John too, Tommy. Take it handy with them. Gentle, no matter how they react."

"What am I supposed to say, like?"

"Don't say anything if you're not sure. The attendant will pull back the covering as far as the chin. John'll ask them. Okay?"

Minogue stepped over to the two women. Mrs. Molloy's face had lost all its pink now. Her arm was twined tight around Irene Lawlor's.

"Mrs. Lawlor. Detective Malone will escort you along with Detective Murtagh here."

He cleared his throat.

"You don't actually need to follow through here. We've already identified Mary from our end. Any time you want to change your mind now . . ."

Irene Lawlor's words came from between her teeth.

"I know what they do here," she said. "I want to see her."

•   •   •   •   •

"No Jack Mullen," announced Éilis. Minogue heard her type something else in. The phone was greasy in his hand. Minogue looked up from the page in his notebook where he had listed the points. Jack (John) Mullen — father. Mary in London. Egans, the gang.

"Doyle was looking for you," she said, still typing. "Returning a call about her."

"I'll phone him in a minute. You're sure about this Jack Mullen?"

"Nothing. He's clean."

"All right," said Minogue. "I'll try his place one more time, then we'll go after the taxi companies. Capitol Taxis, the missus thinks. Ex-missus."

Minogue switched the phone back to standby.

"Nothing on Mary Mullen's da, Tommy. I'll see what Doyler has."

"Darlin' Doyle? Prostitution?"

Minogue nodded.

Malone turned onto Dorset Street. The sun fell on Minogue's side now. He was left on hold for over a minute before he heard Doyle's voice.

"Morning there, John. Matt Minogue, yes. Have you anything to update the file on this girl Mary Mullen?"

"I'm afraid not. She hasn't figured with us here since her last conviction there three years ago. Left the canal trade or maybe got sense."

"Well, now that I have you, maybe you can smarten me up on things. I was wondering if, say, some of the trade down at the canal is done independently, like. Girls on their own, I mean. What are the chances she got the treatment from someone for not paying her way there?"

"Well, we'd probably get to hear about one in, God, I don't know, one in twenty of that. Unless a pimp is beating the head off one of the girls in broad daylight."

"But she could be there for some time and ye wouldn't know her?"

Doyle didn't reply for several moments.

"Well, now, you said it. As regards pimps now, we break up stuff by the canal pretty regularly. But it's gotten right tough to make charges stick. The sting has to be good. Depending on things, Harcourt Terrace and Donnybrook stations take turns at cleaning up the trade. You always get gougers and girls moving through the area though. Girls doing business there very irregular, like. They might do a few tricks one night and that'd be all. Be gone in a few hours with a hundred quid in their pockets. But you'd see a lot of the faces turning up there again and again. Users who need more and more cash to feed the habit or pay off debts from their dealer."

"The dealer and the pimp could be one and the same thing then?"

"Right, Matt. Pimps often double as pushers. Some of them feed the girls, see? But there are girls out there solo."

"How about a crowd called the Egans? Do you know them in your line of business?"

"Does the pope fall to his knees of a Sunday? But this is not their big thing though, is it? Unless they've changed. They're more into the organized crime, I believe. Drugs, moving cars around, fences, all that. Protection rackets and stuff too. That falls more to Serious Crimes really. There's, em, a gale of work being done on that very outfit lately, I believe."

Code for go ask the Serious Crime Squad, Minogue registered.

"Well. Thanks now, John, I suppose."

"Sorry and all but. I just haven't had anyone finger them directly in the trade yet — but here, wait a minute. I'll give you the name of someone who runs a drop-in center up near the canal. For girls on the street, addicts and so on. Sister Joe, do you know her?"

Minogue didn't.

"She might know more. She's a nun. Here's her number."

Minogue scribbled it in his notebook and hung up.

"File on Mary is all we seem to have, Tommy," he muttered. "Doyler and company don't know her since then."

Malone opened his hands on the steering wheel and shrugged. Minogue returned to watching the passing doorways.

"Didn't expect the mother to talk afterwards," said Malone. "Did you?"

"Maybe she didn't believe us. Didn't want to believe us."

"Wonder what Mary was really up to the time she was in England though."

Minogue looked down at the notebook again.

"Hairdressing course, beautician stuff. Well, we can check."

Minogue looked at his watch.

"So we all get together?"

"To be sure, Tommy. Statements, leads, progress reports. Collate, exchange, talk. Drink tea. Evidence, rumors, leads. Dreams you had, even. It's too early for any tight forensic. Depending on how I divide the job, we'll split into teams. And that can change in an hour too. We pull in who and what we need from CDU and stations."

"What about Mary's place? I mean, what happens with that?"

"The gas company, the ESB or someone may have an exact. Éilis has put through a call to the local station too. When we have the number of the place, a station patrol car will go out and keep it for us. Then it's up to you and me, when we've accounted for ourselves back at the ranch. The meeting probably won't take more than half an hour. Get a cup of coff —"

The trill startled him. He picked up the phone off the floor. Kilmartin asked him where he was.

"Five minutes, Jim. Start without us."

"Stay away," said Kilmartin. "You have work to do. That place you got for the girl, the flat. Éilis phoned in for a hold on the place. Turns out that a woman the name of Patricia Fahy phoned in to report a burglary there last night. She's the Mullen girl's flatmate."

"Have you talked to her?"

"Nope. She's up at the flat now."

"F-a-h-e-y?"

"No e."

Malone drove fast. He was lucky with traffic lights. Minogue let his arm dangle out the window. The Nissan's door panels remained hot under his hand. He checked his watch as they turned into Inishowen Gardens: ten minutes. A group of boys was tapping a scuffed soccer ball across the street to one another.

"There's another one," he heard one of them, a boy with protruding ribs and shoulder blades and a Spurs shirt wrapped around his waist, call out.

"There's a squad car anyway," said Malone.

The boys followed the Nissan to a house where the squad car was parked. A small crowd, mostly children, had gathered at the gate. The house had been split into two flats. Minogue stepped up the pitted concrete steps to the open door. Already he could smell perfume. A Guard was coming down the stairs sideways from the flat above. Minogue introduced himself. The Guard headed back up the stairs, the wet patch on his shirt shifting from side to side as he ascended. Minogue thought at first that the flat must have been a chemist's shop or a beauty parlor. The floor was littered with hair spray cans and tubes, nail polish containers, mascara brushes, and shampoo.

A woman with short, stiff, black hair was talking with another Guard. She had a pale face and dark eyelashes. Minogue glanced at her before picking his way through the mess on the floor to peek into the other rooms. A tiny kitchenette similarly wrecked, the fridge door still open, the cupboards emptied onto the floor. Both bedrooms had been turned upside down. Minogue made his way back to the Guard.

"How's the man. Listen, has she mentioned the flatmate?"

"She hasn't. We got the word to hold fire until you showed."

Minogue looked around at his feet. The perfume stung high up in his nose.

"What kind of a place is this anyway?"

"This one worked as a hairdresser. She was always trying out new stuff, she says. Jases. I have two young ones at home and they're just starting off on this stuff. 'Da, I have to get this,' 'Da, everyone wears it this way now.' Jases. Is this what's in store for me too?"

Another Guard came to the doorway and gestured to Minogue. Minogue turned back to the first Guard.

"Do you know this house for anything before?"

The Guard shook his head.

"But she looks like a tough enough young one to me. Been around, like."

Minogue negotiated his way over the litter. Patricia Fahy was still talking to the second Guard. The Guard nodded at Minogue, folded his notebook, and tiptoed around to the door.

"Hello," Minogue said to her. "My colleague Detective Malone. I'm Inspector Minogue. Matt Minogue."

Patricia Fahy stood with her arms folded. She kept flicking her cigarette.

"Are yous with them, then?"

"No, we're not," replied Minogue. Her face seemed to lift a little. "We were notified when you called in to report the burglary."

"Burglary?" She spoke with more humor than disdain. "Jases, more like a demolition squad."

She took a long pull of the cigarette. It came away from her lips with a soft pop.

"So, what are yous going to do about it?"

"We'll do our utmost."

She squinted into the glare from the window. On her shoulder by a strap of her top, Minogue spotted a tattoo of a butterfly. The sun glinted off the jewelery in her nose.

"Goes to show you, doesn't it," she said. "I mean to say we're the ones out working and trying to pay our bleeding way and lookit! Rob you blind, so they would."

Some memory slid around in Minogue's thoughts: Iseult at fourteen, eying him after saying something provocative. She was staring at Malone now.

"Jases," she declared. "I seen you before. You're not a Guard. I know you. Remember? With Jacko and Eileen and? . . . Down in Sheehan's pub? It's you, is'n it?"

Malone bit his lip.

"No. Wasn't me."

Her face twisted up in a sneer of disbelief.

"Bleeding sure it was you! You ended up in the nick too, if I remember. What's that?"

Malone let her take his card. She turned it over, brought it up close, scraped it with her nail.

"Well, it looks like you. Is this a joke or something?"

"What time were you home last night?" asked Minogue.

"Home here? I wasn't. I was with me fella. We were over at his place."

"You came home from work yesterday and . . . ?"

She engaged his look for several seconds.

"What?"

"Was Mary home yesterday?" Minogue asked.

"No."

She drew on the cigarette again and squinted through the smoke at Minogue.

"Not at all?"

"What's all this about Mary?"

The cigarette was shaking now, Minogue noted.

"What's going on here? Yous aren't here just because the place got broken into, are you?"

"When did you see her last then?" asked Malone.

"Day before yesterday. Why?"

"She doesn't spend all of her time here, you're saying," Minogue tried.

"I'm not saying anything. What's all this about? Who are yous?"

Something in Minogue's expression made her frown. She turned to Malone with words framed on her lips, but none came. Minogue waited until her eyes came back to his. She backed away from him.

"No way," she whispered. She pointed at Malone. "You're trying to set me up or something! But I seen you before, I remember you! Yous are trying to pin something on Mary!"

Minogue shifted his stance.

"Why would we want to do that?"

"Oh there you go now! Now you're starting!"

"Why?"

"Just because once she was . . ."

She didn't finish. She let the smoke curl up from her open mouth and she stared at Malone.

"And you," she said. "I don't know what's going on, but it stinks."

"You've got it wrong," said Malone.

"Liar," she murmured. "You're trying to screw me with something here. It won't work, 'cause I know what I know. I remember your face, and I remember you bragging about being a hard chaw — yeah, you were into drugs —"

"That was me brother."

Malone rubbed his nose and looked around the room. She stuck her head out.

"Your brother?"

"That's what I said, yeah." Malone kept biting his lip. "Me brother. We're twins."

She started to smile but couldn't manage it.

"This is bleeding ridiculous! Jesus. I never heard that one before, so I didn't."

"I have some bad news for you, Miss Fahy," said Minogue.

She turned back to Minogue and gave a short breathless guffaw. He stared into her eyes and watched the disdain slide off her face. Now when she blinked she seemed to have trouble raising her eyelids again.

"What are you telling me?"

A droplet fell from Minogue's armpit. The stench of spilled and punctured cosmetic containers had made him groggy. His fingertips came away slick from his forehead.

"Mary is dead. We need your help, Miss Fahy."

Her nostrils flared and she dropped her head. Malone stepped across to her. She jerked her head up but her eyes stayed shut. Tears ran sideways across her cheeks and her stomach began to shudder. Malone reached around her waist. Her sobs gave way to short squeals.

"You're all right," said Malone.

·   ·   ·   ·   ·

The stink of smoke and beer from the open doors of the pubs seemed to follow him down the street. The burger and chips he had downed a half an hour back had formed a greasy lump in the bottom of his stomach. The joint had worn off. He had a pain in his back. He was thirsty again. That moron Jammy didn't know the half of what he could do. Mister Straight. Never taken a chance in his life.

The air around him seemed to be thick and smelly and he couldn't escape it. He watched the buildings quiver above the traffic. He had one joint and a bluey left in his pocket. If he dropped the bluey now, he'd get Jammy Tierney's face out of his brain. Junkie: he couldn't get the word out of his head. Bastard. He should've given Jammy a dig for that, no matter if he got a hiding in return. Show him he still had his self-respect. He looked over the stalled traffic and spotted a bus.

Three business types with their jackets held over their shoulders came down the steps of a new office building. The office had those green windows you couldn't see in. Laughing about something, with their ties loosened, like they were models in an ad. They stopped at the bottom of the steps and he heard their southside accents. See you in Hogans tonight maybe, Jonathan? One of them had a bag with the handle of a racket sticking out. Some of them played squash instead of eating their dinner, he knew. Some day's work. Work? Banging on a computer once in a while, playing with bits of paper and phones. Christ. He stopped and looked back at them. What did Mary say about them? They picked up a phone and made money, that's how it was. Just picked up a phone. As if money were made by magic, down the end of a phone or on a bloody computer screen. Wheeler-dealers. One set of rules for them and a different set for everyone else. They had the inside track all right, just knowing where everything was going down and when.

The traffic began to move. The bus approached but passed the stop. Damn bus was going to the garage. Jesus! The people in the queue murmured and rearranged themselves. An oul one put her shopping bag down again and sighed. Her forehead was shiny and pink and her face looked all swollen, like she was going to burst. The three models were still talking on the steps behind. They didn't wait on buses. Behind them, the office had disappeared. It had been taken over by sky. He stared at it. For several seconds his senses were decoyed. Another suit coming out of the door brought it all back. He tried to see through the reflections on the glass. He couldn't see a thing inside. How the hell did a building stay up if it was all glass?

The traffic was stopped again and the sun glared from a windscreen into his eyes. He stood on tiptoe and looked over the cars for the next bus. Nothing. Fucking nothing. To hell with this. He stepped out of the queue. The backs of his legs were tight from all the walking he'd done this morning. His feet seemed to be swelling up even more, pushing at his shoes by his toenails. Maybe he'd nip into a pub, have a quick pint. He put his hand into his pocket, felt the coins. Down there somewhere . . . The one with the sports bag stepped onto the footpath ahead of him. The handle caught him in the thigh.

"Watch where you're bleeding going!"

"Well, sorry."

"So you should be! You fucking iijit."

Their eyes met. The other two were looking down at him now. The racket guy's brows lowered. He looked him up and down again, sneered, and walked on. The bastard could go off and get into his car. A BMW probably, or whatever car these wankers thought was the cool car now. Drive off to the little woman and the 2.3 brats off in Foxrock or somewhere. Sarah. Jonathan. He imagined grabbing the racket and breaking it across the guy's face. Let him bleed all over that white shirt and stupid tie: that'd sort the bollocks out. He looked back over his shoulder. The three were all looking at him and grinning.

"Fuck yiz!" he shouted.

One of them threw back his head and laughed. He stopped and gave them the finger.

"Wankers!"

He didn't care who was looking at him.

"Fuck off the lot of you!"

He walked faster. Why not, he thought, when the idea hit him: Tresses was just around the corner. What was he rushing home for anyway? God, he was tired. A twist of dust flew up from a building site into his face. He stopped and rubbed at his eyes. Still rubbing, he went into a shop and bought a Coke. He felt around at the bottom of his pocket for the pill. Nothing. His belly ran cold. He took out all the coins and tried again. This time he found the hole in his pocket. The girl behind the counter was looking at him. He had been cursing out loud, he realized. Christ, only halfway through the day: what else could happen to him?

He put his back against the wall and felt the rage melt into that sickly, mixed-up feeling he knew so well, that mess of sorrow and comfort and injustice. The first taste of the Coke reminded him of being a kid again, when Dessie and Jer and himself were out on their bikes all day, nicking stuff from Quinn's shop, setting up wars and forts and ambushes . . . He filled his mouth with Coke and swallowed it in slow gulps. The fizz stung his gums but it didn't take away the feeling that something was pulling him down. He couldn't think straight. He stared across the traffic and caught sight of himself in a shop window opposite. Twenty-three, and he was sliding into nowhere. He thought of the guy with the bag and the racket: a blade, slicing him right down the side of his face, the blood pouring out of him. See the look on his face then.

He shifted against the wall and swilled more Coke. The dole, the job training for no jobs, the nixers he'd done hadn't brought him anywhere in six years. Washing windows. Working off the milk lorries at one o'clock in the morning. Delivering coal. His best chance was to go back to dealing. It'd only be for a temporary thing, of course. He didn't actually need to. It was only junkies needed to deal so they could use their cut straightaway. He thought about Jer. He hadn't seen him for a couple of weeks. Maybe he'd really gone to London like he said he was going to. All those plans he had, all worked out like he was the top banana. H was 30 percent on the streets in London, Jer had told him, twice the bang you got here. Foolproof, Jer kept telling him. He swore he could carry enough to pay everything and walk away with five hundred nicker too. As well as a couple of sessions in London, even! The memory of Jer's laugh came to him. He'd known straightaway that Jer had been high. Jer couldn't handle it. He, Liam Hickey, could.

He drained the can and let the fizz tear at the back of his throat. The resentment crept back into his chest. Maybe he wasn't a goner like Jer, but still he lived at home in a crummy little room with his ma nagging him, with an oul fella who hadn't brought wages home in ten years. He grasped the Coke can tight and crushed it. There had to be something for him. Mary only worked part time in this place around the corner. What if she wasn't there now? He elbowed away from the wall and headed down the street toward Tresses.

Sting, he thought as he pushed the door open. Jases, couldn't they do better than that? A fat guy with a buzz cut was sitting in one of the chairs reading a magazine. Two women were getting their hair done. The woman at the counter was trying to fix a bracelet with a nail file.

"Howiya there," she said. "A trim, was it?"

No sign of Mary. She'd told him not to show up here. She was only in the place a couple of months, part time.

"No, thanks. Not today." Maybe Mary was on a break. "I was, you know, looking for someone who works here."

"Oh, who's that?"

Screw Sting, he thought. Screw the Amazon rain forest for that matter. "Mary, you know?"

Buzz-cut looked up from the magazine. The receptionist glanced over at him and then back. She was still smiling but her tone had changed.

"There's no Mary here."

"Mary Mullen? Kind of tall. Always wears a —"

"Mary doesn't work here," said Buzz-cut. Dub accent, he thought, and he had that glazed look in his eyes that was telling him to get the message.

"Well, she used to, didn't she. Three weeks ago she was working here."

Buzz-cut opened his eyes wide.

"So?"

He stared into Buzz-cut's eyes. Jammy Tierney, the guy who was supposed to be his friend, coming the heavy with him. The tiny hole in his pocket. Going home to be pestered by the ma again. Knowing he'd be out again after tea looking to score. Mary hadn't even told him she'd left this kip. Maybe she'd been in a barney with them here.

"So I came by to talk to her. Can you live with a major crisis like that?"

Buzz-cut closed the magazine and stood. He looked a damn sight bigger standing.

"Hit the trail here, brother. She doesn't work here anymore."

The wet hair and the shampoo, the hot damp stink of hair being dried became suddenly choking.

"I was only asking. What's the big deal? Jesus!"

Buzz-cut flexed his fingers. He kept his eyes on Buzz-cut's as he stepped out the door.

"What's so strange about asking a question about a friend of mine? All you have to say is, well — Jesus! People these days! Must be the bleeding music turns you into head-cases here."

He was out on the footpath before Buzz-cut began to move. Why the hell hadn't Mary told him? Had it been that long since he'd seen her? He looked at his watch. Was there a phone-box around here?

CHAPTER 4

Don't have much of an appetite meself either," said Malone. Bun under his belt, Minogue stirred his coffee and watched his colleague wolf down another sausage roll. The inspector had picked a table near the door of Bewley's restaurant. The late-morning crowd continued to move through the ground-floor section. Many patrons sat slouched, their faces flushed and even slick with the heat. Eyes shone in the clammy gloom. Two men in ponytails and brightly patterned shirts were lining up for coffee. He knew from Peter Flood in the Drug Squad that the taller one was a convicted drug dealer. Both men were elegantly groomed and outfitted. They were enjoying a good laugh. One of them spotted Minogue and his laugh turned to a smile. Minogue saw him elbow his crony and murmur something. The crony began to concentrate on the food he was picking. Some town, thought the inspector. Bananas we should be growing.

A waitress began cleaning up the adjoining table. He watched her blow breath up from under her bottom lip at a stray strand of hair over her forehead. Blonde, he saw, and out of a bottle at that. The roots looked black, same as Mary Mullen's. He sipped more coffee. The image kept soaking in behind his eyes: the killer astride her, slamming her head on the pavement. Minogue stretched and rubbed hard at his eyes. The image was still with him.

"Quite the bullock," Minogue murmured. Malone looked up from his tea.

"Patricia Fahy's father, I meant."

Minogue stared at the question marks he had scribbled in his notebook. He shifted in his seat and snapped his notebook shut.

"Well, Fahy won't get his spake in the next time, Tommy."

"Will we try her later on again this afternoon?"

"Maybe tomorrow instead. People lose it when they get a shock, but still I think that the same Patricia Fahy was being a bit economical with the truth. Not knowing much about where Mary was working or socializing? Doesn't fit."

Malone nodded and squinted at the inspector.

"And didn't know if Mary had a boyfriend? Her own flatmate?"

"Pull the other one, like," said Minogue. "It's got bells on it."

"She's scared, isn't she?"

Minogue nodded. Malone finished his tea and looked at his watch.

"Stop me if I'm being pushy now," he said. "But aren't we supposed to be in a rush?"

Minogue eyed him and sipped at the leftover froth in his coffee.

"Before the trail goes cold and all that?"

"I suppose," said the inspector. "But we're moving along well enough. Forensic takes time. We're getting her father; we're connecting her to criminal associates. We've interviewed the mother. Done a lot of site work, started the secondary search. We're not working alone, man. The teams are out there already."

"Huh," said Malone. "There must have been someone by that part of the canal the other night."

"I hope you're right. I found a rake of spots along the canal where you're out of sight of the street. I was able to walk right under the bridge even. The light's bad."

Malone tapped his fingers on the table, bit his lip, and nodded several times.

"Mightn't even be the site, Tommy. Could've brought her there, slipped her out of a car. Even if we find damn-all from the canal, we don't want to get locked onto assumptions here."

Malone rubbed at his nose and glanced at the inspector. The gesture reminded Minogue of a boxer getting the last word from the trainer as the bell sounded to start the round.

"What do you reckon yourself? So far, like."

Malone began plucking the hairs by his watch-strap.

"Well, I reckon I don't want to make an iijit out of myself with guessing, do I."

"I'm not trying to get a rise out of you," said Minogue. "So I'll tell you what's been going through my mind. With that bruise in the face, he was probably facing her. I'm going on the assumption for now that he's not a *citeóg*."

"A what?"

"Left-handed. If he did that, he's a certain type of person. Strong, of course. More than just a short fuse. I mean, very, very aggressive type of a fella. You go over a distinct barrier as regards behavior when you hit someone in the face. Especially a woman."

Malone rested his cheeks on his fists. "Okay," he said.

"You'd be inclined to expect a pattern. A record, if you follow me."

Malone's fists had pushed his cheeks up to his eyelashes. Minogue finished his coffee. He looked into the narrow slits that Malone's eyes had become.

"How'd you get into the boxing anyway?"

"The, er, the brother got me started." Malone leaned in over the table and frowned up under his eyebrows at Minogue.

"Listen, on that same matter. Do we have a minute?"

"Fire away."

"Well, there's something I wanted to tell you. I didn't know how to sort of bring it up. What she said back in the flat. Patricia Fahy. Thinking she was being set up?"

Minogue smiled.

"About your brother? That was a hoot entirely."

"Yeah, well. Funny to you, maybe. This has to do with the brother, all right. And the Egans. The brother was mixed up with them."

Malone looked down at the fork as though wondering how it had gotten there.

"They got Terry where he is now," he muttered. "In the 'Joy, like. He used to do stuff for them."

He glanced over at Minogue.

"Is it going to, you know? . . ."

Minogue pushed his cup and saucer toward the middle of the tabletop.

"Why should it?" he said. "You're here due your own record, not your brother's."

"Another thing. I can take the slagging about being a Dub. The Molly Malone thing and all. Really."

Minogue nodded.

"But I got to tell you I can't take much stick about the brother."

{ 49 }

"I'll, er, pass that on to the appropriate authorities, Tommy."

Malone looked down at the cup and saucer that Minogue had marooned on the marble tabletop.

"Terry's not a bad person. But I'm sick and tired of looking out for him, wondering what he'll get up to next. He's just finished eighteen months of a two-year for break and enter. He'll be out any day soon. Terry's not even much good at it. He did it to get money for drugs. He tells me that's all over now. Last time I visited, he looks me in the eye: 'I'm clean.' Yeah, right, Terry, I say: prove it, man. I can't afford to believe him. If they find the gene for being a gobshite it'll have Terry's name on it."

Minogue thought about more coffee.

"I gave up getting embarrassed about Terry years ago. All I do nowadays is try to stop him dragging anyone down with him. Me younger brother. The ma."

"How do you mean?"

"The ma? Oh, scrounging money. 'Just a loan, Ma!' The da's dead three years now. The da used to give him the bum's rush. Nearly knocked the head off him with a piece of pipe one night."

Malone picked up a napkin and wiped the corners of his mouth.

"Didn't help the da much, did it? Died of a heart attack on the kitchen floor. I've sisters married. They're doing all right. Then there's Tony. He's nineteen. The baby. He's training for supermarket management. Terry tries, you know, he really does. Then he sees the crowd he used to hang around with . . ."

Malone crushed the paper napkin into a ball and rolled it onto the table.

"Sure what can you tell them and they seeing the likes of the Egans making fortunes out of rackets and drugs and everything? 'Do the right thing'? 'Bite the fucking bullet'?"

He slapped his palm against his forehead.

"Sorry. The ma warned me I'd never go anywhere with the mouth on me. The language, it just sort of jumps out."

Minogue smiled. Malone sat back and looked around the restaurant.

"I've spent half me life trying to figure out how identical twins ended up like we did. This guff about heredity and environment and everything. I don't know how Terry lost it and I didn't. It doesn't make sense. It fu — Excuse me. It *annoys* me. We weren't treated different. We were close. Broke the da's heart. I don't know. I don't ask meself anymore. I just don't."

Malone's voice had dropped to a murmur.

"What I mean is that I try not to ask stupid questions anymore. The meaning of life and all that crap. You know what I'm saying, like?"

War'm'sane, thought Minogue. He nodded. The meaning of life? For several moments he was walking along the lane to the ruins of Corcomroe Abbey in his native County Clare, hardly feeling the asphalt under his feet, the hills and sky all about him, his senses flooded with the fragrances of sea and pasture.

"I sort of came to a funny conclusion a few years back," he heard Malone saying. He noted Malone's sardonic smile.

"Terry's probably the biggest reason for me being a Guard," said Malone.

. . . . .

"So," said Kilmartin. "A definite factor. Two months."

Minogue was still mulling over the news that the autopsy revealed Mary Mullen had been pregnant. They had almost missed it.

"Would she have known for sure herself?" asked Kilmartin. "She'd have noticed the visits from the cousin down the country had stopped at least."

It took Minogue several moments to sort out the euphemism.

"Tell me about the flat being done," said Kilmartin. "Coincidence?"

"I don't believe in coincidences, Jim, and neither do you. Patricia Fahy is missing a bit of money and a ghetto blaster worth a hundred and something quid. But the place was really tossed."

"Do we have any idea of what was taken belonging to Mary Mullen?"

"No. Not yet."

Kilmartin closed his eyes, groaned, and tried to scratch high up on his back.

"Leave aside the idea that this is burglary number nineteen thousand nine hundred and whatever for Dublin this week," he said. "What might Mary Mullen have that someone wanted?"

"Drugs," said Malone. "Kind of staring us in the face, like."

"Attaboy, Molly," said Kilmartin. "Drugs." He opened his eyes. "I phoned Mick Hand and had a chat about this Egan mob. They do more than robbing and beating. Hard drugs, soft drugs, protection rackets, fences, car robbery ring. They have certain parts of the city well terror-ized. Anything they're not into, says I. Jail, says he."

Kilmartin stopped and gasped: he couldn't reach a point high up be-tween his shoulder blades.

"So. Molly. We have to find out what's behind her, who's behind her. Mary Mullen. If she was tied into the Egan clan . . . Ah, bugger, I can't get at it!"

Kilmartin grabbed a biro and found the spot.

"Ahhh . . . Got caught up in a row with a rival outfit. Maybe she fell foul of the Egans themselves. Ahhh . . . God, that's the spot now!"

"Any sign from the PM yet that she was a user, John?" Minogue asked.

"No needle tracks."

Kilmartin scratched the bristles on his chin.

"How soon before the first toxicology?"

"Three, four o'clock," said Murtagh.

Minogue stretched out his legs. There was a check mark and "(P.St.)" beside Jack Mullen's name on the board. It took him a moment: Jack Mullen's statement was being taken in Pearse Street Garda Station.

"We're definite on the cause of death, John?" Murtagh looked over at him.

"Yes. She was unconscious when she went into the water."

"And that bruise again?"

"He said we should consider it very possible that her head was slammed against something."

"How hard?"

"Enough for a concussion. The cheekbone has a hairline fracture in it. No bruises or pressure marks anywhere else."

"Not even her arms? She didn't resist?" Murtagh shook his head.

"She knew him," said Kilmartin. "Proceed as planned." Minogue looked up at Mary Mullen's picture on the board. A punch, he wondered. Facing her. Nothing on her nails, her hands. Unexpected.

Kilmartin elbowed away from the wall and began a slow, measured prowl of the squad room.

"We have Harcourt Street station doing the banks again," he said. "Along with Sheehy and two Scenes men. God help them. I was able to get him a half-dozen from Donnybrook too. He'll need them. Did you see the place in daylight? Christ, what a mess. And the stink! Dear Old Dirty Dublin, my eye. A slurry pit is what it is. Anyway. The lockkeeper — what's his name?"

Malone glanced up at the noticeboard.

"Kavanagh," said Murtagh.

"Him, yes. He's a hundred percent certain. Nothing went through there after lunchtime."

Kilmartin paused and looked around at the three policemen. Minogue thought he recognized the look: the chief inspector's chronic flatulence was about to score again.

"Who's taking Jack Mullen's statement?" Minogue asked.

Kilmartin looked at his watch.

"Conor Madden," said Murtagh. "And the other fella. Larry Smith. Used to be in Store Street. Yes. They took him in an hour ago."

"Any word yet?" Murtagh tossed his biro into the air and caught it.

"Well, I'm going to phone," said Minogue.

He dialed, asked for Madden, and watched Malone while he waited. Malone was writing, frowning at what he had written, underlining, staring at the boards, grilling Murtagh.

"Matt, oul son. How's things?"

"Holding my own, so I am, Conor. Warm, don't you think."

"Hot as the hob of hell. But sure, what harm? We'll be long enough without it."

"Ah, don't be talking. Now. You've had time with Jack Mullen."

"I did that. Will one of yous be by to go at him proper soon?"

"I will indeed. How'd he strike you first?"

"Well, he knew already. The wife had left a message at his job. 'First time she's gotten in touch with me in a year and a half,' says he. 'And it had to be this.'"

"How does he look to you?"

"So far, he seems sound," said Madden. "Broke down a few times. Genuine enough, I thought."

"What's his alibi looking like?"

"He was working that night, he says. The taxi. Day shift, but sometimes fills in on an eleven to seven if he's asked. We can get a log of the fares he had. There are times on it too, a computer printout."

"Does he own the car or just drive it?"

"He owns it, but he works for Capitol."

"How'd he pay for the car?"

"He got a settlement from a back injury when he worked in England. He was on the buildings. To make a long story short, he came back to

{ 53 }

Dublin. He messed up everything with drink but then he was able to beat it. Finally he was able to get an in with the taxi business. There's a kink in him now, I should tell you. He's some class of a born-again. It has to do with being an alcoholic, he says. A club called the Victory Club."

"The Victory Club? Salvation Army? What is it?"

"It's kind of like the AA. He shares a place out in Ballybough with two other fellas. They're ex-alcoholics as well. They're all part of this Victory Club. The idea is, as I understand it so far, that these fellas have to put themselves back together again. They stay together so as to buck one another up against relapsing."

"So it's a recovery group," said Minogue.

"Well, I'm no expert. It has to do with finding yourself and that. I didn't hear him say he'd talked to Elvis or anything of that nature now. Repeated a lot of the same phrases."

"Try a few on me."

"'Coming home'?"

"Okay."

"Something to do with a hole. Not the one you dig, now. Making yourself whole."

"Holistic?"

"That's it. Yep. I thought it was part of the born-again kick, you know. He talks about the time before he gave up the jar as his 'past life.' Later on he says, 'God has decided.' Yep. 'God called her home,' says he. He said that he hadn't been much of a father to her. Broke down again. He was at it a while. That's hard to fake right, I figure."

Minogue watched Malone patting his crew cut while he concentrated on something in his notebook.

"He admitted that he used to tap the wife a bit. I hadn't even asked and he popped out with that one. Now that's odd. Like he was confessing his sins."

"Beat her, you mean," said Minogue. "As opposed to a tap."

"Well, yes, I suppose. He has a bad back now. He's still a big buck of a fella. He goes to a fitness club. He does weights and exercises for the back and goes for physio sometimes."

"When did he last have contact with Mary, according to himself?"

"Said he saw her on the street back in March."

"What, where?" asked Minogue.

"Along Baggot Street, the Stephen's Green end."

"Did he talk to her or anything?"

"She wouldn't talk, he said. He pulled over — he had a fare — and tried to talk to her, but no go."

"Did he know where she lived?"

"No. Not even where she worked. 'Well, I wasn't around when she needed me,' he says. He gave me the run-down on the last few years with the family. He came back from England with a bit of money. Reunited with the wife, but thought she wasn't pleased to see him home, that she had her own fella on the side. Formed the opinion that the wife wasn't a fit mother, that she'd let the daughter go to hell too. Wife's answer was, 'Where the hell were you when she was growing up?' Rows, of course. Went from bad to worse. He thought he could sort things out with his fists. She got a barring order, gave him the F.O. He went back to England."

"Drinking a lot, he says? What, five years ago?"

"Yes," said Madden. "Then he fell off the scaffolding and was laid up in hospital for a while. Said it was the pain from his back sent the drinking right out of control then. This time he came back to Dublin broke. The wife wouldn't have him. He lived with a brother for a while but got thrown out. He hit bottom and ended up in hospital here. Then he got counseling and stuck at the sessions. Next thing is he gets awarded a stack of money — compensation — he hadn't expected. God's giving him a second chance. That's when he got religion. 'Saved,' says he, and he's never looked back."

Saved, thought Minogue — coming home. Born-again. Didn't you have to die first?

"Well, Conor. Thanks. He's not shy of talking then."

"No. We'll have a ten-page statement out of him if we're not bloody careful."

"Oh, before I go. The fellas he shares the place with. Did you run them through the confuser?"

"Very much so. One's completely clean. He even works for a security company. The other one has a record but latest was eleven years back. Break and enter. That one works in a clothes shop, he's separated and he has three grown-up kids."

"All right, Conor. Job well done. I'll be by within the hour."

Kilmartin lit a cigarello. Smokescreen for a fart, Minogue decided. Murtagh opened the door of the photocopier and began clearing a jam.

"Well?" said Kilmartin.

"Mister Jack Mullen claims to be on the side of the angels."

"Arra, talk sense, man! Separated from the wife and daughter, we're just after hearing. An alco. God knows what else will come up. What's angelic about that?"

"Jack Mullen found Jesus," said Minogue. Kilmartin chewed a corner of his lip.

"You make it sound like an affliction."

Minogue bit back a comment.

"Okay, okay," said Kilmartin, and rubbed his hands together. "Howandever. Go and take him on yourself. Now what about that Fahy girl: will I send a car to take her in for round two?"

"Give it a little more time, Jim, if you please."

"Jases, man, we can't be sitting on our hands now. She's had her crying time. She's trying to cod us that she knew damn-all about what her own flatmate was up to? Friends? Boyfriends coming and going? Didn't they talk, for God's sake?"

"I'm not sure how much she knew about Mary's background, Jim, but she's scared."

"Huh. Scared or not, she'd better buck up. She's a key in the lock for us."

Minogue made a mock salute. Kilmartin yawned and cocked an eye at Malone.

"All go here, huh, Molly? Getting the hang of where you fit in the big picture?"

Malone nodded. Minogue imagined Tommy Malone getting up from his corner of a boxing ring, a glint in his eye, to face Kilmartin. The chief inspector waved in the direction of the boards. Minogue sat back. Wreathed in smoke, Kilmartin swept his arm, tapped with his knuckles, and then lumbered along by the notice boards while he declaimed for Malone, who sat, arms folded, watching. Murtagh on his hunkers by the photocopier had turned around to watch the performance, a faint smile playing about his lips.

"We pull it all together each morning and then in the middle of the afternoon — unless we're on the move on one that's breaking open. We'll use anyone and everyone. See that there, Molly? We may find out that Mary Mullen was in tight with the Egans. See that name — Mick Hand? Serious Crime Squad? Resident expert on the Egans. He'll be along tomorrow morning. Doyler, resident expert on Dublin's pavement hostesses, will be here. All the uniforms from the scene — Sheehy's brigade. Plate-glass Sheehy. You'll meet him. If we still can't place Mary Mullen by teatime today, we'll start the door-to-door tonight. Pubs, offices, the whole bit. John Murtagh will go on building our file on her as well as chase the PM. Our very own file search is on foot for MO fits and known offenders; incidents logged in the area; probationers, parolees, and bailed gougers to boot."

Minogue took the phone to the windowsill and dialed Kathleen.

"I meant to phone earlier. Sorry. I've a lot of running around on the menu today."

"Will you be working through on this one?"

He couldn't take his eyes off his Citroen in the yard. The panels. Wheel covers. Squatting down, waiting to be summoned. He blinked and broke his stare.

"I don't know. We're still trying to get up to pressure here."

She told him that she had just put down the phone after a call from Iseult.

"Tell me now," he began. "You're a mother, after all."

"Oh, oh. What's coming up after that class of an opener?"

"No tricky stuff. Could a mother live in the same city as her daughter but be estranged from her?"

"Why would you be asking me?"

Her voice had lost its warmth. Damn, he thought. She thought he was giving her digs about Iseult.

"It's a case where a mother maintains she hardly knew anything about the daughter. Really. The daughter ran away from home. She got herself arrested a few times. She did time. The father beat the mother, and the daughter too, probably. The mother tells me she hardly met with the daughter this last year. What do you think?"

"Well, it's possible, isn't it? Broken homes, abuse. Drink does terrible things, you know."

A retaliatory dig, he wondered. Kathleen Minogue's husband was a bit too fond of a drink for her liking?

"There's guilt, I suppose," she added. "Maybe the mother didn't protect the girl from her husband. Maybe the daughter blamed the mother for something."

He was staring at the writing on the notice boards now. Jack Mullen, Capitol Taxi. Jack Mullen, head-case. Enough, Minogue decided. There were two conversations going on here.

"Thanks now," he muttered. "I'll bear that in mind. How's Iseult anyhow?"

"Odd, if you want to know my reaction."

"Odd? Of course she's odd. Doesn't she have a degree in being odd from the College of Art?"

"I meant *odd*, Matt!"

"Oh. That kind of odd."

"She still misses home. A mother's intuition, call it what you like, but . . ."

Minogue rolled his eyes. Iseult had been living in a flat with her boyfriend for a year.

"Laundry?" he tried.

"If only that," said Kathleen. "No. She's got a look about her."

"A look."

"Yes. A look that tells me she's waiting to land something on us."

"Oh, I see."

"What do you see?"

"I mean yes, em. Well, maybe she misses us. Thinks we need a visit." He waited for her to respond.

"No?"

"Huh. Just tell me what time you think you'll be home. So's I can tell her."

The tone cut through his thoughts.

"I'll aim for eight," he said. "I'll leave a message on the machine if I can't."

CHAPTER 5

Go THE CANAL FIRST, TOMMY," said Minogue. "They'll hold Mullen
down at Pearse Street. I want to have another look at the blind spots.
The bridge and that."

"Okay."

Malone was rewarded for his aggressive driving by a succession of red
traffic lights. It was a quarter of an hour before their Nissan was turning up from the docks toward the canal. On the canal bank at last,
Minogue spotted figures in blue shirts to each side of the canal. He
stepped out of the car and stretched. Fergal Sheehy, Sergeant Fergal
Sheehy, in waders, was perched on the lip of a squad car's boot. Tagged
plastic bags littered the boot. Minogue peered at some. Cigarette pack-
ages, a lipstick container. One held a condom. He eyed Sheehy. The sergeant closed his eyes and shrugged.

Plate-glass Fergal Sheehy was stationed in Fitzgibbon Street and worked
plainclothes. He specialized in street crime. Along with his nickname,
Sheehy had gained some notoriety four years ago when he had disarmed
a cornered knife-wielding pickpocket by throwing him through a plate-
glass window. The pickpocket had very nearly bled to death. He survived
to be charged with attempted murder — Kilmartin, Minogue remembered, suggested he be got for break and enter as well — and to initiate
a suit for damages against Sheehy. The suit was unsuccessful. At the request of Kilmartin, Sheehy had worked on several cases in the last few
years. Kilmartin had even pressed him to apply for permanent posting
to the squad. Sheehy had declined. His reason, the chief inspector had
confided to Minogue, was that he preferred to leave his work in the office.

An eye for detail and a patience that made him appear indifferent and even indolent had marked him as special for Kilmartin. Like many others on the island, the chief inspector had learned early in his career that Kerry people were genetically programmed with the ambition to be boss wherever they were and whatever they did. Kilmartin occasionally cited Éilis as proof. Sheehy was to be his pet Cute Kerry Hoor.

"It's all been said, Matt," Sheehy murmured. "Believe me."

"That stuck, are we?"

Sheehy nodded.

"Unless you want us to take up all the bike wheels and the shopping carts and the tires and —"

"God, Fergal, you're a saint."

"It's staked out in hundred-foot zones from the gates. There's too much and there's nothing at the same time. Look at the rubbish all over the kip. A holy show."

A Guard stepped up from the bank with a comb. Minogue greeted him and returned his sympathetic nod. The worst site: contaminated, traffic, water. Futile work.

"But at least you're outdoors, Fergal. The way God intended."

Sheehy squinted at Minogue.

"There isn't enough soap in all of Dublin to clean myself off after all this shite and rubbish."

Minogue glanced over at Malone, who twisted his lip trying to suppress a smile.

"Two of the lads fell in up to their waists," Sheehy went on. "Man, you should've gotten a whiff off them and they climbing out. And the fucking language out of them! A fright to God."

"I'm glad I wasn't here so. Can't be taking chances at my age. What've you got?"

"Don't ask. Malaria, maybe. A lot of nothing. All soggy at any rate."

Sheehy stood out from the back of the car and pointed down toward the bridge.

"We did a good long sweep up and down. A couple of places that may be — may be, I tell you, and I'm trying to be nice and polite about it — could have been heels being dragged. Couldn't tell anything about any scuffle or the like. No effects that could go with her beyond a million bits of rubbish. Still no shoes or bag."

The inspector looked up and down the banks.

"All right, Fergal. Call it when you're ready."

Sheehy shrugged and shifted his weight.

"Another few minutes," he said. "That'll be that."

Minogue walked down toward the bridge.

"Not like on the telly is it, Tommy."

"Tidy and stuff, you mean?"

"Yep. The gun. The knife. The bad guy in the cheap suit. The good guy with the nice teeth and the winning smile. All wrapped up in time for the end of the show. What do you think?"

Malone held up his hands.

"Four days into the job? Me first active case?"

Minogue picked his way back up the bank until he was almost under the bridge. The water ran fast after its drop from the top of the lock. Bored teenagers, he thought, standing around here over the years smoking and drinking cans of lager. Worse, probably. He took a few steps in under the bridge along the ledge where barge horses must have plodded. The noise of the traffic receded to a resonant sigh. He looked at the wall. There were initials and burn marks on the stones that formed the arch. No paint, oddly enough. Stone loves Jane XXX. Bohs are the greatest. Jacko had had, had wished he had had perhaps, sexual congress with Cathrine: he had not had spelling lessons from Catherine. Kimmage rules. The Doors. Were they big again? Lower down on the wall, on one of the largest stones, he spotted faint colors. He half-closed his eyes and looked again. Now it looked like a picture of a face. He bent over and studied it. No pattern now, no shape. Chalk? Whatever it was, it wasn't paint. It could be years old.

He let his eyes follow the canal banks down toward the docks. If you kept your eyes up from the immediate surroundings, he thought, and if you ignored the stink off the water and the rubbish all about, and if you pretended that no one came down here to piss or to drink or to fight, or to buy or sell sex and drugs, and if you didn't know that a woman had been battered and thrown in here or somewhere near here to drown — if you could forget all that — the view framed by the arch of the bridge was beautiful.

He made his way up the bank. Sheehy was marshaling the bags in the van, checking the labels against the diagrams of the site. He watched the Guards congregate by the van and the two squad cars. He helloed some of them and listened halfheartedly to their jokes and grumblings. The sky over Dublin had taken on the color of milky tea. Haze hung under the trees' canopy by the banks. The sulfury tang of exhausts mingled with the decay breathed up from the water and the weeds. Drivers continued to slow and eye the goings-on. One old man with a terrier on a leash stood on the far bank staring at the Guards while they took off waders and boots. The traffic was beginning to move again. Minogue watched a couple stop by one of the trees to embrace. Something erased their reflections on the surface of the canal. He looked down to see a floating island of scum take over the surface there. He waited for it to go by and restore the image but the floating mass seemed to be getting bigger, broader. The couple moved off.

Sheehy offered him a cigarette and asked after Kilmartin. Minogue read the smile as invitation to a yarn that would glaze the Killer's legend into an even harder monument. He told him that Chief Inspector Kilmartin was in the pink. Sheehy gave him a wink. A Guard began to relate a story he had heard about prostitutes. Minogue looked over to the far bank. The man with the dog was still there.

He crossed the footbridge that was signed NOT FOR PUBLIC USE, pausing in the middle to look at the rills cascading into the lock below. He eyed the dog for a friendly reception. Did dogs take on the character of their owners?

"Warm still," the inspector called out.

The dog didn't reply. The owner looked myopically through his lenses at Minogue. He pulled on the leash. Minogue took in the long nose, the pouches under the eyes, the hair brushed back in a style of fifty years ago. Dubliner for sure, he thought: seen it all.

"I hear there's a chance of rain though," Minogue added.

"You must have come down in the last shower yourself if you believe that one."

Minogue managed a smile. The old man adjusted his glasses.

"A bit late, aren't yiz?"

"Late for what, now."

"Like the saying goes, prevention is better than cure. What are you then, a sergeant?"

"They made me inspector some time back."

"So you'd hardly be patrolling the streets then, would you? To my mind, things went downhill when they took the lads off the beat and put them in cars."

"Well, you're not alone in that opinion. You know the place well, I take it."

"Too well. Make a guess if you like."

"All your life?" Almost a smile.

"Oh, very sharp there. You're a veteran."

"It certainly feels like that this time of the day. Do you live local?" He nodded toward Mount Street bridge.

"The flats in there by the Turk Dunphy's pub." He gave the policemen across the canal a bleak survey. "I was born and reared in City Quay. Do you know where that is?"

"I do."

"Oh, do you now. What age do you think I am?"

"Late middle age?"

"Hah. 'Late middle age.' I never had that one pulled on me before. I'm seventy-six! The wife is seventy-five. Do you know how many times I've walked this canal?"

"A good number of times, I'd say."

He pinned Minogue with a look that told him his measure had been conclusively taken.

"You'd be right. I calculate some days. Something to do in me head when I'm out for a walk. I like it, the mental arithmetic, like. Everybody's talking about exercise and clean living and diet nowadays. All me arse. If you don't have the oul head in order, sure you're bound to fall apart. In one way or another, like. What the hell use is running around and eating bits of lettuce if you're a thick?"

"I think you've hit the nail on the head there."

"You're telling me I have. Rashers and sausages every second day with me. A few pints of the Friday. Have a cigar the odd time. And look at me. Never better. But the wife! The wife's gone a bit slow this last while so I've had to put on the brakes. The better part of seventy years, I've been by here. Now, put your thinking cap on. Do you like doing sums in your head?"

Minogue looked to the reflections of the trees on the water.

"My strong point was more the reading and writing, I think."

"Huh. Say five times a week, say maybe 250 times a year. How much is that?"

"Probably several times around the world at the equator."

He rubbed his chin.

"God, I never thought of it like that. No. The trick is to multiply by

{ 63 }

a thousand. That's easy done, did you know that? You add noughts. Then divide your answer by four. Anyone can do that. Loved sums in school. I like to keep the head working. Even sitting in front of the telly. But, sure, what good does it do you, I ask myself sometimes. You need the bit of exercise, don't you? Me and Timmy. You need a dog with you around here."

"I'm not sure what you mean."

"There's the four-legged rats do be out here. And then there's the rats with just the two legs. Know what I'm saying?"

Minogue nodded.

"The whole place is gone to hell in a wheelbarrow. But maybe you wouldn't see that. Being brass and all. When's the last time you were on the beat here in town?"

"Close on twenty years ago. A bit more, actually."

"Huh. Well, it's die dog here now or eat the hatchet. Dublin's gone. 'Dublin in the rare oul times,' my eye. No comfort in it anymore. Oh, I know the canal was always the place for courting, but you've no idea what goes on here now. It's kind of like, I don't know what. A zoo."

"There's a thought, now."

"Oh, the things you see these days."

"What sort of things now?"

"Well, if you have to ask, it's too late with you, isn't it? Who's supposed to be policing this place anyway?"

Minogue made a guess.

"Harcourt Street station. Maybe Donnybrook at this end. There's plainclothes too out of Harcourt Terrace. Vice and probably Drugs."

The old man gave a breathy sigh and yanked on the leash. The dog sat down, its ears twitching.

"Well, double that — no, triple that — and it still wouldn't be enough. The whores. The types what are on the prowl for it too. Drugs. I've seen men here selling themselves. Boys, I should say. I'll tell you one thing. Yous are never around when ye're wanted."

"Do you see much of that then?"

"What does that mean? Do you think I do be coming around here spying on the types that does be here at night?"

"I meant that you seem to me to be an observant man, Mister, er . . ."

"Byrne. Joey Byrne. You're not telling me something I don't know already there now, pal. The wife says I should ignore the half of what I see.

That I'd be better off, like. I don't go along with that but I can't be arguing with her all the time, can I?"

"You're telling me. I forgot to introduce myself, sorry. Matt Minogue."

"Inspector?"

"I'd prefer Matt."

Joey Byrne fell to watching the policemen by the van.

"Well, what's up?"

"We found a body in the canal."

Minogue watched the glaze fall away from Joey Byrne's eyes.

"My God. Go on, are you serious?"

Minogue nodded.

"When?"

"Last night."

Byrne blessed himself.

"My God in heaven." His tone had lost the Dubliner's protective irony.

"So that's what yiz are up to over there? I should have known. I must be slipping. Well, what I'm saying is, it's bound to happen."

"Were you here at all yesterday?"

"'Deed and I was. Me and the wife and his nibs here. Timmy. Around the eight o'clock mark. Was it on the news?"

"I'm not sure. It probably was. We'd be looking for any witnesses here, you know. Passersby."

"Over there? Well, I don't remember us going up that far now. We sort of sat down here on the bench a while. The wife, you know. She had an operation last year. She's not firing on all cylinders yet."

"Did you see anything peculiar?"

"Well, everything's peculiar, that's the trouble. Do you think she was done in here too?"

"There's the problem now, Mr. Byrne. If I knew that for sure . . ."

"But sure there's traffic here all evening. After dark now, that'd be a different matter entirely."

He pivoted and elbowed Minogue's arm at the same time.

"If you take my meaning. But you wouldn't go down here now, by God. No sir."

"You didn't notice anything different yesterday evening then? On your walk."

"Oh, no! Years ago, you might worry about finding a few tinkers or winos or the like that'd be bothering you for the few shillings. But, sure, even the winos and what have you won't come near the place. They were nothing to the people what come by here these days. God, no. Do you know what I came around to thinking?"

Minogue raised his eyebrows.

"We're going backwards, that's what. Like I was saying to you. Not *rev*-olution, not *e*volution even. It's *de*volution."

He stretched out his arm. Minogue followed the waving hand as it swept across the buildings.

"All this," said Byrne. "All this *stuff*. The fancy new offices and apartments and everything. It all goes fast and looks shiny, doesn't it? Well, let me tell you this. I see through all this. All this rubbitch. Look close up and what'll you see? Fellas with telephones stuffed into their ear and they whizzing along. Women with their skirts up to here. Don't they cop on to the fact they're asking for it if they dress like that? Asking for it, they are."

"Mr. Byrne. I need some way to get in touch with you again."

"Wait a minute there, chief. What do I know?" Minogue took a breath and held back his irritation.

"Just in case, Mr. Byrne." He looked into Joey Byrne's eyes. "Guards can't get anywhere without the help of the responsible citizens, can they now?"

Byrne frowned and looked away.

"Do you have a phone number, Mr. Byrne?"

$$\cdot \quad \cdot \quad \cdot \quad \cdot \quad \cdot$$

"Tell us again, Mr. Mullen," said Minogue. "What she said to you that time."

The chair creaked as Jack Mullen sat back. What was he like when he lost his temper, the inspector kept wondering.

"Again?"

Minogue nodded once.

"Again."

Mullen scratched at his scalp. Aside from the fact that he sweated like a sumo wrestler and that he had ears like the FA Cup, Jack Mullen looked healthy. Three times a week he worked out. Part of the recovery process, he had said. Like hounding his daughter, Minogue wondered.

Mullen let his gaze rest on the dusty windowpanes that looked out over a cut-stone wall topped by shards of glass next to Pearse Street Garda Station.

"You see, if you're going to change your life, you can't leave anything out —"

"Start from when you saw her."

Jack Mullen looked away from the window toward Minogue but his eyes did not stop on him. They traveled on around the walls, over the discolored ceiling and to the floor. Minogue counted himself lucky never to have been posted to Pearse Street Garda Station. He had used this room a half-dozen times before. Here he had watched Kilmartin demolish suspects, gut their alibis and their beliefs that they could leave here without telling him the truth. He had seen Kilmartin throw a suspect in a shooting incident across this room. The smells of polish and paint, of long-gone sandwiches and cigarettes, along with the smells of sweat and desperation soaked into the walls over decades were being drawn out by the heat.

"But that's only a small part of it. You don't understand."

"This was in March, you said. You were driving up by Baggot Street. How long had you been looking for Mary?"

"Look. How many times is this? I'm willing to put up with this, this abuse from yous. And a lot more if need be."

Have a gander at the medical records of Mullen's injury, Minogue decided.

"I can take punishment. Even if it's unfair."

"Punishment for what, Mr. Mullen?"

Mullen sighed again.

"You know. You're slagging religion. I know. You don't understand the recovery process. People pretend they can run away from themselves, don't they?"

Minogue shrugged.

"In denial, that's what it is. And that's sin. It's turning away, isn't it? Not facing up to yourself. Or God. It's only when your eyes are opened to what you've done wrong . . . You have to make amends. You have to come home. God doesn't just pull a miracle out of his pocket, does He? He says, 'Here, this is the way. It's up to you.' He empowers you, like."

Empower, thought Minogue. Relationship. Process. Development. Some days it took almost too much work not to be cynical. He breathed in slow and deep.

"Mr. Mullen. You tried to persuade Mary to come home. To your home? Your wife's?"

"Home to God, that home. Back to God in her heart. That's the first thing."

"She rejected your invitation, you said. In what manner?"

"There you go again. You'll probably agree with everything Irene says then."

"About what?"

"What she told you already about me. You know what I'm talking about. The marriage breaking down. The lies about Mary and —"

"Ah, come on now. You clattered your wife. She says you clattered your daughter. You at least threatened to clatter your daughter. You told us that yourself."

"Yes, I clattered her, as you say. My wife, Irene, was with another fella when I was away working in England. I'm not saying it was right though, did I?"

Minogue said nothing.

"Deep in my heart — even then, when I was a slave to the drink — I knew she'd gone into a life of sin. Deep down, people know what's stopping them being healthy. Everyone has an instinct for good. Everyone wants to heal themselves and become whole again. Sin is a wound, like. To others too, of course."

Minogue pinched the bridge of his nose.

"You can shake your head and everything," Mullen murmured. "I know."

Minogue opened his eyes again.

"What do you know?"

"I know the kind of mind you have as regards religion. I can tell."

"It's the heat, Mr. Mullen. Go back to the actual meeting now. You were driving along Baggot Street. You saw her. She was on her own. Now — go ahead."

Minogue listened. He could detect no inconsistencies this time either. Mullen had finished speaking for several seconds before Minogue looked up from his fingers.

"Since then, Mr. Mullen?"

"Nothing. Like I said. I knew nothing."

"You thought about her a lot?"

"What father wouldn't worry about his daughter?"

Minogue met his eyes. Mullen raised his hands and let them drop in his lap.

"But you didn't try to find her?"

"What could I do? I knew she was in bad company. I prayed. The thing that you forget when you see that your life is out of control is that God gives you choices. But at the time, well, I was lost. Just lost."

But now I'm found, Minogue almost said aloud. He wondered how Hoey was doing in London.

"But now I . . . know there is a path. The drink thing, the alcohol thing, is what you're trying to win over on its own, of course. But that's not the victory you're really looking for, is it? I mean, when you finally get up off your knees and you get out of the bottle, where do you go? Where's home then, if you don't have the bottle to live in — that's the question."

Minogue imagined Hoey motoring around some postcard English dales. Would the heat wave there drive him to sample the local beer maybe?

"It's ourselves, isn't it, our natures. It's sin. Sin is the proof that we're free. I mean to say, God doesn't waltz in and pick up the bits, does He?"

He's asking me, thought Minogue.

"Mary was free, so she was. She turned away. She lived in sin. I knew she had to fight her own battle herself. I knew that in my head. But I wanted to help. I'm her father. I . . . I loved her."

Minogue picked up his biro and drew another box on the paper.

"How long after that when you got the warning, Mr. Mullen?"

Inside the box he drew a circle. Mullen folded his arms and followed Minogue's progress.

"Couple of days."

"Two fellas?"

"Yes. Two fellas. I recognized one of them from a long way back. He was local to us. I couldn't remember his name. A ponytail on the other one."

"Did they say they were from the Egans?"

"No. But I knew. I'd seen them years ago. They'd grown up together. Around the corner from where we — where I lived. When we were together."

"You didn't report it."

Mullen's forehead lifted.

"This is the real world. Who am I going to report to? Lodge a complaint with the Guards? No way. I knew enough about them over the years. You'd hear people talking about the Egans. The fellas who did the work for them. They can do pretty well what they please."

"They told you to? . . ."

"Keep me nose out of Mary's business. To stop pestering her."

"In so many words?"

"How do you mean?"

"They used those words?"

"No. They used, well, you know yourself."

"Nothing physical."

"No. 'Mary doesn't want you hassling her.' 'You can't drive with broken legs.'"

Minogue looked at his watch. Nearly three. The heat was putting him to sleep.

"I know I'm under suspicion, you know. And I don't blame you."

"I'm not persecuting you for your beliefs, Mr. Mullen." Yet.

"You'll probably try anything to make me say I killed my own daughter. Right? You took my car away and I can't work. I just sit at the table and think about everything. And pray. I thought about drinking more times today and yesterday than I thought about it for weeks, probably. You think that's easy? You — well, the other fellas earlier really — run down my beliefs. Call me names, right? Wife-beater. How am I going to persuade you that I'm innocent?"

"You're not going to persuade us. We're going to decide that for ourselves."

"But haven't I got the sheet of me fares for the night, addresses even?"

"It's incomplete, Mr. Mullen. You know better than I do about switching off a meter."

"So if I can't account for ten seconds that night, then I'm still on a list or something?"

Minogue hauled his legs in under him. He put his watch back on.

"We'll be talking to you again, Mr. Mullen. Look, I hope you last it out with the drink thing. Get together with someone, can't you? Your, what do you call 'ems, mentors?"

Mullen rose to his feet.

"Look, let me just tell you one last thing. I don't like this way you treat me. But I accept it because I'm depending on you to find whoever did this. Being treated like I am is a part of my penance for the past, isn't it? You see, I'm not one of those people that thinks anything goes. Right?

Even in the Church, you get a lot of do-it-if-it-suits-you kind of morals. I lost my daughter to that world out there. That's my hell. And you are part of that hell because you don't understand."

Minogue nodded at Malone. Mullen looked out the doorway and then turned to the inspector. The words came out in a monotone.

"Nothing just happens, you know," he said. "There's a reason for everything."

$$\cdot \qquad \cdot \qquad \cdot \qquad \cdot \qquad \cdot$$

"Jesus," said Malone.

"Not quite, Tommy. Just one of His more vocal supporters."

Malone looked over.

"Okay. A looper, then."

"Well. Did you take all that in?"

"Haven't met many of him, I can tell you that."

"Do you believe him?"

Malone gnawed the inside of his cheek while he piloted the Nissan through traffic. Minogue wondered what shape Patricia Fahy would be in for the hard questions.

"Don't know yet. Fella I knew went religious after a car accident. Oh, yeah. Before the crash it was 'fuck this' and 'fuck that.' Then I'd bump into him and him hobbling around on crutches. 'God bless,' 'salvation,' 'love' was all I got out of him then. Told me he woke up in the hospital and God was floating on the ceiling. What about the fifteen pints, I said. Ha, ha, like. No. Not funny."

"Why?"

"Preferred the old way. You knew where you stood. Must have got brain damage, like."

Minogue shifted in his seat. The small of his back prickled with heat. Tiny pieces of grit seemed to be stinging his eyes at regular intervals. The traffic was at a standstill for three minutes now.

A short fat man in a fluorescent vest waved a reversing lorry out ahead of them. Minogue studied the nearly completed block and counted eight stories. The sea-green glass reflected the sky as gray. A crane was lifting more windows up the outside of the building. The load turned slowly as it rose and the sun caught the glass.

"Jases," said Malone and raised his hand over his eyes. He inched the Nissan around a forklift and turned into East Wall proper.

"Those windows'll be a right target for young lads around here. Boom."

Minogue grinned. This area east of the city center and north of the Liffey had been the toughest beat for a century. The adjoining docklands were being redeveloped as Ireland's new international financial center. The glass-clad buildings that had recently sprung up there were epic exercises in New Brutalist style, so far as Minogue could make out. Hope springs infernal.

"A bit hard on the Dublin crowd, there, aren't you, Tommy?"

Malone stood on the brakes as a motorcycle shot through a gap in traffic ahead.

"Ya fucking bollocks!"

Minogue caught a glimpse of the driver. A helmet covered in front by dark plastic, a radio strapped next to his chin.

"'Scuse the language there, er . . . Those fu — those couriers. I must be a bit edgy."

"Don't be worrying. This is your first case."

"Ah, that's not what has me so jumpy — Whoa. Number 27. Here we are."

Malone pulled in abruptly, switched off the engine and rolled up the window.

"What has you so jumpy?" Minogue asked.

"The brother."

"You expect Patricia Fahy to give you more slagging about him?"

"Yeah. And I'll probably get no end of slagging when you-know-who finds out."

"Jimmy Kilmartin? Sure he knows about it already."

"Yeah, I know that. It's a new page in the story though."

Malone's voice had fallen to a murmur. He rubbed his forehead hard with his thumb.

"Terry's time is up. He's getting paroled. Yeah. Terry hits the streets tomorrow."

CHAPTER 6

He slipped off the bus and lit his second-to-last cigarette. He watched the bus turn out of sight down the road. He'd have a bit of something to eat, have a wash-up, and head back into town. He'd try the pubs along Leeson Street. Dwyers, O'Brien's, that Unicorn kip. She might have gone to that club, Stella's. Wash his hair and put on something sharp so's he wouldn't have the bouncer at Stella's looking down his nose at him. But if he had to go to Stella's to look for her, that'd mean money. A fiver cover charge! And she might be sitting with one of the Egans. Christ! He looked up and down the street. She'd throw a bleeding fit if she thought he'd come looking for a freebie.

He drew hard on the cigarette. The steady pulses over his eyebrows were getting stronger. There was a headache on the way, one of those killers. Then his stomach'd go wormy, about the same time he'd get that freaky feeling, like a thirst all over his body. He'd start to think of doing anything. An oul one even, with her shopping bag and a cane, and he'd see himself kicking her in the face just to get her bag. One of these days it'd happen. It was like he couldn't stop it happening the way he had seen it going to happen, like it was somebody else with his face doing it. What was a fella supposed to do, for Christ's sake? Kill someone to get a bit of help or money? His chest heaved with the first impulse to cry out. It frightened him. Was he that close to losing it? This is what a bit of blow does to you? He'd heard stuff but didn't really believe it. The ones that cracked up had their own problems. No willpower. It was just lighting the fuse for a lot of them. Headers. It didn't take much to put them right over the wall.

He had often thought about getting his hands on a gun. Noel O'Rourke had told him he'd get him one for seven hundred quid. Noelie thought he wasn't smart enough to cop on that any gun he'd come by was probably dirty. Maybe even a cop getting shot with it. A gun'd do it, though. He could freelance for a few jobs. The Egans'd look at him different if he carried a gun. No one would *dare* fuck with him. No way: *boom*. You won't do that again, you stupid . . .

He headed for home. He had it all worked out now. Mary had always seen the good side of him, the paintings and drawings he'd done. She liked that stuff. He'd bring her the one of the people with animal heads. Maybe if she was in a good mood, he'd try to suss her out about the chances of selling his stuff to that gobshite she had on the side. Mister Money, whatever the hell his name was. Tony something. Alan? Alec? Him and his mates were the types to buy art, weren't they? If she'd just level with him about what she was up to. How would he say it: Don't you trust me, Mary? Let me in on it. I'll be your backup.

He rounded the corner walking faster. It was when he'd sit down at home, when the ma would give him that look or start nagging, that he'd have to keep a cool head. Another couple of hours, that was all. He could handle that. As long as he was doing something, he was okay. Exercise or something. Running. When he got that stash started up, he'd get a motorbike like Jammy — no, a car. Yeah! No. The stuff about a car was all shite. He'd buy a bike and get fit and everything. They'd laugh at first but then they'd see how organized he was, how he was his own boss. He'd eat right too, then there'd be no stopping him. Basically he was very healthy. It wouldn't take much to get fit —

He saw the Escort a long way off. It was parked five or six houses down from his. It was the souped-up model, new, with fancy wheels and spot lamps. He didn't remember seeing it here before. Maybe it was a robbed car. There was someone in the passenger seat. The back of his neck became itchy. He slowed. There was something familiar about the fella getting out of the car. Two cars passed on the road between them. He was a hundred yards from home. A shortish guy, bulky, with a green polo shirt. Where had he seen him before? Light caught on an earring. The man skipped across the street onto the footpath ahead of him. He stopped as he approached the laneway between his home and the back of Carrick Gardens. The man's hand moved down by his pocket. A signal he didn't want anyone to notice. Something came from around the corner where he was walking by now. Cigarette smoke. The man's eyes met his for a moment.

Which came first, him running or the guy in the denim shirt coming around the corner of the laneway, he didn't know. The panic was like an electric shock. A shout fell in the air behind him. He gathered speed, the balls of his feet bouncing off the pavement. By the bus stop and around the shops he sprinted. He glanced over his shoulder and saw that only the guy in the green shirt was after him. He had to get off the street: the car would be barreling after him any second. He dashed across the road and leaped the parapet into the playground. He ran by a group of children down into the park. He was putting more distance between himself and the guy chasing him but he was getting a stitch. He heard the shriek of tires and looked back. The driver of the Escort jumped out and leaped over the parapet after his mate.

His throat was burning when he came out of the park. Still he kept up his speed. Even in his terror he felt a glow of pride at being able to leg it like this. He remembered the races he had won in school, the only part of the bleeding school he had liked, the teacher who had tried to con him into staying on so he could go on for real training. He spotted the bus taking on its last passenger by Traynor's shop. The indicator was already on before he made it across. He ran in front of the double-decker as it pulled away. The brakes squealed and he ran to the door.

"You stewpit iijit!" The driver reminded him of his Uncle Joe. "Where in the name of Jases are you headed? Glasnevin cemetery?"

.   .   .   .   .

Patricia Fahy's father kept rolling the cigarettes until he had ten made. He worked slowly, pretending to be intent on the paraphernalia in his lap. Minogue looked over at intervals. Fahy's daughter hadn't opened up, the inspector reflected, and he was still undecided as to what to do about this.

"So she didn't even mention a boyfriend," Malone said. "Not even once?"

Patricia Fahy's face looked gray against the glare on the wall outside the kitchen window. Minogue heard children yelling on the terrace.

"No."

"You mean she had no fellas?"

"That's what she said," said her father. He moved his head from side to side as his tongue ran along the cigarette, but his eyes remained fixed on Malone. Neck like the trunk of a tree, thought Minogue.

"Let Patricia answer for herself, Mr. Fahy."

"She did answer. It's just you weren't listening."

"We're doing our best here," said Minogue. "We need Patricia's help."

"She's in no condition to be interrogated."

"She's not being interrogated."

"Then what the hell are two cops doing here in me kitchen?"

"Mr. Fahy," said Minogue. "We're not keen on this."

"Keen on what?"

"You pitching comments around when we're trying to conduct an interview on a murder investigation."

"Too bad then, isn't it? Why don't you leave? And take Haircut there with you."

"You're here as a concerned parent worried about his daughter," said Minogue. "Great. Now shut up, like a good man. Otherwise we'll be conducting interviews on our own premises."

Fahy stood.

"Will you now? Your mug on a card doesn't get you anywhere here, sunshine."

"Da! Give over, Da, will you?"

Her father didn't hear her. His hands came into play. One pointed at the door.

"Cops don't come around here without an armored car, pal. Hair-oil here should know that, even if you don't."

"Da! Stop it, for God's sake! It's only making it worse!"

Patricia Fahy stalked out of the kitchen, sobs tearing at her breath. The inspector turned back to Fahy. He seemed unable to find the words he wanted. His hand moved around the air instead. He sat down again.

"Phone calls," he grunted. "Four or five of them the past couple of days. Two different fellas' voices. Then there was a car. Did she tell you about the car?"

"What car?" asked Malone.

"She's in shock, isn't she, I mean to say. Last night about half-ten. It was parked up at the head of the street. Blue, it was. Stripes, the fancy wheels. New car, I'd say. A telephone thing sticking up out of it."

"You're worried that we can't protect your daughter from the Egans," said Minogue.

"Who said anything about the Egans?"

"Why are you so scared of them?" asked Malone. Fahy's brows dropped.

"Fuck you, Haircut. I'm not afraid of any man."

Malone set his jaw.

"You didn't see the registration plate?" asked Minogue.

"It was dark last night, in case you didn't notice."

"But you saw it was new. Color, fancy wheels. You saw it had a phone aerial."

Fahy maintained his stare but his eyebrows moved up. He licked the edge of a cigarette paper.

"All right, Mr. Fahy. You win. We'll decamp. We'll be off down to Store Street station where we can talk to Patricia in peace."

Fahy was up out of the chair fast.

"Like hell you will. You've no warrant to be in my house."

Malone stood slowly, as did Minogue.

"This ain't Hollywood, brother," said Malone. "Get a grip, there."

Fahy nodded in Minogue's direction but he kept his eyes on Malone.

"Take Junior for a walk there, Kojak, or he's going to be part of the scenery. Rapid, like. Cop or no cop."

"You and whose army," said Malone.

"I'll set your head singing before my daughter is —"

The door swung open again. Patricia Fahy looked over her hanky from face to face. Tears had left streaks down to her jawline.

"God, Da! Go out and get stuff for the tea or something! Jesus! Ma left a list there in the hall."

"I'm going nowhere until these two get to hell out."

"Well, go in the kitchen or someplace then!" Fahy looked from his daughter to the policemen and back. He shook his head and made for the door. He paused in the doorway and his face darkened again.

"Don't you try anything," he growled. Minogue looked at the photos over the table while he waited for Fahy to go. A wedding, a woman who looked like Patricia Fahy. A sunburned couple standing on white sand, an apartment or hotel in the background. Pennants for Spurs and last year's Irish World Cup team. He heard Fahy swear and then the kitchen door slammed.

"The Egans, Patricia," he said. She leaned against the cooker and folded her arms.

"What about them?"

"They're on your da's mind a lot."

She narrowed her eyes and dabbed at her nostrils again with the tissue.

"He doesn't know them," she said.

"What would they want with you? What did they want with Mary?"

"Who says they want anything with me? Or Mary?"

"Ah, Patricia, come on," said Minogue. She pivoted and took a packet of cigarettes from the counter. Her hands were steady as she lit one. She took a hurried second drag down deep in her lungs. Her words came out quickly with puffs of smoke.

"Mary was on the game, wasn't she? Maybe that was it. I don't know."

"What about you, Patricia?"

"What about me, what? You'd know if I was. Same way you'd know Mary was, wouldn't you?"

"We're not here to make speeches, Patricia," said Minogue. "We need to know Mary so's we can find out what happened to her. Don't you want whoever did this to get caught?"

She frowned behind a ball of smoke.

"I can't get over it," she murmured. "Your brother. Jesus! One's the cop and the other's the —"

Malone ran his fingers through his hair.

"What's the use in giving us the runaround," he said.

"Who pimped for Mary, Patricia?" asked Minogue.

Her mouth stayed open for several seconds. She rolled her eyes and looked away.

"Who broke into your place?" Malone asked.

"You're asking me? Amn't I supposed to be asking you that?"

Only her arm moved, Minogue saw, and its arc up to her lips was of such grace and careless accuracy that he could only stare at her. He sat forward and ran his palm across the soft, loose skin on the knuckles of his other hand. Damn, he thought. She thinks she's a bloody ingenue doing an audition for something. Would she be giving him as much grief if he had taken her down to CDU? He turned his hand over and began rubbing at the palm with his thumb. Tiny flecks of dirt escaped the folds of skin and collected in rolls. He didn't look up when he spoke to her.

"Listen, Patricia. We're trying to work from the inside out here. Mary, her friends, what she did, where she liked to go. What she did or didn't do that might be connected to what has happened. It's a lot of stuff.

Stuff you might know but you mightn't think is important. Do you know what I'm getting at?"

He glanced over. Her eyes had glazed over. She drew on her cigarette. He thought of giving up then. Here was a woman with no criminal record being a substantial pain in the arse to the Guards.

"People know a lot," he heard himself say. "They really do. They notice an awful lot, but they need to know something is important before they can drag it out of their memory. You can't beat it out of people either. Things pop up and you can't predict them: 'Yes, she used to do that!' or 'Oh, that was the name of the fella she mentioned that night.' There's another way that's less salubrious entirely."

"Is this the good cop-bad cop bit now?"

Minogue thought of Kilmartin.

"We work from the outside in too, Patricia. It's like cracking an egg. We go after records, suspects, associates. It's a bit like crowbarring into somebody's life, looking all the time for the killer."

He engaged her look. She blinked once.

"But it gets people's backs up, Patricia."

Malone's mouth twitched and he caught the inspector's eye. Minogue rubbed his palm again.

"Cracking the egg often works though," he went on. "But it takes time. Sometimes the inside of the egg isn't hardboiled so it gets messy. Sometimes the egg gets ruined. Ends up on the floor."

"Eggs," she murmured. "I don't like eggs."

"Did Mary seem out of sorts at all the last while?" asked Malone. "Worried, like?"

"I heard her getting sick last week. She said it was the gargle. She'd been out the night before."

"With who?"

"I dunno."

Malone's eyes had narrowed to slits. He was staring at her.

"I fucking don't!" she cried. "I keep on telling you! 'Who was her boyfriend?' 'Who called to the flat for her?' 'Who'd she hang around with?' 'Why didn't she talk to you about her life?' Jesus!"

"You never knew where she went, what pub, or who with?" asked Malone. "Ah, come on now."

"Ah, come on yourself! Don't you get it? I don't fucking *know!*"

Minogue waited for her to lean back against the counter.

"Okay, Patricia. You saw her last yesterday morning. She was in the kitchen?"

"Just before eight o'clock, yeah. I was up late."

"And you said she hadn't been to bed."

"That's right. She was just sitting there at the table. Smoking a fag, drinking a cup of tea. Didn't hear her coming in. She was still dressed from the night before."

"How'd she look again?"

"Tired, that's how. Looked like she'd been up all night. Shagged."

"No remarks about where she'd been, nothing like that?" Malone tried.

"Nothing. Nothing. I knew better than to ask."

Minogue stretched out his legs.

"Patricia. You're telling us that Mary kept to herself —"

"You don't believe me, do you. You're thinking, 'Well, the pair of them were into something, so that's why she won't tell us anything.' Aren't you? Yes, y'are!"

Minogue took in the red-rimmed eyes, the blotchy face. She pursed her lips and lifted her cigarette.

"How long did you share the place with her?"

"A year and a bit."

"Where did she live before she moved in with you?"

"I don't know. Some fella maybe."

"A fella? Did she ever say his name?"

"I don't know! I'm only guessing, that's all! Jesus! Do you think I used to come home here and start firing questions at her the minute she walked in the door? Sure, she was hardly home, ever."

"How long did you know Mary then?"

"Two years, about. I met her doing a thing for manicuring. She was always good for a laugh. Used to see her the odd time after that. Then about a year and a half back I bumped into her in a pub."

"What pub?"

She curled her lip.

"I don't remember. What do you think I am, a computer?"

"You went into a flat with her," Minogue said.

"So? She didn't tell me her life story."

"You knew she worked the trade though," said Malone. "How?"

"I found out one night, didn't I. Met someone. We were talking about people we knew. The usual chatting. I mention Mary and he goes, 'Is she still at it?' So I ask her later. She got mad at me."

"What did she say?"

"'What's wrong with getting money for it?'"

"Freelance, like?" Malone asked.

"I don't know."

"With the Egans?"

Minogue didn't get the outburst he expected. She folded her arms and waved the cigarette around.

"Look. All I know about them is that she knew one of them. That's all."

"That's all?" repeated Malone. "Why should the person who did this get away with it, Patricia? You're helping them."

"No, I amn't."

"You're scared," said Malone. "And it shows. Just like your da."

"Drop dead. What do you know about anything?"

"Mary was your friend, wasn't she?" said Minogue. She pushed off suddenly from the counter.

"I told her, and I told her!" she burst out. "She didn't listen! She wouldn't!"

"Wouldn't what, Patricia?"

"Ah, Christ, I don't know! That's the problem! Can't you get it through your thick skulls? She wouldn't tell me! She had all these secrets. I warned her."

"About what?"

She settled back against the counter and looked out the window.

"So Mary was still on the game," said Malone.

"I don't know. I suppose she was. Maybe she wasn't. I don't know."

"She had no pimp, you seem to be telling us," said Minogue. "But you were warning her against something. Was it people you saw back at the flat, people she told you about? People you heard about?"

"She used the flat as a place to hang her clothes," she said. "So don't be asking me again where she spent her time. All I know for sure is that Mary did manicures over at Tresses. There were times I wouldn't see her for days. A week, even. I was getting tired of it, I tell you. I didn't like being there on me own. That wasn't the idea, like."

An image came to Minogue: Patricia Fahy poking around among Mary's stuff.

"Of moving in together, like?"

"Yeah. It worked out okay, splitting the cost and everything. But you'd want company, you know? I went out with me fella just to have company sometimes."

Malone flipped back a page in his notebook. She glared over at him.

"He's my alibi. Isn't that the word? So's I don't have to keep on telling yous I didn't do it?"

Malone looked up from his notebook. She returned his glare with a studied pout.

"Try to think, now, Patricia," said Minogue. "There must have been people phoning the flat or coming around looking for her. Family, friends — anyone."

She looked up at the lamp shade.

"Look," she said. "Mary told me that the last people she'd want calling around would be family. She told me she had no brothers or sisters. She said her oul lad was a bastard. She wasn't keen to talk about her ma. I thought it was kind of, you know, strange, like. But I wasn't going to be nosy like, was I? She wanted her own life, fair enough, like. That a crime?"

She dabbed her cigarette in the ashtray and then held it under her thumb. Minogue let his cheeks balloon with a held breath. He imagined questions floating around trapped in his mouth. How did she know? What else did she know? What was she leaving out?

"Well, there was one iijit," she murmured as she released her thumb from the cigarette. "Yeah, now I remember . . . I mean, I don't know if he's . . ."

"Who?"

"Just a, well, Mary called him a gobshite. I don't even know his real name. He showed up at the door once. She answered, that's why I forgot until now. Yeah. Skinny fella. What's that artist's name, the famous one, he's dead? Leo . . . Really famous, like?"

"Leonardo da Vinci?"

"Yeah."

"A fella called for Mary," said Malone. "A fella by the name of Leonardo da Vinci?"

"What are you looking at? I told you I didn't know his name. Mary said she knew him years ago. He must have found out where she lived. Scruffy-looking type. No wonder she wasn't keen on hanging around the likes of him."

"Scruffy-looking," said Malone. "Skinny fella? What else about him?"

"Average height. Got the feeling off him he thought he was something, but he wasn't. A gobshite. Wouldn't be surprised if he was into something, you know."

"Criminal?"

"Yeah."

"Did he stay over at the flat?" Malone asked.

"It was Mary answered the door. She was pissed off he was there. I came back later on and he was gone. So was she."

"Not what you thought of as her boyfriend then," said Minogue. She shrugged.

"Said that he was a gobshite, didn't she?"

The air seemed almost watery now. Minogue moved to the edge of the chair and tested his biro on a page of his notebook.

"To your knowledge, Patricia, did Mary take drugs?"

Instead of the sarcasm he expected, Minogue's question drew silence. He looked up from the notebook. She was staring at the ashtray and biting her lip.

"Okay, Patricia," he said. "We'll finish off here for now. Think back more to this Leonardo da Vinci. When he came to the flat, a bit more on what he looked like?"

She glanced from Minogue to Malone and back, but her eyes were blank.

.   .   .   .   .

The air was still full of dust and glare. The sun's orb seemed to have broadened. The inspector hoped that somewhere behind this tarnished air there was a more proper blue than Dublin was stuck with today. His aches had localized themselves in his neck and shoulders. Malone's hair stood out in slick bristles. He finessed his way through the hordes spilling out off the paths by O'Connell Bridge and let the Nissan find its way down the quays toward Kingsbridge.

"I dunno," he said. "I can't tell. Is it shock or is she just plain scared shitless?"

"Well, there was no point in trying to come the heavy."

"I just couldn't figure out how much she was lying. I mean, I'm not totally down on her, like. The Egans are animals."

"Being pregnant," said Minogue.

"What?"

"Being pregnant. That was the fuse lit, I'm thinking."

Malone looked over.

"Tried to get the father to wear it and he wouldn't?"

"Maybe, yes."

"So she laid it on the line for him, he loses the head and clocks her? I wonder how many fellas Mary had on the go."

"Well, maybe we'll know quicker than we thought. This Liam Hickey that Éilis got from the alias search looks good. He grew up two roads over from Mary. We'll know better when we get back to the squad."

Minogue let his eyes sweep along the buildings and the derelict sites turned car parks along the Liffey Quays. Cheap furniture from hucksters' shopfronts cluttered the path. He had a hard time remembering what had preceded the rash of boarded-up buildings awaiting demolition. For every tarted-up pub and pastiche of Georgian facades, there were a half-dozen scutty shops flogging junk. Grime, noise, carelessness. They passed Capel Street bridge and the inspector saw that the tide on the Liffey was beginning to ebb. Soon the people lined up along the quays for their buses home would have the slimy walls of the Liffey banks and the mantle of lumpy masses to either side of the riverbed for company.

The Four Courts, which hid behind its stately facade much of the drab bulk of the State's legal apparatus, slid by the two policemen. With its legions of barristers and solicitors and hard-faced, chain-smoking defendants and their families awaiting their turn in court, the place had always depressed the hell out of Minogue. Though rebuilt after its almost complete devastation during the Civil War, its echoing warren of hallways and rooms smelled of futility from the first day Minogue stepped into a courtroom there. People got lost in there, he believed, and not just criminals either. He didn't want to be one of them.

The Nissan slowed for roadworks. In an alley next to a locked and boarded church whose name he couldn't remember, Minogue spotted a man and a woman swaying and arguing. Both had red, swollen faces and tousled hair. Two bottles stood next to them on the footpath. If he hits her, Minogue thought, they'd have to get out. Couldn't avoid it. Malone was talking.

"Sorry, Tommy?"

"I know Patricia Fahy has no record, but do you want to bet she's on the game too?"

Minogue shrugged.

"Doyle can't help us much there, he says."

Mary Mullen had been pregnant. Pressure on her, a countdown, running out of time. How much did an abortion cost? Did she want one? Some ultimatum, he thought. Blackmail? Her flat had been trashed. An address book, an appointment book. Did anyone write love letters these days? Photos, mementos, letters. Leonardo da Vinci, someone she'd known growing up. Also connected to the Egans?

Malone inched the car by the yellow-and-white oil drums. They had a free run to the squad car park. Kilmartin was writing on the notice boards. Minogue stood back and studied them. The timetable for the last week of Mary Mullen's life was in Murtagh style: bright green and red. Minogue felt something drop in his stomach when he saw the blank spaces. He rubbed his head and looked again.

"Anything?" barked Kilmartin.

"Nothing that'd matter right now. Any news on this Leonardo Hickey fella?"

"A car dispatched to the house. He's not home. I have his record here in front of me. A proper little shite, so he is. Break and enter, possession of stolen property. Drunk and disorderly — he was in a crowd that wrecked a patrol car outside a pub three years ago."

"What's under 'Associates'?"

"Nothing, oul stock."

"Nothing?"

"Divil damn the bit. Hickey is a fifteen-watt gouger. But you never know."

"Give us some good news, can't you? Any yield on the canal bank stuff yet?"

"Four hundred and fifty-two tons of shit, six thousand tons of —"

"All right, Jim. I get the idea. What about Mullen's taxi?"

"Shag-all. Yet. They're still swabbing and poking it. Don't hold your breath, I say. That's why I started the door-to-door already. Murtagh is up to his neck building up likelies from the files. There was a fella released the day before, finished a sentence for rape. He's chasing that one this very minute."

"No fix yet on whether Mary worked after quitting the Tresses place?"

"Wouldn't I tell you if there was?"

Minogue squeezed the bridge of his nose.

"Well, what about this Egan thing?"

"Christ, the questions being fired at me! Amn't I after telling you that I talked to Mick Hand in Serious Crimes? We know her there, says he. She used to come and go with one of the Egans. So I try to finagle the latest surveillance they have on the Egans, see if we can place her for the last while. They're still looking. Some of the stuff is not in the computer yet. 'We're a bit behind in the updates, Jim,' says he. 'Volume of stuff,' et cetera. Sure, says I. The old story: we'll milk our own cows. Anyway. He'll have them done up and copied for us by the morning. He'll bring them along to our powwow."

Minogue flopped into a chair. Kilmartin jammed the cap on his marker and threw it toward Murtagh's desk. All watched it skitter across the desktop and fall to the floor.

"Christ," said the chief inspector. He cocked his head and looked at Malone.

"Don't you love it, Molly? No witnesses. Nobody saw anything, heard anything. And this is a high-traffic area in the middle of Dublin! Gurriers broke all the bloody lights by the banks. Only we know the locks are closed, we'd be faced with the bloody prospect that she went in anywhere along the canal, back up to Crumlin or somewhere — Christ, the River Shannon even! We don't know where the hell this Mary Mullen spent her time. We don't know for certain where she was killed, even. Did she have a falling-out with her fella? How the hell do we know she even had a fella? Her own father and mother hardly knew her this last few years."

Malone shoved his hands in his pockets and leaned against the wall.

"Come on, lads, for God's sake," said Kilmartin. "A whole heap of rubbish, a filthy scene, no sign of a weapon, a girl with a record, a family that fights like cats and dogs . . ."

Minogue stretched out his legs. Kilmartin turned toward him.

"What about this flatmate? Surely to God she knows more about the bloody person she was living with. Didn't they have friends in common? Is this Fahy one on the game too and only letting on? Logic now, lads, logic! Almighty God, can't Doyle and the rest of them in Vice come up with more? Matt?"

"We're not happy with Ms. Fahy," said Minogue. "We'll be talking to her again."

"Okay. But what happened to Mary Mullen? Come on. Save me a headache here. What's going on at all?"

Minogue eyed his colleague. "Right off the top of me head?"

"Where else?"

"In front of the new boy?"

"God between us and all harm! Go on. I'll protect you."

"Why was Mary at the canal at all?" Minogue asked. "To my mind, she shouldn't have been there."

"What do you mean? Chance? Bad luck? The canal's just a place to dump her? Egans, you're thinking? A row?"

"All of the above. Maybe."

Malone scratched at the back of his head, cleared his throat, and glanced at Minogue.

"Someone breaking into the flat is a bit too much of a coincidence," he said. "Maybe she had something she shouldn't have had. Something belonging to someone else."

"Drugs?" asked Kilmartin. "A loan? Was she in hock and she couldn't pay?"

"That might be why she tried to work the canal that night," said Minogue. "A payment to keep someone off her back, maybe?"

"She's no good dead," said Malone. "To a shark, like."

He began patting his crew cut. He sensed Kilmartin's eyes on him and stopped.

"She messed up on something, you're saying?" Malone nodded.

Kilmartin turned away, stretched and groaned.

"God now, Molly, if you didn't go to school here, you met the scholars coming home. Our Mary Mullen is gone down the glen and someone's after sending her. She had more than this Fahy kid for a friend. And they didn't just sell Tupperware, lads. Let's get serious about this now."

CHAPTER 7

An aging Ford Fiesta was parked in the Minogues' driveway. The inspector eyed the rusting paint by the wheel wells before he reversed out onto the road. The laughter from the back garden was his daughter's. He stopped at the end of the garage wall and listened.

"Ah, Ma!" Iseult hooted. "He will!"

"He might," was Kathleen's reply. "You know how it is with him."

"Da! You're surrounded. Come out where we can see you! With your hands up!"

How had she known he was there? He glanced down at the pathway ahead: shadow, yes.

Pat the Brain and Iseult were sitting by the wisteria that had taken over the back of the coal shed. Kathleen sat across from them in a deck chair. Her hand was at her face. The grass was crunchy underfoot. He must water it tonight.

"You can put your hands down now," Iseult said. "What's in the envelope?"

"It's a case about a black Fiesta used in the abduction of someone's daughter."

He made a curtsy toward Kathleen and winked at his daughter's fella. "Howiya since, Pat."

Tea things were all over the garden table but, God help him, no wine in evidence.

"Jim Kilmartin maintains the heat is another grant thrown into the national begging bowl by the European Parliament. Should have kept our own independent weather, says he."

Pat smiled. Minogue tried to figure out what was different about Pat this evening. The T-shirt still hung off his bony shoulders, the hair was as unruly as ever, but the face had changed. Iseult was looking down at the grass not far from where she had discarded her sandals. She was smiling at some secret joke. Would this one sting? A wary, off-duty Garda inspector looked from face to face.

"Ye're ornaments to the garden, all of ye."

"Go way out of that," said Iseult.

Minogue looked at the cups and plates.

"I must say now that I am of an age and humor where I'm interested in a glass of something more bracing than, em, tea. Who'll court a bit of divilment with me?"

No one answered.

"Pat? Red or white?"

"Well . . ."

"What's holding us back here, lads?"

Kathleen had folded her arms. She seemed to be very interested in the apple trees. Iseult smiled again. He made a face at her and sat down.

"All right. Congratulations, then. It'll cost you though."

Kathleen started. She sat up and stared at her husband. Iseult began to laugh.

"Black Beauty out the front, I meant," he said. "The highway robbery of tax and insurance and petrol prices and . . . What do you think I meant?"

Pat's bashful look awakened something in him.

"Iseult," said Minogue. He kept his eyes on hers. It seemed harder to breathe now.

"Is there something I should be let in on? Or am I supposed to go on looking stupid, is it?"

She threw her head back. Her black hair whipped back and settled. She hugged her stomach while she laughed.

"Well, Iseult," he muttered. "Is it what I think it is?"

She recovered enough to nod her head twice. He glanced at her teeth and her bobbing throat. She rubbed tears from the corners of her eyes.

"Da, you're a howl! I told them you'd know! I bet Pat a fiver you'd cop on."

Minogue looked over at Pat the Brain. This was something that only happened on iijity television shows. So this was one of life's moments, something that was already absorbed into family stories: *Will you ever forget the evening Iseult . . . Remember that hot summer, when? . . .* Something was passing, he knew, and it would never return. How was he supposed to react? Pat looked over and smiled. Nice lad, Pat, thought Minogue. Gentle, dry humor. A bit bookish, but his own man. He looked around the garden and thought of the photos Kathleen looked at more often now. Iseult in her First Holy Communion dress, Iseult's graduation pictures. Iseult on a beach somewhere in Turkey.

The sun was behind the trees now. Dulled by the haze, it made the leaves shine and even glow at the edges. Nothing moved in the garden. A grasshopper took Minogue's attention from the birds. He had put in the apple trees when Kathleen was pregnant with Daithi. The rockery with the pirated wildflowers from the Burren in Clare had taken him three years of intermittent, pleasurable work a decade ago. His eyes strayed from rock to rock, plant to plant. He had intended to reform it, recast it sometime, but something in him had resisted. His eyes began to sting.

"I'm very happy for you," he said.

Iseult swallowed and grinned and rose from her chair. Kathleen dabbed at her eyes. He looked over at Pat's distracted smile as he kissed Iseult. Her cheek smelled of peaches.

"That's another fiver," she whispered.

. . . . .

Minogue woke up thinking about Jack Mullen. Jack Mullen was off his rocker. He'd stalked his wayward daughter. He'd argued with her, pleaded with her. She'd refused, and probably ridiculed him. She'd gotten one of the Egans or their gang to lay the heavy word on him: leave our Mary alone — or else. She was too far gone then, wasn't she, and the only way to bring her home, to bring her back to Jesus, was to kill her?

He sat on the side of the bed and opened the curtain a little. Not a cloud in the sky. Day what of the drought was it? Day eleven. The last rain had been a ten-minute shower a fortnight ago. His mouth was chalky from last night's wine. Where the hell had Mary Frances Mullen spent her time? She was a live-in with the Egans or one of their hangers-on, that's what. "Drug-barons" was the latest cliché. Go into this meeting this morning and cobble together a warrant, take crowbars to their places. He tried to shake off his rancor. Wasn't his daughter going to get married? Daithi'd come home for the wedding. Maura and Mick, the whole Clare contingent, would come up, by God. Hoey, Kilmartin, John Tynan. Kathleen's crowd, Iseult's mad friends . . . It'd be one good hooley. My gods are household gods, he thought. He tapped the radio and plodded into the bathroom.

The talk over breakfast was brittle. Iseult had been adamant about the registry office. Pat had maintained the vague smile as he slumped in a deck chair rubbing at his lip. It's more than just the two people getting married that are involved, Kathleen said. Was it too much to expect Iseult to get married in a church? He didn't know, he said. Surely Iseult would realize that when she sat down to think things through. Hadn't she thought things through already, he dared. Kathleen's expression told him that she didn't believe that their daughter had. Couldn't she find some other way to make her statement? She could, was his answer, and it had stopped their conversation on the topic: she mightn't bother to get married at all. He sat in his Citroen relieved to be on the move: my rows are household rows.

Éilis was collating bundles of photocopies. The inspector studied the notice boards that had been wheeled out to the center of the room. He stood up close to the photocopies of the Dublin street map taped next to Sheehy's name. Pink fluorescent, lime green, Blessed-Virgin-Moving-Statue blue for the door-to-door teams Sheehy had set up. He recognised Murtagh's handwriting on a column titled "Bail/released" and the Garda stations he had phoned to tap those suspects. None of the seventeen names was familiar. Only one entry, with a question mark after it at that, under the Incidents column, again in Murtagh's writing. The Known Offenders list comprised twenty-three names. It must have taken him half the night to amass this. He looked toward Murtagh, who gave him a lazy smile in return. Kilmartin's door was shut. Minogue opened his folder and took out the points he had marshaled on a sheet of photocopy paper last night.

"Nice going there, John," he said. "I feel a crushing guilt for leaving early. The daughter announced that she's going to get married."

"Great. Congratulations. Has she anyone particular in mind?"

"She asked if you were still available. Had to tell her no. Sorry and all that now. Don't take it personally."

Murtagh shrugged.

"Is Himself inside?"

Murtagh leaned in closer. He nodded at the door to Kilmartin's office. "He went in there ten minutes ago with Mick Hand. 'Conferring.'"

"The Egans?"

Murtagh stroked his neck and studied the ceiling.

"On the agenda, you can be sure, boss. He came out a few minutes ago looking fit to brain someone."

Murtagh was about to add something when Kilmartin's door was jerked open. Sergeant Mick Hand emerged ahead of Kilmartin. Something about Hand's gait and expression reminded Minogue of teams leaving the field at halftime trailing by three goals. He looked to Kilmartin. The chief inspector shook his head once, stalked to the boards and stood with his hands on his hips.

"All right, all right," he called out. "Away we go. We're going to get an education about the people that Mary Mullen was mixed up with. But first we'll take a few minutes to update ourselves. Can you wait, Mick?"

Hand nodded. He caught Minogue's eye for a moment.

"Thanks, Mick. Site report, forensic and door-to-door for starters. Who wants to go first? Don't all rush, now."

. . . . .

Minogue observed Kilmartin's slow passage around the room. Murtagh talked on. There was no yield yet from Mullen's Volkswagen. Spotless for a taxi, said Theresa Brophy, Kilmartin's favored conduit for early forensic leads. Jack Mullen could reasonably claim to be a conscientious taxi driver concerned with the welfare and comfort of his passengers. Passengers, thought Minogue. He carried maybe a dozen different people a day. That's upwards of a hundred people a week. Five thousand a year. He made another effort to listen carefully to Murtagh. Known offenders, prostitutes known to the police in that area . . . Offenders on bail, recent parolees . . . Addicts known to frequent the area, assaults in the area in the last year . . . Minogue underlined addict.

"Well, why not?"

It was Kilmartin who had barked at Murtagh. The detective looked up from his papers and pushed a strand of hair from his forehead.

"Which now, boss?"

"The brassers, man! The ladies of the night! Why were none of them plying their trade at that hour of the night, we want to know."

Murtagh glanced at Minogue.

"Doyle maintains that there's a hiatus around that time of the night," said the inspector.

"Hiatus?" said Kilmartin. "Isn't that from lifting stuff that's too heavy? Try a bit of English there, Shakespeare. For working men, the likes of Voh' Lay-bah there and meself."

Malone's expression didn't change. He tapped his pencil on his notebook several times.

"The business only really gets going when the pubs close," said Minogue. "Donnybrook station did a sweep of the area three weeks ago. Doyle says the drive-by trade has slackened off there anyway."

"Let me guess," said Kilmartin. "Telephone dates and the Companions Wanted ads do the business now, is it?"

Minogue nodded.

"So says Doyler."

Kilmartin tugged at his ear.

"Fergal?"

Sheehy delivered in a rococo Kerry accent.

"Well now, door-to-door, we have nothing yet. We're doing a quarter-mile radius. We're a bit over halfway through the pubs, clubs, eating houses, hotels. I'm chasing down cleaners and night staff in offices near the canal too. Potentials from residents too."

He turned his notebook sideways to scrutinize a drawing he had made.

"There are video cameras on a place two hundred–odd yards up," he said. "But they're the wrong side of the bridge."

"Speaking of which," Kilmartin broke in and turned to Murtagh, "you're working through the video of the site, aren't you?"

"Yup," said Murtagh. "I've got two fellas from CDU on it. We're about, I suppose, a third of the way. So far, they're all legit. Six cars were parked overnight. We got statements from five."

"All good citizens in that part of town, are they," said Kilmartin.

"As good as you'll get in Dublin," said Sheehy. Hand smiled and crossed his legs.

"Huh," said Kilmartin. "What photos are you using, Fergal?"

"File mugs from her last conviction."

Kilmartin licked his lips and looked down at his cigarette. Minogue yawned but couldn't stop after one. Malone was still writing in his notebook. Kilmartin waved at the notice boards.

"Patricia Fahy. Molly and Matt took her statement? . . ."

Minogue tagged on to the unfinished end of Kilmartin's sentence.

"We're not entirely thrilled. She's scared. Her whereabouts look pretty sound. She spent the evening with her fella, James Tierney, Jammy Tierney. He appears to be a clean bill of goods. John tracked him down handy enough."

Murtagh took his cue.

"They watched a soccer match on the box. Tierney's a soccer fanatic. Arsenal and Everton. He had chapter and verse of the game. She stayed over."

"Say no more," said Kilmartin. "Now, before we move on, a few things to bear in mind. She does not appear to have been a drug user. She had not had intercourse that evening. What she did have was between three and four glasses of alcohol that appears to have been vodka. What she also had was a hairline fracture of her left cheekbone. Mary Mullen was hit hard with something that left no transfer, fragments, pigment, impression — nothing — on, in, or about the tissues. She was very unconscious when she went into the water. She drowned. Her bag's missing. Was she back on the game, for that night anyway? A 'curb job,' as this class of trade is called, I believe?"

He paused and drew on a fresh cigarette.

"Is she short of money? She's jacked it in with this place Tresses. She hasn't applied for Social Welfare. She's pregnant. Does she need money for an abortion? Does she have a pimp who makes her take up the trade again? Do the oul hormones lead her astray?"

Kilmartin arched his back and scratched with his thumb.

"So," he groaned. "No sign of this fella Patricia Fahy mentioned. Hickey."

He nodded toward one of the boards where Leo Hickey's photocopied and enlarged mug shot had been taped.

"Hands up those who think we'll find him belly-up somewhere too," said Kilmartin, looking at Malone.

No hands were raised.

"Well, his mother's plenty worried. He didn't show up at home last night. Hickey's a petty, hang-around type of a scut. He's probably a drug user, to what extent we don't know. But anyway, we'll move ahead. We know from our fine colleagues in the Serious Crime Squad that Mary Mullen has been seen in the company of one Eddsy Egan, in a club called Too De Loos. Mick Hand has several sightings of her in the recent past

there with the little shitehawk. Eddsy Egan. Are we right there, Mick?"
Kilmartin had worked his way around to a seat next to Minogue.
Hand walked to the boards. Minogue looked at the photos of the Egans.
Two of the three were mug shots. There was a definite resemblance be-
tween two at least — Martin and Bobby. Eddsy, the oldest, had a heavily
lined face. He looked at least ten years older than the next one, Bobby.
Minogue scanned the paragraphs and let the pages slip from his fingers
one by one. Tout Des Loups was the spelling of the nightclub.

"Lads," said Hand, and smiled. Now that he was standing, there was
something about Hand's long legs and small, lined face that put
Minogue in mind of a camel.

"Thanks, er, Jim. And thanks for the photocopying there. You should all
have a copy of the summary we did as regards Mary Mullen and the
Egans. It's from the surveillance reports. The phone calls are marked with
three fat dots at the beginning and the end. The stuff is date-ordered. We
went back a month for this. If you turn to the fifth page, I think it is,
there's a surveillance log of Eddsy Egan's house."

Hand flipped the board back and began tapping the marker on some
words. The inspector let his eyes return to focus on them. The Egan
family had been mapped out in red, green and blue.

"Eddsy was number one," said Hand. "Before he was run over. It was
a gang thing. He has plastic knees and pins and bits of things holding
him together now."

"Christ," murmured Kilmartin. "We could have saved the taxpayer a
pile of money if I'd have been driving, let me tell you. At least I know
where reverse is."

"Martin runs things day-to-day," said Hand. "Eddsy sits in the shop.
Martin's on the go. Car phones, faxes, the whole bit. Martin's the brain,
the planner. Eddsy had set up the rackets but he had to bow out. Last is
Bobby. Bobby's a madman. He's into drugs but we don't know if he's into
them on a regular basis. Probably. He has a very short fuse. Bobby scares
everyone, his brothers included. He's the one who looks after the en-
forcement end of things. Mention of him is enough to get the job done."

"So he's the one who looks after the whores?" asked Malone.

"There's a loose confederation of pimps and gougers in the trade. The
Egans decide about some areas. They don't exactly control the pimps or
the trade, but pimps give them some of their take or a quid pro quo, at
least."

"What quid pro quo?" demanded Kilmartin.

"Girls. Information on clients that the Egans could use. We think the Egans pass drugs along a network of girls. For their clients, like, or for the girls themselves."

"What's the extent of that now?" asked Minogue. Hand shrugged.

"We don't know. But we're working on the belief that the Egans are trying to develop new markets for drugs away from the street. It's getting a bit hairy for them there on the streets. So Bobby has two or three fellas on the payroll as enforcers. They move between the operations — drugs, fencing stolen goods, moving property and money around. We've put some away but there are always fellas available. Fellas get out of jail and, bang, they show up on surveillance. Next thing is they're caught again. It's like a merry-go-round with them."

Kilmartin exchanged a glance with Minogue. Tommy Malone was examining the backs of his hands. Minogue wondered if Hand knew of Terry Malone.

"This Bobby Egan character," said Kilmartin. "Drag him in and work at him. Squeeze him awhile?"

Hand scratched at the back of his neck. Kilmartin's eyes had taken on a glint.

"Well, now, I don't know," said Hand. He didn't return Kilmartin's gaze.

"Well, we shagging well do, Mick. Bring 'em in tied onto the back bumper of a squad car for all we care."

Hand cleared his throat and glanced at Kilmartin.

"Well, as I said to you earlier on, Jim . . ."

Kilmartin wasn't budging, Minogue saw. He'd make Hand say it in front of the squad.

"Yes?" said Kilmartin. Hand's tongue worked around his upper teeth. Minogue sat back and joined his hands behind his neck.

"What are we hearing here, Mick?" asked Kilmartin. "A hands-off, is it?"

Hand shifted in his seat.

"God, no," he said. "But there's a very big operation ongoing. Very big thing now."

"Very big," said Kilmartin. "How big? Sure, we're very big here ourselves."

Hand smiled wanly.

"Well, it's really a matter of coordinating your involvement now," he said. Minogue felt a little sorry for Hand. Mere messenger or not, he still deserved to leave with one arrow in his back.

Hand looked hopefully to the faces in the room. "Your investigation could turn out to be a really valuable tool, another bit of leverage —"

"We don't queue here, Mick," said Kilmartin. "Murder's top of the list. Garda Handbook, sweet pea. Page 777. Criminal code. We're in first. All the time, every time."

Hand shrugged and looked down at his notes. Kilmartin looked from face to face and then back to Hand.

"Before you go now, Mick. Bring us back to the house you had under surveillance. Eddsy Egan's place, where Mary Mullen was spotted."

Relieved, Hand sat up.

"Okay. Sure. She arrived the night before in the taxi — actually the morning. Half-two, with Eddsy. No sign of her until eleven then. A taxi rolled up and she came out."

The whole afternoon ahead of her, thought Minogue.

"Now, if you look back to the summary, you'll see that she seems to have come and gone from the house fairly regularly . . ."

·   ·   ·   ·   ·

Hand stopped by Éilis on his way out. Minogue studied Kilmartin's expression as he, the chief inspector, watched Hand give a tentative wave before heading out to the car park.

"To hell and damnation with that," said Kilmartin. "He's bloody lucky not to be leaving here with skid marks all over his arse, I can tell you."

He blew smoke out the side of his mouth.

"Did you ever hear the like? Yahoos. Is this what all the guff about joint operations is about? Let me tell you something. Joe Keane is still top dog over in Serious Crimes. I'll be on the blower to him in a few minutes. Lift him out of it I will bejases. Sending Hand over with bits of paper to keep us quiet. What does he take us for at all, at all?"

None of the policemen spoke.

"I can live with Joe," Kilmartin went on. "Joe's all right. But the rest of them can be desperate messers. Christ, the crap you hear some days! 'European police methods . . .' 'In Germany they do this . . .' 'On the continent . . .' Iijits. Conferences and duty-free hangovers!"

Malone began tapping his biro on his forehead. Kilmartin broke his stare on the doorway where Hand had disappeared and looked over.

"Stop that, Molly," said Kilmartin. "Or you'll be giving me ideas. Now. See those names? I have me own mind on this. Let's be thinking about the runners and hangers-on that the Egans use. The enforcers."

Minogue looked back at the board. Lenehan. Balfe. Malone cleared his throat.

"I, er, well, I sort of know one of them," he said. Kilmartin's brows shot up.

"You do, do you, now?"

Was this why Malone had looked so distracted during the briefing, Minogue wondered. He took in Kilmartin's sardonic grin.

"Yeah," said Malone. "That Balfe fella." He leaned forward and rested his elbows on his knees. "It was years ago. He was in a boxing club."

"Anything you can tell us about him then?"

"I kind of lost track of him. He went the other way."

Kilmartin looked at his cigarette.

"Like that brother of yours?"

Minogue stared at Kilmartin but the chief inspector was looking about the squad room.

"Let's see if we can pin those thugs," Kilmartin said then. "Those enforcers."

He turned back to Malone and eyed him.

"Pick 'em up, even. Spin 'em around, see what falls out, like."

He took a last pull of his cigarette and leaned over the desk to reach an ashtray.

"Who do you think might fall out if we did that, Molly? Our Mary?"

Malone glanced at Minogue.

"Maybe," he said. "Maybe Hickey."

Kilmartin turned and leered.

"Attaboy there, by God, Molly," he whispered. "That's one for the Dublin team."

CHAPTER 8

Here, get up. It's nearly ten o'clock."

His eyelashes had stuck together. He panicked for a moment and began rubbing hard at them. He had been crying last night, he remembered. Was it a dream, or had he heard someone moving around in the night? He looked up into the lamp shade overhead. He remembered yesterday and stale fear broke through his bewilderment. Jammy Tierney was still standing in the doorway.

"Thanks, Jammy. Great. I'm okay now, man. Yeah."

Tierney stared at him. What the hell was up with him?

"I'm going out," said Tierney. "You can't stay. You might rob the lightbulbs or something."

Very smart, Jammy. He rolled to the side of the sofa and sat up.

"You look a right knacker and you sleeping in your clothes."

"Jammy?" He cleared his throat. "Could you loan me a bit of something? You know . . . ?"

"What? What bit of something?"

"A tenner, maybe?"

Tierney folded his arms.

"Fiver? I'll pay you back. All I need is . . ." He stopped then. Jammy had that weird grin.

"A fiver," said Tierney. "Only a fiver? You fall in the door here at eleven o'clock last night, looking like you been through a lawn mower. No explanation, don't want to tell me what has you wrecked. I hear you poking around here last night when you're supposed to be sleeping. In the fridge. Opening drawers. Snooping. Now you want to sponge money off me?"

"Wait, Jammy, that's not the way it is, man —"

"You must be joking. Go home and tidy yourself up. Get a job."

"Hold on there a minute, Jam —"

"And then go to a clinic and start telling the truth! For once in your life, Leonardo."

The urge to scream in Jammy Tierney's face welled up in him. Mr. Fit, with his motorbike and his nixers and his pool sharking. They'd been friends all these years but all he'd done this last while was preach to him about drugs.

"Jammy, I swear to God, man! I don't *do* drugs. I don't! Not the way you think. I mean, man, I wish I could be like you, you know. Really! But a joint never hurt anyone. Takes the sting off things, you know? Christ, you know what it's like out there! But I'm tired of that scene. Really I am."

Tierney gave him a bleak look.

"Jases, Leonardo. Always that hurt kid look. I don't believe I'm doing this."

"I've only got you, man. I'm sorry. I'm going to turn things around, I swear."

"What happened to you last night then? You weren't pissed."

"I ran into a spot of bother at home, like. You know? The ma's giving me stick and all. I just couldn't handle it last night. I had to get out."

"You had to get out, did you."

This bastard, he thought. Leaning against the doorjamb, putting him through this. So bloody smug, so much better than he was. He thought he was doing him a favor lecturing him. He met Tierney's eyes for a moment. He imagined giving him a kung-fu leaping kick right in the snot: *boom!*

"Promise me what I give isn't going into some dealer's pocket."

"Honest to God, Jammy. I've had it, man. I know I need to change."

"How much?"

"Get a job, the whole thing —"

"How much money?"

"Oh." He tried to laugh but couldn't.

"A hundred?"

He followed Tierney through the doorway into the kitchenette. Christ, even this place was spotless. Maybe Jammy did it to to impress his mot. Her stuff there in the bathroom.

"Fifty, Jammy. Fifty?"

"What for?"

"Bus fares. Some to the ma. A shirt maybe. To do interviews?"

Tierney picked up his helmet.

"I don't have it."

"Twenty then —"

"Shut up. I have to go into town anyway. Come on."

He'd been leading him on. He looked around the room. Bloody snob, that's what he was. Always talking of making something of yourself, moving up. It was a bit like Mary, but with her, you knew that she could do it. Jammy Tierney wouldn't. He'd just have the attitude, looking down his nose at the people he'd grown up with. But he'd never be any better than them.

He rubbed sleep from his eyes.

"I'll get you something," Tierney murmured.

"Jesus, Jammy!"

He clapped Tierney's shoulder.

"Great, man! I knew you wouldn't sell me out!"

Tierney glared at him. He was about to say something but he let it go. Weirder and weirder, he thought. Too much health did that to you. Too wound-up, too perfect.

"The back of Charley's, the pool hall, do you know it? Around twelve."

"That's great, Jammy. Brilliant, man!"

· · · · ·

Minogue put down the phone. He studied the doodles he had drawn while he'd been talking with Toni Heffernan. Triangles — was that anger? He crossed out the i and put in a y. Was it short for Antoinette? Short was right: she had been curt, blunt, and short with him. Sister Joe was out on a call. When would she be back? Toni Heffernan didn't know. Minogue had said he would try again — unless she were to phone him first. He made his way to the kitchen, half-filled the kettle, and plugged it in. He was searching for a clean cup when Kilmartin arrived. The chief inspector began working on his ear with his baby finger. Minogue opened the bag of coffee beans and inhaled the aroma.

"Any luck," said Kilmartin.

"I'm trying to get ahold of a Sister Joe. She runs a drop-in center for kids on the street. She might know Mary."

"Uhhh."

Minogue poured beans into the grinder and resealed the bag. He let the grinder run longer than he needed. Kilmartin was still there when he turned back.

"Yourself?"

"Ah, Christ, don't be talking. Politicking. Phoned Serious Crimes, talked to Keane. 'We'd appreciate your input' and all that, says I. Nice to him and all, I was. Still he hems and haws. Huh. Felt like giving him the, well, the you-know-what."

"In the you-know-where?"

"Exactly. I might have to beat some sense into that mob of his soon." Kilmartin rubbed more vigorously at his nose. He stared at the kettle.

"Jack Mullen," he said, and looked up at Minogue. "He's hopping the ball, isn't he?"

Minogue frowned.

"He's a nutter, Matt, isn't he?"

"He has a temper, James. That interests me a lot, so it does."

Kilmartin nodded.

"What's the name of his outfit again?"

"The self-help group, you mean? The Victory Club."

Minogue watched Kilmartin lighting a cigarette.

"Victory over the drink, like. Well, I'm sure that's not a bad thing in itself. But as for this sitting around and crying on the next man's shoulder . . ."

"It's not uncommon these days, James."

Kilmartin coughed out smoke.

"Don't be talking to me. Sure everybody's at it. The psychology racket."

Minogue poured a third of a cup of milk and placed it in the microwave. The chief inspector rubbed at his eyes with his free hand.

"Arra sweet and holy Jesus," he groaned. "Even me own wife is talking about stuff like that. Everybody's-a-victim style of thing. 'Couldn't help it, Your Honor. Me ma looked sideways at me in the maternity ward. Never got over it.' 'Case dismissed. Hire ten shrinks to look after the poor lad.'"

"Maura?"

"Yes. Maura Kilmartin. Got a letter from the young lad. He's in Philadelphia now. Maura got herself in a state about it. I must have put me foot in it somehow. She starts in on this stuff, as if there was something wrong with me — me, the man she married thirty-one happy years ago, bejases! Oh, we've had our spats and everything. But sure, who doesn't?"

Minogue nodded. He recalled Kilmartin's jibe about the stone he had given Hoey and Áine.

"You probably know the routine. 'Let's talk' kind of shite. Babbling on. All this feelings stuff — they make a religion out of 'em. Everyone's their own tin pot God now. We're all victims of one thing or another. Hand out badges, I say. We'd all be millionaires and Shakespeares if only the da or someone hadn't given them a right well-deserved kick up in the arse. Are you with me?"

Minogue looked in at the revolving tray in the microwave. Kilmartin warmed to his subject.

"Oh, yes," he resumed. "It was the sixties done us in if you really want to know. We were all softened up: the ads, the self-esteem crowd, taking away the leather from the schoolmaster. Everything is supposed to be perfect now, isn't it? Everybody deserves everything they want. Want? Demand is more like it! Jesus, we're taken for iijits. Anyway. I thought that at least that kind of eyewash hasn't gotten into my house when Maura gives me one of those looks."

Minogue glanced over.

"Come on now, Matt — you know the ones I mean. Out at a dinner. I'm not stupid, you know. I knew that maybe I was a bit, er, strict and all, but, sure, life isn't all holidays in Greece and wine and 'feeling good about yourself' now, is it?"

Minogue recalled his ten blissful days in Santorini last year. He registered the jibe with a nod.

"That look on her face. Anyway. Right in the middle of eating this very nice bit of dinner, says she: 'Were you very close to your father, Jim?' What do you think of that?"

"A tough enough question. Even when your mouth isn't full."

"You're telling me. Ch-a-rist! 'Not if I could help it,' says I."

Minogue unplugged the kettle and poured water into the jug. The two men stared at the coffeemaker.

"Even if Mullen has fares all evening, he has the few minutes it took to go by the canal and spot the daughter," Kilmartin said.

"His taxi is nearly done, is it," said Minogue. Kilmartin nodded. He pushed away from the counter and pointed his cigarette at Minogue.

"This bloody Victory Club I'm reading up on. Gentle Jesus and all that stuff tagged on to it. 'Charismatics,' yippy-eye-ay kind of stuff. Crying and shouting and floating off the ground? Waving their hands around and singing? These bloody group talks often ended up with his pals telling him he needed to *find* his daughter. I'll tell you what 'find' meant to Jack Mullen, will I?"

Minogue thought of Iseult.

"I don't know, Jim. The social worker fella that sits in on their meetings says it's all part of the recovery deal."

"Huh. Social workers — oh yeah, I forgot. They're in charge of everything now. What does that mean anyway, according to him?"

"'Find,' meaning build a proper relationship with Mary."

"Me arse and parsley, man. I know English better than these frigging social worker experts seem to: 'find' means go out and get her. *Get her.* That's plain English as she is spoken."

Minogue prepared the plunger at the top of the jug of coffee. Kilmartin mightn't be far off the mark, he reflected.

"What did Mullen say again about God lifting her or something like that?"

Minogue thought for several moments.

"'God called my daughter and lifted her out of her dejection.'"

"My God, how you remember stuff like that. Holy Joes."

Kilmartin held out his hand and shook it in a manner that reminded Minogue of farmers at a mart ready to settle on a price. He plucked at his little finger first.

"Let's talk about the real world. One, he has a history of threatening the daughter. Two, he broke up with the wife. He used to beat her up too. Three, he's taken up with a cult — ah now, don't go interrupting me. I know about this 'recovery' stuff. Four, he gets the idea — here, I'll use a big word just to keep you happy — an obsession: he has to save the daughter."

"Saved in Jesus?"

"No need to be disrespectful there now, pal. But yes. He tracks her over time, he finds a pattern. He doesn't need to be James Bond to do that, now, does he. He follows her that evening, tries to talk her into the car or the like. She gives him the F.O. He loses the head and clocks her. Rolls her into the water. She never goes near the taxi."

Minogue pushed the plunger slowly, watching for grounds escaping around the rim. Kilmartin drew on his cigarette and studied the operation.

"So?" said Kilmartin when Minogue had poured coffee into the cup.

"I don't know, Jim. A bit early, let's remember."

"But bear it well in mind, that's all I'm saying. Stick with routine. Pin the alibi to the clock. Wait for the finals from the taxi. Check the site again. Go door-to-door with Sheehy and company if you're too jittery waiting. Pull Mullen in again tomorrow and throw the same stuff at him, compare it with this statement and the tapes. I'm going to give serious thought to a twenty-four-hour surveillance on Mullen for the next week, that's what I'm going to do."

Minogue nodded. Kilmartin blew smoke at his shoes.

"All right there? Look, I'm game if you want to stick it to Mullen hard later on, the three of us. Object lesson for Molly in there."

Minogue's tongue moved to his front teeth. The coffee was stronger than he had planned.

"'One a year,' Matt. Hate to say it, but it looks like one. Do you think?"

Minogue looked up at Kilmartin.

"Well, why don't we just sign it over to you?"

"Nice try there, pal. Like hell you will. Haven't I given you Tonto to help you on this one?"

Minogue returned to sipping coffee. Kilmartin's axiom was that at least one murder case per year turned out to be the most frustrating, difficult and head-banging case the squad had ever handled. There was little point, Minogue knew, in reminding his colleague that this case looked like becoming about the seventh or eighth "one-a-year" this year. James Kilmartin claimed that these cases brought progress and improvement to the squad's procedures. This they did, he explained, by extending the rigorous use of police science and its sundry ancillary support services. He was easily wily enough to turn "one-a-year"s to good account by transforming them into Trojan horses for departmental budget claims. Over a pint, however — over several pints — the chief inspector usually lost little time in putting Police Science in its place: "All very well and good, but a man needs to know when to put it in the P.F.O. file." It was one thing for squad officers as adepts of police science to methodically take everything about a murder case into account; it was quite another to understand what to discount.

"Seven weeks pregnant, Jim. I'm hoping she tried with this drop-in center."

"Short of money for going to England to get the, you know, the job done?"

"The father." Minogue looked up from his cup. "Patricia Fahy has to know him. She must."

Kilmartin stroked his chin.

"This Hickey character," he muttered.

Boots thumped in the hallway. A tall alien passed the doorway.

"Oi!" Kilmartin called out.

The alien returned. Minogue studied the motorcyclist's visor.

"Take off the helmet, man!" said Kilmartin. "How do we know you're not a robber?"

Éilis stood in the hallway behind the Garda motorcyclist. She nodded at Minogue.

"A phone call for you, your honor. A Sister Joe."

The motorcyclist was a smiling, big-toothed motorcycle Guard in his early twenties.

"Ah," said Éilis. "And how's the bold Garda Madden?"

Footballer, thought Minogue. He picked up the jug. Éilis took the envelope.

"Thanks now, Gabriel," she muttered and attacked the string on the flap. Madden stepped backward into the hallway to let Minogue through.

"Gabriel?" Minogue heard Kilmartin say. "A messenger? Is this the Annunciation all over again?"

· · · · ·

He cut across the car park and skipped down the alley toward the back door of the pool hall. He felt lightheaded, happy almost. He sat on the edge of a windowsill and pushed his back against the iron bars. Sweaty already. He began to calculate again. With the fifty he could get a hit off Ginger down on Parnell Street. With the couple of quid he had left of his own, he'd have forty left. He'd try again later on with Mary. Why hadn't she told him that she'd jacked it in with that Tresses kip? He looked up and down the alley. Two skins walked by the mouth of the alley and looked in. One broke his stride and slowed to eyeball him. He was moving toward the door of the pool hall when the skins disappeared. He stepped into a doorway and flattened his back against the metal panel. His knees had gone watery.

So what the hell were those two bastards looking for last night anyway? Maybe they'd mixed him with someone else? Narcs? No: one of them looked familiar. You couldn't tell these days. He thought about the time that a narc who looked like a knacker and smelled like a knacker put the hand on Ginger. In broad daylight, in Stephen's Green, for God's sake, Ginger laughing because he was high and didn't believe it was happening. But those two last night, not a word out of them. They'd just come after him. Why was he shivering, and it like bloody Morocco, for God's sake? Get the money, score off Ginger; phone the ma, see if she knew what was going on.

Steps. He looked out. Jammy was standing in the alley with his helmet in his hand.

"Jammy! Thanks a million, man! I won't forget it, I swear! You and me are —"

Tierney's hand was on his shirt. He looked into Jammy Tierney's face and saw the contempt. Tierney began to twist his collar.

"You lying fuck, Leonardo!"

Tierney pushed him away and laid the helmet down.

"Jammy! Are you mad? Jesus! What's with you, man?"

Tierney closed on him. He took a step backward.

"Jammy! Don't, man! What are you doing? What have I done? What?"

Tierney wasn't stopping.

"Tell me, Jammy!"

Jammy Tierney reached out and shoved. The push caught him as he was taking another step back. He fell. Tierney lifted his foot.

"Jesus, Jammy! Man!"

He scuttled back until his shoulder hit a bin.

"Don't, man! For Jases' sake, just tell me what I've done! Tell me!"

"Get up."

"I'm not going to get up just so's you can start in on me, man!"

"Get up or I'll use me boots on you."

He elbowed around the bin until he was at the wall. He laid a hand on the dustbin. Jammy Tierney was breathing heavily. He tried to decide which way to run.

"Go ahead," said Tierney. "Try and run. See how far it gets you."

A sob almost escaped him. At least Tierney was talking.

"Is it the money, Jammy? Is it? What have I done? Give me a chance here, man!"

"You and your *Mary this* and your *Mary that*. I should have known. Your brain is fried, man! It's gank! You're a fucking menace, that's what you are. You drag everyone down with you."

"What? Honest, man —"

"I shouldn't even be talking to you. Get up, you fucking waster."

He drew himself up until he was on his hunkers. He could get a good start if he went for it. Tierney jammed his hand into his pocket and flicked something at him. Folded paper — money.

"You still going to run?"

"Thanks, Jammy! Thanks! Look, man, whatever I did, I'm sorry. I'm really sorry."

There were more bills than there should be. He tried to smile but Tierney kept staring at him. He looked down and thumbed through the bills. There was two hundred quid. Had Jammy made a mistake? He looked back into his eyes.

"So you're sorry," said Tierney. His eyes had a weird glittering light in them now.

"Yeah, Jammy, you know? . . . Whatever it is . . ."

"What use is sorry to Mary? Tell me that, you fucking bastard!"

"Jammy, I swear to you —"

"What? You're always swearing to me about something!"

"If it has to do with, you know, what I said about Mary and me, that was just, well, I suppose I was just spoofing a bit. It's just a dream, sort of —"

"Shut fucking up!"

"I swear — I mean, really! The truth is, she doesn't think much of me. You know that. Look, tell you what. I'm going around to see her this afternoon. You know?"

Was Jammy nodding or just shaking?

"She's going to talk to Bobby Egan, see if he'll give me a start. Then I'll pay you —"

"See?" Tierney's voice rose. "You're lying again! This morning you told me — You're such a lying . . . You just — Ah, Christ, who cares. Get the boat tonight. Stay away."

"To England you mean?"

"To the North Pole! The Sahara! Fucking Timbuktu, I don't care!"

"Jesus, Jammy. Why would I want to make a move like that, you know?"

The movement was even quicker than he guessed it could be. It wasn't a fist, but it stung.

"Because you'll be fucking next!"

His ear was burning from the slap. He rubbed at it and backed away.

"I don't get it, man! What are you saying?"

Tierney's eyes seemed ready to pop out of their sockets.

"What do you mean, Jammy?" Tierney stuck his face right up against his. "Mary was taken out of the canal yesterday, you fucking bollocks! Can you fucking hear me in there? She's dead!"

He studied Tierney's eyes, the drawn lips, the anger.

"Did you hear me? She's on your conscience! Whatever you did, you and your fucking messing — whatever you conned Mary into. You got her killed, man! Whatever you talked about, whoever you talked to — you're poison, man! Fucking poison!"

He couldn't move. He tried to say something. The whole place seemed to glow. Everything grew sharp and scary. He tried again but only his jaw moved. Tierney's chest was heaving. He looked up at the sky over the alley. He wondered if he was going to faint.

"This isn't really happening, is it?" he whispered. "You can't be serious, man."

"You don't think so?" Tierney snarled. He pushed him in the chest.

"Swear to God, Jammy! Don't make up stuff, man. It's not funny anymore!"

"You're telling me you don't know? The Egans think you do. Talk to them about it."

"How can you? . . ." His throat closed on the last words. Tierney took a step back.

"You're so fucking out of it," he hissed. "I don't know what the hell stuff you do anymore. I bet you don't even remember your name."

Jammy had given him a lot of money. That meant . . . His thoughts rushed back.

"Jammy! She had some fella set up, that's what she told me!"

"What? What fella?"

"I don't know! I don't! She had an in with him. Told me it could go serious. He had money. She was going to take him, you know, like?"

"You don't even know when you're lying! It was you hanging around got her —"

{ 109 }

"Jesus! If you really want to know, Mary was always giving me the brush-off!"

"Not often enough, you bastard! Not hard enough, either!"

He stared into Jammy's eyes. For some reason he couldn't keep them in focus. Smells and sounds and colors kept leaking in somewhere. His head began to feel light. The Egans, he thought. Tierney was still talking to him.

"What?"

"See, you're out of it again! Don't you get it? Get to hell out of here! Dublin!"

"What? How do you? . . . Where was she . . . you know?"

"How would I know? Here I am like a gobshite giving you a pile of money so as you can piss off out from under the Egans."

"Jammy! You got to tell them I didn't! You got to, man! You believe me, don't you? You know I'd never hurt Mary! We're mates, man! You're Mary's friend too, man!"

"Shut up. You're making me puke here."

"But where was she?"

"Read the paper, man, on the boat to Liverpool or somewhere."

"Come on, man!"

Tierney's eyes narrowed.

"Listen! There was a time when Mary had a chance. But she got dragged down, didn't she? And it was you, you were one of the bastards that dragged her under!"

"Come on, Jammy! You know I could never do anything to Mary!"

The anger slid off Tierney's face. What took its place scared him even more.

"Aw, Jesus, Jammy," he whispered. "Jammy! You can't be serious!"

"Do you think it matters what I think? You're the fella telling me you could do anything. Wanted the Egans to know so's they'd take you on. You're the one, man."

"The Egans? The fucking Egans? Jammy. Man! You've got to get the word to them! They won't listen to me! Jammy? Is the whole fucking place gone *mad?*"

Tierney nodded his head slowly. This time he didn't raise his voice.

"Yeah, Leonardo. As a matter of fact, it has. Didn't you notice?"

CHAPTER 9

I have to sit down, Joe."

He yanked on the leash. The dog gasped. She leaned on his arm and lowered herself to a bench. God, he thought, the day would soon come when he'd have to take her to the toilet.

"Grand now," she said. "I'll be okay in a few minutes."

He sat down next to her. The canal was calm and full. Why did she want to go for a walk by the canal this hour of the morning? He took off his glasses and rubbed them with his hanky. The edges of his vision had the familiar blur now. He tried to remember if the eyes had already been like this last year.

"They said that there's low pressure on the way."

What was she talking about? She turned to him and smiled.

"The news, Joey. The weather forecast, I mean. Do you know what that means?"

No, he didn't. Forecast sun and you'd better bring an umbrella. They were as bad as the politicians. Not for him the endless speculation about the weather. Guessology. Facts or nothing. He'd been the happy man in his job. Forty-four years of inventories, lists, parts, serial numbers. Locating, ordering, shipping, investigating.

"Long enough we're waiting, aren't we, Joe? For the bit of rain."

Jennings, his boss, had died four years ago. A big crowd at the funeral, all his kids — grown up, of course. Seven kids, Jennings had had. Lucky number, ha ha. If anything ever happened to him or the wife, he used to say, didn't they have the seven to fall back on? He yanked on the leash again.

"What's wrong, Joe?"

"Nothing's wrong. I was just thinking."

Daughters loved their fathers more, he'd heard. If they'd had a boy, it would have been an Edward. Eddie, his own father's name. Edward Thomas Byrne. Thomas after his uncle.

"Were you thinking about the poor girl?"

He looked into her eyes.

"Why would you think that?"

"I'm just asking, amn't I? That Guard you met."

He shifted on the bench and looked out over the water.

"What about him?"

"You were talking to him, weren't you?"

"That's right, Mary. I was talking to him. And he was talking to me."

She sighed.

"I can tell you're getting annoyed."

"No, I amn't. Why would I be getting annoyed about meeting a Guard?"

The skin around her eyes creased but she didn't smile.

"You get like that when you're annoyed."

He stood and let the dog lead him a few steps.

"He's the one'd be annoyed. 'A bit late in the day for yous to be showing up,' says I."

Mary Byrne rose slowly from the bench. She took a few steps before standing upright. Clutching his arm, they walked toward the lock.

Method, he thought. Everything accounted for, sorted, on the proper shelf. You knew where you were going, what you were looking for, where it would be. A simple rule: there was a place for everything. And that was long before computers too. The wands you wave at a label and that puts the numbers in a computer — they'd taken over completely now. Next step'd be robots getting the parts and taking the bloody money off the customers. Jennings, God rest him. Of course he was fond of the gargle and everything, but a decent man, saying to him: "By God, Joe, you have the most remarkable system here in Parts, the best in Dublin." He'd meant it too. Jennings was the old school, of course. Always had the time of day for you, would ask your opinion and all. Always asking to be remembered to the wife.

"It was on the news," she said. "They asked for anyone who was around the place."

"Yes, Mary," he said.

"Witnesses, like."

Why couldn't people conduct business like that in this day and age? Get organized, be smart about things. Know where everything was, or, if it wasn't in stock, where to get it. He remembered the satisfaction, the joy even, of finding a bulb, a bracket, a clamp — right there on the shelf, exactly where it was supposed to be. Put it right down on the counter in front of their noses. And the look on their faces! How did you do that, Joe, was the usual question. I went to where I knew it was, he'd tell them, to where it was supposed to be. That simple. Oh, you're a beaut, Joe, they'd say. Fellas phoning up from all over the country, looking for parts.

"You heard that, I suppose."

"They do that a lot nowadays, Mary."

Always came to work with clean hands; always left work with clean hands. Nails were important too. Nothing wrong with using your hands for a living, but that didn't mean that you arrived in or went home with the dirt under your nails. Jennings would do that an odd time, yes. Over he'd march with a customer or a bigwig visiting, grab his hands and lift them up, turn them over. Look at these, Jennings'd say. This is Joe Byrne, the best parts man in Dublin. Look at those hands, would you? Not a speck of dirt, not a speck! And do you know why? 'Cause there's no messing goes on here. No dirty work here, sir! The smell of the few jars off Jennings took a bit of the pleasure out of it, of course. He'd go on a bit too much about it by times, especially if he'd started early on the bottle. Once he'd apologized to him but it hadn't clicked with him at the time. It was the apology that had done more damage. But how could he get mad at Jennings for that? Sorry there, Joe, about the "passing it onto the sons" bit. Forgot. It was the drink. A good oul skin, Jennings.

"So you told the Guard, did you, Joe?"

What was she on about now?

"Yes, I did."

Modern medicine, of course. They could do anything nowadays. Maybe it had been psychological. But why was it that men could go at it all the way up until they were ninety? Even thinking about it still got him going. Did Mary notice? What the hell was Timmy nosing around there in the reeds? He pulled hard; the dog yelped. Dirty? No. That's what was so wrong. The church. You couldn't enjoy yourself without thinking you'd go to hell for it. All that was changing, of course. A bit bloody late for him though, wasn't it?

"The night it happened, I meant, Joe."

They were out from under the trees now. The sun felt like hot liquid on his head. He looked at the rows of windows on the new offices. Mirrors. The buildings reminded him of blind people but he didn't know why.

"What are you on about?"

"Oh, all right then, leave it. You're too annoyed, I can tell."

"Leave what, for the love of God?"

She tightened her grip and looked up into his eyes. It was something she'd always done when the going got rough. He used to think it was a move she'd seen in a film, that she wanted to be cuddled or something. It was her way of getting her way, he had learned.

"The oul hip might be shook, Joe, but the head is still working."

"Well, maybe it is, but it's certainly coming out with queer things, let me tell you."

"Where else would you take the dog? I mean to say, where else would you go?"

"What are you saying?"

"I know you go out later on, Joe. Sometimes, I mean. After I'm gone to bed, like."

He let his eyes wander from hers across the water to the reeds. The plastic bags caught there looked full. A black rubbish bag looked like the coat on someone floating in the water.

"It's just that I was thinking of the girl, Joe."

She'd known all along? She pulled at his arm. He turned to her.

"I don't care, Joe! I know you're a good man and all. Don't get me wrong."

"My God! What are you saying? What are you thinking?"

"Ah, there you go. You can't listen."

"Listen to what? You're telling me I go down here every night looking at them?"

She shook his arm.

"I did not. All I'm saying is that she was a girl and —"

"I'll tell you what she was, if you really want to know! A brasser, that's what she was!"

A pained expression crossed her face. She spoke in a murmur now.

"She has a mother and father, Joe. My God, I have to sit down again. I'm locking up."

The anger fled from around his heart. He helped her into a seat. The drill resumed its clatter. They watched the traffic on the far side of the canal. Even the dog seemed to get the message. He sat down and looked up at him. Didn't want to move, that was odd for Timmy. He patted him on the head, lingered, and began rubbing under his jaw. Timmy began to pant.

"Look," she said as the drill fell silent again. The swans had landed up near Baggot Street bridge. They were keeping to the middle of the canal.

"That's what I thought it was at first, you know."

"What, Joe?"

He folded his arms.

"Well, they ought to do something with the bloody lights, shouldn't they? If they were really going to get serious with what goes on around here. I mean there are parts of the bloody canal where it's nearly pitch-black."

"Up near the bridge there?"

"And down by the railings too. It's only common sense! If they're broken, fix them."

"But the young lads are always fecking stones up at the lights and breaking them, Joe."

He looked up beyond the swans at a double-decker bus going over the bridge. He couldn't read the ad on the side of the bus. The eyes definitely weren't this poor last year. A wave of despair washed over him. Soon the strength would be gone from his arms even. He'd end up hobbling around like Mary or something.

"By the bridge, was it, Joe?"

"A white thing," he murmured. "I only seen it for a moment. Moving."

"What was it, Joe? The white thing."

"My God, I don't know! It could have been anything."

He pointed at a passing van.

"Sure, I have trouble reading that. That's the way the eyes have gone with me, for God's sake. What could I tell a Guard about anything I might've seen with them eyes?"

Mary Byrne said nothing.

"Look," he said. "When's the last time you were down there on the bank, by the railings there? You can't see a bloody thing! I thought to meself, well, maybe it's a swan taking shelter there or something — God, I don't know!"

"But they never stay, Joe, they never sleep on the canal. Not anymore."

"I know, I know. You know how they used to stay the nights years ago, how they'd sleep with their heads in under their feathers. Like they were hiding their faces. Ashamed of something, you used to say. Remember? Then I think to meself, maybe it's a ball belonging to a child. Then I hear language. Oh, language like you wouldn't hear outside of a jail or something. It was a woman's voice too. So take a guess at what she was up to, like, what her line of business was, I says to myself. Do you think I was going to go back and get right down there to see if I knew her maybe? Not on your life!"

"How long was that going on?"

"Do you mean how long was I standing there listening? What do you think I am?"

She sighed and rubbed at the back of her hand.

"Sure where would you start telling them stuff, Mary? If we told them everything we saw down here over the years, sure we'd be there talking to them all day and all night. I know what I should be telling them, and that's the class of person what comes down here — I mean the clients, the ones who come by here. Married men and all, business types. Fancy cars."

He sat forward on the bench.

"Should I be telling them about the fancy cars that I see here? Didn't a Mercedes go up and down here the other night, didn't I point it out to you? Going up and down there? The type of creature what comes by here isn't just your average chancer."

She frowned.

"I don't remember you saying that to me, Joe."

"Ah, sure! You and cars, Mary. What am I starting here . . ."

"Maybe you saw it the other night."

A retort was on his lips but it didn't come out. She was right. Surely to God, the memory wasn't going on him. It was her getting up his back, confusing him, caused that slip.

"I think it'd do no harm," she murmured.

"For God's sake, Mary! Sure it's only trouble. They'd twist things around. 'How long were you there now, Mr. Byrne,' and 'What were you doing there anyway, Mr. Byrne.' They could make anything out of it.

Anything! Put you under pressure and you wouldn't know what you'd be saying."

The swans were drifting their way now. He looked down at his wife again. Her lips were set in a tight line, her eyes on something far off. Her lips hardly moved.

"They're not going to think you're a . . . you know, Joe."

He glared at her now but she wouldn't look back. She leaned forward. Her eyes were on the swans now, he saw. He wanted to tell her a thing or two, so he did. But why keep this bloody conversation going? It'd only give her ideas. Her voice was gone soft now.

"Look, Joey, here they come."

．　　．　　．　　．　　．

Even with drops of sweat rolling down his spine he felt cold. His ear hurt from pushing the phone against it.

"Ma! I swear to God! You know me, Ma! Come on now."

His mother interrupted again. He began rapping his knuckles against the doors of the telephone booth. He stopped listening to her and studied the faces of the passersby. He got his chance when he heard her sob.

"I can prove it to you, Ma!" he broke in. "Just give me the chance! Honest! It's just a big screw up! Someone thinks that I — ah, it's too complicated. It's probably someone has it in for me, telling lies or something. I don't know —"

She interrupted again. He tapped his knuckles harder on the Perspex to stop from shouting at her to shut up and just fucking listen. No one wanted to listen.

"No, I won't, Ma. Are you joking? Go to the fu — to the cops! Sorry. I mean, what have I done? Nothing! You know them, though, they'll never believe the likes of me. What if the lads get to hear I talked to the cops. You know what that'd look like? Which? The lads? Come on, you know who I'm talking about. The cops'd never take my word for anything."

He listened again. She needed to get over this part, he knew, to get really worried about him. A shadow fell across the dusty Perspex panels of the booth. He started and squinted into the glare. It was nobody he knew.

"Please, Ma! All I'm asking you is to take the stuff with you going to work. Just throw it all in a plastic bag. The chalk, the rolls of paper . . . What? All right, two bags. Yeah! I need some clothes. Just a change, like. It's only for a couple of days. Aw, Jesus, Ma! Please! Don't ask me again.

I'll tell you when it's over. You wouldn't understand it. It's so stupid anyway."

She told him again about the Guards calling to the house looking for him. Couldn't she cop on that his only chance was to keep away from the bloody house until this mess got sorted out?

"Look, Ma! Ma! Listen! Will you listen for a change, Ma? Okay, look. I'm totally innocent. No. Yes. Totally. I'm not mixed up in anything. Listen, I'm going to do a job search. Really. And while I'm waiting, I'm going to do the pictures again. Remember the summer when I was pulling in fifty quid a day when I had the stuff up by the Green? The Madonna? Yeah, that's your favorite. See? I remember, Ma. You always liked that one, didn't you, Ma?"

That set her crying again. He wanted to scream at her. He bit his lip. Christ, he was the one in a jam and here he was trying to calm her down.

"Show a little bit of faith in me, Ma. Please! You know I have the talent. I've let you down, I know. But I'm going to stay at a mate's house for a while until this gets sorted out. No, I can't tell you! I really want to get back to the art and everything. So will you bring the stuff around, will you?"

She had stopped crying. He heard her rubbing a hanky against her nose.

"Ace, Ma! Make sure no one's, you know, following you. And leave it in the laneway right next to a pile of stuff. Yeah, I want to suss out the place. There's a whole load of black rubbish bags out there. Just drop the stuff in behind them."

He placed the receiver back on the hook. The sweat was just pouring out of him. He felt proud that he hadn't asked her for money. He had standards. He could have phoned his sisters but all he would have gotten from them would be lectures. It didn't matter now. He could handle this on his own. But maybe he should have asked the Ma anyway? No way. She only made a hundred and twenty or so in the restaurant kitchen.

He slapped the door open and headed down toward Capel Street, moving fast. The fear had woken up something in him. He wasn't hungry; his senses were sharp. He still felt that quivery pressure in his chest, but he knew that something had left him too. The streets were crowded but he moved nimbly, his eyes on everything. He watched for fellas standing around street corners. He'd always been a good runner. Brennan, the teacher that had started him on it all those years ago, had told him that he had the ability. What did he call it? Raw talent, yeah. He went through names as he walked, wondering who he could lean on for a couple of nights. Only Jammy Tierney had stood by him, sort of: until today. He stayed close to the edge of the footpath and kept looking to his sides. He went through the names again and that sinking feeling got worse. The money that Jammy'd given him could get him a few nights in a bed and breakfast. If he scored a few hits . . . Forget it. A Garda car sped through the lights at Capel Street. Mary was dead. Dead. The shock came to him as dizziness now, disbelief. He looked around at the shops, the traffic, the hordes of people. The sky was yellow, not blue. He ran his fingers through his hair. Greasy, sweating. Maybe this isn't happening. Maybe this was some kind of a bleeding dream.

· · · · ·

The woman slid the mug of coffee across the table toward Sister Joe and folded her arms. High up by the sleeve of her T-shirt Minogue spotted part of a tattoo. She was gone forty and had dyed her hair. Her stare told Minogue that traffic with Garda officers was not something she liked. He gave himself odds of five-to-one-on as regards her former vocation. She was studying Malone.

"I know you from somewhere," she said to him. "Seen you before, so I did."

Malone poked at the salt and pepper containers.

"Thanks, 'Vonne," said Sister Joe. "Look after yourself."

The woman broke her stare on Malone and turned on her heel.

"Thanks for taking the time, er, Sister," said the inspector. "I hope we didn't? . . ."

"Joe will do fine. It's all right."

Sister Josephine Whelan tore the sachet of sugar.

"Theresa is going to live. She overdosed. There seems to be a more potent form of heroin coming into Dublin this last few months. She was lucky."

"I, em, hope . . ."

Minogue couldn't find the words. She looked up from her cup at him.

"It's as well we didn't meet back at the center anyway. Girls won't come in if there are Guards there, will they now? Even if they are from Clare."

"Ah, go on with you. Are you? . . ."

A smile flickered about her face.

"Kilbaha," she said. "Via London for eleven years. The Irish emigrant community."

Sister Josephine Whelan had the complexion of a waxed Macintosh apple. Her blue eyes became points when she wished to communicate without words. Forty-odd, Minogue decided — young as nuns go — and she had a stiff, assured abandon about her. Did she argue with God, he wondered while he took in her spare and well-considered words, and upbraid Him for leaving his flock to spawn those who hunted and destroyed others? Had it been Kilmartin grumbling that nuns had gone very militant this last while? Sister Joe's accuracy and slow production of words had made the inspector cautious. He expected pointed words from her about Guards before they parted.

"Now," she said. "Tell me what happened to Mary."

Minogue took his time. He was distracted by the stares of the group of women sitting at a table at the far wall of the restaurant where Yvonne had moved to.

"So that's as far as we are now. Have I forgotten anything there, Tommy?"

Malone shook his head. A waitress began removing plates from the next table. Sister Joe pushed her glasses against the bridge of her nose.

"She had not been raped," she said.

"No."

"But she had been pregnant."

Pregnant: in a nun's vocabulary? He could tilt at Kilmartin with this later on.

"Yes. We're taking it into account here. Motives, pressure, expectations. Anger."

She cocked her head as though listening to another conversation. Her glasses reflected the skylight.

"Your Garda Doyle can tell you more than I can," she said. "Mary came by twice as I recall since the center opened. She pretended she was inquiring for a pal."

"Two years ago, you said?"

"About that. Yes. Then she was gone."

Sister Joe sat back and looked high up on the walls of the restaurant.

"God look down on her and her poor family. You'll find her boyfriend then?"

"We don't have a clear view of her companions. We have a high priority on a fella called Liam Hickey, nickname Leonardo. He has a criminal record. He's gone on the run."

Sister Joe nodded. "I'll bear that name in mind then."

"It's possible that Mary was in the life all along, er, Joe. Since you last saw her, like."

"On the game, you mean?"

"Indeed. We're not able to locate her very well that night. Or where she spent her time outside her flat. She had a part-time job up until several weeks ago. She seems not to have taken it very seriously. I think the job was a prop."

"Her job didn't support her, you're saying."

Minogue nodded.

"Girls sell themselves and hold down jobs too," she said. "Married women even."

"Mary had some connection with a gang called the Egans."

"Ah." Her gaze moved down the wall and arrived over to meet his.

"Yes, indeed," she murmured. "I know nothing of them beyond their reputation."

She looked down at her cup and closed her eyes. Was she ill, Minogue wondered.

"Are you all right there now, Joe?"

She opened her eyes, smiled, and sat up and looked around the restaurant.

"I was just using Bewley's as a church there for a moment. I came up here to Dublin to do social work, you know. I used to come in here every Saturday morning for a cup of coffee. It was my reward for surviving the week. I read up on the history of the Bewleys."

"Quakers, were they not," said Minogue.

"Indeed. The Quakers fed people in my home parish of Lisnacree during the Famine. So I think of this restaurant in a special way. How things come around . . . I'll wager good money that other people say the odd prayer here too."

"We'd be fools not to," he said. She frowned at him.

"Girls are beaten, inspector. Beaten at home. Beaten by their fathers and their boyfriends and their husbands. By their brothers and their sons. If they turn to a life on the streets, they're beaten by their pimps. They're beaten by their clients. With Mary, a girl I can barely recollect, I know that God'll see her life and the lives of other trapped girls as their own Via Dolorosa."

Trapped, Minogue considered. He had begun to think of Mary Mullen as a woman with plans and ambition, someone who chose to be close to professional criminals.

"I believe in the resurrection," said Sister Joe. "So I hold out hope. Always."

"Are there women who drop into the center who'd know Mary?"

"Probably. But if you want to find such girls, you'll let me go about the matter."

"I want to find who killed Mary Mullen."

Her eyes stayed on his.

"I understood that from the moment you first contacted us. Do not regard the center as a resource to be mined, Inspector Minogue from County Clare. I'll inquire on your behalf."

"You have my word that I'll do nothing to jeopardize the women in your care."

Her eyes bore down on him. He raised his eyebrows.

"Another cup of coffee there, Joe?"

Her forehead lifted.

"Ah, go on," he chided. "'Come on the Banner County!'"

She laughed but quickly held a hand to her mouth.

"Tommy?"

Malone shook his head.

In the few minutes it took Minogue to get the coffee, lines of fatigue had appeared on Sister Joe Whelan's face. He pushed her cup across the marble tabletop.

"Thank you. Normally, I wouldn't now."

"May I ask now if the woman with the overdose is on the mend?"

"No, she isn't. This is the fourth time, the fourth that I know about anyway."

She laid her spoon on the saucer as though it were a delicate archaeological find.

"I hadn't seen her for a good long while. I began to delude myself into thinking that she was doing better, that she'd gotten out of the life completely. But they've gone beyond the streets entirely, I'm beginning to think. So far as I can gather anyway."

"I'm not sure I get it."

She looked across the restaurant to where Yvonne was smoking.

"I mean that they may have stopped selling sex on the streets. Some of the girls seem to have graduated to being mistresses of a sort."

"You mean another type of criminal activity now, or a group?"

"I know little enough about it. First it's a suspicion, then it's a rumor." She drank more coffee.

"I've heard talk about some girls boasting they could go to such-and-such a club and have everything paid for."

"You're saying there's been some change in the ways that girls do their business?"

"If I knew more, I'd tell you. We might be getting left high and dry in the center. Fewer girls call in. Maybe we need to change our tack. God knows, we're busy enough with drop-ins and crisis interventions for family violence that maybe we haven't been able to notice that girls are keeping away from the place. Maybe we're missing the boat with those girls. They're slipping away on us. The business changes. AIDS. Heavy drug use. More sophisticated types . . ."

Her words trailed off. She watched Malone tapping his spoon on his saucer.

"I have to be off now," she said then. Minogue stood.

"You'll be in touch if you? . . ."

"Depend on it now," she said. "God bless."

Minogue flopped back down in the chair and sighed. A bath, he thought. Sit in the garden tonight with a lot of ice in a glass of something next to him.

"Is she really a nun?" asked Malone. Minogue rubbed his lip.

"The blue clothes are a giveaway, I suppose," said Malone.

Malone looked from face to face in the restaurant. Minogue made another effort to gather his wits. His effort gained him little reward. He swallowed the last of his coffee.

CHAPTER 10

JAMMY TIERNEY STOOD UP and stretched. He turned up the sound on the Walkman, dabbed more oil onto the cloth, and hunkered down again. He shoved the rag in between the exhaust pipe and the axle, grasped it as it showed beneath and then continued buffing. The numbers came back to his mind: how much the bike had cost, how much he'd sell it for, what he could use the money for. Trade it in for the new Suzuki or buy a car? He made a face and looked at its reflection on the exhaust. Car?

He stood up when the figures appeared beside his own onion face on the exhaust. Painless he recognized. The other fella looked familiar. Ponytail, studs along his ear. He pulled out the earphones.

"Jammy," said Painless. "How's it going, man?"

"Oh, great. How's yourself."

He felt stupid with the rag in his hand. He bent his knees to ease the stiffness.

"Going somewhere, are you?" asked Ponytail.

Like who's asking, he wanted to say. He studied the dark patches under his eyes.

"Nice bike," said Painless.

"Thanks."

"Paid for, right?"

"Yeah."

"You up to anything these days, Jammy?"

"The usual, you know. A bit of this —"

"A bit of that?" Ponytail asked. He took a step forward, blew a bubble, and cracked it.

"Like a bit of what?" asked Painless. Tierney glanced back at the sallow, expressionless face of Painless Balfe. Indoors all day, he thought. Probably a user. Psycho.

"Things is slow on the buildings. I get the odd nixer. Then the rock-and-roll."

"Still good with the balls, are you, Jammy?"

He tried to smile. He realized his knees were turning to jelly on him. "You know yourself. Couldn't make a living out of it. But the odd game does the job."

Painless's face took on a quizzical expression.

"Is that the only game you play, Jammy?"

"You know me, man. Just trying to get along. I never went in for the excitement."

Balfe's eyes bored into his now. Again he tried to grin. It didn't come. A trickle ran down his back. He shrugged. Painless's eyes slid down to the bike. He nodded several times.

"How fast does this yoke go, Jammy?"

"About one-thirty."

"A hundred and thirty miles an hour? Fuck me. For real?"

"If you get the road, you know? It's a real buzz if you're into it."

Ponytail blew another bubble.

"Have you ever been on it when it went that fast?" he asked.

Painless's sidekick was grinning. His teeth were yellow. Average size, nothing special if it was a clean fight, but bad eyes. If the Egans had him on the payroll, he had to be the goods. Tierney rubbed at his eyes and looked down at the hands in the pockets. Knuckles, maybe.

"No. Went to one-twenty once, though."

"Not fast enough," said Ponytail. Tierney looked at Balfe. His face was blank.

"Seen Leonardo today?" Balfe asked.

"Well, I seen him the other day, yeah."

Ponytail chewed more vigorously.

"I don't stay in touch with the likes of him, though. I mean to say, he's a fucking header, right?"

Painless's expression hadn't changed.

"He's always messing," he went on. "He's a goner this long time, you know?"

"He's a mate of yours," said Painless. "Am I right or am I right?"

The fear made him vehement now. He jabbed at his own upper arm.

"No way. He stopped being a mate of mine when he started feeding his fucking arm."

"Feeding his arm?" asked Painless.

"Whatever he does. I don't know exactly. I'm not into that. Never was."

"Fella saw you and him in the Eight Ball the other day," said Ponytail. "Charley's?"

He popped one bubble and stopped chewing.

"Who?"

"Doesn't fucking matter who," snapped Painless.

"Well, he obviously didn't hear me give Leonardo the brush-off, did he?"

"Obviously?" sneered Ponytail. "Obviously you're trying to be fucking smart."

His hand slid out of his pocket. Tierney looked down at the rings. Ponytail began a foot-to-foot motion as though testing new shoes.

"Here, Painless, wait a minute!"

Painless's hand was already behind his back.

"I'll help find him for you, Painless, if that's what you mean, you know, like?"

"How?" Balfe's eyes had gone clear and moist. "Said you didn't fucking know him."

"Well, I know him, but I don't *know* him."

"Fuck off out of the way, so," said Painless. Ponytail went by him and raised his arm.

"Jesus, Painless, don't, man! I swear to God!"

He jumped out onto the street. A bread lorry honked but didn't let up speed. Ponytail brought his hand down in a chop. It glanced off the petrol tank.

"Fucking thing," he said. He drew back with his next swing and scraped the side of the tank.

"Painless! Man! Just get him to stop it, for Jases' sake, will you!"

Painless had replaced something in his back pocket. He stared at the motorbike. Ponytail began kicking against the exhaust.

"These bikes," Ponytail grunted between kicks. "You could . . . fucking . . . get . . . yourself . . . hurt tearing around the place on one of these things."

"Lolly," said Painless. Ponytail turned with a mischievous look and smiled at Tierney.

"Be seeing you, there. Stay in touch."

．　　．　　．　　．　　．

He counted the money again and tried to decide. It was too late for laying out the stuff on the paths along by the Green. But the office crowd would be on the move in a little while. He couldn't decide. He flicked the cigarette away. His shoulder ached from lying on the grass. Two kids were throwing crusts to ducks by the pond. He stared at a can floating in the scum on the surface. Christ, the stink.

The ache for a hit ran up from his stomach and his heart seemed to swell. He stood up and lit a cigarette. For several moments he was dizzy; the heat and the glare and the smoke in his lungs made the trees come at him, changing color as they did. He closed his eyes. He'd have to carry the stupid bag with his change of clothes in it as well as the pictures all over the city. Again the craving came to him. He could make himself do it, he thought then, cold turkey. He wasn't really into it anyway, not like people who needed it bad enough to knock pensioners around for a tenner.

The tips of his fingers began to itch and tingle. He began walking around the bench. Eat something, that'd help. It was too hot. He looked down at the bags, imagining them in slow motion falling toward the water, taking his troubles with them. Grabbing the pictures, twisting them to a pulp, watching them sink into the pond. Nobody'd help him. He was out there on his own. People were looking for him. No shelter, the sun beating down on him like it was the Sahara. Through the trees and beyond the dappled walks he caught glimpses of the traffic wheeling around the Green. A man with his shirt open to his waist staggered around the shrubs and came toward him. He almost slipped but held the bottle of sherry upright. He slowed and began heading toward him again.

"Hey, brother. Wait a minute there!"

He grabbed the bags and headed across the grass toward the gate. Where could he go? Take Jammy's advice and get the boat to Liverpool? Stupid bastard. No way: he'd go under there. There was no work. He didn't know anyone. He moved faster down the path now, checking the faces and the parked cars. A faint hope began to leak into his chest and his stride settled. There had to be a way he could talk to the Egans, prove he had nothing to do with . . . Nothing to do with what? The thought of Mary dead made him slow almost to a stop. Nobody'd believe him. There was no safe place. He looked back at the foliage spilling over the railings in the Green. It was like an island away from all this heat and crap and noise, a place he could just walk in, a place where he could lie down to rest. But this was the busiest bloody park in Dublin. It was full of dopers. They closed it up when it got dark.

The idea came to him then as a picture of dense woods. That's where he could go. Hundreds of acres he could get lost in. Did the deer still run wild in the park? And the zoo. If wild animals could do all right in a park in Dublin, why couldn't he? He stepped back out onto the path and headed for the city center. The bags felt lighter now. He'd get a bus down the quays to Islandbridge. There'd be a chipper down there near the gates of the Phoenix Park. He'd even spent a night in the park once. A crowd of lads had gone into the park, drinking and smoking dope. Someone got stabbed, he remembered, and everyone cleared out rapid before the cops came.

There was a charcoal of David Bowie down by the Bank of Ireland. A woman was still working on it, a hippy type he hadn't seen before. There were fifties and pound coins in her hat. She didn't look Irish. He bought cigarettes and a Coke and caught a bus pulling out from O'Connell Bridge. The bus squealed to a stop by Merchant's Arch. He'd laid out his stuff there a lot of times. He spotted another chalkie there, one he'd seen before, a fella who specialized in religious stuff. A man who had been leaning against the railings by the arch turned as the brakes squealed louder. It was the fella who'd chased him from the house. He spread his hand on his cheek and looked down again. He hadn't been spotted.

The bus shuddered as it pulled away. Terror still rooted him to the seat. They were out looking for him. They knew his spots. Maybe he should just go to the cops and hope for the best. But what could he deal with? Even if he signed a statement for the car jobs, the cops'd want to set him up. They'd turn him into a stoolie or something. They didn't care. Nobody cared. The panic made his bladder ache. The whole world was closing in on him, punishing him for something he hadn't done or even imagined. The rest of the journey down the quays passed in a daze. It was suddenly time to get off. He stepped out into a mass of jostling schoolkids. Everybody seem to be looking at him. His bag caught against a kid's shoulder and he pulled it free. He skipped across the street.

He looked over his shoulder, back toward the city center. Was it vibrating? The heat. Jesus. A mirage right here in the middle of Dublin. He passed the park gates and remembered the time he'd been there as a child. The main road stretched straight as an arrow ahead. He trudged across the grass for a quarter of an hour until he reached a small wood. He paused by the outermost trees and studied the shade and deeper shadows ahead. He entered the wood then and made for the middle. It was cool here, it smelled of clay. He let down his bags and lit a cigarette. The open fields beyond the wood were a dull glare now. He sat down against a tree and watched cars pass almost silently in the distance. It was only one of a hundred spots in the park, he thought. For a moment, he felt again as he had when he was a kid: this wood was a vast, limitless forest, a shelter where he could play and live forever.

· · · · ·

"What did she mean?" Kilmartin asked. "Your Sister Joe."

"That girls move from the streets indoors," replied Minogue. "Money changes hands still, of course. Doyler agrees. The whole business is impossible to track."

He looked away from the window. Kilmartin was poised on the edge of his chair looking up under his eyebrows. A smell of salami from someone's lunch hung in the stifling air of the squad room.

"Hnnkkk. This bloody flatmate of hers. Patricia Fahy. Christ, she has to start talking."

Minogue sat back and watched Murtagh writing on the boards: addresses for hard cases and enforcers in the Egan clan. Next to one was the address of a shop owned by Eddsy Egan.

"Probably. We need to go to her with something, Jim. Something that will make her cop on to the fact that the Egans can't touch her. Something to make her wake up and realize that we're all she's got. Any word on Hickey yet?"

"Not a sausage, and bugger-all new from the lab about Mullen's bloody taxi either. I've been going through his log again, minute by minute nearly. We're down to three or maybe four significant periods of time he could've had a chance. Murtagh's got the file searches for regulars by the canal, the customers, well in hand. The gougers on the parolee list as well as ones on bail are coming up empty. We'll have to widen the net. Open it up to a year even. Go through the logged incidents reported into stations. Jesus."

Minogue caught Murtagh's eye.

"This Balfe character uses the Egans' shop as his HQ? 'Painless' Balfe?"

Murtagh nodded. Minogue swivelled back toward Kilmartin.

"We're okay to jump on the likes of him, aren't we? If we can't poke the Egans directly?"

Kilmartin blew out smoke in small, measured puffs.

"Don't ask. Talked to Keane again. Last resort, says he. And I have to go through him if I want to. Holy God, says I, we have her in and out of one of the Egans' houses — right from his own surveillance! 'I know, I know, Jim,' says he. Told him I could get a warrant as easy as kiss hands. ''Course you could, Jim.' All that shite. I talked to him for twenty minutes. Finally he drops the clanger: 'Well, Jim, you'd really need to get good advice on going it alone with this.' In other words, check upstairs or I'll be pissed on. Trouble is, I knew that bloody Keane is right. But I didn't let on, did I?"

He snorted and stood. A smell of sweat and long-extinguished cigars wafted over to Minogue.

"I checked already with a certain party in HQ, you see. Turns out that Keane has all the trumps in the bloody deck. It's a combo between Drug Squad Central, Revenue Commissioners, Customs and Excise, Serious Crime — with their automatics stuck down the back of their shagging trousers! Then, to put the tin hat on it, I find out that it's the personal initiative of you-know-who, the Iceman himself. He set it all up. If I want to take the Egans in, it's bloody Tynan himself I'd have to ask!"

"Well, did you phone him then?"

Kilmartin's eyes opened wide.

"I could as easy have a nice chat with Tynan as my wife could walk by a shoe shop."

Minogue looked down at the names again.

"Well, let's pluck these fellas then."

He flicked a glance at the boards. Kilmartin looked at the names.

"Doyler put them in order of severity. John's got their haunts. Start with Balfe there?"

Kilmartin guffawed.

"'Painless.' Christ."

"I'd like a poke at him too," said Malone. Kilmartin and Minogue looked over at him.

"What class of a poke had you in mind there, Molly?"

"I knew him years ago. He'd remember me. Maybe I can get somewhere with him."

Malone spoke with no trace of humor.

"Painless is an animal. The other one is a total loop in his own right too. Lollipop Lenehan."

"Why not, Tommy," said Minogue. "Will you arrange the pickup then?"
Malone nodded, looked at Kilmartin and picked up the phone. Minogue stretched.

"God, the air in here," he groaned. "I have to go out for a bit of fresh air." Kilmartin followed him out to the car park.

"Listen, Matt. Don't let Molly off the lead so quick now. Here he is asking his pick of —"

"He's volunteering, Jimmy."

Kilmartin grimaced.

"I'm saying he's inexperienced. I don't want this case banjaxed due to a trainee dropping the ball. It's bollocky enough yet with all the blanks we have to fill in."

"Ten-four, James."

"Here — why'd he ask to see this Painless fella anyway?"

"Maybe Balfe knows the brother — Terry."

"The squad that used to be all business seems to be a holding area for comedians. If you ask me —"

Minogue didn't. He held up his hand to be sure he had heard Éilis's summons to the phone.

"Da."

"Hello, love."

"How's it going?"

"A minute ago, I was looking for the jacket I never brought with me this morning. The heat has me addled."

"Don't be talking," said Iseult. "I put paper on the windows here to keep the sun off."

Minogue remembered that the window frames in Iseult's studio were old metal ones. He had seen a crust of frost on them just after Christmas. Winter meant air thick with the smell of a gas storage heater and the sundry oils and dyes, the wood shavings and stains, the scents of hemp and paper. He had held off opining about the place as a health hazard. Iseult shared the studio with several others. He had been bewildered to find her working with chisels and awls last month, helping one of her fellow tenants to finish a wooden construction that looked, in sketches at least, to be a tank trap from a Normandy beach.

"Well, how are you anyway?" she asked. He forgot the ache in his back, the stale smell of sweat that clung to his shirt. Iseult wasn't in the habit of calling him at work.

{ 131 }

"For my age, do you mean? Or my occupation?"

"In general like."

"Oh, as ever. Happy-go-lucky. Early dotage maybe . . ."

"Fibber. Are you working late?"

"It's hard to know. The usual. Waiting, checking, talking, thinking, cursing . . ."

"I was just wondering."

"Well, if I had known you were in the market for tea, now."

"It's all right."

He waited for another hint. Malone waved at him, stepped over to the boards and tapped his marker against a name. Painless Balfe. Minogue put his hand over the mouthpiece.

"We can pin him, Tommy? Right now?"

"Surveillance at Egan's shop saw him go in five minutes ago. They called it in for us."

So Kilmartin had bargained something out of Serious Crimes then, Minogue reflected.

"Okay. Pick him up — only when he comes out though."

"Here, I'll leave you," said Iseult. "You're busy enough."

The brisk tone made him even more alert.

"Busy? God, no! Where do you want to meet?"

"I don't want to, you know, get in the way now."

"Well, I do. What's that black-and-silver place in George's Street? Music from the Andes, the stuff on the walls, avant-garde and what-have-you?"

"Back Then? Are you sure? It's gone completely vegetarian, you know."

He rolled his eyes.

"A quarter to six?"

"Done," he said. "Will you be on your own?"

"To all intents and purposes. I'll see you, Da."

The connection was lost before Minogue could utter a word. Was that humor he had heard in her answer? He replaced the receiver and gave a sigh. Phone Kathleen. Tell her that Iseult wanted to see him. Him alone? How would he manage this one, he wondered.

. . . . .

The straps of the plastic bag had cut deep into his fingers again. He stopped to change the bag to his other hand and looked through the grove at the cars passing in the distance. He wiped his forehead with the back of his hand and lowered the bag to the ground. Did it get cold at night this time of the year, even with a heat wave? If he found some newspapers, that'd help. He sat down and rested against a tree trunk. Something had come between that world of busy commuters and the trees about him. He looked up into the canopy and imagined a tree house there. The chestnut leaves overhead were so dense that he found no bit of sky at all. Like a roof, he thought. Even if it rained, the trees would shelter him.

His hand searched out the bag but it landed among pieces of metal. There were beer cans all mangled up under the grass, cigarette butts. He moved over and took out the biscuits and the Coke. They didn't taste as good as the first time. They had lost that magic that had brought him by the back of his tongue to the age of nine again. He stopped chewing. The bastard could have given him the money, the loan of money, without acting the bleeding Rambo about it. It'd been a long time since Jammy had been that mad at him.

Jammy was scared. Mary. Small pieces of biscuit caught the back of his throat. It began to tighten. His eyes prickled. What a mess, what a fucking mess. The crushed biscuit turned to paste as he cried. He tried to gather it at the front of his mouth to spit it out. Everything was stacked against him no matter what he did. He imagined going into a Garda station and yapping his head off, trying to do a deal to keep him on his own. They'd find out soon enough that he had nothing to do with Mary's . . . Mary getting killed. They'd nail the bastard who'd done it. Then he'd be all right.

Even as that hope rose in him, he felt himself falling deeper into something. He swilled Coke around his teeth. Didn't matter what he'd done or hadn't done, nobody believed him, not even Jammy. The cops would use him and if he got nailed by any of the Egans, they wouldn't lose too much sleep over it. He squeezed his eyes tight and sucked in air through his teeth. Fucking bastards, the lot of them. Whatever Mary had been into had left the Egans pissed off. Maybe she had told them some yarn about him just to buy time or something and they had done her in then . . .

He stood and took a few steps into the grove before peeing. The panic came back to him in an instant and it swept all hope away with it. He'd never make it, not tonight out here in the park, not tomorrow — never! He'd been too cocky about using, even bragging that he could go weeks without a hit. Sure, he had once, but he had been climbing the walls. Junkie; user; scumbag; addict. He still had nearly a hundred and fifty quid. Go down to the Bell and score off Brannigan. Then what? Stay in the pub and blow more money? He could pick out a boozer and knock him outside when he left the pub. He slapped at the tree branch. If only he could talk to one of them, one of the Egans, without any danger he'd get done in, he could explain. He leaned against the tree. Birdsong erupted above. What the hell was he going to do here all night? The foliage seemed to look back at him, to draw him in.

"You fucking iijit," he heard himself say. What time was it? He wasn't hungry. Was he going nuts? Here in the middle of Dublin, in the six hundred acres of the Phoenix Park, he'd never felt so lost.

·   ·   ·   ·   ·

"Well, look at that," said Painless Balfe. "The Kremlin."

Malone looked around from the passenger seat. Balfe sat with his hands on his knees between two CDU detectives. The Nissan turned into the car park of Harcourt Square.

"I'm going to miss you, lads," he added. He looked from one to the other. "We've grown very close." Malone turned back as the barrier came down behind the car.

"Do I get the chauffeur treatment on the way back too?"

"You lead, will you," Malone murmured to the driver. "I still don't know my way around here."

A Garda in uniform met the car at the entrance to the lift.

"Any word from my solicitor?" said Painless.

"What do you want a solicitor for?" asked Malone. "Are you in trouble?"

Balfe's expression didn't change. The Guard held the door open.

"Hey Tommy," said Balfe.

"Say hello to the brother for me, will you, Tommy? I hear Terry's taking the air tomorrow."

Malone watched the doors slide together.

"Maybe I'll be seeing him before you do, of course," said Balfe. "By the way, he didn't mention to you about getting AIDS in the 'Joy, did he? Maybe he wants it to be a surprise."

"Get yourself a fucking future, Painless," said Malone. Balfe looked to one of the detectives.

"Did you hear that?"

"Hear what," said the detective.

The group followed the uniformed Guard to an interview room.

"Hey, there's a phone," said Painless. "I could phone him here myself."

"Only internal calls there," said the Guard. Minogue appeared around the door.

"Sit over there, Mr. Balfe —"

"*Mr.* Balfe? Is this going to cost me money?"

"— and shut up."

Balfe's face suddenly twisted into a look of hatred.

"Don't you fucking talk to me like that, pal! I'm here because I co —"

"No sign of an up-to-date tax disc for Mr. Balfe's Sierra yet?" Minogue asked one of the Guards.

"Sierra?" snapped Balfe. "Such a shitbox. Only cops drive them. I drove one four years ago."

"Do you own a blue Escort XR3?"

Balfe shook his head. Minogue flipped open a folder and gave the top page a quick look.

"There's a discrepancy in your car's tax book, Mr. Balfe. Who did you buy the car off?"

"Oh, Christ, here we go. What's it going to be this time?"

Minogue sat heavily into a chair opposite Balfe. He nodded at one of the detectives to go to the monitor room. Painless Balfe's eyes slid around the room before resting on the mirrored glass.

"Hello, Mammy and Daddy," he said, and leered at Minogue. "Will this make me a star?"

Malone dragged his chair into the end of the table.

"So, Tommy. What are you up to these days, oul son?"

"Cleaning up the streets, oul son," said Malone.

Balfe put up his fists and made a mock feint.

"Still at the you-know-what?"

"Matter of fact, I am, yeah."

"Not the real thing though, right?"

"That's right. It's only sissy stuff, Painless. I only take on fellas who know how to box."

Minogue studied Balfe's reaction. His face slackened and his eyes became very still.

"You're such a fucking smart alec, Tommy. You probably think you're even funny."

"Last Monday, Mr. Balfe," said Minogue. He sat up and grasped his pencil.

"Yeah? What about last Monday?"

"Where were you?"

"I don't remember."

"Try. We certainly would appreciate the effort."

"Got up. Had a cup of tea. A smoke."

"You were at home Sunday night? Twenty-one Oriel Street, Bally-bough?"

"My jases. The fan club's really up to date. Yeah."

"Alone?"

"With someone."

"Theresa Joyce?" asked Malone.

"You said it. That was fast. I must tell her she's getting famous."

"And?"

"Well now. Monday. Went into town. Met me friends. Had a smoke. Et me dinner. Went to the bookies, watched the ponies. Played a few games of pool. Had a few jars. Had me tea. Went to the boozer. Oh, I forgot. Had a haircut." He winked. "The whole thing: shampoo and blow dry. Ever get one of those, Tommy?"

"Haircut's a haircut."

"Well done, Mr. Balfe," said Minogue. "Start again now. This time we'll try the time element."

Balfe looked from Minogue to Malone.

"Who's Gentleman Jim here, Tommy?"

"Excuse me, Mr. Balfe. I forgot to introduce myself. I'm Inspector Minogue."

"You're not one of my normal fans."

"Serious Crime Squad, Mr. Balfe? Oh, no. They're the tough guys to be sure. I'm much more reserved and genteel really. Murder Squad."

Balfe frowned.

"Murder Squad?"

"Let's begin again now, Mr. Balfe. Start us Monday morning and take us with you all the way through until you woke up Tuesday morning."

CHAPTER 11

Minogue listened to Kilmartin's rationale. An hour and a half with that head-case Balfe and he was no wiser. The phone slid around in his hand. He pushed Polaroids of Mary Mullen's trashed flat around the desktop with his biro.

"What about the other character, the sidekick? Lenehan."

"No sign of him. To get back to Balfe here."

"What do you want to do? Put him to the wall or through the wall?"

"Through the wall, James. Doyler ranks him number one in the bully league."

He spun one of the photographs. He heard Kilmartin flicking a lighter.

"He talks like he has a wallet full of alibis, Jim. I haven't found a gap yet."

"So? You can't put him near Mary Mullen in the recent past?"

"Not yet. He said he met her once but that he didn't know anything about her."

"Well, you got that out of him. Fire it back in his face if we find out different later on. The way you talk it's obvious we need more. This Lenehan fella, he'll turn up soon enough."

"Any word on Hickey yet?"

"No. Still on the run, it looks like. Look, Matt. Push this clown Balfe on any association with the Leonardo fella. Tire him out, catch him — the routine."

"I've done that," said Minogue. "There's no sign of a giveaway. He didn't try to dirty anyone. No hint of a deal either. He seems willing to take the hard option."

Kilmartin said nothing.

"I want to pitch him out, Jimmy. I'm tired. We can hammer away at the alibis and his statement on paper and then work from there."

"Fine and well then."

From the tone, Minogue knew that Kilmartin felt different. He waited.

"Well," said the chief inspector. "You could round up a couple of lads there from CDU, lads what *know* Balfe. Then take yourself off for a little walk. Down to Bewley's, your usual shirking zone. Come back in a while and there might be a different tune. Falling down the stairs can do a lot for a man's tongue."

"Come on now, Jim. All those conferences on methods? The tour of the FBI college?"

"Get smart there, Hair-oil. Do you think they never take the gloves off over there?"

"Balfe knows the routine. He's been broadcasting about his solicitor since he got here. Either we hold him now and get serious or we call it a day."

"Umhhk," said Kilmartin with a soft belch. "Well, far be it from me, et cetera."

Far indeed, thought Minogue. He trudged back to the interview room. The air was stale. Arms folded, Malone had slid down the chair. He was staring at Balfe.

"Aha," said Balfe. "You found a phone that makes outside calls?"

Minogue glanced at Malone.

"Okay, Mr. Balfe. That'll be all for the moment."

Balfe gave him a blank look. He blinked and sat back in his chair.

"Just when we'd got to the interesting bit, huh, Tommy?"

Malone gathered himself up and stood. Balfe also stood.

"You think I'm messing, Tommy, do you? Not this thing, the girl who got killed. I mean the psychology thing. Very interesting, no joke. How come you're the Lone Ranger and Terry's not?"

Minogue leaned against the wall. Whatever that was about, the tape would have picked it up.

"What did she have belonging to you, Mr. Balfe?" Minogue asked.

"Who?"

"Mary Mullen. When you went through her flat, Mr. Balfe. Did you find it?"

Balfe's eyes seemed to recede a little into his head.

"You'll have to do a lot better than that if you want to try stitching me up, pal," he said. Minogue thought about Kilmartin's suggestion that he go for a stroll and leave three or four Guards from the Hold-up Squad with Balfe.

"I'll show you out, Mr. Balfe," he heard himself murmur. "That way, next time you're back, you'll know the way yourself."

.   .   .   .   .

Minogue swung around South King Street and turned into Drury Street. He registered the plastic bottles and beer cans lying in the doorways, the pub doors wide open to admit more of the sultry air. Two men in shorts and copies of Ireland's national soccer team's T-shirts staggered by. He levered the car into Wicklow Street and parked it.

Back Then was dark. Hot air thick with the smell of cooking vegetables washed over his face. His eyes began to adjust to the light and he navigated toward a table against the wall. World music came on strong from the ceiling speakers. He ordered a tumbler of water and looked about. The restaurant could pass for a workshop or studio. Bold design with haphazard *objets trouvés* seemed to state that this was a provisional setup and would remain permanently provisional. Work in progress. Iseult was suddenly composing herself in a chair opposite.

"Will we stay?"

"Didn't we decide to?"

"All right." He watched the waitress approach, the glitter of something on her nostril.

"You don't like it?"

"I'm not used to the idea that the restaurant is not finished but merely abandoned."

"God, Da, the older you get! What'll you eat now?"

"Your mother was asking for you."

Iseult cocked an eye and held the glass of water to her cheek.

"I'll phone her tonight," she said.

"She's excited about the wedding. So am I."

Iseult searched his face for sarcasm. He kept his gaze on posters across the room.

"I suppose I should get her more involved. Plans and everything. It was to be the Registry Office, I hope you know."

Was, thought Minogue. Her hands searched around the table, touching the vase and its single flower, the tumbler, the cutlery.

"'Was,'" he said. Iseult arranged her knife, fork, and spoon in over-lapping patterns. "Did I hear you right?"

"Pat's parents dug in their heels. They won't go unless it's in a church."

She picked up the knife and stared at it.

"I had a monster row with him over it," she said.

"And?"

She began to finger the handle of the knife. The tip held some fasci-nation for her.

"I thought I knew him."

Minogue said nothing. Thin, clear soup arrived.

"So what are you going to do?"

She blew on the spoon.

"What I told him I'd do." She put down the spoon and joined her hands over her bowl.

"He comes home the other evening and starts hemming and hawing. I thought he was having me on."

She sighed and returned to her soup. Minogue thought of Pat's par-ents. He had met them half a dozen times. The mother, Helen Geraghty, was from Meath and was very active in community groups. She liked amateur theater and took classes in writing. The father, Des, was a bank manager in Terenure. He liked golf and expressed keen interest in the Minogues' visits to France. He had buttonholed Minogue after a few jars at the Christmas and spoken darkly of the state of the country's coffers and conscience. We have to pull up our socks here in Ireland or we'd never be taken seriously in Europe — or anywhere else for that mat-ter, according to Des. Minogue had become used to the prospect of knowing the Geraghtys better as in-laws. Kathleen and Helen main-tained correct and cordial relations. Compliments were plentifully ex-changed and neither woman allowed earnest discussions of politics and other contentious matters to blunder into argument. Both sets of par-ents were punctilious in maintaining the open secret that Pat and Iseult lived together.

"His parents are gone barking mad since the abortion referendum," Iseult said.

Minogue had tired of the soup. Barking mad, he repeated within. Pat's parents, those golfing, innocuous, and charitable suburbanites, those people with generous and tolerant instincts, had declared themselves committed to following Church teaching. Helen Geraghty had referred to the matter with almost apologetic earnestness, he recalled, but he hadn't missed the glint in her eye: "Really now, Matt. When it all comes down to it, there's only one choice, isn't there?" He'd been stunned later to hear Des Geraghty reading the lesson at Sunday mass broadcast on RTE. Was Des Geraghty in that thick with the Church, he'd spluttered to Kathleen. What did he mean "in that thick," was her reply. He glanced at Iseult.

"Maybe Pat doesn't want to hurt anyone's feelings."

"Oh, really, Da? I thought that principles are supposed to cost you something. I told him to sort himself out and then get in touch with me when he's ready."

The waitress laid down bowls of vegetable casserole. Minogue lost heart at the sight of the steam rising from them.

"Get in touch?" he asked. "Is he banished back home to think it over maybe?"

She poked at cauliflower with her fork.

"No. I left."

Minogue looked down at her fork working. This food was too good for you, he thought: lentils, cauliflower, beans. Iseult's moody excavations with her food brought him back twenty years. *Ma, I hate cabbage, I hate it!* Either by design or indifference, her hair was all over the place. Her mauve T-shirt and worn jeans looked like she'd worn them gardening. The heat had made her eyes glisten and brought color to her cheeks. There was a smell of turpentine or paint around her. She glanced up at him.

"Don't you like this stuff?"

He was too far gone to prevaricate.

"A lump of meat in the middle would do the job. A bit of a caveman, I'm afraid."

Iseult began to describe the panels she was planning for an installation in the hall of a gallery. She wasn't being paid. It would be great exposure.

"The idea is why we keep things to look at," she said around a piece of carrot. "We kill them with our minds. We interpret them and we classify them. Do you get it?"

Minogue chewed on the half-cooked stalk he couldn't identify. "Back Then" indeed: like starving peasants who'd eat roots and bushes during the Famine. Chic.

"Not really. Did you say you'd moved out of the flat?"

"No, I didn't say." She speared broccoli.

"So you have."

"Temporarily."

"Until your intended gets some sense."

"Precisely."

"And if he doesn't?"

"He can fuck off, so he can."

Minogue dropped his fork. Iseult twisted away a smile.

"Listen to me, now. Maybe if we gave some thought to Pat's reasoning?"

"I'm not going to analyze anything, Da. To hell with that. That's just rationalizing."

"Sorry for trying to be reasonable. I rather like Pat."

"Good for you."

"Well, where are you staying for the moment then? What's the name of your friend, the photographer, I'm always forgetting her —"

"Aoife. No."

"Which friend then?"

"I'm like you, Da. I've no real friends. Scared them off, I think."

Minogue sat back and folded his arms.

"You know, Da," she said. "I have that thing too. The difference is, I'm still not used to it."

She ran her fingers through her hair.

"What are you talking about?"

"Oh, Da," she said. "You pretend you don't understand because you're afraid I can't handle it or something."

"Did I fall asleep and miss —"

"You know what I'm talking about," she broke in. "Don't treat me like a kid. Don't protect me, I don't need that. Teach me. Teach me about being alone."

· · · · ·

Every part of Ryan's Pub seemed to be oozing out smells. Minogue tried to take stock of them while he waited for the barman: varnish from the stools and counters, the hop tang of beer and stout from the taps, the ashtrays, hot dishes and glasses from the dishwasher, even diesel fumes? The doors had been jammed open. The sky to the west was orange on the dusty windows. He looked back to where Iseult had commandeered two stools. Modern primitive, he thought. Drinking orange juice in a pub must be the latest outrage. He carried the drinks over.

"Well, how bad can it be," he said after his first swallow. "Trying to please people is not the most ignoble of things. Pat has parents, doesn't he?"

"What do you think? The Immaculate Conception or something?"

He bit back a comment about Our Lady of Perpetual Succour.

"Try that one on your mother, why don't you," he said instead.

"What I mean is that Pat doesn't believe in this crap anymore than I do. And you're only making excuses for him. You like Pat, that's the problem."

"Problem, is it. Fight your own fights, love. I've had to recover from too much friendly fire over the years."

"Big help you are. Maybe Daithi was right." He looked up from his glass.

"Now what does that mean?"

"You know. You were allergic to telling him what to do."

He took a gulp of his drink and glared at her.

"See?" she said.

He tried to steer the conversation away. She shrugged off questions about jobs. The talk drifted to his holiday in Greece, the fact that traffic in Dublin was out of control. Iseult's best friend from primary school had just gotten married. Minogue was dopey from the beer. Would she have another orange juice? No. Thanks. She had detected no sarcasm in her father's offer.

She slipped off the stool. He followed her outside and took his bearings. The new car smell in his Citroen still held its own. Iseult began fiddling with the electric sunroof and then the windows.

"God, the laziness," she said. He thought about phoning the squad room.

"What do you want to do? Will you come home with me?"

"Remember the Sundays we used to go to the zoo," she said.

"The zoo."

"We had lemonade and crisps and chocolate and ice cream. I remember all of it."

Minogue looked over at her. Hormones, he thought. She hadn't brushed away the strands of hair that had drooped as she had fiddled with the dashboard.

"The installation I'm doing. It has the zoo in it. The animals looking in at the people and the mess they're making of things. How we ruin everything."

"That's clever," he said without thinking.

"Clever?" she cried. "I don't want clever, Da! I want fucking *real!*"

He turned the car without a word and drove through the lights onto the Main Road that ran the two and a half miles through Phoenix Park. He knew that she knew the zoo was closed. True, he thought with a tight ache around his heart: I think I have that thing too, Da. All the while preparing to forge her own bonds — and Minogue believed that she loved Pat and wanted him to win her in this trial — his daughter was still driven to untie them in advance. Contrariness, the family heirloom. She was laughing now.

"Remember the ice pops and the salt and vinegar crisps?"

"How could I forget."

"Gallons of lemonade and everything? Chocolate? God, we were spoiled! How did we ever keep it down!"

"Ye didn't always. I well remember carrying Daithi one warm day in the Botanical Gardens . . ."

She guffawed. His sadness moved off. He kept the Citroen cruising along in second gear. Shrubs and trees had thickened in the dusk. An oncoming car flashed headlights at him. He had forgotten.

"I can smell the elephants," she said. "Or something. Dung."

He coasted by the railings set into the hedges that marked the boundaries of the Dublin Zoo. The car seemed to be gliding now. He glanced over at Iseult's arm draped out the window. Over the lisp of tires he heard a screech alien to Irish birds.

"Hear that?" she whispered. "Macaws, I'll bet you."

She fell to staring at the passing trees. The Citroen seemed to have found its own speed, its own route. They heard the birds' screeches again. Minogue looked across the grass toward the coppices and groves where deer occasionally sheltered. Her hair hid her face from him. She drew in her hand from the window and held it folded over the other. The bob of her head alerted him. He heard the first sob.

"Will I stop, love?"

She shook her head but didn't look up. He headed back to the Main Road. She sniffed, blew her nose, and pushed her hair back. He wondered if she wanted him to say something. Plenty more fish in the sea, love? Pat means well? As well you found out now and not later?

"I always wanted to set them free," she sniffed. "Find the keys and open all the padlocks. Let them run somewhere they wouldn't be gawked at anymore. Where they could be themselves."

She turned her head and gave a wan smile.

"Can you imagine elephants trying to hide and live normal lives in Ballyfermot?"

"Nothing to that, love. I work with a buffalo inside. Jimmy. Speaking of which, I must head back there now. Come in with me, why don't you? Phone Mammy from there."

"How late are you staying?"

"I wish I knew. We're waiting for information. People to show up, witnesses, call-ins. New yield from forensic tests, breaks from door-to-door work. It's our second night at it."

"Not going so well, is it?"

He shook his head.

"I'll just go in and see if there's any new information that can't wait until the morning. I'll let John Murtagh and the new lad show their mettle tonight. Okay?"

"I'll wait in the car."

He hadn't the heart to ask her who'd phone Kathleen to tell her that her daughter was coming home. She brushed her hair back from her face again.

"You know," she said, "I meant that about the alone bit. How you turn in sometimes. You think I'm not old enough to figure it out. But I am."

He struggled once more to avoid saying something stupid. He mustered a smile.

"I don't know," he said. "And I know even less about you artist types. Just take damn good care that your stronghold doesn't turn into a prison when you're not watching."

•   •   •   •   •

A tremor jolted him against the tree. He'd dozed off. He rubbed at his burning eyes. The crappy yellow light above the trees made the city look like it was on fire. He could see a few stars. He shifted his back against the trunk. He could smell his breath. He returned to rubbing his stomach. Great. All he needed was the runs now on top of the itchies and the sweats and the . . . Birds squabbled overhead. Oh, Christ, something had to give.

He got up slowly. There was that weird groaning and grunting again. Elephants, he thought, big, smelly elephants. Rhinos. Giraffes. The stink off the gorillas; the way they looked like people. How come he could hear them and the zoo a mile away? They'd like this heat, of course. Maybe they were at it in there, the males and the females. Did all of them sleep though? No. He sniffed carefully again. A stink of manure. Monkey piss. How'd he know it was monkeys? After things got back to normal, he'd get a laugh out of telling them about the night he spent up by the zoo. They'd laugh, all right. They? There was no one waiting for him to talk to, no one to share a joke with. Not even Ma: she'd had it. All his stuff in plastic shopping bags around the back of the restaurant, dumped like rubbish. Nobody wanted to hear from him, and nobody — nobody — had ever asked him — not once, nobody — how he felt. Like he had no feelings. Like he was the type of bastard who could do that to Mary, who could even *think* of doing that to Mary. Like he was some kind of an animal.

His throat was killing him. He found the bottle of Coke and finished it. Christ, it'd be better to sleep in the day and stay up at night, not bother trying to get to sleep and worrying. Sleep: the more you want it to come, the farther away it gets. It must be well after midnight now. At least he hadn't bumped into down-and-outs or courting couples. In a way, he wanted some to be here so's he'd know the place was safe. He fingered his cigarettes. Twelve, enough even if he couldn't sleep at all. He cupped his hands around the lighter. With the cigarette lit he glanced at his watch. Half-one. The Coke had left an awful furry taste on his tongue. He hawked several times but couldn't summon the spit. The cigarette was doing a little dance in the dark. That meant his hand was shaking. He imagined dark figures slouching by the park gates, fanning out across the fields, tiptoeing from tree to tree. He got to his knees. He could see nothing in the darkness under the city's glow. He slapped his knuckles against the trunk.

Minutes passed. It had worked — he had calmed down. He sat down again. He began to think about the few times he had slept out before. They'd put together a sort of a hiking club back when he was eleven or so. That social worker fella that was always hanging around, the bearded fella who never got mad. Finn. Hiking up in the Dublin mountains. Jammy, him, the lads. Joe Ninety, Spots, Tommo. Had Pizzaman been with them on that? He couldn't remember now. Pots and pans and half the bleeding furniture they stuffed into them bags. O'Reilly and the vodka, Christ! Walking up by the Hellfire Club, Finn spots O'Reilly handing it to someone. War. Bleeding war, man! We're all going back. Who else has stuff? They'd sung as they marched along, dirty songs some of them. Finn pretending to be pissed off but smiling. Even the other fella, the priest who never put on priest's clothes. What was his name? Four eyes. Goggin — that was it. Camping up in the Pine Forest or something, everybody shagged and ready to hit the sack, sitting around the fire, Goggin came on with the fucking sermon. How did it go? Jesus in the bleeding garden of what's-the-place. Praying, yeah. Just before the big thing. Cavalry — Calvary. "Won't one of you stay up and keep me company?" And the apostles all shagged off or fell asleep or something. And Jesus woke them up or something and asked again . . .

He forced himself to let his eyes close. Orangutans had orange hair, faces like oul wans. There were all kinds of ones that looked like cats or squirrels or mice or something. Lepers — no — lemurs. Come to think of it, we were monkeys too. He suddenly ached for someone beside him. Talk about anything. Jammy, so he could see that he had all his marbles, that he was just as quick and smart as ever. There was a time when people admired him for the stuff he knew, for all the facts he could remember. Lemurs. Krakatoa; the Vikings; Jesse James. All the stuff he knew: different types of clouds, makes of cars — he could guess the age and model of any car with just a look at the bonnet. Two seconds, that was all he needed. That counted for something, didn't it?

An ambulance siren made him open his eyes. He watched its blue lights flashing as it raced toward the city center. Some poor bugger in an accident. His eyelids slid down again. Images flared suddenly in his mind then: himself covered in blood lying on a stretcher in the ambulance. The driver booting it, the other one looking down at him. *Jesus!* He writhed and stood up and squeezed his eyes tighter. He's a goner, one of them was saying. My God, look at the blood. They must have used razors on him. They sliced his eyes and everything. We're too late. Take him to the mortuary.

CHAPTER 12

A HALF CENTURY and more of mortal existence and he still hadn't copped on to the basics: you cannot make yourself sleep. Minogue opened his eyes again and looked at his watch. Seven, not bad. Last night's shandy had left him gassy but without the melancholy wake-up he expected of Guinness.

He loaded the coffeemaker, switched it on, and stepped into the garden. His forsythia had cascaded even further over the walls into the neighbors'. No problem. He ambled by the potato drills. British Queens, Duke of York. Leaves looked starchy. Drought in Ireland, he thought. That he should live to see it. He remembered Kathleen fussing over Iseult last night: would Iseult like a nice bubble bath? Apple tart with real cream? All Iseult wanted, damn it all, Kathleen, was to slip into the house and be left alone.

The phone sounded shriller than usual. He skipped back over the grass.

"Are you awake?" It was Murtagh.

"No. Go ahead."

"Sorry. Just thought I'd wait until after seven. We found the other hard-chaw, Painless Balfe's sidekick. Lenehan. Call him Lollipop."

"Where is he?"

"We took him up to Fitzgibbon Street. Five o'clock he came rolling on home."

"Oh? You waited for him, John?"

"Me and Doyler. We had a grand old time of it. I even got a couple of hours' kip."

"Have you talked to him yet?"

"Talk, is it? He was high on something. He threw shapes right there in the street. Fab, it was." Minogue heard the coffeemaker hiss.

"How fab was it?"

"He didn't buy the ID. He thought we were hit men or something. He pulled out knuckles. Swear to God, boss. We had to call in the cavalry. It took four of them and then the two of us. When he saw the squad car screaming up, he went berserk."

"Are ye all right?"

"Never better. Such a row! It was Doyler who finally gave him one in the nuts. Had to tie the feet and all then. Three fellas sitting on him all the way back to the station. What a madman. Ponytail, face like a crocodile. Acne. The mugshot didn't do him justice."

"So we can have him for the long haul?"

"Yep. Weapon. Assault. Assault with intent. Battery. Resisting. Causing a disturbance. Malicious damage. He's a goner."

"Does he know he's up the creek?"

"Yep. He's been dropping hints. I think he's trying to suss out a deal."

The excitement came to Minogue mixed in with the scent of brewing coffee.

"Great, John. Great. Now tell me, is he our man?"

"Could be. Christ, he's a reptile. Vicious. He could be our man."

Minogue put on the boiled eggs. If Lollipop Lenehan was a lifer, he could clam up and take the charges without a word. One of the eggs popped. He looked in to see the albumen issuing out into the dancing water. Iseult stood in the doorway.

"Did I wake you?"

"I wanted to be awake. Will you give me a lift into town and you going?"

She sat at the table. Her mother's dressing gown was a foot short on her.

"I'll get stuck into me stuff and I'll be right as rain."

He poured her coffee. He listened for Kathleen's step on the stairs.

"Did you talk to your mother?"

"A bit."

She threw her hair back. There was a glint in her eye to match the edge in her voice.

· · · · ·

The Citroen crested the Rise and began its descent toward Foster's Avenue and the Bray Road into Dublin. From the Rise, Minogue caught glimpses of a city webbed in haze below. Spires and towers, cranes and blocks of flats stuck out of the mantle. The sun reflected dully back to them from faraway windows. He turned up the radio.

Iseult remained silent until Leeson Street.

"I'd like to travel, Da."

"Yes."

"Tell us about Greece again. The bit about walking around early in the morning."

He made up bits but she didn't seem to mind. She insisted that she wanted to be left by the Green. He watched her stride through the gate. She didn't turn back. He almost nicked a lorry thinking about her later.

Malone was in the squad room before him. He wondered if the detective's hair was wet from the shower or gelled.

"Another scorcher," said Malone.

"Yep and why not, Tommy?" Minogue saw Murtagh's feet on the desk. He leaned around the cabinet.

"How's John. No ill effects from the barney with Lenehan?"

Murtagh yawned and smiled. The three policemen headed down the hall.

"Is the Killer up to date on this?" Minogue asked.

"Yep," said Murtagh. "Says he'll have a look-in sometime this morning."

"What's the condition of our Lollipop then?"

"Sour enough," said Murtagh. "But I think he knows the stakes."

Two Guards were lounging at the door of the interview room. Another two were inside with a man in a loose-fitting, black-patterned polo shirt and a ponytail. Lenehan turned as the door opened. Pale and yellow around the eyes, he had a flat look to his expression that put Minogue in mind of priests and gangsters. The three detectives took the place of the two Guards. Lenehan's halitosis reached halfway to the door. There was also a stale sugary smell. Minogue showed him his card.

"You've been advised of the charges against you, Mr. Lenehan?"

Lenehan nodded once.

"You have a criminal record, Mr. Lenehan."

Lenehan began picking at something on the knee of his trousers. Minogue sat opposite him.

"So you can expect little leeway, if any, in court."

Lenehan's lips puckered slightly. His eyebrows went up.

"Does that interest you at all, Mr. Lenehan?"

Lenehan looked up with a quizzical, almost amused expression. Minogue waited while Lenehan looked from face to face. His eyes stayed on Malone.

"Is this fella for real, Tommy?"

Malone exchanged a glance with Minogue.

"He's the one to bury you for eight to ten," said Malone. "So, yeah, I'd say he's for real."

Minogue studied Lenehan's acne. Lenehan looked high up on the walls.

"You've really hit the wall this time, Mr. Lenehan."

"Did I, now." Malone spoke before Minogue could continue.

"Yeah, you did, Lolly. Head-on, man. Get yourself organized. You know what I'm saying?"

Crocodile, thought Minogue, but baby-faced. He liked to cut people up.

"Give up on Mary Mullen, Mr. Lenehan, and that could make the difference."

"What are you fucking on about? 'Give up on Mary Mullen.' What kind of shite is that?"

"As it is, you're going to get hammered for last night. Then we're going to put the murder on you. Save us some time, man. Clear the slate."

"Fuck you, pal," said Lenehan. "Take me off and do whatever the hell you're going to do."

"We can do the business right here, Mr. Lenehan. There's no taking off anywhere."

Minogue's gaze lingered on the ponytail. Lollipop Lenehan examined the skin on his knuckles.

"Now. Where were you that night?"

"Down at the pictures or something. I don't know. Ask around."

"Ask who? Bobby Egan?"

Lenehan looked up with a pained expression.

"You can't make me wear this, for God's sake. Grow up."

"Wear what?"

"Mary Mullen is what."

"Who told you about her?"

Lenehan shook his head.

"You did. 'Give up on Mary Mullen.'"

Minogue looked again at the copies of the records from Lenehan's file: aggravated assault; resisting arrest; threats of bodily harm.

"But before that. How'd you know?"

"The papers. Someone told me. I don't know."

"How well did you know her?"

"Not well enough to do her in."

"Who can vouch for you on Monday night?" Malone asked. Lenehan closed his eyes.

"Catherine Hennessy. 3592764. Now, happy?"

Minogue glanced at Malone.

"Why were you hanging around Patricia Fahy's place?"

"Who's Patricia Fahy?"

"You and who else?"

"Take a fucking walk, why don't you."

"Who were you expecting there?"

"Where?"

"At Fahy's."

"Who's Fahy? Is this a quiz? Don't open the box — I'll take the money and go."

"What was Mary's problem with the Egans?"

Lenehan smiled and held in a breath.

"Jesus Christ, Tommy. What kind of a thick are you paired up with here, man?"

"Come on now," Minogue went on. "Are you that well paid you're ready to go for eight years and not even wonder what the Egans think of you, now you messed up? You fell on your face, man."

"Yeah, well, I wasn't expecting two fucking detectives, two ugly-looking bastards, sitting outside my house at five o'clock in the bleeding morning, was I?"

"Show me the rule book on that, why don't you."

"How the hell was I supposed to know they were the law? They didn't identify themselves, for Christ's sake! What kind of a law is that? They could have been anybody!"

"Oh, you were expecting trouble? Someone wanted to settle a score with you?"

"You're talking through your bleeding hat."

"And was it you turned her place upside down too? Or is that beneath you?"

Lenehan took a breath but said nothing. Murtagh opened the door and beckoned to Minogue.

In the hall was Chief Inspector Kilmartin. He held a cigarello cupped behind his back.

"The hard," he greeted Minogue. "Maggot Number Two in there?"

"Don't be talking. A double-barreled gurrier. A good hiding is what he needs."

"Huh. There was high jinks enough when they picked him up, I believe."

"There was that. There's plenty to throw at him, but the initial reaction is poor."

"A record on him the length of a nun's drawers?"

"Every commandment broken. Rank poison. Long day ahead of us, I'm thinking."

Kilmartin studied the tip of his cigarello.

"Run shifts on him all day then," he growled. "Sweat it out of him, why don't you. Did he call for a referee yet?"

"No. But he doesn't seem to care if his goose is cooked."

Kilmartin cleared his throat. He gathered the phlegm behind his front teeth.

"Maybe the Egans'll send in some brigand of a solicitor when they find he's been taken in. Send him my way, why don't you."

"Lollipop Lenehan?"

"No, the bloody solicitor. I'm in the humor of barracking someone. Move Lenehan somewhere if a solicitor shows. Do you need me here?"

"Thank you, no, Jimmy. I'll only use you for a big threat later on."

"Ho ho ho! You're only jealous."

"Still no word on this Leonardo yet, is there?"

Kilmartin cut short his chortling.

"Neither hide nor hair of the little bastard. He'll be Case 2 now, wait'n'you see. Turn up in a ditch with his throat cut or something."

Kilmartin stared at the floor as though committing something sage to memory.

"Oh, well, what the hell," he said. "Y'all have a nice day now, y'hear?"

Minogue watched Kilmartin's jaunty walk back down the hall. Then he looked through the oblong safety glass set into the door. Lenehan was talking to his hands it seemed, and didn't notice the inspector looking in. Malone did, and his eyes widened for a moment as he glanced at Minogue. The inspector reciprocated. Malone nodded once. Minogue elbowed into the monitoring room.

"Listen to this now," said the Guard on the tapes. The inspector picked up the headphones and looked through the one-way mirror.

"Yeah, so you knew her that way then," Malone was saying. Murtagh pushed his chair back on two legs and cast the odd furtive glance at the glass.

"Well, fuck, everybody knew her," said Lenehan. "Isn't that the whole idea, like? I mean to say, do you know any other reason why a woman'd want to peel off her clothes in front of a camera?"

"I don't know," said Malone.

"You don't know? Modeling, man. Sure, everyone's at it. Fucking Madonna's gotten everyone in on the act this time. Everyone thinks they're stars. Jases."

"There's more than the family album changing hands in this business though," said Malone. "Isn't there now, Lolly?"

"Like what?"

"Drugs?"

Lenehan looked up under his eyebrows at Malone.

"You ought to know, Tommy. Unless you were walking around blindfolded since your mother got kicked out of the Rotunda with you under her arm."

"What do I know?"

"The only real fucking drug is money."

"Who has pictures of Mary?"

"I don't know. Tell me."

"Come on, Lolly. Who?"

"Don't know. I seen some of them, that was all. They looked like the real McCoy too. Hardly recognize her."

"How do you mean?"

Lenehan shrugged.

"Seen one, you seen them all, man. Or didn't you know?"

Minogue gritted his teeth. Malone was slipping. He was challenging Lenehan too directly after finding out that he was a veteran head-case, someone who knew something from the inside.

"You're fucking lying," said Malone.

He was staring at Lenehan now. Minogue unhooked the headset and headed for the door. The Guard on the switches grabbed his arm as he passed. Minogue picked up the headset again. Malone went on in the same mild tone. Lenehan was licking his lips.

"I can't believe you're such a gobshite, Lolly. Here you go, sitting here, looking down the hole, and all you can do is lie through your teeth. You're such a liar, I can smell it off you."

Lenehan's voice came out as a whisper.

"Fuck you, Tommy. You're nothing more than a thick shit rozzer."

"Oh, yeah? What about you? You never could make it with real people. Couldn't go in a ring without a knife."

"I know all about your fucked-up mind from Terry. You're the one's screwed up. Mr. Morality. Take a fucking jump."

Malone laughed. Minogue exchanged a look with the Guard.

"And you think you're tough," said Malone. "You think that because you're a lying fuck that's going away for eight to ten, for real years, that the Egans are going to have a marble statue put up to you? You stupid iijit. They'll leave you buried in there, Lolly. You'll get out and you'll be, lemme see, thirty-six, thirty-seven. Christ, you might as well jack it in here and now. If you can do your time without going stupid or getting an ugly boyfriend, you'll stagger out of the 'Joy just in time to get walked on by fellas who aren't even teenagers right now. Smart move there, Lolly. I've got to hand it to you there, man. Here — I'll do you a favor: I'll smuggle you in a shank so's you can top yourself."

"God, the language," Minogue murmured. But Lenehan still hadn't called for a solicitor. Malone's eyes traveled around the room, stopped for several moments on the glass, and then went on to Murtagh.

"Let's get this gobshite a solicitor, John. Start burying him now. He's good for nothing."

Lenehan's eyes were slits now. Minogue watched, appalled. Malone was throwing a key to this murder investigation out the window. Maybe even the killer. Whatever Minogue himself thought, Kilmartin would hit the roof. Murtagh seemed to be playing along but kept looking to the glass.

"What's the fuss over a few bleeding snapshots, for Jases' sake?" Lenehan burst out. "You'd have no trouble finding them if yous were real cops!"

Malone leaped out of his chair.

"Yeah, well, let's say I *was* a real cop then!" he shouted. Lenehan looked up at him and his mouth opened. "Where would I get them? Where would I start?"

"Well, I don't know, do I," said Lenehan.

"What *do* you know, you fucking waster? When did you meet her? Where was it?"

"I didn't *meet* her, meet her! I seen her in a pub. Someone said

something. I don't know! Then I was looking through pictures somewhere and I seen her again."

"Where?"

"Where what?"

"Where did you see her in person?"

"Some pub."

"Come on, Lolly."

"I had a few jars on me! Some pub we called in to, near Baggot Street.
I don't know. I never said a word to her. He says to me —"

"Who says?"

"Painless. Says to me, 'Not as nice as her family album.' Nudge nudge,
wink wink, like."

"And you remembered her."

"So? You would too. If you were normal."

"Where'd you see the pictures?"

"I don't know. Some place. Something to do with Ali Baba. What do
you call it?"

"The forty thieves?"

"Fuck, I don't know! It was a couple of years ago."

"Okay. Some place called Ali Baba's. What is it, a knocking-shop? A
club?"

"It was just an office, a place with a phone. Up a few flights of stairs
somewhere. Near Mercer's hospital. Where the rag trade is."

"That's all you can do? Something about Ali shagging Baba?"

"A hundred nights . . . something like that."

"What is it, a telephone job? Rent-a-girl?"

"'Models.' Yeah. Dates and stuff."

"All the way?"

Lenehan shrugged.

"I suppose. What's 'all the way' for you?"

Malone continued to stare at him. Lenehan kept stroking his bottom
lip. Finally he looked up.

"What about a smoke or something," he said.

"No, thanks," said Malone. He strolled to the door. "I haven't had a
smoke since I was ten or eleven, Lolly."

Minogue dropped the headset and went into the hall.

"I'd prefer you didn't pull that stunt again, Tommy. I thought he was
going to go by on us."

"Sorry."

"We'd be nowhere if he'd clammed up."

Malone's frown, his downcast glance, suggested defiant contrition to Minogue. The detective's head came up and he smiled.

"Feels good though," he said. "Doesn't it?"

Minogue grinned back.

"You've more in common with the Killer than either you or he would like to admit."

"I want a word with him," said Malone. "Lenehan. With the tape off though."

"Can't do that, Tommy."

"I'm not going to put the heavy word on him or anything."

Minogue eyed him.

"That's right. You're not, Tommy."

"Just a bit of advice for him? A minute?"

Minogue continued to give Malone the eye.

"I'll be listening in then. I'll scrub the tape for one minute. Don't mess with your good luck, Tommy. And get John Murtagh out of the room. He shouldn't have to carry anything."

The inspector returned to the monitoring room. Murtagh gave a blank look at the glass as he left the room. Minogue put his hand over the recording button.

"Did you find the number then?" Lenehan asked.

Malone stared at him.

"What number? I came back to tell you something."

Lenehan blinked and drew in his legs. Malone leaned over the table between them.

"Do you know why you're in here, Lolly?"

"I got nailed, that's why. Bad luck. Am I missing out on something deep here?"

"Why you're in such a bleeding mess, is what I mean."

"Yeah, I do as a matter of fact. I was set up by the cops. Is that news around here or something?"

"No, no, no. You just don't get it, do you?"

"Tell me then, know-it-all."

"It's because you have no discipline, man —"

"Aw, fuck, is this school or something? What the hell are you on about? *Discipline?*"

"You had to slip up. That's just how it is for iijits. You think you're smart, that you get away with the odd trick. A lot of tricks even. All you gougers are the same. You're going away for a long time, pal. And if I find out that you did for Mary —"

"I fucking didn't! Who's the iijit around here now, that's what I'd like to know!"

"Or if you know who did, or if you are covering for someone who did . . ."

"Yeah?"

"I'll be all over you, Lolly. You're messing with me, I'll fucking land on you." Lenehan let his legs out again. He nodded as he drew on the cigarette.

"Oh, now I get it. This is *personal,* man. In that case, I hope Terry fucks you over, man. I really do."

Minogue noticed that a line had appeared on Malone's cheek.

"Well, seeing as you brought up the matter. You know Terry, right?"

A smile flickered around the corners of Lenehan's lips.

"Yeah, I heard of Terry."

"This is a message for anyone visiting you. Leave my brother alone. You got that?"

Lenehan blew a very flawed smoke ring.

"It's a free country," he said. "What can I do?"

Malone stood.

"A bit late to be asking me, isn't it?"

· · · · ·

He was on his feet and moving before he was certain it wasn't a dream. His heart raced and now the weakness that followed the moment's terror was flooding up from his knees. It was his own breath he heard snorting out. The dog stood off with its nose jabbing the air left and right. He took a step toward the tree and eyed the owner. The man didn't want to look him in the eye.

"Sea — musss! Sea-mus!"

He looked back at the dog. It was a mongrel, but mostly spaniel with those big eyes, a yapper.

"Fuck off now, dog," he muttered. "Or else."

And the dog trotted off. Smart dog. The rest of the morning began to arrive to him: steady traffic on the Main Road through the park, the sun over the trees. He tried to swallow. It was like swallowing sand. He looked at his watch: half-eight! He'd actually slept? Right here, in the dark, out in a wood in Phoenix Park? It was the dog's panting woke him before the calls of its owner.

His back was as stiff as a board. It felt like he'd been fighting with a thousand video Ninja madmen in his sleep. But he was alive, he was standing up. He had made it — whatever that meant. He found his cigarettes and lit one. Two left. He counted back. He must have been awake until three o'clock or even four. If he had fallen asleep with a fag in his hand and then woken up with that bloody dog lifting its leg on him! Get a laugh out of that someday.

The first pulls on the cigarette had him lightheaded and hawking. His stuff lay crumpled on the ground. The extra shirt he'd tried to cover himself with, the other jeans. His head began to clear. He remembered walking out to the road just to be near the lights for a while. Fragments from his dreams came back to him. Dreams about animals: hippos, ostriches, lions escaping from the bleeding zoo.

He spotted two joggers running along next to the Main Road. He imagined himself there with them. He could still run. Maybe if he just changed his name — how did you go about that, anyway? Stupid idea. It'd cost a lot of money for starters, and then he'd lose his dole. If he could only slip out there into Cabra or somewhere, get a place, find a bit of work. Grow a beard. They'd never find him. He watched the joggers until they descended through the trees into a hollow.

He ground the butt into the clay. There was no Coke left. He bit into a biscuit but the taste on his lips turned him off before he even chewed. He tossed it into the trees. He'd left the chalk drawings all wrapped up in plastic bags at the back of a demolished building down the quays. Why the hell had he asked the Ma to bring those stupid drawings anyway? Rolling them out on some footpath next to Grafton Street, trying to get a few quid in his hat? Everyone in the bleeding city could see him there. What had he been thinking about?

The panic began to creep up on him. What the hell could he do, just sit here waiting for things to sort themselves out? He looked about at the empty Coke tins, the cigarette butts, the plastic bags of clothes. He'd often passed tinker camps by the side of the road and wondered how they could live like that, with clothes and rubbish thrown all over the place. He eased himself up slowly and began gathering the bags. He'd leave them hidden near here somewhere. It was about a twenty-minute walk to the gates. Once he got close to the gates, he'd make a quick dart out onto the quays. Down Stoneybatter toward the Markets, get a bit of something to eat there. A cup of tea at least, buy fags.

He stepped out from under the trees and headed across the fields. The Wellington monument came up out of the trees ahead like the top of a rocket. Either the hunger or the cigarette had made him alert. He kept his eyes on the rooftops and the spires he could see over the trees.

The stiffness in his body had eased by the time the park gates came in sight. He had made it, he'd kept himself in one piece and even managed to sleep a few hours. So what if he was going to be knackered by the afternoon. Through the traffic he saw a stand with a big board on it. He waited his chance and ran across. It was a map of the park. He studied the roads and traced where he had come from. His eyes fixed on a word in a box to the side of the map: Garda. Cop headquarters were back there, opposite the zoo! Right in Dublin, right under their noses. He studied the map again. The Hollow, some place over the far end of the park called the Wilderness. This place was even bigger than he had thought. How come he'd never known that?

The noise of an accelerating motorbike startled him. He walked fast by the gates to the park. Soon the city's buildings began falling into place alongside him. He realized that he had been almost running. He knew what he would do. No way was anyone going to corner him or try to put one over on him. He was going to stay free, like an outlaw.

CHAPTER 13

MINOGUE PUT DOWN the phone, drummed hard with his biro, and then pitched it in the air. Kilmartin looked over.

"What's the matter with — Hello? Hello? Yes. I'm trying to get in contact with someone who'd know about modeling agencies. Yes. Well, that's the problem now, this one is gone out of business."

Kilmartin's unseeing gaze roamed about the squad room while he listened.

"Exactly," the chief inspector went on in a pleasing tone. "I'm out of Dublin a while and I wanted to look up a person I used to know. Yes."

He winked at Minogue.

"Oh, yes. A very nice girl she was. That's right — What?"

Kilmartin's face darkened and he slid off the edge of the desk.

"What did you just say to me?"

Minogue heard the line go dead. Kilmartin dropped the receiver and stared at it.

"Gave me the F.O. Did you ever hear the like? The nerve of him!"

"Maybe it was the genuine article, James. A real modeling agency."

Kilmartin picked the receiver up and laid it gently on the phone.

"Huh. Any luck, you?"

Minogue shook his head. Kilmartin pulled a face.

"Sure, there's no jobs in the country," he said. "Wouldn't surprise me if a girl'd turn to you-know-what. The trade."

The chief inspector's eyes closed. The fart, a prolonged one, reminded Minogue of a rusty door hinge. Kilmartin opened his eyes again.

"At least inflation's holding steady," he whispered.

Minogue made for Malone's desk behind the room divider.

"Are you there, Tommy? Let's try that place."

"Which one?" Kilmartin called out. "That 'Just You' one?"

"That's the one, Jim. On George's Street. It's the only place so far with an address. The rest are just phone numbers: 'We'll meet you at so and so's.'"

Kilmartin lumbered up behind Minogue.

"Telephone girls, hah?" He yawned. "They're getting to be like the banks. Pick up the phone, by God, and they make money. Not a stroke of work, real work as you and I would understand about."

"Stroking's hard enough work," said Malone as he wrote. "If it's done right."

"Ha, ha, ha. Let me tell you, I know fellas do their day's work on the phone. And they're well paid too. Sure, that's not the real world, I tell them. Know what they tell me when I ask them what the hell goes on in the line of *real* work in those bloody glasshouse-looking places? Like those efforts made of glass you can't even use to look through? Christ, they'd blind you, and you trying to see where you're going."

"You can see out but you can't see in, Jimmy."

"Oh, a genius amongst the common rabblement here. Thanks. Well, anyway. Do you know what they say, cocked up in the chairs in the lounge with the Jag parked outside and the boxes of wine and the daughter married to the doctor, et cetera, et cetera?"

Minogue was wary of another fart. He beckoned to Malone.

"The suspense is killing me, Jim," he muttered.

"'This is the Information Age, Jim,' they say. La-di-da. Like I'm a gom just in from the bog, you know? 'The borders are coming down, Jim.' 'Jim, you only have to be in the right place at the right time.' 'Timing is everything, Jim.' 'Jim, the basic ingredient for making money is time.' All paper money, says I. Tricks. Magic money with nothing behind it. The eighties gone mad: all money, no value."

"Well, Christ," he added as Minogue and Malone made for the door, "says I to one of them, a fella I know well and would ordinarily take halfway seriously, they were wrong about the oldest profession in the world. Do you get it?"

·　　·　　·　　·　　·

Malone let back the seat and leaned his arm out the window. Minogue drew a squeal out of the tires as he accelerated through the amber light onto the quays.

"Wouldn't mind spending the rest of the day up in the park," said Malone.

Minogue looked at the greenery of Phoenix Park as it receded in his rearview mirror. The Citroen picked up speed. He opened the sunroof completely. The breeze which blew his hair asunder barely stirred Malone's crew cut.

"Were you in the park for the pope's mass there, back whenever?" asked Malone.

"Kathleen went all right," murmured the inspector. "I sort of prefer watching the deer myself."

He took in Malone's turn of the head, the second's scrutiny.

"Okay," he went on. "Tell me how you'd like to work this call now."

· · · · ·

The car was an oven. He thought about parking it in the shade somewhere, but Malone might not spot it. He looked at his watch. He'd give him ten more minutes. He couldn't shake scraps of the conversation he'd had yesterday with Iseult out of his head. He checked the standby and the charge light again and shoved the phone into the door pocket of the Citroen. The sun was hot on his head, too hot. He turned the ignition and pushed the button to close the sunroof.

Malone opened the door, climbed in, and slammed the door in one fluid movement.

"Thanks," he said. "Got something anyway."

"Yes?"

"Yeah. I let her know right off the bat that I could come in heavy if she wasn't on the ball here. Swore on a stack of Bibles she had nothing to do with brassers or that."

"So why did she give you the come-on over the phone?"

"She thought I just wanted pictures."

"That's what she has?"

"Yeah. 'What sort of a project do you have in mind?' says she. 'Project.' That's when I flashed the card. Big change. Anyway. So far as I can read between the lines, she's an agency for models. No actresses or that, just fashion and advertising. It's a room with fancy chairs and stacks of fake flowers and all. There's folders like you get when you're going to get married, photographs and all, with her clients. Models. Nothing wild now. Bikinis is as far as they go. She didn't know anything about Mary

Mullen. I tried the names of the other places we've dug up so far. '1001 Nights' got her going. Turned up the nose, admitted she'd heard of it. 'One of those places that gives the business a bad name.'"

"What do you think then?"

Malone scratched at his bristly crown.

"Hard to say. Says she, 'You have to be very careful these days.' She'd heard that 'organized crime' had moved in and was dragging the profession into the dirt."

"'Profession,'" said Minogue.

"She said she'd thought of getting out of the 'profession' but couldn't do it to her clients."

"Is she scared?"

"Hard to say. She's happy enough to pass a fella on to someone who does a different kind of photography though."

"What's in it for her?"

"I reckon she's in on it somewhere. Far enough out to be able to hold her nose and walk away from any poking we can do. But I bet she gets a backhander for passing someone on to the other end of the business."

"Just a front?"

"No. I saw ads and clippings in the model's port . . . what you call it. I suppose she's legit."

"Portfolios."

"Well, I got a phone number that we didn't have before."

Minogue started the engine and the Citroen rose up smartly on its suspension.

"Lift-off," said Malone. The inspector worked the car down off the curb.

"What are we looking at, Tommy?"

"Pictures. 'Models.' Mary Mullen. Prostitution. I don't know."

"Who tossed her place?" asked the inspector. "What did they want?"

Malone tapped the door panel.

"And was she already in the canal when the place was done?"

Minogue took the phone out of the glove box. Murtagh was back.

"Thanks, Éilis," he said. He studied the crowds on South Great George's Street.

"Johnner? Me and Tommy are out here baking away in the car. How'd it go with Lollipop?"

"Oh, we kept after him but little else came of it. It was Tommy woke him up in earnest."

"We're still working that angle about, er, modeling, John. Did Lenehan spit up any more about this modeling thing?"

"No. He was talking about dirty pictures, he said."

"Of Mary."

"Right. That's the same as he told us earlier on. He didn't budge on it."

Minogue heard the yawn.

"Book off, John. You've been on all night, man. Call after a snooze, will you?"

. . . . .

There was nothing in the paper. Where would he get hold of yesterday's? He should get batteries for the Walkman and get some news. He looked around the restaurant. The lunchtime mob had gone and the shoppers and the unemployed and the chancers were sitting around. What was that long-haired bollocks looking at? He got up and stepped out onto the footpath. Probably trying to score a hit, thought he looked the part. Jesus. Did he look that obvious?

He moved along Capel Street close to the shops. The hamburger and milkshake were moving around like snakes somewhere in his guts. He stopped by the open door of a pub and squinted into the dim interior. A pint of something, anything.

He ordered a pint of lager and drank half of it in his first draft. The barman eyed him as he loaded the fridges. He could stay here all day just nursing pints, that'd be perfect. He'd be off the streets; he could think, figure out a plan. What was the bloody barman looking at? It felt like the cold lager had slushed around his brain. He looked around the pub at the handful of customers. There were two fellas with aprons from the Markets. A middle-aged guy with his tie loose and his face all rubbery from the drink was moving in on a woman with a tube skirt. She kept trying to laugh him off, crossing her legs and talking to the barman who was trying to ignore her. Maybe there was a reward. He saw himself talking into the phone, a cop at the other end. His eyes came back into focus: he was staring at his face in the mirror. He grabbed his glass but one finger jabbed it. It whirled before falling.

"Shit," he hissed.

"Look here," the barman said and stood up.

"You think I did it on purpose?" he muttered to the barman. The barman stared at him.

"Well, do you?" His voice was louder than he'd expected.

"Get off the premises, now. Or I'll call the Guards."

He was moving toward the door, a bit dizzy but full of the strength his anger had brought. Out in the street with the door swinging behind him he stopped and stood. Two women with shopping bags gave him a wide berth. The sunlight hurt his eyes. He began walking but blundered into a teenager.

"Hey," said the teenager. He thought about turning back and giving him a rap in the snot.

He spotted a phone-box at the corner of the next street. Some pages of the Dublin phone book had been torn out but he found the Guards' one. He took out his change and placed the coins on a ledge. He lit a cigarette, shoved in the coins and dialed.

"Yeah?" he replied to the voice. "Which of yous does murders and stuff?"

·　　·　　·　　·　　·

Malone was doubtful. He pulled at the hair sticking up over his forehead.

"I'm not the expert," he said.

"You look the part," said Minogue. Malone gave him a sidelong glance.

"Thanks very much," he said.

"We can't go together anyway. So go on in and get what you can."

Malone moved off reluctantly from the car. He pushed open the door and moved around the partitions to the deeper recesses of the pub. A tall man with thinning, light-blond hair turned on his stool. On his own it looked, Malone thought, a pint of beer in front of him. Blondie gave him the once-over and nodded. Malone slid onto a stool and ordered a pint of lager.

"Howiya," said Blondie. "Was it you phoned?" Dub accent, but not the real thing, Malone decided. Late thirties. He looked like a clapped-out pop star.

"Yeah. I was looking for, you know. Did you bring any?"

"Any what?"

It flashed through Malone's mind that the one from the modeling agency might have tipped Blondie off. Why would he show up then?

"You know yourself, like." He shrugged and glanced down at the floor. No bag. Blondie took a slow drink from his glass. Malone paid the barman and started into his pint. He felt the eyes on him while he drank. Maybe he should act like a creep.

"Well, what sort of stuff are you into?"

Malone kept at the pint for several seconds.

"Well, I'm kind of into sports a bit. You know?"

"Sort of figured that," said Blondie. His face stayed blank. He continued to stare at Malone. "You're either a fucking cop or a fucking gangster."

"I could be a fucking priest too, couldn't I?"

Blondie's stare was unblinking.

"So who do you know?"

Malone looked from the row of bottles back into the man's stare.

"Painless. Painless Balfe? Lollipop Lenehan. Them."

His gamble seemed to register in Blondie's eyes. Was he going to smile? No.

"That'll cost you."

"What?"

"Extra, that's what."

"So?"

"If you're into the same stuff as those guys. It costs money to play rough, pal."

"Well, I'm not totally into that, man. I mean, there's lots of stuff, right?"

Blondie's eyes glazed over. He looked around the pub.

"I'm not a fucking shopping center, pal."

"Well, all I want is to get an idea of what stuff I can get."

"You want rough trade. What else?"

"Christ, I don't know."

"You're new, are you?" He swilled the beer around in his glass.

"Well, I like the outdoors and stuff," said Malone.

"'The outdoors.' Motorbikes? Farm shit? Girl-girl? Black and yellow? I don't care what you're into. Just make up your mind."

The anger rose up in Malone's chest.

"Well, I like them to look like, you know. Girls you'd meet. Next-door types, I suppose."

"Ugly, you mean."

"Well, I mean . . . I just broke up with someone. She wouldn't, you know. Turned her off and stuff, like? If I could find ones that remind me or, well, look a bit like her."

He stopped. The blond-haired guy was eyeing him again.

"So you're going for a resemblance or something, is it?"

Malone let go of his glass.

"You looking to leave through that fucking window, pal, just keep talking like that. All I fucking said was —"

"Yeah, yeah, yeah. Relax. So you're not the expert. Okay, okay."

Malone settled back in his stool. Blondie finished his glass and slid off his stool.

"So how is Painless anyway?" he said.

"Same as ever. You know yourself."

Blondie gave a half-hearted grin and dipped his chin to release a gassy belch.

"Come on then."

Malone gulped more lager and followed him.

．　　．　　．　　．　　．

Minogue followed the two men's progress with one eye open until they turned the corner. Then he started up the Citroen, reached for the phone, and let it rest in his lap. A bus let him out. He made the turn down toward Mount Street and cruised by on the far side of the street. The blond-haired fella didn't seem to be bothered. He moved quickly. Malone kept up with him. Minogue placed them in the side mirror as he passed. Minogue stopped at the end of the block and took a torn manila envelope from the backseat. With the phone in his pocket, he stepped out onto the curb, and began looking up at the office windows and down at the envelope.

Blondie stopped by a Celica and squeezed a remote. The sidelights flashed on the car and Minogue saw him nod Malone over to the passenger side. Minogue put on his best pissed-off look and got back in the Citroen. He dithered with the phone. Was the blond guy going to take off or do the business there and then? He adjusted the mirror and deciphered the registration plate. He clicked the call button and stared at the Celica while he waited. It looked as if the sky had been pasted on the windscreen. Damned tinted glass or something: he couldn't even see an outline through it.

"Ah, Éilis, a stór. Key in this car number, will you. I'm in a wicked hurry."

"Fire away then, can't you."

He stared at the Celica, willing it not to move. Maybe this Ryan gazebo had a mobile office full of smut. How was Malone playing it? Éilis's voice sounded from his lap.

"Yes, sorry, Éilis. I'm just staking something out here."

"Like the real police do? That's nice. Here it is."

He scribbled on the envelope.

"And it's straight?"

"Yes, indeed, your honor. All paid up and properly belonging to same."

"I'll get back to you. Thanks."

The Celica hadn't budged. Dermot Ryan, Howth. No record. He looked back down at the address. The Moorings was swanky, wasn't it? Way to hell out in Howth. Malone was out of the car. He walked slowly along the footpath back toward Baggot Street. The Celica pulled out abruptly and was driven hard in the opposite direction. Minogue drove after Malone, passed him and turned on to Baggot Street where he pulled in. Malone took his time crossing the street.

"Enjoy yourself?"

"Not much," said Malone. "He showed me a few magazines. German or Danish or something, asked if I wanted to get some."

"Can we can him, Tommy?"

Malone breathed out heavily, making a whistling sound against his teeth.

"He was vetting me. He says he'll be back here in an hour. Same pub."

"Careful, so he is."

"Yeah," said Malone. "He has his little car phone and all. Not the grubby little bollocks in a raincoat you'd expect."

"Dermot Ryan, Howth. He's not the only fella in Dublin with a phone in his car."

A double-decker bus slid by within six inches of Minogue's mirror and let off its passengers.

"Get this," said Malone. "He wanted references, if you don't mind. I fed him Balfe and Lenehan. He knew their idea of fun too."

Malone's head swiveled around and he looked into the inspector's eyes.

"Rough stuff with girls."

Minogue noted the clouded look in Malone's eyes.

"Well, now," he murmured. "Isn't that the curious piece of information to be sure."

"Maybe I should have put the heavy hand on him in the car," Malone said. "Then tossed the gaff out in Howth, see what turned up."

Minogue leaned heavier into the armrest and looked about the street. "We'll see. Don't be worrying."

The policemen fell silent for several moments.

"Let me ask you something, Tommy. Patricia Fahy?"

"Yeah?"

"Do you think she's good-looking?"

Malone looked over his shoulder at the inspector.

"Why?"

"I'm not asking if you want to marry her. Do you think she's good-looking?"

"I suppose."

Malone frowned.

"You put her in the game too?" he asked.

"What if?"

Malone stretched.

"It could explain why she's clammed up, I suppose."

Malone began stroking his chin harder. "Who paid the rent, like."

Minogue nodded. Malone stopped rubbing his chin.

"What do you want to do?"

"About fifty things," said Minogue. A fireball had been trapped where the small of his back met the seat. "All at the same time. Number one is to keep this going with Ryan."

"If he shows up here, he's moved from just having it to selling it, right?"

Minogue paused before answering.

"That's right. See what he can give you here on the spot. Or in the car. Then he's ours if we want him."

"And if I think he's holding out?"

"Well, then, in my judgment, Garda Malone, Mr. Ryan is asking for it."

•　　•　　•　　•　　•

"Curse-of-god device," Minogue grumbled. "You get so's you actually depend on the thing."

Malone sipped at his coffee and nodded at the phone.

"Beats playing Relevio on the radio," he said. Minogue shifted in his seat.

"Okay," he said. "We have a crew waiting behind the ESB place."

He had moved the Citroen around the block into the shade of the Bank of Ireland.

"Ryan has the office out in Howth. Weddings, school pictures, et cetera. I wonder if he does the smut himself or is he just a middleman."

Malone cleared his throat and spat halfway out into the street. Caught between admiration and revulsion, Minogue looked away. Boxing habit, he wondered.

"Hope to God he doesn't check up on Balfe and the other head banger," said Malone. He checked his watch. "Uch. I'd better go out and try this stunt."

Minogue tapped him on the arm as he yanked the door handle.

"Are you okay, Tommy? Even the slightest inkling he might turn Turk . . ."

"What's he going to do to me? I'm a big boy now."

"He might go haywire if you have to lay the card on him."

"Like hell he will," said Malone. "I've got his fit. Mr. Semi-detached. Fuckin — excuse me, sorry. Bloody hairdo on him. Bet you he was never in a barney in his life."

"I'll be on the street with the car."

Malone moved off down the path. Minogue pulled away from the curb. He coasted by the parked cars and pulled in within sight of the pub. No sign of the white Celica. He turned off the engine. Five minutes passed. His mind began to wander again. Weddings, Iseult. He let his head back on the headrest. There was a warren of streets here, lanes plenty wide for a car. He rubbed his eyes. The canal was behind those buildings there. He stopped rubbing and looked down at the sweaty pads on his fingertips.

The white car coming down the street had dark windows. Minogue stayed still and watched the Celica. Ryan stepped out of the passenger side and stood stooped in the open door talking to the driver. Then he slammed the door and strode empty-handed into the pub. Minogue saw the driver indistinctly behind a half-opened window: a man, sunglasses. The Celica drove off but came to an abrupt halt and was reversed into the curb. The driver got out and looked up and down the street. Mid-twenties, chunky and sunburned, liked his clothes. Film director gold-rimmed sunglasses. He strolled to the footpath, put a foot against the wall behind him, and lit a cigarette.

He eased away from the wall and began pacing slowly up and down the footpath. Occasionally he kicked at things he found in his study of the path. The head came up and the sunglasses swiveled with the head

as he looked up the street. Minogue shoved his head back into the headrest, closed his eyes and let his jaw sag. He counted to six and allowed
the eyelashes to part a little. The sunglasses were still facing his way.
Bugger, he thought: sussed. He couldn't look away. Sunglasses took out
keys and opened the driver's side. Minogue reached for the phone and
glanced down to locate the memory button for Mobile Dispatch. He'd
asked for the squad car to stay off the street. Sunglasses was winding up
the window. He stepped back, slammed the door, and set the alarm on
the car. Minogue dithered and dumped the call. Sunglasses had sauntered into the pub. Minogue would go in after him himself.

He eased the Citroen out onto the road, reversed, and parked it across
the front of the Celica. He walked around the back and stuck his face
against the glass of the Celica's hatchback. He shifted around and
cupped his hands better against the reflections. He even tried standing
back. All he could make out was his own disgruntled frown.

The pub was air-conditioned. He let the door swing shut behind him
and tried to adjust his eyes. A barman wearing a dress shirt nodded at
him. Minogue moved through the pub, trying to remember if there were
other doors out. There was a dozen or so customers but no Malone. He
rounded a partition wall and saw Ryan walking away from the bar. Behind him he saw the driver, his glasses dangling in one hand. His other
hand, fingers spread, was almost touching Malone's chest. Malone's eyes
went from Minogue to the driver and back. He took a step but the driver
blocked him. Ryan slowed and his eyes searched Minogue's face. Malone
said something to the driver. Minogue saw the splayed hand push at
Malone's chest, the sunglasses being flicked away from the other.

Ryan's mouth was open now. Minogue had his card up.

"Ryan," he said. "Hold your horses there, pal —"

The driver's hand flashed up but Malone was ready. His head darted
across and down to one side and came up again. The sound of a grunt
and breaking glass caused Ryan to look back. The driver's legs were up
and rolling across a low table.

"You're under arrest!" Malone called out. "I'm a Guard!"

The driver wriggled off the table. Malone kicked him under the ribs
as he came up. Ryan's eyes bulged. Minogue pointed at a seat. Ryan said
something but Minogue didn't hear him.

"Fucking stay there this time," he heard Malone say.

CHAPTER 14

"WARRANT FOR WHAT?" Minogue asked.

Ryan looked over at the squad car. The Guard standing by the open door, a red-haired recruit with pimples and a mobile jaw, looked to Minogue for guidance. Ryan's sidekick — and Minogue recalled the tremendous kick that Malone had given him — sat next to another Guard in the backseat.

"It's my car," said Ryan.

"Of course, it's your car, Mr. Ryan. That's why I'm going to examine it."

"I haven't done anything. Charge me."

"All right," said Malone. "Assaulting a police officer in the course of his duties."

"I didn't touch him! Matter of fact it was him did the —"

"Resisting arrest," said Minogue.

"Obstruction of a Garda off —" Malone added.

"Oh, come on," Ryan gasped. "You must be fucking joking!"

"Swearing," Minogue went on.

"What?"

"Breach of the peace," said Malone.

"I'm going to fucking phone a solicitor!"

"More cursing and swearing."

"It's my right to call one!"

"Fire away — but don't use that car phone. We have to impound it too."

"I'll go to another phone then."

"Phone from the station," said Minogue. "But only after we have full confidence that the call you make won't allow related criminal and indictable acts to be concealed or engaged in."

Ryan began to say something but stopped himself. Minogue studied the patterned shirt. Fifty quid, he guessed.

"You can't do this," Ryan said. "It's entrapment!"

The Guard holding the door of the squad car shifted his feet.

"Let us into the car, Mr. Ryan," said Minogue. "The stuff you brought."

Ryan looked at the Garda by the open door, sighed, and held his hand out. Minogue handed him the keys he had taken from the heavy. He nodded at the Garda. "Go ahead there. Hold him on assaulting a Garda in the course of. We'll be in touch by teatime."

The alarm beeped once and the door locks popped up.

"Get in the back there," said Malone, "and start handing us the goods."

The interior smelled of a soapy aftershave. Minogue took in the leather seats, the sound system, the phone from Star Trek. He sat behind the wheel. There were tapes of rock groups he'd never heard of.

"Nice," said Malone. He took a folder from Ryan. "How'd you pay for it?"

Ryan folded his arms and looked out the window.

Minogue began leafing through a photo album. He wondered but didn't much care about whether Ryan or Malone would notice his reactions. He realized that he was holding his breath and he made the effort to breathe normally.

"Christ," said Malone to nobody. "Nothing they won't do?"

"It's a private collection," said Ryan. "That's perfectly legal."

"A collection of privates, you mean," said Minogue.

The inspector didn't always look at the faces first. The fake smiles began to get to him. The phony ecstasy, the makeup, the lie of beckoning, of need, clouded his lust more and more. There were few who didn't look painfully amateur. Some couldn't hide their shame. In others he thought he saw a fear beyond the feigned helplessness. It was Malone who spotted Patricia Fahy first. There were two pictures of her. Her face was red, her eyes glistened. He exchanged glances with Malone.

"These don't look like Scandinavian furniture to me. Are these all the Irish girls?"

"All I've got," said Ryan. He turned from the window. "Look. What are you really after?"

Minogue said nothing.

"Look, is it such a major crisis if I have pictures? All of them are over eighteen, I hasten to add. You're obviously working on something. I'm nobody really but maybe, you know, I can help out?"

"What does hasten mean?" asked Malone. Ryan frowned.

"What gives?" he said. "I mean, what do you want to know?"

"I think you should hasten to wake yourself up, pal. Who are your customers?"

"Who said I had customers?"

"Do you know all these people?" Minogue asked. "These women?"

"Of course I don't. But if you're looking for someone, maybe I might know them."

"How can you tell who's who here then," said Minogue. "It looks like the camera was an inch from various crotches half the time."

Ryan sat back.

"Well?"

"The people who commission them, well, they want the pictures for their own sake usually."

"'Commission'?" said Malone.

"I don't know anything about any other stuff," said Ryan.

"What 'other stuff'?"

"Whatever it is you're getting at. I think you're trying to frame me for something."

Malone guffawed.

"Frame you? We don't need to frame you for anything, pal. You're the accessory to all the charges that landed on Tarzan, there. He works for you, right?"

He closed the folder and shook his head.

"Here, give me another one. I'm nearly getting used to this stuff. What was the name of that folder I just had?"

"'All for one and one for all,'" Ryan muttered.

"I think that's the one I have," said Minogue.

"Yours must be 'Sports' then," said Ryan. He handed him another folder.

"What's this one?"

"'Work out.'"

Malone rolled his eyes and grabbed the new folder.

"This is the stuff you said you wanted. Painless and them."

Minogue looked up from his album. Malone opened the folder. A woman who looked like she'd just stepped out of a steam bath was tied by her ankles and wrists to what seemed to be a row of bars in a prison cell. The beads of sweat or water glistened in the harsh light of an overhead bulb. Painted on her breasts or real, Minogue couldn't tell, were weals from a whip. Malone's frown deepened. He turned in the seat and glared at Ryan.

"Don't take this too much to heart, Ryan, but you're a fucking slug."

Minogue followed the pages as Malone turned them.

"Where do these come from?" asked Malone. "Who are these girls?"

"People phone me. I bring the equipment and I do the photography."

"Where?"

"Different places."

"Don't be jack-acting around here," said Malone. "Talk in English."

Minogue closed the folder and adjusted the mirror. Nice car, he decided. Wouldn't mind a blast out the Naas Road with it. He watched Ryan's face.

"I get a call to come to a place and that's it. Flats, apartments, hotels. Offices even."

"Yeah, but who are the people that call you?"

"How do I know? Hey, look, I'm just a hired hand."

"So you go to these places and? . . ."

"I go to the address, set up and do the routine."

"Then?"

"I hand over the rolls of film or negs I have from the session. Then I walk out the door."

"Who do you give the stuff to?"

"Whoever's at the door."

"All out of the goodness of your heart. Do you tell the girls what to do too? Is that your kick?"

Ryan let out a sigh.

"A lot of the time it doesn't take much to get them going."

"Ah, come on now," said Minogue. "These girls look like any girl you'd meet walking down O'Connell Street. They're hardly professional models. You're trying to tell me they're volunteering?"

"Volunteering? Jesus, you're definitely out of touch."

"Tell me more," said Minogue. Ryan began nibbling on a fingernail.

"That's all there is. I told you everything."

"'Doesn't take much,' you said. What do you mean?"

Ryan still held his hand up under his chin, looking at the fingernails.

"Well, you're not going to get much done without a leg opener, are you?"

"What kind are you talking about?" asked Minogue.

"I don't know. A few jars. Whatever. Did I ask? I just showed up and took pictures."

"How'd you get paid?"

"Who said anything about getting paid?"

"I did," snapped Malone. "Because I say you wouldn't lift a finger if you weren't getting money for it."

Ryan seemed to be deciding which fingernail to nibble.

"Sometimes I'd get a set of negatives. Not all of them, only some. Then the fee in an envelope. Be delivered to the office."

He stared back into Minogue's eyes in the mirror.

"How many girls are there in these books?" the inspector asked.

"Twenty-five, thirty. Around that."

"And you run off your own photos of these and sell them."

"Sell them? Who says —"

"Shut up with that rant. Are these all the girls you've done this kind of work for?"

"No."

"You're telling me that, whoever your employers are, they only bother with some of these girls?"

"I suppose." Minogue glanced at Malone.

"So where are the pictures of the rest of them?" asked Malone.

"I don't know."

"Do you know a person by the name of Mary Mullen?"

"No."

"Patricia Fahy?"

"I don't ask names. Look, I'm only a middleman. This is a business."

"Who calls you?" Malone asked.

"I told you. I don't know."

"The Egans."

"I don't know."

"Record's stuck," said Malone. "Get with it there, pal."

"You know them," Minogue went on. "You know their do-fors."

"Well, I heard of them. Who hasn't?"

"You asked me who I knew and I gave you two names," said Malone. "You remember them?"

"Maybe I do. Tell them to me again."

"Like hell I will," retorted Malone. "You knew them well enough to tell me they liked this stuff. Tying up and that. Do they visit you?"

"No."

"How do you know them?"

"Same as how you came along today. A phone call, a meeting. I showed them samples."

"Listen," said Minogue. "Think very carefully about what I'm going to ask you."

Ryan blinked. Minogue looked down the street.

"I've a feeling that you've dealt with Guards before. Am I right?"

"Spoke with some, yes."

"You know Detective John Doyle?"

"Heard of him."

"Umm. I note that you have no criminal record, Mr. Ryan. I'm impressed. I'm impressed because I believe you hang around the fringes of criminal groups and individuals. You've been trying to persuade Detective Malone and me that you were not aware of these dimensions. All very nice. Happy events. Wedding photographs. Do you do graduations?"

"Yes, as a matter of fact."

"Baptism, First Communions? Confirmations too?"

"Done plenty of those."

"That's nice. Car, home out there in Howth. Nice. I'll bet you good money that you're thinking we can't do much to you. Get yourself a good barrister and push the private collection bit? Maybe there's a grand, big, flexible law has landed on us from the New Europe guaranteeing our individual rights and freedoms in the line of dirty pictures?"

Ryan almost smiled.

"Who knows," he said. "It's time we caught up with the rest of the world, isn't it?"

"Is it?" asked Minogue. "What's the worst, you're thinking maybe. These two Guards sell me off to the Revenue Commissioners. I pay up, say, even a couple of thousand quid on undeclared income. Who's to know, right? I bet you see that as the soft option to be sure. Compared to the other option. Right?"

"What option?"

"I believe you know exactly what I'm talking about —"

"What? The photos? What's the big deal? Christ, Ireland's not some bloody backwater with everybody shuffling off to Mass all the time! Look: people do what they *want* to do now. Life's what you make it these days. Those girls weren't forced into doing that. So it's not like they didn't know what they were into. Everybody wants to make something of themselves. That's human nature, isn't it?"

"Tell me about human nature then, Mr. Ryan," said Minogue. "But some other time."

Ryan's face grew flushed.

"I'm doing a fucking service to those girls in actual fact!"

"Now, now, Mr. Ryan. Language."

"I am! You don't know a damn thing about life out there. A lot of these girls have nothing! Working in shops, no prospects. They want to get into, you know, modeling and stuff. It's a free choice."

"'Modeling,'" said Malone. "You're a model, Ryan."

"Nobody made them do it. What's wrong with them wanting things? Clothes, money, a good time? You guys are all right, you have jobs. What if you're twenty or twenty-one and there's nothing coming your way?"

"What the hell do you know about growing up in the flats?" Malone demanded.

"It's all about selling yourself," said Ryan. "Everybody does it in one way or another."

Minogue thought of the lipstick, the fake rapture. He was groggy with the heat now. He felt himself slipping into a stupor. He pushed buttons but the windows stayed up.

"You have to turn on the ignition," said Ryan.

Minogue did so. He opened both windows. Malone was nibbling on his upper lip.

"Okay, Mr. Ryan. How many of these folders do you have?"

"The four you see there."

"That's all?"

"Yeah."

"Don't believe you," said Malone.

"Swear to God."

"We'll send a squad car out to your place in Howth and give it a good shake to be sure, then."

"I told you —"

"Who else has stuff like this?"

"Christ, I don't know! Whoever sets up the sessions, whatever they do with it. I don't know!"

"Have you ever seen your stuff around? With other people?"

"No."

"You're a liar, Ryan," said Malone. "And I'm going to find that out for sure. And when I do, I'm gonna be all over you."

"What's the charge?"

Malone looked over at Minogue. The inspector rubbed at his eyes as he spoke.

"Obstructing police offers, inciting and abetting others to assault police off —"

"Aw, come on! You can't be serious, man!"

Minogue took his fingers away and opened his eyes.

"And accessory to murder." Ryan sat very still, staring into Minogue's eyes.

"You're bluffing," he whispered.

"Me?" said Minogue. "Oh, no. You're the one's bluffing. Hot and grumpy — and the rest of it — I may be; bluffing, I am not."

"I don't believe you. I just don't."

"I don't care," said Minogue. He began rubbing his eyes again. He heard the soft clicks as his eyelids stretched and relaxed across his eyeballs.

"In your, em, collection there, Mr. Ryan," he went on, "there is a picture of a woman who was associated with a murder victim. It is my opinion now that this associate of the murder victim may have concealed information vital to our investigation."

He paused, glanced at Ryan and resumed rubbing.

"Do you want to tell us again you don't believe us, Mr. Ryan?"

Ryan swallowed.

"I don't know anything about this," he whispered. "I *swear* to you."

"A slippery slope, this, Mr. Ryan," said Minogue. "If I had a pound for every brigand and smart-arse that's come my way with their routines, their cat-farting around and lying and making fools of themselves, well, I'd be on my yacht parked below in the Mediterranean. I don't like the idea that someone concealed potential evidence from me, Mr. Ryan. I really don't. But she's frightened. If I were her, I might be the same way. But you? I won't be putting up with any tripe out of you."

"But what do you want from me?"

"All your little collection."

"It's all here. Every bit. Who was murdered?"

"Someone that I believe you took pictures of. We want all of your stuff."

"You didn't find her here? Let me look . . . no, I don't even know who she is."

"You say that you only get some of the pictures back."

"Right. Yes. Only some of them."

"Your employer, for lack of a better word, kept the ones he liked best, do you think?"

"I suppose. Look, really. The most I'd ever know might be a first name."

"Try 'Mary.'"

Ryan blinked and scratched at his forehead.

"Well, Mary's a common name like, isn't it? I can't really say I remember."

"Maybe a session down in Harcourt Street station would refresh your memory."

"I'm doing the best I can! A lot of the time you wouldn't really re-member a face even. Honestly, it gets like that. Then there's makeup."

"Who put it on?" asked Malone.

"Themselves, or to one another. Some of them really pour it on so as they won't be recognized. It'd get all messed up then and we'd have to wipe it off."

"'We'?"

"Me and Danny. Danny, the fella driving my car. Look — have you got a picture of this girl that was, you know? . . ."

"Murdered?"

"Yes."

"Before she was murdered, Mr. Ryan, or after?"

Ryan bit his lip.

"Bring over both if you please, Tommy," said Minogue.

He watched as Malone reached into the Citroen for the folder.

"Are you nervous, Mr. Ryan?"

"It's boiling here. I'm not used to being . . . to being talked to by the Guards. That's all."

Malone slammed the door and walked to a traffic warden who was surveying the parked Citroen. It was almost rush hour.

"You know the kind of things the Egans get up to, don't you," said Minogue.

"Yes."

"You're scared of them, aren't you."

Ryan stopped rubbing his hands. The parking attendant scrutinized Malone's card and nodded.

"Well . . ."

"Was it Lenehan and Balfe together used to, er, supervise these sessions of yours?"

He kept his eyes on Malone but he heard Ryan swallow.

"Well," his voice turned to a creak. He cleared his throat. "Four times out of five, it'd be, em, Lolly — Lenehan."

"He likes to hurt girls, right? Or see them hurt."

When Ryan didn't answer, Minogue turned around. Head down, Ryan was rubbing his thumb and forefinger through his eyebrows. Minogue studied his scalp.

"He'd show for the other stuff usually," said Ryan. "The props. The bars and stuff."

"Has he got some of these photos?"

Ryan's fingers now ran up from his forehead through his hair.

"Wouldn't surprise me."

Malone flopped back into the seat and opened the folder.

"Before," said Minogue. Malone handed him a photocopy of Mary Mullen's record. Minogue folded the sheet until only the face was uppermost.

"Just the face now, Mr. Ryan. Do you recognize this person?"

He studied Ryan's frown in the mirror.

"Sometimes it's hard to tell. . . . Makeup and hairdos, you know. That's a good photocopier, I tell you. . . . I think she was in one of the sessions. Yes. I think so."

"You think so," said Malone. Ryan raised his hands.

"You're trying to trap me," he said. "I'm being totally on the level with you. I can't be certain and I have to tell you that. Jesus, I wish I could say 'no' but I want you to know —"

"When?" asked Malone.

"Wait a minute now," said Ryan. "No matter what I say here, how do I know you're going to take it the right way? I mean to say. I can't remember 'when.' I just think she was one. Obviously she's not one of the ones I got back."

"Obviously," said Malone.

"She's graduated then," murmured the inspector. He handed the photocopy back to Malone.

"Pardon?"

"She passed the test."

"What test?"

Minogue took the keys out of the ignition.

"Is this over with now?" Ryan asked. Minogue glared at him while he muttered to his partner.

"A word outside, Tommy."

CHAPTER 15

Malone followed the inspector around back of the Celica. Minogue rested a foot on the bumper and began massaging his neck. Malone looked in at Ryan.

"Will we book this Ryan yob and let him sit in the system awhile?" Minogue looked at his watch.

"Great minds think alike, Tommy."

"You think he's playing with more than the one deck here?"

"I'd say he's trying to cover himself, yes. Keep an eye on him while I phone in."

Minogue ambled over to his Citroen and retrieved the phone. He sat with his feet resting on the footpath. Éilis told him that he was just the man she was looking for. He asked her if he was the first man she'd told that to today.

"That's a different matter entirely. Do your business with his Lordship, can't you, and I'll give you your messages after. I have a message for Master Malone, too."

"What?" said Kilmartin a moment later.

"A fella called Ryan took the pictures. So far I haven't found ones of Mary Mullen but I have ones of Patricia Fahy."

"Aha, the flatmate. Are they any good?"

"The pictures are bad, Jimmy. We call them pornography, remember?"

"Late in the day to be playing the iijit with me, head-the-ball. Are you going to the Fahy one with this under your belt?"

"Eventually, yes. But I'm phoning so's you can —"

"Who's this Ryan?"

"The link is Lenehan, the gouger who went haywire this morning. He was at some of the photo sessions, I suppose you'd call them."

"What else?"

"What else yourself. That's why I'm phoning. Where are we as regards filling in all the holes? What Mary Mullen did all day, for starters."

"Huh. I tried the mother again, just on the phone. She stuck to it, got a bit annoyed. Didn't know what the daughter was up to at all. I almost lowered the boom on her, let me tell you. Ready to take her down to the local station and do the talking there. I told her to try hard and remember, as I'd be phoning again later on, begob."

"Anything turn up at the flat?"

"Nothing of note. No money. No checkbook. No bank cards. No drugs for that matter."

"And no sign of the handbag?"

"Divil damn the bit."

"Sheehy and company, door-to-door? . . ."

"Don't ask."

"The quare fella, Leonardo?"

"Am I repeating myself here? No sign. John Murtagh talked to the mother again. She's very agitated but still no lead on where he might be. Johnner has the impression she didn't want to tell the whole story at all. I tell you, Matty, there's a quare lot more people scared of gangsters than they are of us good guys."

Minogue stared at the people leaving the offices along the street. He felt the phone slipping along his palms. He changed hands and wiped his free hand on his knee.

"Well, James. We're going to sandbag this fella Ryan for a while. Then we'll move on to Patricia Fahy."

"'We' my eye," said Kilmartin. "You might end up doing a lot of running around on your own."

"Why? What's up?"

"Your new sidekick. Voh' Lay-bah. Éilis got a call for him. Personal, but I got a whiff of it though."

Minogue opened the door and labored out onto the street. He returned the pedestrian's glances, the phone still jammed against his ear.

"Something to do with the brother," said Kilmartin. "He's out of the nick."

He knew that rubbing it wouldn't help, but it was driving him mental. He shifted around on the cement and shoved his knuckle into his eye. He stopped rubbing and looked across the car park at the dust rising from the building site. Rubble had been bulldozed up into a heap and a JCB was loading it into dumpsters. He tried to open his eye again, but it hurt. He covered the eye with his palm and looked about. There was grit mixed in with the sweat on his forehead.

He watched the car park attendant adjust the headphones on his Walkman. He thought of taking a crack at it, right here in broad daylight. Straight over, slide the knife out as he got into the doorway of the shed, right up against his belly, smiling all the time, grabbing the cash, walking off. Maybe even leave a nick on the guy's belly to let him know he meant business. No knife, but. One-eyed too. Dreaming. He fingered out another cigarette. Instead of lighting it, he rolled it around in his fingers. He couldn't see straight, couldn't think straight either. He thought of the park, the trees and shadow. Where was that herd of wild deer in the park? And the bloody Guards' barracks, headquarters actually, next to where he'd spent the night. Funny; dangerous. Maybe he could take a dip in that little pond he'd seen near the playing fields. No. It'd be scummy, and he'd catch some . . . He thought of Mary's face with those creepy weeds across her face, those slimy green things that grew like anything, the dirtier the water, the better. Stupid, she'd gotten in over her head. But why hadn't she told him more about what she was doing? It wasn't like he would've screwed up on her, for God's sake. And she'd thought she was so tough and everything. How nothing was going to get in her way.

He lit the cigarette and sucked fiercely on it. If she'd only trusted him a bit more, she wouldn't be dead. He imagined her calling him out of the shadows by the canal: Liam — and it wouldn't be Leonardo either — Liam, this guy thinks he can mess with me. With *us,* Liam. Do for him, Liam. Show him. And he'd clatter the guy before he knew what hit him. Karate: flying kick in the belly and then straighten him up with a boot in the snot. One for good measure in the nuts, then take the wallet or whatever. Roll him into the canal himself, see if *he* makes it. Go off laughing with Mary, have a few jars with your man's stash. If she . . .

Stupid bitch, no! How the hell could she do it, be so stupid as to put herself in danger? It was such a mess. Such a mess. Her oul lad caused it all. He should be had up. Mary wouldn't have been on the game at fifteen if her oul lad hadn't been such a thick shite. A thick, fucking alco bastard. Yeah, her da should be charged with all this. The bastard. There was no justice.

He took his hand off his eye and tried again. It was watering and scratchy but the lashes parted halfway. He let them part further. Gone! At least something, some stupid bloody thing, was going his way. Maybe just closing his eye had done the trick. He explored in the corner of his eye and found the grit. He looked at it. So small, so much trouble. Maybe that was what happened to Mary: one tiny thing. A word, a look, bad timing. She thought she knew the guy but maybe she didn't. Had she been doing a nixer out there by the canal, just to turn a hundred quid she needed in a hurry?

The end of the cigarette tasted awful. He flicked it out onto the street. Maybe the cops were doing the exact same as he was, trying to figure out what had happened. Yeah, but they weren't sitting here on the side of the bleeding street, baking in this idiotic weather, with no place to go, not even a place to sleep tonight. Should he try again? They probably had a lot of calls like his. The stupid cop on the switchboard had given him the phone number of the Murder Squad. Didn't give a damn, didn't even try to con him into talking a while. As if they didn't want anybody's help at all, like they knew everything or they'd do everything their own way, in their own sweet fucking time. Typical. But what could he tell them? If he sat on the phone somewhere, they'd trace him in a few seconds, Christ, everybody knew that.

He got up and stretched. It was like putting on two or three stone weight overnight, this bloody heat. He should be out at the seaside somewhere, sunning himself. He still had that kink in his back from sleeping crooked last night. What the hell time was it anyway? He walked over to the car park attendant. He could hear the guitar riffs out of the headphones even over the noise of the traffic. The guy must be stoned. He looked at his watch. Four? Already? Christ! Had he fallen asleep somewhere along the line? The day had been a succession of tins of Coke, cups of coffee, biscuits. A hamburger, yeah. That stupid phone call. He'd walked by the pool hall a few times too. He'd nearly gone in once. To hell with Jammy in anyhow. Even the money. It was like what's the guy in the place they drag Jesus into and he washes his hands? Punch us the Pilot they used to call him.

He tripped on the edge of the footpath. His legs were tired, his back was aching. He stopped by a shop window and looked at his reflection against the camping equipment. His eyes came to focus on the gear in the window. A lot of this stuff would be handy for the park. Maybe he'd get some of this stuff and head up the mountains, up the back of the Pine Forest or somewhere. A sleeping bag, waterproof pants; a compass so he wouldn't lose his way off the paths and stuff. A gas thing to cook your dinner up on the side of Mount bleeding Kilimanjaro, boots you could probably wear in space. His eyes stayed on the knives. He studied the blades. The one he liked had a jagged bit on the top side. He fingered change in his pocket, heard it click. It was a Bowie-type knife, for skinning bears or something. Just showing a blade like that would do the business. Eighteen quid though? He would have felt a hell of a lot better last night if he'd had one of those in his hands.

All the ideas that had been buzzing around in his head stopped. The blade shone. He wasn't just going to sit back and bleeding roll over for anyone. Everyone took him for a gobshite, Mary even. But that was history now. He wasn't going easy, he wasn't going to take anything lying down. He'd phone the cops. Give them a minute or two, let them have it with a few facts. Get them fucking thinking for a change. Then they might just wake up and see that it was the Egans they should be picking on. And phone Jammy Tierney too: tell him to get on to the Egans. Tell them to smarten themselves up or else. He moved toward the door but stopped and moved back. It was a small reflection of himself he had seen moving across the polished surface of the blade.

. . . . .

"You're all right," said Minogue.

Malone stood leaning in through the open door. "It's not going to, well, you know?"

The inspector shook his head.

"The job? No, Tommy. It stays personal. Don't worry."

"Christ, I could just kill him."

Minogue took in the lines on Malone's forehead.

"I mean to say. Look at him. He's hardly out of the bleeding nick and he's a walking breach of the peace again. It's got to be drugs. It's got to be."

Minogue shrugged. Malone's eyes swept down from the sky. His fist thumped on the roof.

"Fuck it! Goddamn it to — sorry. The new car and all . . ."

"Listen, Tommy. I'm off before you beat the car to a pulp. I'll go to Patricia Fahy. Call in when you get the chance, okay? Home number too — any time up to about eleven."

"Are you sure? I'd hate to think —"

"Family's first, Tommy. Just go."

With words rattling loose in his mind, Minogue drove off. He was still thinking about Iseult when he reached Fahy's house.

Patricia Fahy's father was itching to say something. He stood with his arms folded in the hall looking at Minogue. Missus, a compact, harassed-looking woman with a big chin and a sagging neck, had gone upstairs to get Patricia.

"Hot again today, Mr. Fahy."

"Too hot," said Fahy. Minogue tapped the envelope on his palm.

"Is the kitchen free maybe?" Fahy shifted his feet.

"Free for what? Yous were here with her already, in case you forgot."

Minogue heard murmurs upstairs. The house was tidy and newly decorated. One of the advantages of having an unemployed father.

"Oh, no, Mr. Fahy. I didn't forget. It's Patricia who did the forgetting."

"And what does that mean?"

Minogue nodded in the direction of the top floor.

"Does she always take a snooze in the afternoon?"

"The doctor gave her a sleeping pill. What was that about —"

"Any unfamiliar cars or people hanging around the street since we talked?"

"Wait a minute there . . . As a matter of fact, no."

Minogue heard scuffing from upstairs, feet crossing a rug or a carpet. He eyed Fahy.

"We can nail them, Mr. Fahy," he said. "We can, you know."

Fahy nodded his head several times but the eyes told Minogue it was scorn. Patricia Fahy's feet moved hesitantly down each step. She had a long dressing gown on. Veins stood out by her heels. She stopped on the bottom step, one hand on the dressing gown by her neck and the other on the banister.

"Yeah?" she said. Her voice had a sleepy, fearful alertness to it.

"Hello, Patricia. I need to talk again."

"But I told you everything. I mean . . ."

"Just a chat, Patricia, and I'll be on my way."

She looked down at the floor in the crowded hall. Minogue tapped the envelope on his palm again and saw her eyes dart over.

"The kitchen, is it?" He turned to Fahy and his wife in turn. "Just the two of us, thank you."

Patricia Fahy's hand slipped on the handle of the teapot as she poured. The clatter of the cup and saucer brought a question through the door from her mother.

"No, Ma," she called out. "It's only the teapot!"

She pushed her hair away, glanced at the envelope he had laid on the table, and lit a cigarette.

"Well, what is it?" she said.

"I found the photos of you, Patricia. I'm still looking for the ones of Mary."

Her head lowered. She stared at the envelope. Minogue watched her eyelashes.

"It's time to talk, Patricia. We need to move on this."

She drew on the cigarette but did not brush her hair back.

"Don't be afraid," he said. "We'll see you right. Just quit stonewalling."

She pulled on the cigarette again.

"It's bad for everyone, Patricia. For you most of all right now."

She seemed to curl up. He could see her scalp. Her head was almost on the table now.

"Patricia?"

She let her forehead fall onto the edge of the table. Her hands came around under her armpits. Her back began to shake. The cigarette burned in the ashtray. He looked around the kitchen again.

"Patricia? Patricia. I'm not here to threaten you. Do you understand that?"

She shuddered and sniffed.

"I have a daughter your age. I'm talking to you sort of as a parent, Patricia."

"Oh yeah?" she sobbed. "You're here to put the law on me."

"Why didn't you tell us about this stuff before?"

"I don't know! All I know is that you can do what you like."

"We want to get whoever killed Mary."

"And you're going to trample all over me for that."

Minogue looked around the kitchen again. She blew her nose.

"Here," he said. "Take the envelope. It's your stuff. Do what you want with it."

She kept pulling at strands of hair by her ear. Crying had made her face puffy.

"So," she said. She fished out the cigarette and took several drags from it.

"Nothing's for free. What do you want?"

"Who has pictures of Mary?"

She shivered and looked out the window.

"Eddsy Egan, I suppose," she said. "Bobby, maybe."

"Do you know for sure?"

"How could I?" Minogue stared at her.

"Where was Mary on the night she got murdered?"

"Don't know."

"Listen, Patricia —" She turned toward him with her hands wringing the air.

"I swear to you! Jeesis! What am I supposed to say? You want me to make up stuff for you so's you can go away happy, is it? Look — that was just her way! She wouldn't tell anyone, would she? I remember once she said that. 'Don't lean on anyone. They'll let you down when you need them the most.' Something like that. She never let on where she was going or who she was with. I used to think that — well, I don't know."

"Tell me."

"Christ, I don't know — that it was just a put-on."

"I don't get it."

"Ah, come on. Like she was the Southside, glamor-doll type. Putting it on, you know? 'You take the bus,' she used to say. 'I prefer my Mercedes.'"

"A Mercedes —"

"It was a, an expression with her, wasn't it?"

"Maybe you saw her once in a Mercedes, did you?"

She squinted at him.

"Are you joking me? Didn't I say it was just an expression. The way you'd say, I don't know, 'Bob's your uncle.' Yes, she'd say that the odd time: 'I prefer champagne.' Messing, you know?"

Minogue examined the scribbles in his notebook. His biro slid around like wet soap against his fingers.

"Don't you ever hear people talk like that?" she was saying. "Well, younger people, like?"

He glanced up at her. Younger people. Huh.

"'Ooohh, Alan wouldn't like that.' Putting it on, like."

"Alan?"

"Joe, Pat, Alan. Anyone."

"Why 'Alan'?"

"It's just an example. Don't you get it?"

Her forehead wrinkled.

"Everyone has their own expressions. Families, like?"

"Mary said that: 'Alan wouldn't like that'?"

She blew smoke from the side of her mouth and looked away.

"Could have been Mary. I just heard it, you know, the way you remember things in bits? It's a snotty-type name. 'Alan.' 'Jonathan.' You know what I'm saying? Maybe it was her who said it, maybe that's why it sticks in my mind. I don't know."

"But it could have been Mary? Try to remember, Patricia."

"I *am* trying! Jases. I can't even think straight with that pill. I told you the last time."

Minogue sat back.

"How did Mary get around?"

She took a deep breath and let her eyes close.

"We're not going to go through all that again, are we?" The biro slipped from Minogue's fingers onto the table. He'd had enough.

"It's here or in an interview room down at the station."

Her breath came out in a rush. She sagged in the chair.

"I don't know how she got around," she groaned. "Like anyone else. Bus. Walking. Taxi. I don't *know!*"

"Well, she didn't stay in the flat every night, we know that from what you told us."

Her hand went to her forehead. Her jaw began to quiver.

"It's no good crying now, Patricia. Let me get it right this time. I just can't believe that you didn't wonder about her and then ask her things."

"She didn't like that, I told you. She told me to mind me own business more times."

"You never worried about her those times she didn't come home?"

"She was an adult, wasn't she? I mean, she'd been around, right?"

Minogue thought of the slime on the canal water. Mary Mullen shouldn't have been there: why did he keep thinking that? His eyes came back into focus on Patricia's cigarette. Her head was aslant, eyes steady on his now.

"She was doing," she was saying. "Except for the once, I suppose."

She let go of a strand of hair over her forehead.

"Why did you move in with Mary, then?"

"It was more she moved in with me."

"Why did she move in with you, then?"

"I don't know. What was I going to say to her: 'Why'd you move in with me?'"

"Why do you think, then."

"She — what difference does it make?"

"Any detail helps, Patricia. You say Mary kept things to herself, things beyond the usual day-to-day chat. We have to dig around for something."

She examined a picture of Torremolinos, flicking her cigarette several times.

"She wanted a place, I suppose, didn't she? Maybe somewhere ordinary, away from her other life. The high life, whatever she had going."

"Tell me again about who called for her."

She closed her eyes and let her head roll back.

"Phone calls, Patricia. Try and remember."

"Fellas. Always the same."

"Who were they?"

"Nobody. 'Leave a message for Mary. Bobby'll send a taxi around.' Or, 'Tell Mary to phone Bobby.' That was it. I already told you that before."

"Before? How do I know you're still not holding back here?"

For a moment he thought she would hit him. After several moments, she shrank back in her chair. Her hands still gripped the tabletop. He saw her Adam's apple go first. Her arms went slack and her hands dropped away from the edge of the table. She elbowed the ashtray away and laid her head down on her arms.

"Bastards," she wailed. "Yous'll never give up, will you?"

Her father yanked open the door.

"That's enough," he growled. Minogue turned and stood.

"Enough of you listening in at the door, you mean."

"Get out of my house this minute!"

"I'll have a squad car around within ten minutes to pick Patricia up."

"Like hell you will!"

"Obstructing police is a lot more serious of an offense than you seem to believe there, Mister. Turn down the volume and wait outside."

"My daughter's not going anywhere!"

{ 193 }

"That's what I was hoping to hear. We'll conclude our chat shortly — as soon as you get yourself settled down and out of the way."

"That's what you think, pal."

"If you've nothing to do for about six months, just stay right there and make a bigger iijit out of yourself. I go, Patricia goes. So do you."

"Harassment! Look at her, she's in tears!"

Minogue looked down at his shoes.

"What do you say, Patricia?" he asked. "Can we move on here a bit or? . . ."

She lifted her head a little and nodded. Her father jabbed at the air.

"If you —" he began. Minogue looked up. Fahy backed out the door, still waving his finger.

"As true as God," she whispered. "I knew nothing. The nearest I got to knowing anything was them pictures. And they were the biggest mistake of my life, 'cause now you think I'm like her, like the way she was, I mean. And I'm not."

She wiped her eyes with the back of her hand and lit another cigarette.

"Okay, Patricia. Let's try again. Mary and you were talking one evening."

"It was before Christmas. I remember, because I was thinking of the presents I was going to buy and all. I sort of wanted to know how I could, well — I'm not saying I wanted to live like Mary did. No way."

"She told you about it then. The photography."

She nodded and held in the smoke she had drawn so deeply.

"She brought me along. We'd had a few drinks, you know? I wanted to know and everything, sure, but I didn't want to be too nosy, did I? And she told me too. 'Just do what they tell you. Don't be asking questions. They don't like that.' Yeah, right."

"'They'?"

"That fella with the ponytail. She told me he worked for them. The Egans. Anyway. She puts on that face, the face she'd have on when you wouldn't know if she was thinking you were a gobshite or if she felt sorry for you. She says: 'I bet you don't have the nerve.' Like it was a dare. And I knew, I knew that she thought, well, this'll teach the kid a lesson. That's when I knew I'd go through with it. We go into the hotel. There's more gargle —"

"Just the drink? Were there drugs produced?"

"No, there weren't! Jases! I wouldn't even know what they looked like!"

"Go on then."

"There's makeup and stuff on a table. It kind of looks like the set of a film. It doesn't look like what I expect, you know? That blond-haired fella at the camera: he was a prick. And the guy with the ponytail just standing around. I thought he'd want to try a few moves, you know? So I tell Mary, look, I says, I don't want anything to do with that creep. No way. She sort of smiles and says something to him."

"Did she call him by his name?"

"No. She just says, 'Don't be getting ideas there. Eddsy wouldn't appreciate it.'"

"Meaning?"

"I don't know, do I? I make one slip and now I'm supposed to be the expert on this?"

"Go on."

"Go on with what? That was it! It was more than I expected but it wasn't as bad as I expected. I'm telling you straight out that I was pissed by the time it was over. Mary had a few drinks too but I don't think she was drunk. I cried me eyes out all the next day. And it wasn't just the hangover, let me tell you."

"Mary took part in the session, you said."

"Yeah."

"And you both, as a pair? . . ."

"That's right. I didn't really know what I was doing. It looked like Mary did. I was gargled by then. Not completely locked, now. But, you know . . ."

"You said that you talked to Mary about Eddsy Egan. Afterwards. About his likes and dislikes in this line."

"Well, I didn't *talk,* talk, did I? I just mentioned to her that, well, I'd heard that fellas got off on that and all . . . She said it was as good as it got for him or ever would get for him."

She let the cigarette roll about between her fingers.

"For him, like. He'd been injured or something." She looked up from her cigarette.

"That was it? Nothing came of this?"

"All I know is that nobody called about them. I was glad too. I felt like a right iijit, didn't I? I mean, I asked Mary once or twice. Even asked her if I could get the pictures. So's, well, no one'd get them. Know what I mean?"

Minogue nodded.

"Did you hear me?"

"Pardon?"

"I didn't want anyone getting them, I said. Those pictures. Mary told me that if Eddsy liked them he'd want more or something. He never got in touch, though. I never got any pictures. After a while, I stopped worrying. A lot of makeup and that, you know?"

"What else did you get involved with as regards Mary?"

"I don't like the way you're talking."

"You'll like the way one of my colleagues talks even less then. Ready to pack and go?"

Her eyes narrowed. She drew slowly on the cigarette, barely moving it from her lips between drags.

"I'll say one thing. It was only later on I got the feeling that Mary did it to shut me up. To turn me off any ideas I might have, you know?"

"About getting in on the good life or whatever you call it?"

"The good life. Christ. Look where it got her."

He watched her run her fingertips across her eyebrows and back several times. Her elbow rested on the envelope. She drew herself up in the chair. Her tone had changed.

"I'm off, Patricia. For now. You have my number?"

"Yeah, I think." There was something in her eyes which irritated him.

"Are these the only copies of, you know? . . ."

He looked down at the envelope under her elbow.

"I don't know."

"Come on! What kind of an answer is that?"

"It's no answer at all really, I suppose. I want you to phone, Patricia. Any small thing you remember."

"What does that mean? What am I supposed to remember?"

He raised an eyebrow. Her eyes were bright now. Yes, he noted, definitely there alongside the relief: scorn. She lit another cigarette. Number five, he thought. He turned on his heel and opened the door into the hall.

"Where's Hard-Chaw today then?" asked Fahy. "Did he jack it in?"

Minogue didn't slow down.

"Blasting away at dummies out on the shooting range, I imagine."

The door closed quickly behind him. Most of the other doors on the terrace were open in the late afternoon heat. He keyed off the alarm, sat in, and took the phone out of the glove compartment. Great. He had forgotten the number for the incident room in Harcourt Street station. He dialed directory and waited. Alan Long-Shot, he'd call him, Alan Long-Shot driving a proverbial Mercedes. An apocryphal Mercedes. An it's-just-an-expression Mercedes.

CHAPTER 16

YES, WELL, SPARE ME the rest of it," said Kathleen. "It sounds like a very difficult case."

Minogue found a piece of garlic stuck to the bowl. He fished it out on the end of his finger and slipped it onto his tongue. Iseult chased crumbs of garlic bread around her plate. The guilt at his truancy from the squad room was beginning to ebb. It had taken Plate-glass Fergal Sheehy to put the tin hat on matters: nothing yet. Nothing? That's right, Matt, came the slow, musical reply. Nothing.

He had felt like apologizing just after he had hung up. Fergal Sheehy and his team were not responsible for the fact that there were no useful tips, leads, or evidence from their door-to-door work. Minogue resolved to phone him in the morning, have a chat. An interview with a recent parolee was in progress in Crumlin station, Murtagh had told him, and it looked like the fella was spoken for. All the alibis completely sound, had been Minogue's unbelieving query. Seriously, John? Seriously. What news on Jack Mullen then? Murtagh and two detectives from CDU had found and talked to some of Mullen's fares. His alibi now covered virtually all the time that evening, with only scattered periods of five and ten minutes when he wasn't either sitting in a taxi rank or with someone.

"Pardon? I'm sorry."

"Away with the fairies," said Iseult. "Again. Maybe it's petit mal."

"So you had it with the heat and the runaround," said Kathleen.

"Well," he sighed. "In the heel of the reel, what we had seems to be slipping away. The suspects, I mean. And then, what we haven't found . . . This girl kept things very much to herself."

"Well, doesn't that make you suspect she was involved in, you know, something, let's say, illegal?" asked Kathleen. Minogue eyed Iseult.

"Easy for you to be so smart," he said to Kathleen. "The word from on high as regards the organized crime stuff, well, that sort of tore the ar — it, er, sort of knocked the stuffing out of it for me. I can start fresh in the morning."

"Please God," said Kathleen. Minogue looked out into the garden.

Please God? Did God, seeing everything, see what went on at the canal then? At night?

"Cooking for three is as easy as cooking for two," said Kathleen.

"Not to speak of a fresh face at the table," added Minogue. "And the chat."

"I don't want you to sell the house," Iseult declared. Minogue kept a garlic belch to a muffled report by letting it linger around his larynx. Kathleen said nothing.

"I think those apartment things are bloody stupid, so I do," Iseult went on. Minogue's face twitched but Kathleen had spotted him. Iseult stood up.

"Leave the stuff, Ma. I'll do it. I'm just going up the garden."

Minogue watched his daughter's progress up through the garden. She strolled with her arms crossed, by the shrubs and the trellis, one of his earlier follies now engulfed by creepers years before he had expected it.

"She's making up for all the times we haven't seen her since she moved out," Kathleen said. "The bit of security now, I suppose. I don't mind telling you, but I feel for Pat. I do. Now that he's putting his foot down as regards the wedding. I never thought he would go for it myself. But God works in strange and mysterious ways."

Put his foot down, thought Minogue. On a land mine, if he only knew.

"What mysterious ways do you mean, exactly?"

"Stop that. You know what I mean. God looks out for people. We don't always understand His ways. If we did, they wouldn't be mysteries, would they?"

Minogue rubbed at his eyes. He had flunked Irish Catholic logic a long time ago. Mysteries indeed: what were the ones they had recited again at Lent? The Sorrowful Mysteries, The Joyful Mysteries? Which were which again? The Immaculate Conception, The Passion and Death of Our —

"Do you think she wants us to bring up the subject?" Kathleen repeated. "I have the feeling she wants to tell us something."

"It's only company she needs, love," he said.

"Well, she knows what my opinions are. My beliefs, I should say. Not that I'd force them down her throat, now."

Minogue opened his eyes again. She glanced at him.

"I sort of wish she'd move back," she said. "But I could never say it to her."

"You could, but you'd better put your fingers in your ears after you say it."

"You tell her then."

"I will not. But I'll let her know it."

"What are you saying? You'll tell her, but you won't tell her?"

"Something like that. How did you get on at work?"

Kathleen rested her chin on cupped hands. Minogue smiled.

"Huh. Those apartments in Donnybrook are selling like hotcakes. We were run off our feet."

"Investors no doubt."

"A lot of them, yes."

"Spelled with an F, as the bold James Kilmartin might say."

"They stimulate the economy, Matt."

"My economy's not for stimulating. It's trying to get rid of stuff I am."

He spotted Iseult's head above the lilacs. She stooped. Had Iseult inherited, learned to mimic, his unease with the world? At least she had that flair for life, that appetite and gaiety that he now remembered had been native to his mother. It had come to him late enough. There was no knowing. It might well be one of those mysteries Kathleen fortified herself with. But Iseult, she had a lot of living to do to get to that stage. He suddenly feared for her, for the bills she'd be presented with daily for being different and averse, bills she could never pay. An innocent, for all her tough talk, and she hadn't a clue about the price of things. Her words, the look on her face, had stayed in his thoughts: teach me how to be alone.

He launched himself up from the chair.

"Come down to Dun Laoghaire," he said. "We'll do the pier. I'll buy you ice cream."

Kathleen stayed looking at the garden.

"Be still my heart. I'll go and change, so I will."

"Thanks now. Thanks a lot. Stonewalled at work, sarcasm at home."

"What about Iseult?" Kathleen called out from the foot of the stairs.

"I'll ask her."

He trudged up the garden. Iseult was examining the underside of a leaf. She declined his invitation with a murmur. He didn't ask a second time.

"Slugs," he said. "There better not be. It's too dry, sure."

"Maybe they're under one of the leaves. I was looking for Pat."

"Ah, give over. Are you going to get a voodoo doll next?"

She let go of the leaf and the stem swished back. There was a glint in her eye.

"He let me down, Da. I'd never tell him how much either."

"Consider it a free installment in the marriage preparation classes."

"Go to hell. You think it's funny."

She jerked her head away. He felt ice in his veins. A swarm of midges moved in under the hedge.

"Sorry," she said.

"It's me that's sorry," he said.

.   .   .   .   .

"Well, I can take the details," the cop said again. He had a culchie accent. Probably a big fat lug with the shirt hanging out of his trousers. He took another swig of the vodka. A belch came up from deep in his belly. Christ. Maybe he shouldn't have started so early, but he'd started only to try to stay clear of going looking for a hit. And it wasn't early anyway, it was after tea. He realized that he was swaying slightly. He leaned his shoulder against the side of the telephone box. The cop was still jabbering away.

"What," he said. "What are you fucking rabbiting on about there?"

The cop's voice stayed the same. It was like he hadn't heard him.

"Leave me a number and I can have them get in touch with you very shortly."

At least he hadn't tried asking for the name again. As if he was stupid enough, or pissed enough. He focused on the window where the phone was telling him he had two pence credit left. The telephone box stank. Someone had pissed in it. He watched the traffic turn up Hatch Street. His stomach gave another wormy twist. Christ, enough is enough! He'd been on the phone too long already.

"But why isn't there someone there right now?"

The cop kept talking in that careful, polite voice.

"Well, it's the kind of section where people are on the go at irregular times now. Calls are routed through that number you dialed if —"

"Are you fucking deaf or something? You think I don't know what you're trying to do here? You think I'm a gobshite or something, is that it?"

Another belch stole his words.

"I'm not exactly sure now what you —"

"Shut up a minute! I'm talking. You hear? This is fucking important. This is about someone getting killed, man, someone getting *murdered*. Did you get that? You're trying to keep me talking here so as yous can trace me!"

"Wait, wait a minute. What would we want to do that for? We're always glad to get calls from the public now —"

"Sure you are! Fucking liar! Listen! This is the second time I've called and still I'm getting the runaround! You'd think in the case of a bloody murder that you'd be on the ball here, you crowd of —"

"All you have to do is —"

"I don't *have* to fucking do anything! Just tell them that we have to talk. Only over the phone, a coupla minutes at a time."

He was breathing hard now. He took another gulp from the bottle. This one burned worse. He squeezed his eyes tight and leaned his head on the glass. He felt giddy when his eyes were closed. The cop was saying something. Still spinning it out, trying to coax stuff out. Everything'd be on tape, probably.

"Well, at least let me have an idea when you'd be calling so I can pass it on. To be sure someone's there to handle the matter, like."

"Sometime in the morning then, that's when they better be there."

"You'll phone in the morning —"

"Yeah. Maybe. And tell them another thing, okay? You listening?"

"Yes. Go ahead, now."

"Tell them this. I had nothing to do with it. Nothing! I'm getting the fucking rap but I'm not going to take it sitting down. No way, you hear? No fucking way! You tell them. Tell them the Egans are after me too, so I'm not just going to sit here like a fucking —"

The warning beeps sounded.

"Hey! Did you get what I said!"

The line was dead. He threw the receiver against the base. It swung and clattered again and again. Had to get out of here. Jesus Christ! Nearly nighttime and it was still frigging boiling. It was like someone had put a wet rag around his face and he couldn't breathe. He had a headache. He stepped out of the booth. Definitely not too steady on the feet now. It could have been the last few swigs, took them too quick. He stopped to think. Now: how the hell was he supposed to get back to the park? At night?

He found himself heading along Baggot Street toward the Green. He began to count the pints he'd had since the afternoon. How much was left of the vodka? Poxy, cheap shite, it was only fit for . . . The next belch brought a sour burn to his throat. There was something in his chest, something moving. He began to walk faster but it seemed he was hardly moving. He heard his shoes scuffing on the footpath. He was startled when a car bumped into his leg. It was parked. He pushed away from it. Things were beginning to slow down and slide around on his eyes like they were smeared on with grease. People were looking at him, every bloody light was shining into his eyes. He turned down a laneway. The streetlamps were still moving when he sat down. He reached in and took the knife from his pocket. Maybe he should have another pint or something to settle the stomach, get him over this bit. The thought of it made his belly go airy again. He began passing the knife from hand to hand until he dropped it.

His cigarettes had been squashed. He had to rip off half of one to get a proper smoke out of it. The first pull on it made him shiver. Christ, he was knackered enough to sleep right now. If he didn't try to have a rest he'd be shagged, wouldn't be able to think even. He thought of the trees and the long grass in the park. He was imagining a tent there when something shot up his throat. He got to his feet before the second spasm came. His hand scraped along a wall. He heard the vomit splatter by his feet and felt little pieces stir against the bottom of his jeans. The loathing and the stench twisted his stomach more. He staggered away from the wall with the spasms coming still.

He thought he heard someone say, "Look," but when he opened his eyes there was no one. He was vomiting dry now, his stomach twisting every few seconds. He had turned into a doorway and was leaning against the metal door. His eyes and nose kept running but his stomach had stopped heaving. The lights had stopped swimming around. Everything looked cold and ugly and foreign now. There was puke on his shoes. He had no hankies or anything. The smell drove him away from the doorway. He pushed off and headed down the lane. Against one doorway were stacked collapsed cardboard boxes and black rubbish bags. He kicked at them. They were full of shredded paper bits. That was it, he thought. Office stuff, clean. That'd do the job. He'd try for a bit of kip here maybe. Clear the head a bit anyway. Even if he didn't actually fall asleep it'd still be okay.

He built a tunnel lined with the bags of shredded paper and pulled cardboard in over them. He lay down and pulled some cardboard closer about him. It felt warm. He took out the knife, opened it out and left it by his head. His shoulders flattened more against the cardboard. Minutes passed. The sounds of the city seemed to become fainter. His stomach hurt like he'd been kicked. He didn't care where his thoughts began to take him now. Mary, that look she'd give him when she'd had enough of him asking her stuff. Questions he really wanted answers to: can't you talk to one of them for me, Mary? Come on, you know I'm sound. I could even work for you, or with you. When are you going to talk to them, then? It was like she enjoyed keeping things from him, hearing him ask, beg even. If only she'd taken him on, she wouldn't have . . . Panic flooded through him in an instant: those bastards who had been waiting for him by the house, would they be waiting for him wherever he went —

Footsteps, women's, with the quick click-clack of the heels, getting closer. Where was the bloody knife? Sounded young, walking fast. Maybe she was taking a shortcut and she was scared going down the lane. He strained to listen for other footsteps. The footsteps hurried beyond him, fading into the hum of the city. Far off he heard a siren. He lay back again and closed his eyes. The smell of the cardboard stung his nose now. There was no way — no way — he was going to go to one of the hostels for down-and-outs. A decent sleeping bag and some kind of plastic if it rained, that'd make things a lot easier. It was only for a short while anyway, wasn't it? It'd take money. Maybe it was time to think about using the knife to make a bit . . . He jerked himself up when he heard the rustling sound. He settled onto his hunkers, with the knife grasped tight and waited for several seconds. He heard nothing beyond his own suppressed breath in his nostrils. He knocked away the roof with his free hand and kicked his way out onto the lane. He was alone. Maybe it had been the stuff settling in the rubbish bags. Rats? He stared into the pools of darkness down the lane and shivered. His chest was still heaving. He leaned against the wall. Three or four people passed the mouth of the laneway singing and shouting. It must be closing time.

His legs began to feel rubbery. He leaned against the wall and looked around at the bags of rubbish and the cardboard. Did rats eat cardboard? Only if they were stuck, maybe. When was this stuff picked up anyway? Hardly at night. Slowly he gathered the cardboard again and rearranged it as he lay down. He was too wasted to sleep. He lost track of the time he lay there staring through a gap in his cardboard roof at the slice of blue and yellow night sky. The car horns and the shouting from the street didn't seem to matter much now. It grew quiet in the laneway after a while, how long he couldn't tell and didn't care. Many times he wondered if he was having a dream, if it was him lying here in a laneway with a knife in his hand. It was rubbish, and he was part of it. That was the truth and he couldn't pretend different. As the minutes and hours passed, something else moved around in his mind, something he couldn't get a fix on at all. Maybe he'd never be able to explain it to himself even, but somewhere inside himself he felt light and clean.

. . . . .

Minogue switched off the radio. Did he really need to be told that the high pressure system still remained over Ireland this morning? A possibility of thunder? That had to be a joke. A cement lorry at the site of new apartments in the Coombe made him detour by Thomas Street.

Kilmartin's tie was ambitious. His jacket was too up-to-date, however.

"What's that thing around your neck, Jim?"

"For your information, smart-arse, that tie was a present from the wife. So keep your smart remarks to yourself, you. Unless you like fast trips in ambulances, like. Now. You have work to do, let me tell you, and you'll have to do it on your own this morning. Molly Malone phoned in. He won't be in until later on. You know yourself."

The brother, thought Minogue.

"Now: the real business. There was a call in to you here at ten o'clock last night. A Mrs. Mary Byrne. She said it wasn't urgent. Your name is tagged to a Byrne fella you met there?"

Byrne, the old man he had talked to by the canal. Had the wife seen something?

"She lives down off the canal there. Vesey Court. Put that aside now a minute and cast your eye over this one, but."

Minogue took the photocopy. It was a print of a call to Central last night. It was made from a public box by Hatch Street. Kilmartin tapped him hard on the shoulder.

"It's that Hickey fella," said Kilmartin. "Mr. 'Leonardo' himself. He's alive and well. He wants to play tough guy over the phone too."

Minogue noted the smile along with the glint in the chief inspector's eye.

"I was onto CDU," Kilmartin went on. "They have units ready. Fella the name of Cosgrave will handle it. That's his number there. Sergeant. Let him know you're on, okay?"

Minogue continued scanning the transcript of Hickey's call. He felt his spirits rising.

"Not bad," he murmured. "Not bad at all."

"'Not bad'? It could be the go-ahead, man! And Hickey was drunk. He's on the run. He'll sing, that's what I say."

The chief inspector hoisted an arm and withdrew it with a delicate shrug from the jacket. He settled the jacket carefully on his arm and tugged at the collar of his shirt.

"Oh, yes," he muttered. "We'll have that scut sitting across the table from us signing up for this one."

"Nothing new come in on Jack Mullen? Any give on the car tests?"

Kilmartin shook his head.

"Leave Mullen for the time being. He may be a bit cracked, but that's normal. It's only religion with him."

Minogue put down the photocopies.

"Has John Murtagh stitched him up tighter as regards alibi yet?"

"What, what?" exclaimed Kilmartin. "What am I hearing? Are you still trying to soak Mullen for it?"

Minogue didn't answer but stroked his lip instead. Kilmartin shrugged.

"Ah, I'm not sure. Last I heard — and that was eight o'clock last night, when you were safe at home in bed — Johnner had him down to four gaps. One was about twenty minutes, near the nine o'clock mark. Put the bloody collar on this louser Hickey," he said. "Maybe he could lead us to the Egans. There'd be no stopping us then, wait'n'you see."

Minogue studied the chief inspector's tie again. Éilis entered the squad room.

"Good morning all," she said. "Glorious bit of sun again today."

"To be sure, Éilis," said Minogue. "You're an adornment to the facility this fine morning."

Kilmartin rolled up his shirtsleeves.

"I'm telling you," he said. "This is the go-ahead day. I can feel it in me *water!* Here, what was this thing from the Fahy one I saw: this 'Alan' someone you're looking for?"

Minogue was explaining when the phone rang. Éilis lifted the receiver after one ring. Kilmartin held out his hand. He and Minogue stared at Éilis's face. She waved the phone at Minogue.

"Kathleen," she called out. Kilmartin slapped his knee.

"Shite," he said.

"Pardon?" said Minogue.

"Sorry. I was hoping it was the Hickey fella."

Kathleen related to her husband how Iseult had left the house, the family seat in Kilmacud, in a huff not ten minutes ago.

"She was still asleep when I left," he said.

"Well, she was. And I thought she'd be well rested. She came down the stairs and I had her favorite breakfast ready for her. She's eating away, so innocently enough I try to, you know, have a little chat."

"'A little chat'? Don't you mean a big chat?"

"Oh, stop that! That's not one bit funny! All I said to her was, 'Darling, isn't it time to get whatever's bothering you off your chest.'"

Minogue felt his jaws lock. He stared at Kilmartin but didn't see him.

"Kathleen," he murmured. "Listen. This thing about getting things off one's chest —"

"I can tell by that tone that you're annoyed now. I can!"

"Listen to me: all this guff about openness and sharing —"

"Oh, stop, stop! This is the twentieth century, Matt! People need to talk it out, for God's sake! I'm sorry now I phoned."

He had to make an effort to breathe. He rubbed hard at his eyebrows. What was the bloody point of another tilt at pop psychology? It was a lost cause.

"It's you and her," Kathleen said. "It's coming out more in her as she gets older. Contrary, God!"

"We can't be meddling. We just have to wait."

"Talk to her, would you? Please?"

"I'll listen, that's what I'll do."

"Oh, Matt! Why are you so bloody obstinate?"

"I'm not. Everyone else I meet is, that's the problem."

"All right, all right. Anyway. I hope I haven't taken your mind off something."

"Ah, don't be worrying. I shouldn't have . . . Well, let it rest for the moment. Is she gone to the flat?"

"I think so."

Minogue replaced the receiver and stared at the desktop. Kilmartin came into view.

"Okay there?"

"No. Yes. Maybe. Eventually. I don't know."

"I think you got them all there."

Minogue looked up at his colleague. Kilmartin squinted at him. Minogue sat back.

"Iseult dug in her heels about getting married. Won't go near a church."

Kilmartin rubbed at his nose.

"Ah, don't worry. She'll get sense."

"I hope not." Kilmartin shook his head and began rearranging his rolled-up shirt-cuffs.

"Nothing's good enough for you today, bucko," he declared. "Saddle up now, and we'll chase bad guys."

Minogue winked at Éilis, lifted the receiver, and keyed in Byrne's number.

"Tommy Malone won't be in 'til later, Éilis," he said. "If at all today. And I'll be going out on a lead now in a minute, I hope. Make sure the boss tells you about a call we're supposed to get — a big prospect in the Mary Mullen case is going to phone, or so he says — Hello? May I speak to Mrs. Byrne?"

CHAPTER 17

MINOGUE TURNED AWAY FROM the canal and let the Citroen freewheel down the lane. Vesey Court was a working-class enclave surrounded by a palisade of offices, mews houses, and apartments. The Byrnes' place was on the ground floor of a two-story block of Dublin Corporation flats. Through wrought-iron gates Minogue caught a glimpse of a forest-green BMW squatting on an interlocking brick forecourt. Skylights with sharp angles erupted from several roofs; a glossy, lilac-painted door stood out from a gray pebble-dash wall. He glanced at the dashboard: ten o'clock. Cars were crammed everywhere in the laneways. He'd have to jam some in to park the Citroen.

He set the alarm and strolled down the terrace. There was a faint smell of rotting rubbish in the air. A pneumatic drill began hammering away somewhere in the adjoining streets. Movement behind the coffee-colored glass on the top floor caught Minogue's eye. He kept his gaze there while he stepped out onto the laneway proper. Sudden movement to his side made him start. The motorbike swept by within inches of him. Star Couriers, proclaimed the rider's jacket: "Consider it there."

The fright ran like cold water down to his kneecaps.

"Goddamn you and your bloody machine!" he called out.

He spotted the curtain drawn back before he reached the door. He rang. Why was it taking so long to answer? The door opened to show Mrs. Mary Byrne, stooped and shuffling.

"You're the Guard? The one was talking to Joey there the other day?"

Her face was damp, her eyes were small and intent.

"I am that. Mrs. Byrne?"

"Oh, none other. Do you use those cards now, like on the telly?"

"We do indeed. The card says I'm Matt Minogue."

"Go on into the kitchen, will you. I'm a bit slow on the pegs."

"Same as myself, by times, Mrs. Byrne."

"Oh, yes. But I'll bet you don't have plastic things for hips now, do you? Sit down there. God, you're a bit tall, aren't you? Oh, well. Find your own way."

Minogue eased himself into a kitchen chair.

"Does your husband know that I'm coming by?"

"No. I sent him down to the shop for rashers. He'll be back in ten minutes, give or take, like. So you're a Guard, are you. Which crowd do you work for?"

"You'd probably know it by its old name, Mrs. Byrne. The Murder Squad."

Her eyes left his and Minogue looked around. The kitchen was spotless. The cooker gleamed and the counters were clear, what's more. She had noted his appraisal.

"Oh, I can't really take the credit for that! Joey does all the stuff around the house."

"You're well set up then, Mrs. Byrne. Is your husband a Dublinman?"

"'Deed and he is. Right down to his toenails."

She grimaced as she shifted in her chair and squeezed out the words.

"Salt of the earth, he is."

Her eyes were still closed.

"Are you, em . . . ?"

She opened her eyes and smiled.

"Ah, I'm grand. It's the hip. No. My Joey's a man in a million. Doing housework all his life. Likes to be busy. Nicest man you could meet in a long day's walk. Amn't I lucky?"

"To be sure you are. Is he long retired now?"

"Eight year, so he is. You'd never guess to look at him but! And I'm not just saying that. Oh, no! I'm the oul wan in this family, so I am. Ha ha! I put on the wrinkles for the both of us. Joe's the same today as he was twenty year ago. Oh, yes."

"That's great."

"He used to be a ringer for Victor Mature. What more could a woman want?"

Minogue smiled and looked around the room again. Maybe all the grandchildren's First Communion pictures, et cetera, were in the front room. His eyes returned to her face.

"Seventy-six he is. Oh, but you'd never guess! Sure, didn't he lift me out of the chair the other day?"

Minogue's wandering thoughts slowed.

"Swept you off your feet, did he now."

"Ah, go on with you. Ha ha! No. I sort of got locked into position, don't you know. The joints, like. And I'm no featherweight, I can tell you."

He smiled.

"Great for a man of his age," he said.

"Of course, being tidy and organized is second nature to him," she went on. "A place for everything, everything in its place."

A key was inserted deftly in the hall door. It opened immediately. Paws slid and scratched on the lino.

"I'm back, Mary!"

"Keep Timmy on the lead now, Joe. I have a visitor here."

Mrs. Byrne's eyes darted from the cooker to Minogue and back.

"Who?" Joe Byrne called out. The dog barked. Minogue heard metal tinkle — the lead, he decided — and a door close. The next bark was muffled.

"Come in and don't be shouting at me, Joey."

Joe Byrne appeared in the doorway. Minogue half stood and watched the frown slide down Byrne's forehead. He felt that familiar voltage course through him, and he looked for that sign, that recognition of contact, from one who might be or might become his quarry.

"Hello, now, Mr. Byrne. We met the other day, you and I."

Byrne's eyes disappeared behind the reflections of the window in his glasses.

"The, em, canal? Oh, yes."

Minogue kept staring at the dual images on the lenses.

"On the news, Joey," said Mary Byrne. "They were asking for any . . . The poor girl!"

Several moments passed. Byrne's eyes seemed to have locked onto his wife's. Minogue still couldn't see through the reflections on his glasses. His lips twitched once. He turned to Minogue.

"I don't know what she told you, but you'd have to take it with a grain of salt now. I mean, you know the way the women are."

"Will we sit down and have a chat maybe?"

For a moment he expected Byrne to tell him to get lost. The lips moved, the tongue pushed at a denture. Byrne dipped his head and his eyes came into view again. He blinked several times.

"All right. So's I can set you to rights here now."

Mrs. Byrne moved stiffly around the kitchen, filling the kettle and taking down cups and saucers.

"Are yous, I suppose, getting along with it?"

"Not as I would like — as we would like, I should say, Mr. Byrne."

Byrne pushed his glasses back up his nose. Big hands, thought Minogue. The dog began scratching at the door.

"Mary. I'll finish the tea now. We'll let this man talk here with me, won't we? I'll bring you a cuppa there now in the front room."

Mary Byrne scuffed her way over the lino, blocking the dog's entry while she closed the door behind her.

"What did she tell you?" Byrne asked.

"That you took a walk there later on the night Mary was murdered."

"So? . . ."

"So it sounds like you wanted to hide something."

Byrne's eyes left his and went to the bottom of the door.

"So it's a matter of getting our facts and information straight now."

Byrne looked up and rubbed his nose.

"Are yous going around the area, like? To see if anyone knows anything?"

"We need to take a walk down by the canal, you and I, Mr. Byrne."

Joe Byrne's lips began to move again but he closed them tight. He had been carrying a carton of milk from the fridge. He raised it and looked at it before placing it on the table.

"But tell me first about that night."

·   ·   ·   ·   ·

"Nice," said Byrne. The alarm yipped as Minogue pressed the remote. He dropped the keys into his pocket.

"Dear enough, the Citroen," Byrne went on. He looked down at the styled aluminium wheels while they waited for a truck to pass. "But they lose their value quick."

"You were in the motor trade, Mr. Byrne?"

"'Deed and I was. I remember those Citroens during the war. They were a good yoke back then."

Byrne had gotten over his sulk anyhow, Minogue concluded. They crossed to the canal bank. Byrne took off his glasses and began wiping them with a hanky.

"Up by the bridge here, you said?"

Some faint movement around Byrne's mouth lodged in Minogue's mind. Byrne stepped down onto the bank ahead of him.

"I don't know what Mary told you, now, but —"

"You went for a walk later on. After she had gone to bed. Half-ten or thereabouts?"

"Well . . ."

"Well what? You didn't think it worth your while to phone us after you had learned there was a murder here? Even after I bumped into you the other day?"

Byrne put his glasses back on. He cleared his throat.

"Well, like I was telling you earlier on, Mary now, she doesn't have the full run of herself, you know."

Minogue stepped in front of Byrne.

"Mr. Byrne. Give over complaining about the state of the nation and get down to details. It was half-ten and you going out that night, right?"

Byrne bit his lip.

"After the news. I don't need much sleep this last while. When you get on a bit, you know? . . ."

He nodded toward the railings by the bridge.

"Anyway. Down there, where you can't see. There's a little corner there. As a matter of fact, you can get in under the bridge there if the water's not up. There's a path."

The inspector looked down at the dry grass that had been trampled into the ground. God Almighty, the worst place. The patches of clay were flattened, packed hard. He spotted squashed cigarette butts, foil bubble-gum wrappers.

"Were you down here on the bank?"

"God, no! I wouldn't go down there. I was up above on the footpath."

Minogue stared at the ground again: look at the grid and get the lads who had gone over this part. Maybe it wasn't too late.

"Half-ten?"

"More like a quarter to eleven, actually."

The streets would be empty as people ran into the pubs for last call, Minogue reflected. He turned back to Byrne.

"Listen, Mr. Byrne. I want you to do something for me. Go back up onto the street there, up by the bridge. Go the way you were walking, the pace especially. I'm going to call out to you from that corner there. I want to know whether you can see me. Keep me in sight there until I give you the billy to go on."

Minogue studied the ground ahead of him as he made his way forward. Weeds; beer can; broken glass. He squatted down. Bits of newspaper two weeks old, yellowed already. He stood, leaned in and peered around an abutment that formed a retaining wall for the railings and wall overhead. A torn plastic supermarket bag. More cigarette butts, a tin squashed, its brand unrecognizable. He turned around and saw Byrne's head and shoulders above the wall.

"Okay," he called up to him. "I'm heading around this thing here and I'm going to move right over to the wall by the bridge. Count to ten or more so's I'm there ahead of you. Start your walk then, the same way you did the other night."

Byrne pushed at his glasses and nodded. Minogue stepped around the pieces of rubbish. The noise of the traffic receded as he closed on the corner where the bridge met the wall. The water eddied out toward him from under the bridge, dark and sluggish. He finished his count.

"You up there, Mr. Byrne?" His voice echoed.

"What?" faintly from above.

"Huh," Minogue muttered. "You can't hear me either."

He retraced his steps back around the abutment. Not an accessible part of the waterway for the aimless stroller. He stopped at the foot of the steps. The rot by the canal banks had a sharper tang to it here. If Byrne was on the level, whoever he had heard that night must have been shouting. The same Joe Byrne was at the top of the steps. Byrne was gnawing on the inside of his cheek, one hand a fist by his side. Not a happy man to be caught out. Night vision was the first to go in most people, wasn't it? He must get Byrne's prescription.

"Are we right?" asked Byrne. Minogue didn't answer. He took the steps slowly.

"Tell me again what you saw."

Byrne shifted his weight from foot to foot.

"Look now," said Byrne. "If only I knew what Mary was jabbering on about, I'd know where to start and set you straight. She runs on and on and makes a big deal out of nothing."

Minogue held up his hand.

"Listen, Mr. Byrne. You saw us working up and down the canal here the other day. Do you have any idea how much work is involved in searching both banks here, up and down, all day long?"

Byrne poked at his glasses.

"You don't. Well, I'll tell you. It's too much, that's how much. It's dirty and it's hard and it's discouraging. It's the kind of place that makes us want to give up. But we do it. It's all we can do."

"But lookit," said Byrne. "If yous had've listened to ordinary people like me and Mary and cleaned up the place here and put Guards on the beat here, then this wouldn't be going on."

Minogue narrowed his glance.

"Doesn't wash," he said to Byrne. "Ordinary people are what count. What good's a uniform on its own? You should have phoned me. You should have told me the other day when I bumped into you. That spot down there might be useless to us by now."

"Well, I mean to say. I didn't think there was anything out of the ordinary, did I? There's a hell of a lot of this class of thing going on here these years. There does be people down there. Up to no good, like. Don't ask me what, now — the trade, I suppose. And every night of the week too, I'm telling you."

"Every night?"

Byrne folded his arms.

"I don't be out every night of the week if that's what you're trying to get at."

"All right, all right. Tell me again."

Byrne took a deep breath.

"Well, now. The lights down there are useless. I been at the Corpo years to do something about them. Bits of that bloody place are pitch black, so they are. Well, maybe not totally black like — I mean, years ago, you'd be able to see the swans there, how they'd go in there for the night and tuck in their heads like. But then there's the water itself. You know what I'm saying? Sure, that gives off the queerest reflections by times. Especially if there's a breeze. I was over here by the steps —"

"Wait. Were you on your way down the steps?"

"Are you joking me? I wouldn't go down there in the dark for all the tea in China, man!"

"You heard voices."

"Yes. A woman's voice. Only the one — and she was cursing. I told you —"

"What words?"

Byrne's nose wrinkled. He fingered the arm of his glasses.

"The exact words?"

"The exact words, Mr. Byrne."

"You mean I have to? . . ."

Minogue nodded slowly. He looked around Byrne's face. The tight lips, the frown: prowling around here at night, then probably going to early Mass every Sunday. He was very close indeed to calling for a car to take Byrne down to Harcourt Square.

"Well. 'You!' That was what I heard for starters. A shout, like."

"Like she knew who it was?"

"I suppose. I didn't hear every word what was spoken. Shouted, I mean."

Minogue looked at the water. Sic Kilmartin on him, he thought. He turned back. Byrne seemed to have picked up on his mood.

"The, er, F-word," said Byrne. "A lot of that."

"Fuck, you mean."

"Yes. Like I was telling you. No names now. 'That effin' B,' she said."

Minogue looked back and met Byrne's eyes.

"B for bastard? B for bollocks? B for bitch —"

"Bastard. Yes."

"Not 'You effin' bastard'?"

Byrne's lips flickered again.

"No. 'That effin' bastard.'"

"*That* effin' bastard?"

"That's right."

"No other voices? No one arguing with this woman? Protesting? Name calling?"

"I didn't hear anyone, no."

"You're certain you didn't hear sounds of a row? People moving about down there?"

"No."

"How long were you standing here listening to that?"

"I never said I was standing there listening to this —"

"Slowed, then. Paused. Lingered."

"Ten seconds maybe."

"And how were you able to see anything at all down there, Mr. Byrne? I was down there and you could barely hear me. You certainly didn't see me."

Byrne blinked. The inspector's stare became more intense.

"I know, I know," said Byrne. "Didn't I tell you that the place is out of sight of the path?"

"Well then? You told me that you didn't go down the steps at all."

"That's right."

"So how'd you do it? How'd you see anything at all?"

Byrne shifted on his feet.

"Well, I saw in bits, didn't I? You know. I sort of, well, I sort of like hopped up once or twice."

Byrne looked down at his shoes. Minogue saw more color welling in behind the pink skin on his forehead. Here was something to offer Jim Kilmartin, a quirk, a vision of human behavior that would set the chief inspector laughing in derision for the day.

"You hopped? You're seventy-six years of age, Mr. Byrne."

Byrne looked up sideways at him.

"Doesn't mean I'm an antique, does it? I just don't want you or your crowd getting the wrong idea."

"What is the wrong idea?"

"That I'm one of those, you know, gawkers. Perverts. Personally now, speaking for myself like, I'm nothing but disgusted by the goings-on in this city. Dublin's gone to hell. There. And that's a Dublinman telling you. You can quote me on that."

"You thought then that what you saw was a swan. You said that to your wife."

"That's right. What I'm saying is there used to be. Years ago. Before things started . . . Ah, sure . . ."

"Go on."

"Go on with what?"

He plucked his glasses off and thrust them at the inspector.

"You try them — go on. Amn't I trying to tell you it's no use? And didn't I tell that wife of mine the self-same thing?"

Minogue held the glasses up close. The trees swam far-off, the buildings floated as though underwater. Byrne was rubbing his eyes.

"I knew this'd happen," he said. "That's why I told her. And it's ten times worse at night."

Minogue handed him his glasses.

"Tell me again what you heard."

"What? The language? God —"

"No. Traffic. Splashes. Talking. Music. Anything." Byrne sighed and shook his head.

"Traffic . . . Let me see. There does be a kind of a lull about the ten o'clock mark, you know, with the pubs. Then all hell breaks loose after closing time, of course. The usual. Cars flying up and down here a hundred mile an hour."

"You didn't hear anything going into the water."

"No. Not a thing."

"People shouting, singing even? People coming out of pubs?"

"Coming out of the pubs, is it? You must be joking. Just this one with the woman. This woman cursing. Sounded young. 'Effin' B.' 'Liar.' And the rest of it."

Minogue looked down at his notebook.

"'What the F would you know?'"

"Yep. That's it."

"'Stupid'?"

"Right."

"No 'Leave me alone' or 'push off'? Any rebuff like that?"

"Is that a rebuff? No."

Minogue looked across the street at his Citroen. With its suspension fully down, his fire-engine red automotive folly looked as if it had collapsed squat on the roadway like a spent voluptuary. Technical site team, he remembered. He stared at Byrne when he spoke now.

"You'd best go home now, Mr. Byrne, and await our call shortly."

"What call?"

"I'm going to call for a Guard to take your statement proper. He'll take it in full and he'll type it up. Then you'll sign it."

"Wait a minute there. I done me bit."

"He or she will bring you to a Garda station, Harcourt Terrace most likely —"

"Me? A Garda station?"

"And you'll tell the Guard every detail of what you told me. You'll also suggest any changes that are needed to make it more accurate and detailed."

He let his eyes rest on Byrne's for several moments longer.

"I'll take you back to your place now."

Minogue crossed the street without waiting for Byrne.

. . . . .

Kilmartin was working his way through a sandwich. John Murtagh was on the phone.

"Hopping," the chief inspector chortled again. "Oh, Jesus, I love it! Hopping — ha ha ha ha! Seventy-what is he?"

"Seventy-six. No word from Hickey?"

"Wouldn't I tell you if there was? Aren't me and John Murtagh all revved-up here by the shagging phone waiting to jump? There are three cars sitting out there too. Four motorcycle lads from Traffic on standby. Tell me about this Byrne fella hopping again, though — here, is he one of those fellas robs knickers off the clotheslines?"

"Ask him yourself."

Minogue took a half of a sandwich, sat down, and examined it.

"So we have a half-blind pensioner walking his dog," said Kilmartin.

"A half-blind pensioner with high moral standards walking his dog," said Minogue.

"Huh. What's going to stay standing in this fella's statement then?"

"Mr. Byrne believes he saw something white. A swan, perhaps."

"'A swan,'" said Kilmartin. "Jases, he has you codded! Why not a Martian spacecraft with the *clooracaun* at the wheel, and —"

The chief inspector let down the remains of his sandwich, nodded at Minogue, and picked up the receiver.

"Technical Bureau, C.I. Kilmartin."

Minogue watched the chief inspector's expression slide into a scowl.

"I'll get him for you," he drawled. He hit the hold button hard and held the receiver out toward Minogue.

"Voh' Lay-bah. He wants a word with you."

Minogue gave the chief inspector a glare. He took the extension by the window.

"Tommy," he said. "Howiya."

"I'm all right. Just to let you know I'm coming in. Give me half an hour, all right?"

"You, em, sorted out the issue at home, I take it."

"Not what you'd call sorted out. Terry got out in the morning but he never showed up at the house until late. Arrived in steaming drunk. We had a row."

Minogue looked about the squad room for something to say.

"Do you want to book off a bit of sick leave, Tommy? It sounds like you need to set things straight a bit. Are you all right where you are, what you're doing?"

"I'm trying to decide what to do. Terry's sleeping it off still. Yeah. The ma's in bits. She's no match for him, like."

"Is it any use getting him in treatment or anything? He's on probation, isn't he?"

Malone didn't reply for several moments.

"I've half a mind to get him for breach, yeah. I don't know. I don't want to do it. I've an idea he kept a habit going in the nick. If I send him back, he might go under even worse."

"Is that what? . . ."

"Pretty sure. He was really throwing shapes. Anyway. There's something I have to tell you. This might throw a spanner in the works. But I have to. It affects the case, like."

Minogue watched Kilmartin tearing the crust off the last of his sandwich.

"Terry gets out, right?" said Malone. "So guess where he goes first? They were waiting for him outside, the car, the reception committee. Welcome back and all . . ."

"The Egans?"

"Right. They gave him some freebies and set him off. He came in the door looking for me. 'Bobby says hello.' Thinks it's funny. They'd set him up to get at me. And he thought it was funny. That's when I clattered him."

"You? . . ."

"Right in the snot. Nearly broke me bleeding hand. He wasn't that out of it that he didn't get up off the floor and go after me though. He connected a few times. The neighbors came in. Joey Cuniffe next door. He's a brickie. He had to sit on Terry. Jases."

"The Egans," said Minogue. "Bobby Egan."

"That's them. The fuc — the Egans. Their idea of a joke or something. Terry said they knew about Lenehan, Lolly Lenehan, getting picked up. And they knew it was me involved in that too. Says Terry, 'They're going to look after me. They're going to give me a job.' Christ. They'll probably try to get him in on some muscle job or take up some of the slack from bloody Lenehan. It's sick, man."

"Setting him up, just to get back at you, you're saying."

"Yeah. I'll fucking kill them, so I will."

Kilmartin was eyeing him now. Minogue focused on stains on the window.

"Nice, Tommy," he murmured. "That'll come out very clear on the replay."

"Sorry. I'm seriously pissed off. Hey. Did you mean that about the tape?"

"Just keep those comments to yourself."

"Okay. But I've bollocksed my first case, haven't I? I have to get off it now, won't I?"

"Let me think about that. What are you going to do?"

"Dunno. I don't want Terry back inside. He'd do something really stupid. But I don't want him falling into the Egans' hands either. And I can't watch him every day, can I? Jases, such a mess! Those fucking — excuse me. Am I screwing everything up?"

Minogue didn't want to answer. He met Kilmartin's mocking eyes across the room. Molly Malone screws up big time. The Dub's a dud: told you so.

"I swear to God," Malone went on. "If I'd a thought Terry was going to go ape-shit, I mightn't have been so bloody keen to apply for the posting on the squad and everything. But now here's Terry going around like an unexploded bomb. And he's taking me and my career down with him. The Egans know that too, I know they do. The bastards!"

Minogue bit back any words of consolation. Malone remained silent.

"Don't be getting ideas about the Egans, now. You have to cool off."

"Okay."

Minogue replaced the receiver and looked down into the yard. No Iseult sitting in the passenger seat waiting for him. He couldn't tell her how much he liked having her at home again. Kilmartin was standing behind him.

"What's with Molly?"

Minogue didn't answer him.

"It's the brother, isn't it? Trouble, right? Didn't I tell you? The genes, man."

Minogue turned and opened the file on Jack Mullen.

"So it is the brother," said Kilmartin. Minogue glared at him.

"Amongst other things, Jim, yes."

CHAPTER 18

MINOGUE POURED MORE COFFEE and turned over the Victory Club papers again. Jack Mullen had brought them to his first interview and used them by way of telling his life story. The stuff reminded Minogue of the twelve steps from Alcoholics Anonymous, but loaded with a heavier dose of God. It was also peppered with terms that he, Minogue, had grown queasily averse to. Denial — in denial; empower; self-esteem; grieving; relationships; homecoming; breaking the cycle — something that would have many puzzled Irish men looking for a puncture-repair kit or a set of bike-spanners? No. Unfair, he thought. Irish males — even Irish policemen, middle-aged Irish policemen, middle-aged Irish policemen from the west of Ireland — were not ignorant of the wider world. There had, after all, been a *Time* magazine spread several years ago on men, film stars included, going into the woods in America to share their feelings with other men. Mullen had said several times that he wanted his life back, that he wanted his family back. He wanted to start fresh. The wife obviously hadn't been impressed with fresh starts and she still didn't want anything to do with him, sober or not. And if Mary hadn't wanted anything to do with him? Didn't want to be "recovered"?

Minogue was beginning a second reread of today's update of the forensic findings from the state lab when the phone went. He watched Éilis's expression as she put the phone to her ear. She slowly sat upright and stared at her monitor for several moments. He sat forward in the chair, placed his hand on the extension, and waited. Is that him, he mouthed. Her eyes came back to focus on his. She nodded. He picked up the receiver and pushed for the call.

"Matt Minogue speaking, hello?"

He listened for street noise on the other end. Someone breathed.

"You're a cop, right?"

"Pardon?"

"Are you a cop, I said!"

"Yes, I am."

"What are you, a sergeant?"

"Inspector. I'm —"

"Well, I know you're not the only one on this. So don't try to lie to me!"

Minogue said nothing. Kilmartin had emerged from his office.

"Did you hear me?"

"Go ahead there now. Liam, is it?"

"Fuck you and your 'Liam' stuff! Shut up and listen! I didn't do nothing. You're chasing an innocent man. Totally innocent! Yous're too stupid to go after Bobby Egan and them! Or yous're too chicken. That's what I'm telling you!"

Minogue listened to the sharp intakes of breath. Leo Hickey was holding his hand around the mouthpiece. Kilmartin was tiptoeing toward him. Éilis, he noticed, had a line ready for the call from Communications.

"Hey! Are you listening?"

"I am indeed. I thought you wanted —"

"You think I'm going to take this shit lying down, man? I been framed! So get that!"

Minogue tugged at his eyebrows. Kilmartin was staring at him. The phone hadn't been sourced yet. How long did it take them, for God's sake? Weren't they talking about fifteen seconds from the reverse directory computer now?

"I hear what you're saying there. If you'd just —"

"I'd never harm a hair on Mary's head, so I wouldn't! Did you get that? I don't know what crap yous've been told but you can't believe it."

"Well, why not meet me and we can have a chat —"

"Shut up! I knew yous'd try that!"

High, Minogue wondered, but the voice was clear.

"Oh, yeah, sure! I come in and yous nail me. Oh, very smart. Yous stick me in a cell somewhere 'cause you don't like what I'm saying. Right? And what happens then? I get it from the Egans! Even if I get remand, they can get in. No way, man! That's a death warrant!"

"We can protect you, Liam."

{ 223 }

"Like hell you can! I walk back out on the street and it's worse even, 'cause you'd put it out that I'm a stoolie or something! Yous do it all the time!"

Kilmartin was waving. He began jabbing his forefinger into the desktop.

"Listen, Liam, you're upset —"

"You're bleeding right I'm upset! Here, I'm jacking this in!"

"Just a second. Please! Give us where you were that night. We can check it. If it's sound, what have you to worry about?"

"Are you deaf or something? The *Egans*! Everyone thinks I done for Mary too!"

"Do you know what an alibi is, Liam? Give me an alibi I can check. We're not interested in any other stuff you're into."

Minogue heard a horn from Hickey's end.

"Alibi? What if I don't have one?"

"Well, try me."

Minogue tried to read into the few seconds' silence.

"I fucking can't!" Hickey blurted out at last.

"Look, Liam. We're not going to come on heavy on any minor stuff you're into. Come on, now, put yourself in the clear."

"I was out that night."

"Who with?"

"On me own — aw, fuck, this is stupid, I'm —"

"Just give us a chance, Liam."

"I was doing cars! Don't you get it? That's why I don't have a fucking alibi!"

"Where then?"

"Yous'd only use it on me anyway . . ."

The voice trailed off.

"That's nothing compared to murder, Liam. Don't let it —"

"Don't give me that! Yous don't give a shite about the likes of me! You think I don't know yous're after the Egans. And that you'll use me to get them! And now you're trying to keep me talking so's you can corner me here!"

"Liam! The street, the time, the car — anything. You name it."

"Liars! You're trying to get me to wear the murder or else use me to take down the Egans! I'm not stupid, you know, I know what's going on, you know!"

"No, no, Liam. Give us anything. What street? What type of cars, do you remember?"

"Ahhh . . . Mount Street. I done a Golf, a GTI. There! I got a camera and stuff. Leather jacket. Ah, fuck!"

"Where did you fence the stuff?"

"Go to hell. What if I did?"

"If it checks out Liam, then —"

"I'm gone, man! I already said too much!"

"Call again, Liam. Give me time!"

The line was dead. Minogue released his grip on the receiver. Kilmartin threw his jacket over his shoulder.

"Come on," he said. "The standbys are up and running already."

"Where is he?"

"Up the road," said Kilmartin. "A phone-box in Cabra. Come on, for the love of God!"

"Will you get that off the tape, Éilis, the car make?" Minogue called out as he rose. "And see if it fits? But work any address in Cabra belonging to family or associates of Hickey first, will you?"

They took Kilmartin's Nissan.

"A bit of a dogfight there, pal," said Kilmartin. He accelerated around a slowing bus. "But you got him handy. Minute and a half he jabbered on. We can land the bugger!"

The breeze in the window of the speeding car fanned grit into Minogue's face. He rolled up the window halfway and pulled his seat belt tighter over his shoulder.

"If he'd put another ten pence in the phone, he could have put a bit of weight in that alibi he pitched at me."

"Alibi, is it?" snapped Kilmartin. "Ah, Jesus, man. One of his cronies did it and fed him the details."

Kilmartin was late on a red light turning onto Infirmary Road. A van driver gave him the finger.

"Wait'n'you see, Matt. It'll fall asunder in ten seconds flat when we have him sitting across the table."

He looked over at his colleague.

"Come on, now. Don't get to thinking we're chasing a shagging genius here. Sure, look what he let slip! Mount Street, he says he did that car. Bloody Mount Street is only a stone's throw from the canal, for God's sake! Hickey's just stupid. Smashed, maybe. He probably doesn't know what the hell he's saying, man. Sure isn't he a junkie?"

"Stupid is too often the sorry hallmark of the truth, James."

"Oh, will you listen to frigging Aristotle here. Stop worrying, will you. We'll get him."

· · · · ·

They didn't. Guards were still going door-to-door in the streets around the phone-box an hour later. A shopkeeper came up with a jittery young man close to the photo. Hickey had bought a Coke and a packet of Major cigarettes there. That was a half hour before the call had even been logged. Kilmartin and Minogue cruised the area until three. A scene-of-the-crime technician had taken prints, many prints, from the phone-box. Kilmartin pulled in beside it.

"Well," said Minogue. Kilmartin ran his hands down his cheeks. His face had gone puffy in the heat.

"The bastard," he grunted. "Either he legged it into the park to hide out with the bloody monkeys in the zoo or he had some class of an out ready here. Still none of his pals have a flat here in Cabra?"

Minogue shook his head.

"Ah, Christ," sighed Kilmartin. "Our stuff is out of date, I bet you. They move, these people . . . Bloody nomads."

"I checked with Eimear at the lab though," said Minogue.

"Majors he bought, right?"

"They're the ones. Four of the butts from the canal bank were Majors with the names still on them. There are still thirty-something awaiting analysis."

Kilmartin smacked the steering wheel and looked over at his colleague.

"Ah, he'll phone again," he declared. "The bollocks. But when though, that's what —"

The phone interrupted Kilmartin. Minogue was pleased to hear Tommy Malone's voice. Minogue stared back at Kilmartin while he listened to Malone.

"Great," he said when Malone had finished. "We'll be back in ten minutes. Thanks."

"Molly's back on board?"

"None other," replied Minogue. "He just fielded a call from Fergal Sheehy. One of his got ahold of a fella who works in a club in Leeson

Street. Over the Top is the name of it. Fergal's been plugging the Alan thing and a Mercedes that Patricia Fahy coughed up the other day. He might have an Alan from one of the barmen at a club."

"How so?"

"A fella came back from his holidays yesterday. He knows an Alan who comes to that club, or used to go clubbing there. He wasn't sure about the surname. Kenny, Kelly, Keneally. Something with a K in it. Drives or used to drive a Mercedes."

"Has anyone attacked the computer with this?"

"Tommy got a search and showed up an Alan Kenny. Mr. Alan Kenny drives a Mercedes."

. . . . .

Frigging Guards! Because they were thick culchies, they thought people from Dublin were all stupid too. Gobshites! As if he'd never heard they could trace a phone call, for Christ's sake! He stabbed hard at the earth between his knees and let the knife stand for several seconds before he yanked it out.

He shifted his spine away from the tree trunk and finished the cigarette. The smoke seemed to give up on trying to go anywhere and hung in the air instead. Midges' and flies' wings glittered in the sunlight. The blot of shadow he sat in was within sight of the Garda Headquarters. Funny if it wasn't so stupid and serious. What the hell had brought him back down here to Phoenix Park again anyway? He thought back to waking up in the laneway. Wrapped up in cardboard and bits of paper, right in the middle of Dublin, and he'd slept until bloody eight o'clock! He might have slept even longer if that delivery van hadn't come down the lane. No hangover, even. He'd probably puked everything up. Mental, he was. But what was he doing back here? It was the clothes, right, a change of clothes. Or was it something else? He remembered that creepy kind of feeling he'd had when he'd stepped off the bus next to the park this morning and looked at the trees hanging over the wall. They'd looked like they were waiting for him or something. It had taken him a while to scout out a good phone-box he could use.

Meet, said the cop. Have a chat. And that smoochy kind of voice, like a priest or a teacher fobbing off advice on you. If that cop ever got ahold of him, it'd be a hell of a different story. They'd batter him around until he signed a confession. He stared at the cars passing along the main road through the park. He couldn't hear any one of them over the background murmur of the city. His eyes moved from the far-off traffic to the branches overhead. The leaves had rusty spots and little holes. He thought of the conkers he used to gather and carry home in bagfuls as a child. Treasures. What had happened since then? The waste. His throat suddenly hurt. He tried to swallow but he couldn't.

The traffic looked like it was floating over the grass. He imagined one of the cars turning off the road and drifting over the grass toward him. His stomach tightened when he thought of the car chasing him the other day. He felt his bladder turn weak. A bird swooped down out of the tree and landed near him. He stared at it, willing it to step nearer. It could just fly off in a flash and be above the trees in a few seconds, flying over the whole city and looking down at all the iijits sweating it out there.

He got up slowly and walked to the far side of the tree. He kept strolling around the trunk, trying to think. Within a few minutes he realized that he was circling the tree. Soon he settled into a rhythm. He heard himself whispering, swearing. The whisper turned to a murmur and he began to repeat the words: a matter of time . . . wherever you go . . . He stopped and looked out toward the main road again. The lump in his throat was gone. He was thirsty again. He scratched the handle of the knife with his thumbnail. There were bits of dried clay in the hinge now. He looked down at the knife and then dropped it into his pocket. He had started something with that phone call, he realized. He couldn't just stand here. It was late enough. He was going back into town.

·　　·　　·　　·　　·

Malone's lower lip was still swollen. He fingered the Elastoplasts on the knuckles of his right hand and stared at the passing traffic. Minogue was still surprised that Kilmartin hadn't fired a few jibes Malone's way when he'd seen him. Just a look, he recalled, a look a zookeeper might give an ape who had unexpectedly pinched him as he was delivering the day's food to the cage. The two detectives were parked across from the offices of Kenny, Doody Chartered Accountants. They were waiting for Kilmartin's call. The chief inspector needed time to dig up any muck on Kenny he could before Minogue and Malone walked in. Minogue didn't ask Kilmartin what he could unearth beyond what he had himself seen looking back at him from the computer monitor: no criminal record.

He suspected Kilmartin could filch credit info from one of his cronies in the bank.

"Yeah," said Malone. "That's about the size of it. Hickey knows the score the same as anyone else coming from his side of the street would. Sees the likes of the Egans running the show, Guards or no Guards."

He took a swallow of the can of 7-Up he had brought with him from the squad room and grimaced.

"You have to live in the place to know what I'm saying really. It's no good talking in the abstract and stuff. If you're in a neighborhood and it's run by gangs, I mean. You can't move out, you don't have a job. You can't go crying to the Guards because they can't protect you in the middle of the night. You know what I mean?"

Minogue glanced over at him. *Yah know whar ah mee-ann?* He had missed Malone, his Dublinisms.

"Two generations of men unemployed where I grew up. Nothing to lose, the young fellas. Rob a car, get a thrill. Joy-ride it, torch it. Get pissed and start a fight. Bang up. Do time. Me, I was a skinny little bollocks, so I was. Very much the Mammy's boy. So I got into the boxing. Now, with the boxing club, I tell the kids to save their best for the fellas coming by with the needles and the dope. I tell them to beat the living shite out of them and I'll take care of the rest."

Minogue gave a breathless laugh. Malone swished more 7-Up around his mouth. He gave the inspector a rueful look.

"Not the official line there, don't you know."

Malone seemed to be suddenly distracted by the traffic. He began tugging gingerly at his lip. Minogue looked at his watch. They'd been waiting ten minutes now.

"So what are we going to work on this Kenny fella with?" Malone asked. "Mr. Accountant. The fact that a barman or bouncer working there saw him talking to Mary a couple of times over the last few months?"

"It's a start. Dropping the name of the Squad is a good opener."

"I noticed."

"Him seeing how serious we are when we ask him for the car too. Watch him."

"What if it pans out into just a client thing? You know, Mary doing a call-girl or escort type thing with him?"

"We work another angle. Follow other, ahem, lines of inquiry. Leads."

"That's it?"

"That might be it for the Mercedes thing. We have Hickey to find, don't forget. We need to go back over Jack Mullen and his timetable again. There's Lenehan — he might crack. The teams might pick up something more from the door-to-door. Maybe we'll turn up an associate we haven't seen yet. Just go at it again."

"Huh."

Malone suddenly crushed the can in his fist. Minogue looked down at the knuckles and back up at Malone's frown. The detective continued to stare at the top of the can. Minogue decided to wait for Kilmartin's call no longer.

The phone went as Malone was locking the car.

"Just going in there, Jim. Yes. No, I didn't want to wait anymore . . . . For what? Nothing? Okay. Yes. He's what? I think I remember that one, yes. About a fishing village and a ghost or something? We'll go ahead with the walk-in. No. Okay."

He switched the phone back to standby and handed it to Malone.

"Seems Kenny is as clean as a whistle. Among his accomplishments are doing the money end for films and theater His finances are in good order. Unfortunately."

"Bet you he jumps on the phone for a solicitor," said Malone.

"Do you think, now."

"Yeah. Southside prat, isn't he?"

"Aha. You've been to the night courses on psychology? Okay, let me try you on this. What if Mr. Kenny does not wish to help the Gardai with their inquiries?"

"Give him the chop, boss."

"Give him the chop," said Minogue, nodding. "Phone call?"

"From the station. He'll open the car for us first or he'll give us his keys."

"You're a fast learner there, Tommy."

"No messing," said Malone. "Do the business."

Minogue grabbed the detective's arm as Malone made to push the plate-glass door.

"Tommy. By the way, like. Perhaps Mr. Kenny didn't kill Mary Mullen. Okay?"

Minogue took in the glass portico, the metalwork, the polished granite in the foyer. Sharp, no nonsense. A man in his early twenties, with a badge high up on his short-sleeved shirt and a marine haircut, sat behind a granite-topped console.

"Are you all right?"

Minogue held out his card.

"Grand, thanks — can't complain. Yourself? The one door at the back, as well as the goods entrance?"

"Er, yeah."

The man tugged at his tie. Malone was taking in the sculpture next to savanna grass.

"Hey, is this a bust, like?"

Malone turned around, a puzzled expression on his face.

"I don't know what it is. What's it supposed to be?"

Minogue smiled at the security man.

"There'll be no fuss now," he murmured.

The lift smelled of cologne. The doors opened out onto a peach carpet, black doors, gray walls, and more dried flowers. Malone plucked at his shirt under his arms.

"Air-conditioning," he muttered and nodded at the nameplate. The secretary's anteroom breathed out more perfume. Macintosh computer, black furniture, and a leather sofa for *gámógs* to cool their heels while they waited to be told what the firm of Kenny, Doody could or couldn't do with their tax messes and their proposals for film funding. Show business, thought Minogue, paperwork: he and Malone, two sweaty detectives, had been beamed to Los Angeles. At least there was a homely layer of dust on the windows outside.

The secretary had a tan, wholly bogus eyelashes, and a direct look. She tapped at a dangling earring.

"Hello?"

Minogue smiled.

"Mr. Kenny within?"

"Is he expecting you?"

Minogue drew up his card from his side.

"It wouldn't surprise me. But I can't be sure, now."

Her expression changed to a bewildered suspicion. She reached for the phone.

"I'll let him know you're here."

Minogue raised his hand.

"Prefer if you didn't, thank you now. As a matter of fact, I insist."

"He has a client there."

Minogue smiled again.

"As do we. Kindly do not use the phone for the next couple of minutes or so."

Behind him he heard Malone open Kenny's door.

"Yes?" he heard from within. None too pleased, Minogue detected.

"No," he heard Malone reply.

· · · · ·

"And it'll be, em . . . ?"

Kenny sat forward, his hands out on the seat to either side. Malone started the Nissan.

"It will not be damaged, Mr. Kenny," Minogue repeated.

Even with the windows open, Kenny's stale breath came to the inspector again.

Malone's good eye slid around toward the inspector. Kenny sat back.

"We'll be passing Over the Top, Mr. Kenny. Just beyond the lights. And there's Tout des Loups. A grand spot too, I believe. I have a colleague who's more into the club scene. Young fella, of course. What do you think of the Tout des Loups place?"

Kenny blinked and squinted at the doorways. If he's sitting in an air-conditioned office all day, maybe he's entitled to sweat, thought Minogue. Give him a fair trial, then hang him.

"It's all right. Is that where? . . ."

"You heard about the case then?"

"Well, I'm just assuming that you're pointing it out for a reason," said Kenny. "You told me you're investigating the death of a woman called Mary Mullen. Right?"

A woman called Mary Mullen. Kenny might give him a headache yet.

"We believe that Mary frequented that place in the past, the recent past. I have a photo of Mary here now. Take a look at it, why don't you."

Malone slipped it out of the folder, turned in the seat, and handed it to Kenny. Minogue watched Kenny's face carefully in the mirror.

"You know Mary, Mr. Kenny. Right?"

Kenny drew in a breath and let it swell his cheeks. Like he's assessing a prospect, thought Minogue, a balance sheet, maybe. Malone jerked the wheel to avoid a parked van. Keep your eyes on the road, not on Kenny. He glanced at him again as the traffic drew away ahead. He hoped that Kenny would lie outright. Kenny let out his breath.

"Well, I mean I wouldn't want to say now, I mean, what if I were to tell you something here and you well . . . You get the idea?"

"Not really."

Kenny tossed a long swath of hair back up off his forehead. Something he saw in Malone's face caused him to drop the ironic expression.

"Am I under arrest now, is it?"

"God, no, Mr. Kenny. Why would we arrest you? Have you done something?"

Kenny let go a brief smile.

"You've agreed to be interviewed," said Minogue. "To help us with our enquiries. Which we appreciate."

"And my car?"

"And a fine car it is too. Like I say, it will be returned in tip-top shape."

"Was it seized?"

"Borrowed. A routine check." Kenny flicked back his hair again.

"How many other cars have you applied this routine check to? In this case, I mean."

"You have the honor of being the second."

"A forensic study is hardly routine now, is it?"

Minogue looked at Kenny's tie. Silk? It had little planes on it. To judge by his build, Kenny was no layabout. Tennis, Minogue guessed — no, wait a minute — squash.

"The favorite Irish pastime there, Mr. Kenny."

"I don't get it."

"Jumping to conclusions. Who says your car will be subject to a forensic examination?"

"I read or I heard somewhere about this thing. That's what forensic is for, isn't it?"

"For what?" He gave Kenny a dull stare.

"Murder," said Kenny.

"Amongst other things, yes."

He watched Kenny's eyes narrow a little before they turned back to the window.

"I think I'm beginning to detect a certain tone here, Serg —"

"Inspector."

"A certain tone which suggests, I'm not sure. Pressure? Suspicion? Intimidation? I don't know. That's not what I believed, or was led to believe, back at the office when I agreed to help. It seems the closer we get to your, em, headquarters or whatever, the less, well, positive the atmosphere."

Minogue scratched at his scalp.

"Ah, Mr. Kenny. I'm sure you're not taken in by the charm here now." The breeze had draped Kenny's glossy mane back down over his eyes. He flicked it back up less often than he could, thought the inspector. A ladies' man. Malone slowed for the entrance to Harcourt Square, gave a halfhearted wave to the Guard by the kiosk and started up again. Minogue was out first after Malone parked. Kenny climbed out slowly and looked across the roof at Minogue.

"I've been thinking," he said. Well, that's sure to mean trouble, Minogue almost said.

"And I want to phone my solicitor."

The inspector nodded, turned around and rolled his eyes. It had started.

"Certainly, Mr. Kenny. As is your right."

He strolled around to Kenny's side.

"But why the rush into the arms of the legal confraternity? You're not under arrest. Save your money, I say."

A confused look registered around Kenny's eyes. Minogue summoned his most avuncular manner.

"I should tell you again how grateful we are that you have offered your help. Of course, I imagine anyone would be a little apprehensive, wouldn't they? Especially a man like yourself, Mr. Kenny, a man who's never been in trouble with the law, being in a building — no, a complex — full of policemen."

Kenny searched the inspector's face for a giveaway smile.

"I'm the same myself, Mr. Kenny. I actually can't stand coming here at all. It's like a fortress or something. I'd sooner be out on the streets."

Kenny tried to smile.

"If you only told me exactly why you've picked on me," he said.

"Picked on you?"

"I mean, why you want to talk to me specifically."

So you can prep your five-hundred-pound-a-day pain-in-the-arse solicitor for when he can come storming in here to hand out migraines, Mr. Kenny.

"All in good time, Mr. Kenny. Will you go a bit of the road with us here? Tea, maybe?"

CHAPTER 19

Malone kept pulling at the ends of his Elastoplasts. Kenny looked over at him often.

"You're taping our conversation, aren't you," he said to Minogue. The inspector nodded.

"Is that allowed?"

Minogue nodded again. Kenny's eyes had a dull shine on them now. They weren't five minutes into the interview. Kenny coughed.

"It could hardly be just the Mercedes now, could it?"

"A bit more, Mr. Kenny. You frequented a nightclub that Mary also patronized. Now, we located a person who saw you in conversation with her. Several times, over time."

Kenny sat back and crossed his legs.

"Did this, er, person see anyone else talking to her? Or me talking to anyone else in the place?"

Minogue rated the performance. Irritated: good. Little bit of hurt dignity, incredulity: good. Can't a man have a bit of fun, et cetera.

"I mean," Kenny went on. "People who go there are sociable, I would have thought. By definition?"

Mild enough sarcasm yet, Minogue considered. A bit of condescension toward thick Guards. All to the good.

"You knew Mary Mullen then, Mr. Kenny. Outside the club too?"

"When you say *knew* her . . . No, I didn't *know* her."

Kenny's folded arms lifted and dropped back to his chest.

"From the little I knew of her, she was there with a couple of regulars. I found out that they were, you know, beyond being shady."

"Shady?"

"Oh, come on now. I think you know. A family called the Egans."

"How did you know them?"

"I didn't know them. I heard about them somewhere. Someone told me. In the club, probably. I forget when. You meet all sorts there. There are people who get a kick out of that mix of customers in the clubs. I mean, accountants mixing with artsy types and shady types. It's all color, isn't it? Adds an edge."

"You like an edge, do you, Mr. Kenny."

Kenny let out a breath.

"I suppose I do. For me, it's business too, sometimes. I'm dealing with film people, theater people, so I go where their scene is. It's play and it's work."

With his elbows on the table and his cheekbones resting on his knuckles, Malone had been eyeing Kenny. He raised his eyebrows now. Kenny stared back.

"Hey, I'm a workaholic," he said. He raised his hands in mock surrender. "I admit it. You know, I work on average about eleven hours a day. In the car even. Two phone lines at home, fax and everything. So I just can't buy all the moaning and whinging we go on about in this country, about unemployment and all that. Sometimes I'm working until eleven or twelve. It's crazy, I know. So I go to places like Over the Top to let off a bit of steam. Maybe I'm getting too old for it though."

He shrugged and looked around the room.

"Oh, to be sure, Mr. Kenny," said Minogue. "To be sure. The night Mary was killed now. Was that a work night for you?"

"No. Like I said. I was in Tobins. There in the Temple Bar?"

Like I said, thought Minogue. Petulance was making a dent in the performance.

"I had a meal with a client at the Marco Polo after that. I'll give you his name. He's actually a film producer, you know. Great guy. Ended up at . . . Well, you've already got that there, don't you?"

Minogue looked down at his notebook and back up at Kenny.

"How right you are. I do. Slatterys. Then you went home. Eleven. Ms. Julie Quinn."

"My fiancée, yes."

"So it was an early night for you then. Considering."

He glanced up from the notebook again. Kenny's stare was cool now.

"Mr. Kenny? I need to hear from you on this. We need to fill in the gaps that night."

"Gaps?"

"By my reckoning, you were in transit a lot that night. Twenty minutes here, ten minutes there. You went from place to place."

"Well, those times I gave you may not be exactly accurate, down to the second, I mean. I've been doing my best to be accurate about the times but maybe I was out on a few of them. I mean, when I got into the car and drove from Marco Polo's . . ."

Kenny's eyes had become fixed. He broke his stare with a slight shake of his head.

"What if I can't account for every single minute of that night? Until I got home to Julie, I mean?"

Minogue took his time sipping the tea. That Mercedes had better cough up enough to float a warrant for Kenny's house by a JP, he thought — and soon. He laid down the mug.

"What do you know of Eddsy Egan, Mr. Kenny?"

"You didn't answer my question," said Kenny. Minogue smiled.

"Nor you mine."

Kenny moved back up a little in the chair. His jaw moved from side to side.

"I've nothing to hide," he said. "In spite of this, well, I don't know if it merits the word provocation . . . This atmosphere of suspicion. Yes, I've heard of him. Eddsy Egan. I've seen him. In the clubs. He's the guy I was talking about. Someone told me Mary was his moll."

"Moll?" said Malone.

"She hung around with him. He looked to me like a fat dwarf with a walking stick. Pasty-faced. Didn't look much the gangster, I'd have to say."

"Ever talk to him?" asked Minogue.

"No way. Jesus. The glamor is fine at a distance, thank you very much. I found out that he and his brothers are rough customers."

"That they are, Mr. Kenny. That they are."

"You also know Bobby Egan then?"

"I know of him, yes."

Minogue looked over at Malone.

"Wouldn't want the likes of Bobby Egan on my case, now, hah, Tommy?"

Malone nodded solemnly. Minogue laid his hand on the file folder he had taken from the car.

"Do you know a man called Dermot Ryan, Mr. Kenny?"

"I don't think so. No. Is he a criminal type?"

"He works as a photographer. Precious Moments is his business."

Minogue paused to observe Kenny's expression.

"Do you mean in the film business, is it?"

"Not that I know of," Minogue replied. "I understand he's much sought after. In a certain sense."

"I don't get it."

"Ah, it's a long story. It has to do with the Egans. A modeling agency. A shocked wife somewhere. A disgusted fiancée maybe. Photographs. Rackets — no, not squash. Prostitution, I suppose. Protection. Blackmail."

Minogue slid the photos out face down. Kenny's eyes stayed on them until Minogue's stare awoke him.

"Drugs, Mr. Kenny."

"Sounds awful."

"Oh, it is." He nodded at the cell phone that Malone had parked on the table.

"We're all in the Big Time here now, Mr. Kenny. Our place in the sun. Standard of living, et cetera."

Kenny's eyes seemed to be getting brighter. Minogue waited some more. Kenny was shrewd enough. It wouldn't be too long before he would realize that outside of the rigors and the all too often dogged procedures of police science, there were no rules of conduct in a murder investigation. It was useless to guess at how much Mary had or hadn't told Kenny about her own life, how much she had shown him. It was probable that Mary Mullen had lied to him, lied a lot. Kenny mightn't be in any of the photos.

"Look," said Kenny, and swallowed. "You've been beating about the bush here. Why don't you just come out and say what you have on your mind. Get all this, I don't know what to call it, all this crap out in the open."

Minogue turned over the first photo. Kenny tried to keep his eyes on the inspector but he couldn't.

"A rather poor shot," murmured the inspector. "But I'm hardly a good judge. I mean to say, what would I know? I'm your sort of suburban type, am I not, Tommy?"

Malone nodded.

"A culchie too?" Malone shrugged.

"Not your fault, boss."

"Thanks, Tommy. Anyway. The blurry stuff there are clothes, I am told by our imaging experts here. Thrown off rather precipitously I imagine. This was in a place called the Cave. There's no name on the door now. Do you know it?"

Kenny's expression didn't change. Minogue sat back and stretched.

"I bet you're wondering how it's done, aren't you? The actual photography, I mean. Not the actual, well, you know what I mean. The recreation there."

"Not really."

"You aren't? Well, my goodness, I was, I can tell you. I thought of the old Hollywood stuff, of course. The one-way glass masquerading as a mirror and all that. But, sure, fool that I am, I'd look straightaway for something like that. If I were interested in that class of an encounter, I mean. The way I was reared, I suppose. Here, Tommy, what about you?"

"Definitely," said Malone. "First thing I'd check. Yeah. Be a fool not to."

"Did you check, Mr. Kenny?"

"What?" snapped Kenny. "I've never been to this Cave place in my life."

"Ah. You know the place then?"

Kenny turned away. Minogue sat up and leaned on the table.

"To make a long story longer now . . . Those Japanese wizards. Miniaturizing everything, I'm told. They'll soon be making them so small that you won't even see them. The camera is wrapped in a piece of sponge, slipped in behind a small mirror and hung on the wall. The pictures are all taken remotely. Hardly a peep out of it."

Kenny didn't look over. He kept up his study of a corner of the ceiling.

"Don't know what the color is like," Minogue went on. "Very grainy without the flash, I'd say. But sure, who needs color? Oh, by the way, do you know this fella here in the picture? Just on the off chance, now?"

Kenny didn't answer.

"No? We don't either. Yet. We've been having a kind of a lottery in the office there since we got hold of these pictures. I have fifty pence on this man here being a Tipperary dairy farmer. No?"

Kenny turned his head. There was a vague suggestion of pity on his face. He looked from Minogue to Malone and back.

"Up for the mart here, I decided. The Spring Show maybe. The wife out shopping in Grafton Street, most likely. Your man had enough of the tractors, et cetera, early on in the day. He even has the look of a heifer about him. A bullock maybe, though."

"It's a good story," said Kenny. "At another time."

Minogue put on a startled expression and turned to Malone.

"As a matter of fact — no, it couldn't be. Could it, Tommy?"

"What?" asked Kenny.

Minogue dismissed the thought with a wave of his hand.

"Couldn't be. Ah, no! It just struck me that this man bears a passing resemblance to a man we work with . . . Well, Tommy, what do you think?"

Malone didn't crack a smile. He half stood and examined the picture.

"Well, the build, maybe . . ."

"No, couldn't be," Minogue declared. "He's Mayo. I'm forgetting the basics here. It's the married men are the meat and potatoes of operations like this, Mr. Kenny. If I can use that expression. But you're not married, so what harm."

A glaze had fallen over Kenny's eyes.

"That's just about enough," he said. "If you want to talk to me again, phone my solicitor. I've sat here long enough. Do you know what my time is worth? I charge — ah, what's the use. Here I am, doing my best to cooperate with the Guards and what do I get —"

"Twenty years, Mr. Kenny. Probably."

Kenny's head tilted to one side. Minogue sat forward in his chair and joined his hands.

"Pardon? What did you just say?"

"You asked me what you could get," replied Minogue. "Average it out at about twenty years. Depends a bit on the demeanor of the defendant, of course. The posture he takes as regards cooperating with the police."

Minogue watched the changing expressions cross over Kenny's face. His jaw began to go from side to side again. When Kenny spoke, his voice was hoarse.

"You know, I'd heard rumors that this was how the Guards worked. Sometimes. When they were stuck. When they were desperate to get someone, anyone, so they could claim they were getting on with a case. I tell you, I used to discount this kind of blatant intimidation. That was probably because I had some faith in cops. I mean, maybe the Guards knew more about the clientele, the background, than the man in the street, like. One thing for sure, though: I never expected that a Guard would try this crap on the likes of me. Some illiterate with a record maybe, someone who didn't know his rights — sure. But I never imagined that this day would come —"

"*Carpe diem*, Mr. Kenny."

"I beg your pardon?"

"Loosely translated, 'Let's get going.' Sort of a way of saying —"

"I know what it means. I want to know what this latest installment of weird and unbelievable —"

Minogue turned to Malone again.

"Tommy. Do you think Eddsy has the pictures?" Malone continued his scrutiny of Kenny's face.

"Hard to say," he said. "Not hard to get though."

"Oh? Mr. Kenny here does not appear to be unduly alarmed," Minogue went on. "So presumably he is of the opinion that Eddsy Egan —"

"What the hell are you talking about?"

"'The hell,' Mr. Kenny?"

"Cut the crap. You can delay things here a bit, but it won't stop me phoning my solicitor."

"God between us and all harm," said Minogue.

"Do you think you can get away with this?"

"With what?"

"Your colleague here is a witness. Unless he wishes to perjure himself."

"No, thanks," said Malone.

"Your tape of this conversation is also evidence. You've presumably logged in here for the use of this room. Need I say more?"

Minogue loosened his collar. Water the garden tonight, even if he had to do it in the dark. A big tin of very cold beer in the fridge. Like America at home, by God. He stood up and faced Kenny.

"You need say nothing at all that you believe could be used —"

"Aha! So I am under arrest!"

Kenny's eyes had narrowed. His lips tightened in ironic satisfaction.

"You seem well-versed as regards your rights," said Minogue. "Not to speak, my God, of the most mundane procedures here in Harcourt Square. Logging in for the use of this room. How did you know that?"

Kenny said nothing. He began tapping his fingers on the chair back. Malone had eased himself up now. He leaned against the wall by the door.

"You'll naturally be aware then, Mr. Kenny, that the State does not proceed with posthumous convictions. Sort of obvious, isn't it?"

"What's going on here? Come on!"

"You want me to charge you, arrest you? Do you, Mr. Kenny?"

"I dare you."

Minogue tugged at his earlobe.

"I'll have to turn you down on that one, Mr. Kenny. Yes, indeed. The edge, no doubt. You're a gambler and a risk-taker, so you are. No. You can go back out there and take your chances."

"Unreal," said Kenny. He shook his head. "I'd never have believed it. That real cops, Guards, would act like this, talk like this."

"Act, Mr. Kenny? We're not doing auditions here." The inspector turned and nodded toward Malone. The detective's expression wavered between amusement and contempt. "No makeup, no special effects. The unvarnished truth."

"As you picture it, you mean," retorted Kenny. "It's not how my solicitor will see it."

"Oh, well," said Minogue. "Maybe we're wrong." He returned Kenny's look.

"I mean about the snapshots," he added. "Maybe Eddsy Egan hasn't a good shot of your face. If so, I can't imagine what parts of your anatomy he might trace you from. For your sake, I hope the light was bad. Maybe Mary never let slip enough about you to anyone who could give Mr. Egan a trail to your door."

The inspector drummed his nails in a quick tattoo on the chair back. He stopped abruptly.

"You're free to go, Mr. Kenny. Take care now. Detective Malone here will drop you off. And your Mercedes. It's a Two . . . ?"

"It's a 190."

Minogue beamed. "Ah! The pocket Mercedes. A gem entirely. Tell me, how do you find it at speed? On a twisty road, more particularly?"

Kenny's cheeks inflated. Minogue maintained the smile. It'd be some recompense to hear a good, rich curse from Alan Kenny. Nothing.

"Your car should be processed by midday tomorrow, Mr. Kenny. If all goes well."

Kenny let the air out from his cheeks with a pop. He bit his lip.

"Are there facilities?" he said. "A toilet, I mean."

Minogue almost smiled. He looked over at Malone but the detective shrugged. Right, thought the inspector. Malone didn't know his way around the place.

"Follow me, Mr. Kenny."

.　　.　　.　　.　　.　　.

Kenny closed the door behind him. Minogue stepped over to the urinal. He was happier than he wanted to admit to have discovered that he was dealing with a fastidious man. Kenny was probably up in a heap about being monitored in the toilet by a cop. Doubtless a chartered accountant would do his best to piss to the side of the bowl.

Minogue zipped and headed for the washbasin. There was no sound from the cubicle.

"Are we right there now, Mr. Kenny?"

The intake of breath stopped Minogue dead.

"Fine. Yes."

Like hell, thought Minogue. He studied his own reflection in the mirror.

"You're er? . . ."

Minogue heard the vomit an instant before the gagging sound. Damn, he thought, had this bugger swallowed something? Another scratching sound from Kenny's throat now but less puke this time. A sweet, soupy stench reached the inspector's nostrils. He pushed up from the handbasin. Well now: Mr. Hairstyle Mercedes had come undone. He had better make sure that this clown didn't damage himself on police premises. Did drug users have episodes like this? Maybe Mr. Hairstyle was proof they did.

"Mr. Kenny?" The answer came in a wheeze.

"I'm okay."

He ran water over his hands and rubbed the soap around his knuckles. The soap made slurping sounds as he worked it toward a lather.

"I'm serious about the Egans, Mr. Kenny. And I'm serious about the photo sessions."

He waited for Kenny to say something.

"When I find photos of you and Mary, you'll be glad it's me walking by your secretary's desk first."

Sounds of toilet paper being tugged and torn. Minogue turned the tap on high. Drops of water splashed onto his shirt and trousers but he didn't care. He glared at the reflection of the cubicle's closed door.

"Me and not Eddsy Egan, I mean. Can you hear me?"

A whistley, choked-off sigh sounded from behind the door.

"Listen now. If you're that worried, you should talk."

Kenny said nothing. The inspector swore under his breath, shook the water off his hands, and walked into the adjoining cubicle. He let down the seat and stood on it. With his feet to either side of the seat he jammed his cheek against the ceiling and tried for whatever he could see in the three or four inches between the cubicle wall and the ceiling. Kenny's glossy hair was all that he saw. It moved down over his forehead until he shook it back.

"Come out and wash your face. You'll be the better of it."

With the shudder and the wheeze, Minogue realized that Kenny was sobbing. His wet hands on the wall felt colder. Kenny's hair began to tumble forward again. He sniffed and flicked it back.

"Talk to me, man. You can't just hide in the corner, for the love of God."

Kenny turned and looked at the door.

"Up here," said Minogue. "I don't normally do this class of thing, mind you."

Kenny's watery, red eyes turned up toward him. He stood and rubbed at his face.

"She told me that he could do anything," he whispered. "Anywhere. Anytime. I wouldn't even be safe behind bars."

The stench began to make Minogue woozy. "Almighty God . . . Open up the door, man. We can talk outside."

"Do you think he knows?"

"Who? Eddsy Egan?"

"Yes."

"Possibly. Probably. Don't bet that he doesn't. Or can't find out."

Kenny was drawing the door back when Minogue stepped out of the cubicle. Minogue watched him roll up his shirtsleeves with his fingertips. He turned on the hot tap for him.

"You're going to talk to me now."

Kenny cupped water in his hands.

"I need guarantees," he said.

"You want what?" The inspector took a step back and pointed a finger at him.

"Do you think you're buying a new kettle or something? I'll give you guarantees then. If and when Eddsy Egan finds out who you are and where you fit, that he will call on you when you will be least able to escape his attentions. Is that the kind of guarantee you're talking about?"

Kenny grasped the edges of the basin and let his head drop. He let out a deep sigh.

"You don't understand," he whispered.

"What — the meaning of life? Enough of this caper: you're under arrest."

Kenny stared at the inspector's face in the mirror.

"How can you do that?"

"You killed her, that's how."

"No, I didn't! I couldn't! No!"

"You hung Mary out to dry, that's what you did. You left her out there, didn't you?"

Kenny's jaws worked but no words came.

"No deals! Dry up there and let's get going. Mr. Alan Kenny, I am placing you under arrest in the death of Mary Mullen. It is my duty to inform you that anything you say can and will be used —"

"She never told me! Never! I swear to you!"

"— as evidence against you. You have the right —"

"Never! She just said . . ."

Drops of lather still fell from Kenny's outstretched hands.

"Said what?"

"If I didn't take it off her hands, she'd say that I'd ripped her off. She did!"

"What?"

Kenny began shaking his head.

"Look. She thought . . . she thought . . ."

Kenny seemed to buckle at the waist. His hands sought the washbasin and he hunkered down before it, shuddering. Minogue looked down at him. He had been right: there were highlights in his hair.

CHAPTER 20

THAT WAS HALF-EIGHT, right?" Malone asked. Kenny nodded. Malone ran the tip of his biro along the lines in his notebook while he read. "'I'll phone Eddsy if you're not back here with all the money at ten.'"

"Yes."

Kenny had left his sleeves rolled up. He was rubbing his wrists. He tossed his hair back every now and then. The mannerism was driving Minogue to distraction.

"You knew all along you'd never come up with the rest of it, the rest of what she wanted."

"The three thousand? Yes. I mean no. I knew I couldn't."

"You're certain that you never actually told her that?"

"Right. I mean, what did she really think? She thought I had that kind of cash lying around the kitchen?"

Minogue shifted in his seat.

"You never told Mary anything that would lead her to believe that you actually wanted it, that you might be interested in selling the stuff —"

"Absolutely no way."

"— or using the stuff."

"Impossible. She was just coming the heavy, straight out. She'd tell the Egans if I didn't cough up. I couldn't believe it when she turned on me like that. Just unbelievable."

Took the words out of my mouth, Minogue said within.

"She was really scared, you said. Scared she'd be found out?"

"Yes. Either the cash or the stuff had to be there. She said Bobby didn't

{ 246 }

mind if she did a deal without advance warning. As long as the money was there right away. They'd been burned before, he'd told her. She said, anyway."

"Look," said Minogue. "How would she form the opinion that you were in the market for this stuff? She told you she'd done something dangerous by taking the stuff from Bobby's. Why'd she pin you for this deal?"

"Wait a minute here! You agreed earlier on that in no way was I dealing just because I took the package off her hands for a little while that night. No way! The worst thing I did, if I did anything wrong at all, was that I'd tried the stuff once or twice. Right? I mean, is that the crime of the century? You told me that wasn't an issue here at all."

"Stop, stop, stop, Mr. Kenny. What I'm trying to understand here is how you got yourself into this mess. You haven't told us everything."

"Ah, come on. You're the cop! You know human nature, surely?"

Minogue eyed Malone.

"Everyone wants risk, don't they? Oh, come on! Danger even. Mary was an attractive girl. She was ambitious. Anyone could see that. I grew up in a different way, a different world really, I suppose I'd have to say. I never really had to . . . you know?"

Minogue wondered how long she had been playing him. Was he hers or was she doing it for others? Mary Mullen had persuaded herself that this was her chance to cross into his world, the black furniture and the air-conditioning and the money that lived in the computers, real money that was clean and just as powerful as the worn and worried-over twenties she'd earned as a prostitute.

"It probably started and ended with me being stupid," Kenny was saying. "Pretending I'd tried the stuff before. Or that friends of mine, people I know, had used — had said they'd used — stuff."

"Stuff," said Malone.

"All right. Drugs."

"On one of those 'one or two occasions,' you used Ecstasy when you were with Mary. Am I right?"

"Yes. I admitted that. Right."

"Did she?"

"No. She said she wanted to stay straight, that she liked it better that way."

"She shoved this package into your lap when she got out of your car that evening," said Minogue.

"Right. At first I hadn't a clue, but then I squeezed it and I knew."

"So you handed the package back to her."

"Bloody right I did! Like a hot potato. But she threw it back in and walked off. More like ran off."

"But not before she told you that you had to come up with the cash or else?"

"Or else Bobby'd know about it and there'd be big trouble."

"Your reaction again?" said Malone.

"Well, like I said. I was, well, totally flabbergasted. I mean to say. It was so out of character for her. I really thought she was strung-out or something. Just nuts, she was. The look on her face, I mean."

"So you didn't put much store in her telling you that she was dead against drugs, that she never used?"

"Up to then I thought, well, she was admirable, I suppose. She hung around in that, em, subculture, like. I never saw her stoned. At least, if she was, I never knew. Never saw her overdoing the drink either. But at that moment, I knew I couldn't reason with her. She was just nuts."

"You decided to get a thousand quid together," said Minogue.

"Not right then, no. I mean, I was late for the dinner with the client and everything."

"When did you decide again?"

"All during that dinner, I was trying to decide what to do. I don't think I tasted one dish that I ate. I knew it was time to get out of this, you know. I made up my mind that she could have the thousand quid. It'd be a way of saying good-bye, sort of. I had to ferret around a few bank machines, I tell you."

"But you planned all along to go back to the canal at eight to meet her?"

"Yes, but I wasn't keen to, I tell you."

"So. Eight o'clock rolls around. You have a thousand quid and the package."

"I gave her the envelope with the money. I *tried* to talk to her. She ripped open the envelope, saw what was in it and then she freaked again. I tried to tell her that we should, you know, give things a rest? That I didn't like the direction we had been going in."

"By this time, you're steamed up, aren't you?"

"Sure, I was annoyed — I mean it was pretty clear she'd set out to take me, right?"

Kenny held his hair back over his head with two hands. Minogue stared at the shine on his forehead. Kenny let go. His head drooped.

"I was working too hard," he said. "Everything was too fast. I didn't weigh things. I realized that it was time to —"

"Settle down?" asked Malone. Kenny looked up at him and frowned.

"Yes, settle down. But I resent the way you make it sound. I was ready for a serious, long-term —"

"Relationship," said Malone. Kenny gave him a hard look.

"Marriage, actually. You can understand that, can you?"

"Mary knew of this?"

"Not in so many words. But I think she knew something was up. Women's intuition and everything, right?"

Minogue studied Kenny's tentative smile.

"It might account for her rotten humor though, wouldn't it?" Kenny added. "Timing, I mean, trying to get whatever she could before it was too late."

"So. You tried to give her the package."

"Right — as well as the money. The thousand quid. I told her that I guessed she was under some pressure and would this help her. Told her I just couldn't get into this kind of thing. There was absolutely no way. Imagine, I said to her, me trying to get rid of this stuff to clients and friends and the like. I mean it would be funny if it weren't so, well, tragic, I suppose. Accountants — the high life! Really? Christ, how naive. I really couldn't figure out where she'd gotten the idea that the likes of me . . . Television, maybe? I don't know."

He glanced at Malone. The hostility lay like a shadow over his colleague still. For a moment he saw Mary Mullen and thousands like her, tens of thousands like her probably, standing at bus stops for late buses, full buses, to ferry them home to blighted suburbs. Mary had seen too many Alan Kennys cruising by in their Mercedes.

"Maybe I yapped too much," said Kenny. "About deals, the film business." He looked from Minogue to Malone and back. "Maybe it's when you guys, you know, finally crack a case. Yes. Do you know what I'm saying?"

"Crack a case," said Minogue.

"When you've just pulled off a big deal, I mean. When you've gotten it on paper? The deal. You've just got to talk about it to someone."

"You boasted to Mary Mullen about your deals."

"What I *meant* was that Mary might have picked up a false picture of the work I do. She *thought* it was just a matter of picking up a phone, talking big talk, and then you went home rich."

"Oh," said Malone. Kenny's lips tightened.

"It might *look* like that to someone on the outside," he said. "She used to pick up on strange phrases. 'The inside track' was one. She wanted to be in on deals, deals she'd never understand. 'In the know' was another one. I bought an apartment, right? I kept it, I rode the trend and got out with a tidy sum. Okay? Is that so awful?"

Minogue looked at the wall above Kenny's head.

"But Mary — people like Mary, anyway — they think it's easy. They think it's magic! They can't *see* how it's done. Don't you get it? She said, 'But you don't use the apartment, you don't even live in it.' You see what I'm trying to get at?"

"Maybe, Mr. Kenny. Maybe."

"So I tried to explain to her that money was made in buying and selling merchandise and services. Products. An expert's time and training. Property. Information. Investments. Her eyes would glaze over. So when she shoved those pills at me and I told her I could never use them, she tells me, 'Well, you told me it was all about buying and selling stuff you didn't need.' Why couldn't drugs be just another commodity there, you know?"

"They already are," said Minogue.

"Yes, but not legitimate business, not in the sense of . . ."

He let the words trail off. His eyes still blazed as they bored into the inspector's.

"Okay," said Minogue. "There you were. You gave her the money, you gave her the package. It's eight o'clock."

"I gave her the money, yes. I *tried* to give her the package."

"That was when things turned, let me see . . ." He looked down at his notes. "'Really nasty'?" Kenny nodded.

"I told her I just couldn't do it. She could keep the money. I *told* her, *tried* to tell her, that it was time to, you know . . ."

"Go our separate ways," said Malone. Minogue glanced at him. The detective's face was blank.

"That's right," snapped Kenny. "And, by the way, I've heard your accent there."

"And?" said Minogue. Kenny kept his eyes on Malone.

"Haven't you heard of inverted snobbery?"

Malone shook his head.

"Well, maybe you can't credit anyone who happens not to have been born on the Northside of Dublin with any feelings, any positive feelings, I mean. Is it my fault I grew up in Foxrock or something? Is it my fault I have a good job? Christ, man, you don't know the hours I put in! But hey — I'm not complaining!"

Malone's expression didn't change.

"A thousand quid," he said.

"Yes! A thousand quid. That's a lot of money for me. A lot."

"You tried to buy your way out," said Malone.

"Buy my way out? That's a damn lie! I reckoned on it being enough to get her out of whatever scrape she was in. Enough for her to forget that stupid stunt she was trying to get me into."

Scrape, thought Minogue. What was the going rate for an abortion in London anyway?

"'Scrape.'"

"Whatever she wanted to use the money for, I don't know. Maybe she had debts?"

"You keep on saying, or suggesting, that Mary was under pressure. How so?"

"I don't know. I don't."

"What did you suspect?"

"I really don't know. Maybe they told her to hurry up. The Egans, I mean."

"Um. It was at that time that she became, shall I say, explicit about threats?"

"Yes."

"Go through it again."

"Do I really have to? We've been talking . . . Oh, I get it. You want to find inconsistencies and then jump on me, is it?"

"Maybe," said Minogue. "Do we, Tommy?"

"Don't know about you. I wouldn't say no to a bit of that. Yeah."

"So, Mr. Kenny?"

"Number one: She'd tell the Egans that I had stolen the drugs — the package. They'd believe her, she said. Her word counted for a lot more than mine there. 'When it really counted,' she said. Maybe mine might count with the Guards, I remember her saying, but where it really mattered, hers would. Kind of ironic, isn't it?"

"Deeply," said Minogue. "Go on."

"This Eddsy Egan would do a number on me, personally. He was a sadist she said. He'd, well, he'd . . ."

"'Chop your fucking nuts off,'" Malone murmured. Kenny frowned at him.

"Yes. So I began to get more annoyed. I mean, who was she to threaten me like this? I mean, what had I done to her that I deserved that kind of thing?"

Done to her, Minogue reflected. Given her hope, maybe.

"I mean, all she has to do is bring the damn stuff back," said Kenny. "Then she can keep the money, right? Go her own way. I mean to say, Mary knew how to take care of herself, didn't she? But no. She goes into a tirade about us, how I was the scum of the earth."

Malone began to recite, his finger following the scribble across his pages.

"'Southside fucking bastard . . .'"

"Yes, yes — whatever. That's when she comes up with the photo bit. She tells me she has photos of a night in the Breffni hotel. I don't care, I tell her. Well, Eddsy Egan does, she screams back."

Kenny broke off to rub his hands alternately through his hair.

"You knew before then that she did photo sessions for the Egans?"

"No. She told me that Eddsy, the crippled-looking one, was the one who started her on them. Apparently he can't, well, you know what I'm getting at. All he can do is look on, I hear. He likes to know the girls he's looking at. The crazy one, Bobby, is into it as well. He gets prospects for the brother. Bobby'll go, how can I put it, all the way. His harem. Him and Mary. As well as others, of course."

"Back to the threats. The break-every-bone-in-your-body bit."

"You make it sound trivial. Like it's funny or something."

Minogue and Malone stared at him.

"She said, 'I know a guy who can break every bone in your body.'"

"'Every bone in your fucking body,'" said Malone. He wasn't looking at his notebook now.

"This is separate from the threat about Eddsy Egan?" asked Minogue.

"Well, I didn't know, did I? At that stage I was thinking that she was so shrill about the Egans that there was something strange going on. More than just her anger and everything. She was losing it. Panicking. I got the idea then that she wouldn't dare tell the Egans. That she'd get into trouble with them if they found out what she'd done, what she'd tried to do. That she was bluffing."

"So the other threat was her own, sort of?"

"I don't know. I really don't."

"You used the term 'double-cross' earlier on. You said you believed that Mary had been caught in a double-cross."

"Yes, I did."

"And that you were annoyed enough — the money, the threats — that you decided to just drive off."

"That's right."

"With the drugs in the car."

"With the package in the car, yes."

"You wanted to teach her a lesson."

"I never said that. I planned to come back later and try again. See if she had cooled down. See if I could talk some sense into her."

"You made no attempt to find more money."

"Absolutely not. No way! Look. You know I'm telling you the truth. I'm not going to grovel. Just look at the proof I've given you!"

"Proof? Sorry. Proof of what, now?"

"Proof that I'm telling you the truth! Proof I had nothing to do with what happened to Mary."

Minogue looked down at the tabletop, at the random marks of a biro from some other interview. Couldn't the cleaners get them off or what? He rubbed at them with the heel of his hand.

"Mr. Kenny," he said, and rubbed harder on the marks. "I have to tell you that I'm puzzled."

"Puzzled? Okay. I mean, why? I don't get it."

"Puzzled. You are not obviously a stupid man. You have waived, or at least not exercised, the right to be represented by counsel. You have tendered information to us here, all building up to a substantial and useful statement, a statement I'm assuming you'll sign your name to this evening."

"I stand over everything I said here, that's right."

"Good, Mr. Kenny. Very good. Listen, now. You are right to be afraid of the Egans. It is a sensible and natural reaction. It's an adaptive behavior that has brought us out of the mud and the jungle to a fine city like ours here. With all its faults, of course. Many people are afraid of the Egans. That is business for the Egans. They make money out of fear. Now you seem to recognize that your rashness had led you to a pretty pass here. It's after bringing you over the line where the law is concerned."

"Technically, maybe," said Kenny. "But you'll see the package with your own eyes. It hasn't been touched by me. Where is that Guard anyway, the one who I gave — you gave — my house key to? He should be back by now, shouldn't he? I never gave you or any Guard permission to search the flat for anything more than that, to retrieve that package, I mean."

"Traffic," said Minogue. "You know how it is. Dublin wasn't designed for traffic."

Kenny tapped his fingers flat on the palm of his other hand.

"Look. I swear it was never opened. Don't you understand? It was Mary who made the arrangement, the time. If she had been there, I would have given it back to her. I would have dumped it on the path at the very least if she was still nuts. If she had just *been* there! You see? She should have *been* there when she said. I keep thinking that. She should have *been* there."

Wrong, thought Minogue. Mary Mullen didn't belong there. She had worked her way out of that place. She had been determined never to go back.

"You were late, Kenny," he murmured. "That's what did it."

Kenny's stare slid to the tabletop. His hands began to work through his hair again.

"You wanted to teach her a lesson," Minogue went on. "Didn't you?"

"I never thought . . ."

"You wanted to show her that you weren't going to be pushed around by a — well, Mr. Kenny, perhaps you have the word for her? No? 'Who does she think she is,' right?"

"You've got it wrong. The most of it anyway."

"Okay, Mr. Kenny. This is why I said I am puzzled. You have told us things that could incriminate you further. And still you haven't gone baying for a solicitor."

"I've nothing to hide."

"I've worked on the squad awhile, Mr. Kenny. I have this picture of you in my mind's eye, driving over to the canal. On time. Ahead of time, even. I see you annoyed at her. Ready to lose your temper. You look after yourself, Mr. Kenny. In the physical line, I mean. Bet you have a substantial arm from that squash, don't you?"

"Squash? What does that have to do with anything?"

"You have means, Mr. Kenny. You have motive. Client or no client, dinner or no dinner, you cannot yet account for all of your movements that evening. So now I see that you have opportunity."

He stopped and looked at Kenny's head going from side to side. Were the roots a different color?

"All right. Let's go at it again. The first time, she dropped the bag onto your lap . . ."

·   ·   ·   ·   ·

"Are you sure?" asked Kilmartin. Minogue's mug slipped and hit the desktop with a bang.

"Not once," he repeated.

"Ah, go on with you. I bet he knew, the bugger. Accountants aren't stupid, you know. He'd have guessed you'd be looking for the giveaway. 'Expecting'? 'Pregnant'?"

Minogue said nothing. He looked over at Malone. The detective was still talking quietly into the phone. Leaning in over the desktop, Malone seemed to be trying to smooth the deep lines in his forehead.

"Not even 'in trouble'?" said Kilmartin. "That's a good old reliable, isn't it?"

"No. He thinks he had been set up from the beginning. He puts it down to pressure on her from the Egans to rope him in good and proper."

"Huh. Maybe he thinks he has us codded. Kenny. Any percentage in us picking him up again and working on him tonight?"

Minogue looked down into his own mug. *Paris: capitale du monde.* Kathleen had bought it for him four years ago. He had mended the same break in the handle twice now.

"No, Jim. Let him sit in it. A sleepless night will do him good."

"Joseph Byrne," said Kilmartin. "The oul lad with the dog and the honest wife. He hears the row at ten o'clock. Kenny gets there late for the showdown, the final payment. It could fit."

Kilmartin pushed a folder in toward the center of the desktop and folded his arms. He stared at Minogue's mug from Paris for several moments. Then his face wrinkled up and he twitched.

"Ah, Christ," he hissed. "What am I thinking? Sure Byrne is half blind! I saw a copy of his prescription that you got. Jesus, he couldn't see the Holy Ghost if He appeared to him at the end of the bloody bed. Couldn't put Byrne in a witness box, man. It'd be a circus."

Minogue took another mouthful of coffee. He held it at the back of his mouth before he let it drop down his throat. Malone was nodding slowly now. He could see the mark of the earpiece on Malone's ear as he shifted it. He looked at the clock. Phone Iseult's again. Kilmartin rubbed his eyes.

"Kenny didn't think she was bluffing about getting a heavy to work him over," said Minogue.

"I'll buy that all right. He believed her enough to rake up a good lump of money."

"So did she, could she, would she?"

Kilmartin looked across at Malone. Still yakking away. Looked worn out.

"If it was a planned job from the start, in with the Egans, I mean, she would have called in the likes of Lenehan . . . Ahhh. A load of crap!"

"What is?"

"Almighty God!" Kilmartin cried out. "Maybe he didn't clock her, but by God, he knows more than he's told you! This Kenny creature . . . He's lying, lying, lying. Frigging lying! Come on, man. Hold him over. Let him get as scared of us as he is of the bloody Egans!"

Minogue shrugged off Kilmartin's pique.

"I still say leave him out there. Let him sweat."

"If she's freelance trying to put a con on Kenny, would she bluff about calling in a heavy? I don't know . . . Hhhnnnkkk. God, the wind."

A whiff of Kilmartin's burp came to Minogue. Bluff, he wondered; would she have given Kenny another chance to come up with the money? Or had she run out of time?

"Never screeched for the solicitor in the end."

Kilmartin wheezed and coughed and belched again.

"Huh. You'd expect the likes of him to be all over the shop, calling in the UN. Stampedes of barristers running down the halls."

"Point in his favor, I had to conclude, James."

"Really, Captain? So's the fact he puked all over the jakes, you'll be telling me next."

"So's the fact he pu —"

"All right, all right! Very smart."

"Tell me something now before I go, Jim. Do you remember Maura being pregnant?"

"Maura? My Maura? My current wife?"

"Yes. That Maura."

Kilmartin gave his colleague a flinty glare.

"There are some things I don't mind forgetting. What about Kathleen? Shouldn't your memory be twice as good as mine? Sorry. Three times, I meant to say."

"I remember Kathleen being sick with Iseult."

"Long before she got to be a teenager?"

"I'll tell her that one, James. She'll love that one. Your timing couldn't be worse."

"What is this anyway? Are you after joining up some group to get in touch with your feelings or something? Who was it put out the idea that life is a shagging holiday anyway?"

Kilmartin paused to wipe his mouth with the back of his hand.

"'Cause if you're into that stuff, you better keep way to hell away from me. I can't abide that shite."

"You do remember then."

"Damn right I do."

He leaned toward Minogue to whisper.

"Why do you think we have only the one?" He sat back again and examined his nails.

"World War III around the house, as I recall. Jases, we could have had the Russians beat into the ground with a platoon of expectant mothers. Honor of God, man! And the humors! Floods of tears and then the next thing she'd look like a holy picture or something. All cuddly and what have you, full of plans, talking all night long. Oh, well I remember that bit. Too well! 'The nesting instinct.' New curtains, crockery, furniture, paint the house — God in heaven, man, sure I was years paying it off! Running around like a red-shank I was. She was ordered off the feet in the finish-up. Swelling in the legs."

Kilmartin swilled the remains of his tea in the mug.

"Hormones, man. Sure you know yourself. Giddy: pure giddy. Wild out by times."

"Did she ever offer — threaten, I mean — to maim you? In a red-hot row, like."

"Mind your own business. That's personal."

"Did she, Jim?"

Kilmartin gave him a limpid stare for several seconds.

"What kind of a question is that? Of course she did. Is there a married man above ground that hasn't had that? Wake up there. It's par for the course, that stuff."

"Out of character for Maura, of course."

"To be sure it was. Oh, now I get it! You're playing doctor! This diagnosis of Mary Mullen flying off the handle due to having a bun in the oven?"

"Pressure, Jim. She was desperate."

"Christ, she's not the only one. You're telling me that she lost the head? It's not the same these days, you know. 'In trouble': I'll tell you who's in trouble — it's the likes of you and me what's having to pay Social Welfare for these single mothers sitting around the house on their fannies."

Kilmartin's epiglottis issued a wet flap as he downed the last of his tea. It was followed by another gassy belch between his teeth.

"Plenty of work to be done," he growled. "I don't care what they say in the lab. They're going to go over the videos again, bejases. And all this talk about computer enhancements! Sure, the frigging machine does everything. What are they complaining about?"

It took several moments for Minogue to realize what his colleague was talking about. The video footage of the site, the gawkers that night, the parked cars.

"What about the Big Bust, James."

"What are you on about now? Elizabeth Taylor, is it?"

"Keane. The police officers here and in our brethren European countries who are waiting for D-Day on the Egans."

"Oh, very clever. Ask me something else."

"Plate-glass Sheehy's brigade. Have they new stuff?"

"Nothing since this Kenny lead."

"No bag?"

"No bag."

"Jack Mullen?"

"Much as it pains me to tell you, pal, Holy Jack Mullen is almost in the clear. John Murtagh traced a fare last night, a drive-off what never showed on the meter."

"No Hickey?" Kilmartin cleared his throat.

"No Hickey. But maybe these Egans'll get him first."

Minogue picked up his mug and stood. Malone was walking in arcs the length of the phone wire now, nodding and listening. Minogue eyed Kilmartin.

"Listen, you big Mayo bullock. I'm taking time to rake over all the statements again. We've missed someone or something. I'll even pick up Patricia Fahy again. Kenny. Anyone. Who could Mary have called in, if she wasn't bluffing — that's what we have to know."

Kilmartin began pushing his mug around the desktop.

"Listen to you," he muttered. "You Clare *gámóg*. Tough guy, are you? Maybe the answer is right under our noses but we're too busy gawking all over with binoculars. Think Hickey, man. What have you got stuck in your brain there with him, anyhow? Is it just because he does a bit of the art stuff that you think he could never commit a murder? Sure man dear, the wind is whistling through his alibi."

Minogue decamped to his own desk. Malone was still on the other phone. By the look on his face, Minogue judged that he was trying to explain something that he knew his listener couldn't or wouldn't understand.

CHAPTER 21

Minogue phoned his daughter's flat. He let it ring seven times before he hung up.

Malone was peeling back the Elastoplasts from his knuckles, rolling them back on. He looked up as the inspector sauntered over.

"A bit more of the other stuff, Tommy?"

Malone nodded.

"Trouble all right. Terry. He's left the house. Said something about going over to see Bobby Egan. What am I going to do?"

Minogue shrugged. Malone nodded at the door to Kilmartin's office.

"It could screw up everything," he said. "What do you think?"

"I don't know what to tell you. Except to keep away from him. Can you do that?"

"Christ. It's like a game they're playing. I could kill them for this."

"How's your ma?"

Malone sighed. He yanked one of the plasters clean off his knuckle and studied it.

"In bits."

"Go visit her then."

"Aw, Jesus — excuse me. I can't. Really. I mean I've already taken time off yesterday —"

"Go, will you. We'll be okay."

Malone looked up from his raw knuckles at the inspector.

"You think I'd better get away from here so's you-know-who in there doesn't get under my skin enough to . . . You know?"

Minogue nodded.

"What am I going to do though? Here's me own brother being pulled into this crap and I'm going to sit by? I can't. But if I have him picked up . . . I don't know. I just don't."

"Go to your ma's, Tommy. Phone me."

"You sure?"

"Go. I'll square it with the Killer. But phone me."

. . . . .

"Well," said Kilmartin. He capped the marker and stepped away from the board. Minogue put down the copies of the statements. He looked at Kenny's name and followed the line for the evening.

"Julie Quinn," said Kilmartin. "Kenny's fiasco. Spotless alibi all evening."

Minogue pressed his fingers harder onto the desktop until the nails went from pink to white.

"Does she know anything about his extracurricular activities, the nightclubbing? Mary Mullen?"

"She said that she's been to the clubs with Kenny. Never heard of a Mary or anything about the case. I told her then what was up. She came on strong, Matt, I tell you. Shocked that his name would have come up at all. She started giving me a list of people I could call to check on her little Alan. References, the story of their romance, what she had for breakfast —"

"They live together, right?"

"They do," replied Kilmartin. "Didn't hesitate to tell me either. She's as clean as a new brush."

Minogue stopped pressing down with his fingers and watched the nails turn pink again.

"So Alan Kenny has all the more to protect then," he said.

"Meaning?"

"That we really don't know how he'd react if Mary Mullen tried to blackmail him with snapshots. Would he care a damn? Would this Julie Quinn? I just don't know. He's no mug. I think he's the kind of fella who'd want to see them, to prove they exist."

"So there's still the two separate worlds: Ms. Quinn the fiasco, all the linen and lace, and then the slumming and slagging around with Mary Mullen. How'd he hold it together?"

"'The edge,' Kenny calls it."

"'The edge'? Slinky suits and hairdos. Telephone in the pocket. I see

more of them every day. The type'd cut you in two in the traffic. Frig-
ging counter-jumpers. And they want everything now, right this minute.
A crooked breed we're rearing these days, with our United Europe shite.
Christ, man, we were better off in the bog."

"You were maybe."

Kilmartin's eyelids drooped.

"Is that the way with you? Busy pissing on the Kenny blackmail idea,
but I don't seem to remember you leaping across the floor and into my
office there with the case cleared. Did I miss that?"

Minogue kept his gaze on the statements on his desk. Kilmartin
turned his head.

"Whose is that?"

"Tierney, James Tierney. Patricia Fahy's beau."

"Are you getting anything from it maybe?"

"A headache."

"Speaking of which, where's Molly? Voh' Lay-bah, the owil yuunion's
nummbahr waahn!"

The chief inspector suddenly waltzed across the floor.

> *"He wheels his wheelbarrow*
> *Through streets broad and narrow*
> *Crying cockles and mussels*
> *Alive-alive-O"*

He turned on the balls of his feet and let his imaginary partner rest on
his arm.

"Next dance, please. Well, where is he?"

"Jimmy: give over. He has stuff to deal with."

"And we don't?"

"Don't come to me looking for half your jawbone if you push him
over the edge. Call it quits."

"No sticking power, that's the problem. If Molly can't —"

"Who scored the winning goal for United on the night of Mary
Mullen's murder?"

"What? Who cares? Why the hell would I know that?"

"James Tierney knows. It's in his statement."

"So?"

"And the other goal-scorers. The penalty that was missed. The fella
given the yellow card."

"Oh, great. Soccer is a load of cobblers anyhow. Gurriers, beer cans, riots. Like England."

"I wonder if his girlfriend is so keen on it. Patricia Fahy."

"On what? The you-know-what?"

"The soccer."

"I hope not —"

Minogue grabbed the phone before it had finished its first ring.

"My God, you're fast," said Kathleen. Minogue sat back and let out a breath.

"For a married man," he said. "Is it yourself that's in it, love."

Kilmartin nodded and moved off. Kathleen asked if he would be home for tea. The inspector didn't know whether he had an appetite or not. He told her he'd probably have to stay late. She talked about an apartment that had come on the market today. He felt the outside of his coffee mug. The back of his tongue was still sour and chalky nearly an hour after he had drunk the last cup. He looked down at the file folder of statements he had been reading and began to push the cup around it. Like a boat trying to land on an island, he thought. The mug slowed. He pushed harder and it tipped.

"Goddamn that bloody! —"

"Pardon?" asked Kathleen. "Pardon?"

He grasped the corner of the folder and yanked it up. Sheets slid and darted out, floating down to the floor. The coffee spread in a pool the size of a saucer. A map the shape of Africa, he thought.

"Spilled something," he said. "Give me a minute." He laid the receiver down and dithered. Kilmartin reappeared by the desk.

"Christ, you're an awful messer," said the chief inspector. He took out a packet of paper hankies, dropped them on the desk, and began picking up the statements. Minogue dropped the tissues at strategic intervals over the spill.

"Use the tail of your shirt," said the chief inspector. "Like the rest of the Clare crowd."

Minogue lifted a saturated hanky and squinted at Kilmartin.

"Jim. Thanks. Now go out and play on the train lines. There's a Cork train due."

"Ah, howiya there, Kathleen," Kilmartin called out. "Take him home, will you. He's losing the run of himself here."

Minogue spoke between clenched teeth.

"Jim says hello."

"Do you see an end to it all soon, love?" she asked.

"Not really. I'm trying to find anything we might have missed."

"Ah. Well, have you spoken to her?"

Minogue looked down at the brown mess where his coffee had been. Definitely Africa. He wondered if his headache would get worse.

"Who?"

"Iseult. Your daughter."

"Sorry. No. I tried the flat, but there was no answer. Listen, did she drop a hint as she flew the coop?"

"She just leaped up from the table and out the door with her. It's the wedding. The cancelation, I mean."

"Yes."

"Maybe there's some way to talk her out of it. Get her to see reason. Talk to poor Pat maybe?"

Poor Pat? He studied the flash of the outside line on his phone, its constant glow as Murtagh picked it up.

"I'll try her again around teatime," he said.

"Yes. And you could suggest to her —"

Murtagh was waving and pointing at the receiver in his left hand. Kilmartin walked smartly to Hoey's desk and grabbed the extension.

"Have to go, Kathleen. Got a call. I'll phone you back."

"It's Hickey," Murtagh whispered. He tapped at his head. "Sounds like he's out of it." Minogue's heart began to beat faster.

"Ready to try again then?" he whispered to Murtagh. He pushed down the button.

"Liam? This is Matt Minogue. How are you?"

He heard the dull bass of television voices nearby.

"How do you fucking think I am?"

Murtagh waved. He had the line open to Communications.

"I'm glad you called, Liam. I was hoping you would."

"So's you get another chance? I seen yous racing around the place two minutes after I dropped the phone, man! What kind of fucking treatment is that?"

Slurred all right. Minogue bit his lip.

"It's police procedure, Liam. Straight out."

"Wait a minute there, you! Just hold on there a minute! This isn't how it's supposed to be. Why amn't I getting more of the social worker crap?

'Come on, Liam, I understand your problems.' Huh? 'Let's talk about it, Liam.' What if I just drop the bleeding phone right now?"

Minogue waited for several seconds.

"Then you'd be a damn liar, Liam. You're no friend of Mary's."

The inspector looked around the squadroom. Murtagh was rubbing his ear. Kilmartin's brow had lifted and the inspector caught a glimpse of teeth as they scraped on his upper lip. Hickey wasn't talking.

"So prove me wrong, Liam."

"Don't . . . you . . . fucking talk to me like that! What gives you the — I could just drop the phone —"

"Listen to me, Liam. Your alibi is coming out pretty clean. Tell me who you fenced the stuff to, the camera and the jacket."

"Why? So's I get the guy into trouble and have him and his mates after me too? All he'd tell you anyway is the opposite of what I'm telling you. 'Never heard of the guy.' Christ, that's what I'd say if the cops landed in on top of me, man! Forget it."

"Well, give me something definite then. I mean, someone else could have robbed the stuff and told you about it. Tell me what else you took out of the car."

"What do you mean, what else?"

"If you're lying, you don't know what I mean then, do you?"

"A Walkman. I kept it."

"What kind of a Walkman?"

"Sony. The batteries ran out."

"What tape was in it?"

"What kind of a fucking question —"

"What tape was in it, Liam?"

"What's the guy. He has a group. The guitar guy. Ahhh . . . Dire Straits. *Brothers in Arms.*"

"What did you do with it?"

"I still have it in the . . . Wait a minute. What are you trying to do here? You'll pull me in on robbing the car and then throw me somewhere the Egans can nail me!"

The drone of a conversation blended with the bass, excited and indecipherable tones of a television ad. Minogue looked down at his scribble. *Brothers in Arms.* Had he heard that one before?

"Come on in, Liam. We can put you in a safe place."

"Where, for Christ's sake? For how long? My only chance is out here!

But you guys are out there, still trying to run me down as well!"

"Meet me, Liam. Just me."

"You're nuts! Even if I did, what good would it do? I don't know anything about Mary. I come in, you want answers that I don't have! I don't *know* what she was into, man!"

"You might know something we could use and still —"

"To hell with you!"

"Give me a middleman then. Someone you trust."

"Like who?"

"Your friend, Tierney. Your ma says you and he are pals, right?"

"Jammy? Hah! We used to be. But he hates my guts now. Jesus! When he found out about Mary, he treats me like AIDS man. Christ! He always . . . Forget it."

"He always what?"

"Forget it, I said! I'm going to drop this fucking phone —"

"Why not Tierney?"

"Jammy's a gobshite like anyone else. He heard the Egans were on the warpath. He's so straight, he's like a fucking . . ."

"What?"

"Ah, they were opposites. Mary liked the life. Jammy's thick. He couldn't figure that out. He doesn't know how people work. That's just the way with some people."

"You all grew up together —"

"'Course we fucking did! As if you didn't know that already! That's ages — way back, yeah. Everything's mad when you're thirteen. A few jars out in the back fields before they built the cardboard factory out there. Next thing you know is you're doing it, like. The girls, you know? But Jammy couldn't get near her. Ah, what am I talking about?"

Minogue's hand closed tighter on the pen. He began to stab it slowly and deliberately into the mess of tissues and coffee. He didn't want to see the expression on Kilmartin's face.

"Don't leave it hanging, Liam. You can help. You can."

"I'm no fucking mug! I got to look out for Number One, man!"

Thoughts flew faster through Minogue's mind.

"We have to talk, Liam. There's got to be a way. Pick a spot —"

"I'm gone, man. I'm gone!"

"Pick a time, Liam. Any time. I guarantee —"

"Fuck you and your guarantee! Eddsy Egan had a guy's throat slit in the 'Joy three years ago! And Eddsy's still walking the streets!"

Minogue squeezed the pen tight and closed his eyes. The line went dead. He flung the receiver on the desk. Murtagh leaped up out of his chair. "Pub phone," he called out. "Barney's, in Capel Street."

. . . . .

Minogue handed the note to Éilis.

"Will you kindly get ahold of the fella with the GTI Hickey says he did?"

Éilis looked up at the ceiling and drew on her cigarette.

"Travers," she murmured. "Blackrock." Minogue winked.

"There's the name of the tape that Hickey says he got in the Walkman he robbed. First see if the actual name of the, er, the artist, is inventoried on the Stolen Vehicles report. If you please, Éilis."

She squinted at the sheet and turned it upside down.

"I'll be needing it translated, your honor. 'Brothers . . .'?"

"*Brothers in Arms.*"

Minogue returned to his desk and flopped into his chair. He rested his chin on his fist and stared at the phone. Kilmartin sat on the edge of Minogue's desk looking down at the floor. Minutes crawled by. The phone didn't ring.

"Damn," said Minogue. "They'd be on to us by now if they'd nabbed him."

"Ah, hold your whist," said Kilmartin. He seemed to be scrutinizing the inspector's forehead. Perhaps it had just dawned on Kilmartin that Barney's was on the edge of a warren of streets and alleys that led on and through the Markets up to Smithfield.

"A little unorthodox there on the phone, weren't we, Watson?" he whispered. Minogue glared at him.

"No, we weren't."

"What was the rationale to driving into his face the way you did, then?"

"He was drunk, Jim. I thought I could go direct while he was out of it. Maudlin and the rest of it. Prolong the call."

Kilmartin threw his empty cigarette package across the room. It missed the bin by two feet. He stood.

"Maybe there's a Guard off the Olympic team on foot patrol up there in the Markets."

"Maybe," sighed Minogue. He rose from his chair. "I need some air. Out of the way or I'm going through you."

"Oh, the tough talk is out now, is it? Hold me back. Learn to relax, man."

The air was muggy and thick with the tang of exhaust and hops from the Guinness brewery. He strolled about the yard, his thoughts on Iseult. Drive by her studio, that's where she'd hidden out. Entice her out for a walk and a pint? That'd get her talking. He was leaning against the boot of his Citroen when Kilmartin emerged. From the chief inspector's wary hangdog gait, Minogue concluded failure.

Kilmartin paused to light a cigarette.

"Well, Jim?"

Kilmartin shook his head. Minogue swore.

"And the rest of it. He's alive, he's scared. We'll find him."

"He's also smart, James. He picks his phones very damn well."

"We'll bag him yet, old son. Barman put it at about two minutes between him hightailing it and a Guard bursting in the door. Left a half pint of beer on the counter behind him too, the little shite. But it's not over, old bean. There are a half-dozen cars in the area."

Kilmartin blew out smoke, cleared his throat in a long, modulated gurgle, and spat across the yard.

"Look at the time now, for the love of Jases," he groaned. "No wonder you're gone crooked. Are you lost without your new sidekick?"

"Keep it up, Jim. You'll probably get your wish."

There was an outbreak of hurt innocence on Kilmartin's face.

"Oh, is it my fault for trying to insist we hire dependable and dedicated staff?"

"He can't help it if he has a family, for God's sake, or if his brother ran amok, can he?"

"Oh, I forgot — everybody's a victim these days. Quick, fetch me a consultant — a counselor!"

"In case you forgot, Jim, you're not supposed to take family details into account from his personnel file. It's strictly performance, commendations, record —"

"I know that, Professor."

Kilmartin, in his truant, shifty schoolboy incarnation, let his tongue swell his cheek.

"What's the latest bulletin on this soap opera of a family of his anyhow."

"Terry the brother is all over the place. He has a drug problem. He's gotten in with the Egans. They got to him right when he walked from the 'Joy. They're going to destroy him. Tommy thinks they're trying to take him down in the job too. Quits for arresting Lenehan."

"Well, there's a thesis now. This is real Egan style, I daresay."

Minogue nodded.

"That's right. Nobody's immune."

"You think they might be blackguarding our Molly somehow, using the brother?"

"They might try but he won't go."

Kilmartin's eyes lingered on his colleague's for a moment before he looked down at the Citroen.

"Here, let's climb aboard this rig and I'll buy you your tea."

"Sorry, James. I'm going to drop by Iseult's studio."

"Fine and well. I didn't want to be seen in this frigging nancy-boy spaceship anyway."

Minogue held up his fist. Kilmartin shoved the cigarette into the corner of his mouth and made a feint. Minogue went into a crouch.

"Plan for six months in traction there, you bullock! Tommy Malone gave me tips."

"Go to hell, you Clare lug! It's yourself that'll get the astronomy lessons here!"

• • • • •

Christ! Couldn't a fella read the bleeding paper anymore? He tried again to ignore the barman. The gobshite behind the bar must have wiped the counter twenty times since he'd come in. Maybe he was drinking too fast or something. But it was a hot day, for Jases' sakes! He was still jittery after the row on the phone, the running from Barney's. He peered over the top of the paper again. What a kip. Things living in the carpet. The stink of the place was made even worse by the smells of the rotting fruit and vegetables and fish hanging in the air all around the markets. They should knock the place down. He finished the pint. Which one was that, number three or four? Three. He looked at the clock. Three pints in a half an hour. He watched the two oul lads cocked up on stools by the bar. At least they weren't bothering him anymore, trying to put talk on him. Another fella had come in a few minutes ago, a big fella with an apron. The barman had a pint ready for him and he downed it in about ten seconds. Not a word out of him. At first he'd thought it was a cop and he

{ 269 }

was up out of the seat before the guy had stepped through the door properly. Yeah, maybe that's what had done it.

He studied the leftover froth on the sides of the glass. Maybe the barman was trying to fit him to some picture he'd seen but didn't remember enough. Surely to God there weren't pictures of him up, in the papers. Up on walls: "Wanted Leo Hickey. Murder." Jesus! He folded his paper and looked down at the seat beside him for his cigarettes. He didn't want to go, he realized. He didn't want to be out there in the streets. He didn't want to go back to the park. He let himself lean back against the seat. He hadn't been ten steps from the phone when he'd heard the the tires of the squad car through the open door of the pub. Straight out the side door into the laneway and through the markets. What a pack of lying bastards, the Guards. They must have had the cars ready again, waiting for him. That could only mean they had him fitted for this, for Mary. Even that guy, the culchie who'd told him straight out: standard procedure, Liam.

Why was the guy still looking at him, for Christ's sake? He stood up. The bar seemed to move with him. Hey! He felt in his pocket for the knife. The bar seemed brighter now. The barman was rubbing the counter again, but slowly now. He saw his own face in the mirror. A sight. No wonder he'd been keeping an eye on him. The anger began to drain out of him. He let go of the knife and grasped the coins instead.

"Here. Give us another pint there."

He watched the barman pouring it, pretending to watch the filling glass but watching him at the same time.

"Any grub here, man? Sandwiches or stuff?"

"Crisps —"

"Okay. Three crisps. Smokey Bacon?"

The barman looked up from the glass. The two old geezers had stopped talking. Christ, why was the kip so quiet? Didn't they have a telly or anything?

"— or peanuts," the barman added.

"Yeah, well, all I want is the crisps, see? Smokey Bacon."

The barman placed the pint on the counter. Why was he moving so slowly? He turned aside to get the bags of crisps.

"Three bags of Smokey Bacon," he said. He turned back, placed them next to the pint and rested his hands on the countertop to either side of the glass. Now he was looking straight at him. What the hell was this guy's problem? Like this was such a fancy place they didn't want riffraff or something? Like, it was so fucking exclusive or something? He let his hand slide back into the pocket. His fingers closed on the knife again. He imagined his hand coming out of the pocket so fast, the blade opened already and coming down on the guy's hand: right through it, pinning it to the counter. Right into the counter.

His hand came out with the fiver crunched up inside. He dropped it on the counter. The barman spoke in the same flat voice.

"Five pounds."

What had he ever done to this guy? Was it just the way he looked or something? Did he stink and he didn't even know it? The bar seemed to be changing around him. Christ, he really should get a decent meal before he . . .

"That's a hot one, I'm telling you all right," someone was saying. He turned. One of the oul lads. His forehead was shining.

"Yeah," he heard himself say. "Isn't it."

"But there's going to be rain like was never seen before, I read."

Something about the oul lad's face reminded him of something, of someone he knew. Keeping the peace, he was. He must have been reading his mind. Could he know about the knife?

"Rain . . ."

"Oh, that's a fact! If you're to believe those chancers what give the forecast."

The glass was cool and wet in his hand. He saw the downpour beating down the leaves of the chestnut tree that he had hoped would be his home. Of course it had to piss rain, he thought. It was always that way. The minute you thought you were getting somewhere. It came to him as a pain then, like that heartburn he used to get when he was a kid. Everything wrong. Just impossible. He brought the crisps and the pint back to the table and flopped down in the seat. He'd go out later, he decided. He had money and he had a knife. He didn't really give a damn anymore.

·   ·   ·   ·   ·

Her eyes filled with tears. Coming here, he said, but his lips didn't move, coming here to surprise her was a very, very stupid idea. No sleep tonight if he were to tell Kathleen. If? When. He'd have to tell her. He stared at her. Paint had dried under her nails. Strands of hair had escaped her hairband. Some part of him must have known already, he understood.

"Is that all you can say?" she whispered. "Try to say something funny."
Things crashed about in his head. Grandfather; babysitting; bottles; nappies. He would always remember this time, this place. The big windows with peeling paint and putty that kept the studio like a fridge in winter — the landlord's hint to Iseult and the co-op of just how annoyed he was that he had given them such a lease before the area had become so suddenly trendy several years ago.

"Sorry," he said. "I only meant the Immaculate part."

He turned aside and looked down into the street below. A cluster of young people whom Minogue took to be artists of some kind crossed the street below and disappeared into the pub. A girl with hacked hair and a green tuft shooting up from the crown pedaled by. The windows in the studio were wide open but it was still uncomfortably warm. Everything seemed very far away: the rest of the buildings, the streets and laneways already gray, the traffic noise from the Liffey quays a street away, his memories of Iseult's childhood.

"Well, maybe it'd be funny some other time," she said. She pulled the apron over her head. "I'd never thought of Pat as the Holy Ghost."

She walked over to the windows and stood next to him. That cloud was there again, the one that looked like the mushroom cloud from an atomic bomb. It must be far out at sea.

"You get really tired," she said. "I didn't know that happened so much."

"Well, this is your first time."

"Don't tell Ma — ever — but I thought straightaway of going to London. You know?"

He nodded. Like a hunter in the blind, dozing, he thought, awakening to a stampede all around him. Over him.

"It's true," she said. "The thing about Clare people. How they're different. The sixth sense."

"Clare people are cracked, Iseult. Everyone knows that. Exhibit number one here. Can we go out for a stroll or something? The fumes here are getting to me."

She stopped in the middle of the Ha'penny bridge and leaned against the railings. The Liffey below was close to full tide. Vibrations from the passing feet came up through Minogue's knees. A bus screeched on its way down the quays. There wasn't a breeze.

"We must be in for a change of weather," she said. "I've had a headache all day."

Minogue let his eyes wander down the quays, taking in the sluggish swill of the river, the quayside buildings in a wash of honey-colored light. He felt that Iseult and he were on an island in the middle of Dublin.

"I knew you knew," she sniffed. "I felt it anyway. Really."

"I didn't really know," he said. "I sort of thought maybe . . . Well, it doesn't matter. It's great news. I'm thrilled."

She eyed him.

"Are you okay for walking here?" he asked.

"Of course I am. Typical man! It's not an illness, you know."

Minogue glanced at her.

"Is Pat excited?"

"He was, last time I saw him. Then he was worried. Then he went into his moron stage. Holy water and rosary beads next. Jesus, I'm still bowled over by it all."

Minogue did not rise to the bait. He kept his eyes on O'Connell Bridge.

"Pathetic, isn't it," she said. "'I'm 'in trouble.'"

He looked over. Her nostrils were still red.

"In trouble," he said, and frowned.

"Well, isn't that the expression? Or is it only old fogies talk like that anymore?"

"Why ask me? Come on down the quays a bit, can't you."

She fell into step beside him. They waited for the lights at Capel Street.

"You like Pat, don't you?" she asked. "Still, I mean."

"Yes."

"Even with this church stuff?"

He shrugged.

"Well, yes. Clumsy maybe, but decent, I say. Give him a chance, will you?"

Iseult stepped away from him and folded her arms. Others had clustered around them waiting for the light also. He fingered the button again. Why was it taking so long to get across here?

"What's so 'decent' about wanting to get married in a church, for Christ's sake?"

He bit his lip and kept his finger pushed against the button.

"I could still kill Pat, you know," she declared.

"A little louder there," he said between his teeth. "They may not have heard you in Wales."

"I don't bloody well care, do I? I could *kill* him!"

"You told me that before. The more you say it, the worse it sounds."

"I could! I'd break his neck, so I would."

"Stop, Iseult. That doesn't help."

"Huh. You just don't like to hear it out loud. Whose side are you on, anyway?"

"I don't even know there are different sides really. It's not like your mother would want to shanghai you either, you know —"

"Oh, come on! Are you going to fall into line with Holy Ireland too?" He glared at her.

"Well?" she prodded. "Don't you ever take sides? Huh? Whose side are you on, Da?"

"Homicide, Iseult, if you really want to know."

CHAPTER 22

KILMARTIN HAD GONE home. Minogue perused the note the chief inspector had left him. Jack Mullen was now down to one twenty-minute span — trouble was, the time was around nine o'clock. The note from Éilis was cryptic but complete. GTI — Br. in A. — yes. *Brothers in Arms* was the title of the tape. Hickey was closer to being in the clear. Now, how the hell was he supposed to get back on board if Hickey turned out to be going nowhere?

Murtagh was reading the evening paper. The inspector saw no sandwich but he could smell onion somewhere.

"Well, John."

Murtagh looked up. Minogue became suddenly baffled. What had he wanted to tell Murtagh that it looked like he was going to be a grandfather? Iseult had rebuffed his pleas to come to Kilmacud for the night at least. No amount of talk about croissants, hot baths, sitting in the garden, doing nothing, or catching up on her reading persuaded her. He had left her at her studio. She had not asked him in. He had nearly clipped the end of a van coming down through Kilmainham, a place he shouldn't have been in but that he couldn't remember turning into. Was this the same as being drunk?

"Well, boss?"

Murtagh was still looking at him.

"Sorry, John."

"Are you all right there?"

And what did that mean? Giddy. Everything so vivid and changed as he'd driven through the streets.

"I think so. Yes. You're er? . . ."

"I was going over the timetable again, looking for cracks."

Minogue looked up to the notice-board. Kilmartin had updated the line for Mullen. The gap began with "20:45?" and the thick green line resumed with "21:20 (log)." He walked closer, looking down the names. Lenehan filled in completely, three names to account for him. One, a J. Mahon, did not have an X for criminal record. His eyes slid down by the Egans to the orange line leading out from Leo Hickey's name.

"Still no word on Hickey?"

"Nope," said Murtagh. "He did a natty disappearing act after the call, and that's a fact."

"Talk to anyone about him recently?"

"All the patrol units have the description. The Killer got Central to leave two cars set aside. They're out there until midnight."

He let down the paper, stretched, and scratched at the back of his head.

"What's the world coming to?" he sighed. "No United in the cup. The first time in five years."

Minogue flopped down at his desk and stared at the notepad he had left. Ryan — photo files; Alan Kenny — he looked back up at the notice board. The gaps for Kenny remained but the alibis had names now. He recognized the names of the two pubs in brackets. Upmarket, he believed, all the rage in the lotsamoney eighties. Weren't they too bloody busy in those pubs to reliably keep track of the likes of Kenny? Murtagh was looking at him.

"Yes, John?"

"You're, er, well, you're sure?"

"Sure of what?"

"That you're okay, like?"

Minogue blinked.

"You're gone kind of red . . . Is it sunburn, maybe?"

Minogue began moving the folders and papers about. Murtagh took up the paper again. Would Iseult's baby be a few lines in the Births, Marriages, and Death columns early in the new year? His eyes stayed on the headline over the photo of a sweaty headed player holding his head in his hands. "The Good Life Over."

"What's that good life they're talking about being over, John?"

Murtagh smiled.

"Ah, United had their name on the F.A. Cup this last few years. Injuries done them in this year but. They're out of the running now."

"Since?"

"Last night really. Ah, sure it was time for them. They were in trouble from last month when what's-his-face got a broken ankle. Brown. Downtown Brown? He was the heart of the team. Should have seen the tackle that brought him down. Oh, yes. That'll go down in history books, so it will."

"When was that?"

"Last Thursday three weeks. It was about seven minutes to go and . . . What? Did I say something?"

"How do you know it was seven minutes?"

Murtagh smiled.

"Taped it, didn't I."

"I didn't know that this soccer mania had taken over in the Guards too."

"Are you, er, finally going to break down and take an interest in the oul soccer, boss?"

Minogue remembered Murtagh's good-natured jibes at the height of last year's hysteria when Ireland looked like making it to the semifinals in the World Cup. Dublin had closed down on the days the Irish team played its matches. Novels were written around the World Cup fever that gripped Dublin. Housekeeping money disappeared into pubs. Newspapers reassigned staff — even their luminary pundits normally only content in their great task of reprobating everyone and everything — to issue *pensées* on the skills, accomplishments, history, status, and future of Irish soccer. Pubs became choked with guff about whether one player's ankle was up to par, another's knee. Had Eddy Gagan, our glorious full forward, looked a bit peeky on his last outing? What about that Danish striker, the one who had destroyed England's defense? Well, the Irish would show that fella a thing or two about defense: offense too, for that matter!

Minogue had watched and wondered while Ireland suffered and enjoyed another of its galvanic spasms of underdoghood: weren't we great, our gallant little country taking on the world? Soccer had floated the entire nation on a rising tide of hope and pride. He had heard Kathleen detailing scores, moves, prospects, and hopes at great length on transatlantic calls to Daithi. Unwise enough to query what all the fuss was about, Minogue had staggered into a blitzkrieg of taunts from Kathleen and Iseult alike: Stuffy! Snob! Culchie! Begrudger! Cynic! Get wir' it — soccer's bleedin' brilliant!

"Have you got a copy of the press release we fired out the day after the murder?"

Murtagh yanked open a drawer and began flipping through files. Minogue phoned Kathleen.

"You're serious, I take it," was her reply to his request.

"As ever."

"You sound a bit odd, that's why."

"Odd?"

"Something in your voice — ah, don't mind. Look, try and get to bed early. You want newspapers for the night this girl was . . . ?"

"Exactly."

"They'd be gone, Matt. Sure bin day was yesterday."

"Would you forage around there with the Costigans or somewhere?"

"Tell me again."

Murtagh laid the copy of the press release on Minogue's desk. Stapled to it was a clipping from one of the evening newspapers.

"I want to know about a soccer match on Monday night."

"What match?"

Minogue tossed the file papers to find the copy of Tierney's statement.

"Hold on a minute. Here. Everton were playing Spurs. Did I say that right?"

"Yes."

"When it was on, when it was over, et cetera."

"All right, love. Listen, were you sitting in a draft or something? Your voice, well — are you a hundred percent?"

Minogue was trying to find the times in Tierney's statement.

"Draft," he said.

"Oh, don't mind me! Listen, did you get ahold of you-know-who?"

"Who's you-know-who?"

"Je — ! God forgive me! Who do you think!"

"Oh, yes. Sorry. She was working in the studio, so she was. She's going home to the flat tonight."

"And how is she? Is she going to at least visit us in the next fifty years?"

Only once, he recalled, had he found himself imagining the baby. Not as a boy or a girl, just as a toddler learning to walk.

"Probably."

"And how does she look?"

"Never looked better, I thought to myself."

"You mean she's over the row with Pat?"

"Not quite. She still wants to claw his eyes out so far as I know."

"Well, how do you mean she never looked better, then?"

Minogue groped for decoys.

"Well, you know how she is when she's talking about something she feels so strongly about, how she's so full of life."

"Full of life? She's supposed to be depressed, if you ask me."

He let her words drag about in his mind.

"Can we talk later, love? I'm a bit addled here. I only stayed late out of guilt really. John Murtagh's been here every evening since, and I was gambling that maybe a suspect would be picked up earlier on in the evening."

Minogue put down the phone and sat back.

"Highlights, John."

Murtagh swiveled around in his chair.

"The football?"

"Yep. There'd be highlights on the news or the sports part of the news, wouldn't there?"

"Yep."

"More than the one station?"

"Oh, sure."

Minogue sat forward, elbows on his knees.

"Okay," he murmured. "Okay."

Murtagh was still looking at him.

"Thanks, John."

He pulled his chair into the desk and grabbed the phone book. It might take awhile. He could probably get the numbers of the British stations from RTE anyway.

·　　·　　·　　·　　·

Five pints he'd had, not four. He belched again. And only the crisps for grub. What time was it? He moved his arm about to get enough light from the lamp at the end of the laneway. Half-nine. He shifted his stance. Something broke underfoot. He stared down and saw bits of glass. A needle. Christ! He moved off into another doorway. The sheet metal felt good under his palms. He lit a cigarette. Maybe the guy'd have a stash with him too. He'd have to remember to hold the knife away from him, against the blade. No, no, no: this was stupid. Just score, pay up, and split. He could phone his ma then. She'd have an idea. Maybe there was some relative she had that he had never been told about, someone in Australia or something. How long did it take to get a passport?

There was that whistle again. He leaned out and looked down toward Mary Street. That was him all right. He could tell by the shape of the hairdo. About bleeding time too. He stepped out into the laneway.

"How's it going, man?" The guy nodded.

"You still want that stuff?"

"Well, yeah. I'm waiting long enough. Where were you? I could have gone off and sorted it out in a half a dozen other places, man."

The guy wasn't more than eighteen. He'd followed him into the jacks back at the pub. He wouldn't be a narc if he was eighteen. Sure, he'd said. He needed ten minutes to sort it out. Friend of his, et cetera. Meet him down Jervis Lane there. Pimples and an attitude; big shirt, baggy pants, high-tops.

"So? How much'd you want?"

"Gimme two. Twenty right?"

He watched him rummage in the deep pockets. It was the scuffing of the shoes behind that alerted him. The other fella was running fast.

"Hey!"

He had his hand on the knife but the guy with the topknot had already hit him. It didn't hurt but somehow he was against the wall now. The second guy came right at him, kicking. He turned sideways and took a kick on his leg. Did they have knuckles?

"Fuck off!" he shouted. "Or I'll do you!"

He kicked back but missed. The first guy had taken something out of his pocket and he was swinging it. A stick? Looking down at the hand for that moment cost him. The kick came in just above his hip. The laneway went suddenly bright with the pain. He couldn't stop himself staggering and sliding along the wall.

"Stop! I'll give you what I got, just don't . . ."

It was a chain, he saw.

"Turn 'em inside out then!" the second guy was shouting. What? Pockets. He had a glimpse of the second face as the guy circled around. Twenties, no pushover.

"Fucking do it, man, or you're gonna die right here!"

If he let his hand down, they might come at him again. He couldn't stand straight. If they'd only stop moving around him . . .

"Okay, okay, I will! Just don't fucking —"

"Drop everything you got there, man!"

He scattered the money on the ground and pulled his pocket out.

"The other one too, you bastard! Come on!"

Where were the cops? Where were the million people who lived in this bleeding city? If he hadn't stayed in that kip and had all those pints . . . He should have just bought cans or something and gone back to the park to have a think. Christ! He thought of the shadows in the grove of trees, the fields . . .

Hairdo was on him and he was trying to knee him in the nuts. He saw the older guy coming in now. The knife slipped out cleanly and he had the full swing of his free arm. It ran along the shoulder and the kid started screaming. He fell back, tottered, and looked down at his hand.

"He's got a knife, Andy! He's after cutting me, man! I'm bleeding like fuck, man!"

He couldn't take his eyes off the kid. He watched him reeling away down the lane holding his shoulder. Was it that easy, he thought. What if he'd cut across the kid's neck. There were drops falling from the kid's elbow and he watched them. The screaming turned to groans and wails.

"Andy! Man! I got to get to a hospital! It won't stop!"

Too late he realized that the older guy hadn't been taken up watching his mate staggering around like he had. The kick cracked against his cheekbone and he went over. He felt the concrete of the laneway on his cheek now. There was a noise like running water all through his head. He knew he had to get up. The guy was calling him names now. The next kick caught him under the armpit and his arm buckled under him. He held on to the knife as he rolled and tried to get his knees under him. The groaning and crying was further away. He got one knee down but everything exploded when the boot connected with the side of his head. This is it, he thought, this is the end of it. He couldn't see now but he knew he had let go the knife. He felt around for it on the pavement. A kick caught him in the shoulder. The kid was back to shouting now.

"It won't stop, Andy! It's bad, it's really bad! You got to help me, man! It's all over the place."

He had to keep the other guy from getting the knife at least. His fingers closed on it at last. The boot came down. It was his own screams he heard. The boot turned and he felt the skin being torn by the cement. The guy was screaming at him now. He twisted and grasped the guy's leg with his other hand. The boot came up. He tried to roll away. The kick caught him in the head again. He couldn't take it. He shouted but it wasn't words now. Another kick. He felt the money under his face now and he grabbed it and flung it into the laneway. There was a whistling sound all around now, like wind around the house. He wriggled away, drawing his arms up about his head. No kick came. Footfalls next to his ear, the sound of the bills being picked up quickly.

"Andy! You've got to, man!"

Footsteps again, in a hurry. Was the guy going away? They stopped.

He rolled around again. The kick seemed to stop everything. Colors, noise, the stink of his own sweaty clothes. His mother's face when she'd be asleep in front of the telly. The trees in the park. He was falling now, and there was nothing he could do.

· · · · ·

"Well, you seem to know what you want," said Kathleen. He eyed her.

"We're having a heat wave, Kathleen. And it's a celebration."

"Any excuse."

Minogue nodded to the barman. The Minogues were in Gerry Byrne's pub in Galloping Green. Minogue liked the place a lot less since the management had banished darts from the bar. With the darts had gone the working-class clientele. Bar and lounge alike now routinely housed clutches of men in golf sweaters.

"You're taking it very well," he observed.

"What choice do I have? I often thought it'd lead to this. Her and Pat. Their arrangement."

He pushed his empty glass with his forefinger.

"We can't live in the past, Matt. God is good."

He closed his eyes for a moment. He had expected fireworks, tears, a call to arms. It was dusk when he had rolled into the driveway. He had hurried her out. For a drive, she had asked? At this time of the evening?

"She's never had a real job," he said. "And Pat looks like he'll stay a student another while."

"Listen," she said. "I'll tell you one thing about Pat. His decision to be married in a church stands to him. He must have known, and that's why he insisted. Whatever else he's done, he's gone up in my estimation, I can tell you that."

The barman let down a fresh pint.

"She knows how we think anyway," Kathleen went on. "She can never say that she didn't. God knows we've had enough rows about this and matters like it this last while. Woman's right to choose and all the rest of it."

Minogue took his change and a mouthful of the lager. Who would sleep the least tonight, he wondered: Iseult, Kathleen or himself? What about Pat? He took another gulp.

"I want to talk to her tomorrow," she said. "So make sure you phone her early."

"Yes, Kathleen."

"Now! I didn't mean it to sound like that. I won't get dug into her."

"I know you won't."

She frowned as she examined some part of his shirt collar. Her voice fell to a murmur.

"She could never do wrong by you, could she?"

He looked down at the stain left by the glass.

"She couldn't, Kathleen. She could not."

He looked up from the counter and met her eyes. They were hard and tired. She blinked and looked away again. She reached in under her cuffs. No hanky. She slid off the stool and made her way to the toilet.

"Rain, Matt," said the barman as he filled another pint. "Can you believe anyone these days — is that yours, that bleeping thing?"

Minogue switched off the pager, unhitched it from his belt and looked at the message. The squad number. Kathleen passed him as he picked up the phone.

"Have you a twenty pence piece for this thing?" he asked her.

· · · · ·

The Guard was a lanky recruit with a recent haircut. He was reading the paper when the inspector walked in. He stood and dropped the paper on the chair behind him.

"Howiya," said Minogue. He studied the face on the pillow. One eye was completely closed. Iodine stains all down the same side of his face. The lips were swollen, held together at their corners by dried blood.

"Is he sleeping or is he —"

The eyes flickered but only one opened.

"Ah." Minogue walked closer. A bandage had been tied under his arm and then across his other shoulder. The bruise seemed to be spreading away from the bandage as he watched. Broken rib or ribs, Minogue guessed. Collarbone maybe. The one eye was covered in a film but it followed him as he leaned in over the bed.

"Well. They really did a number on you. Any idea who?"

The eye stayed on his face but it remained out of focus. Minogue turned to the Guard. The Guard shook his head. Minogue sat down on the edge of the bed.

"I'm Matt Minogue. An inspector down at the Murder Squad. We've talked before, Liam."

He scrutinized the eye for a reaction.

"You nearly left it too late there, Liam."

The eye slid away but the lips moved a little.

"Who did that to you? The Egans?"

The eye traveled across the ceiling, lingered on something, and drifted off to the far side of the room. Minogue got up again and motioned to the Guard. They stood by the window.

"Not a word, huh? Well, can he talk? Is his jaw broken or something?"

"He was talking to the lads who found him. He told them he was okay and to leave him alone. He'd had a row with mates of his but it was okay."

The Guard had halitosis. Minogue held his breath.

"Then he collapsed again?"

"Yep. Hasn't said a word since. No ID, no money. Kind of pissed. It was Mooney who thought he'd seen him somewhere before. Mooney used to work out of Crumlin. He'd arrested him a few years back. He remembered the last name so he sent it in on the way here to the hospital. Your mob had the name tagged. Is it the fella you're looking for?"

Minogue had to breathe again. He stepped back and turned to the bed.

"I think so."

He let his eyes linger on the man he believed was Leonardo Hickey. The eye was still open, staring at the ceiling.

"Liam?"

He could see the effort the man was using not to look over.

"Liam. You won't make it a second time. Don't throw yourself away, man."

The eye began its slow tour of the ceiling again. Minogue took another step back toward the bed.

"They'll kill you next time, Liam."

The eye found Minogue.

"You don't believe me?"

The lips began to move but they didn't part. Minogue sat on the bed again.

"Tell me about Mary in the old days, Liam. Before she got mixed up in the life. Before you lost her."

The jaw quivered and the eye closed. A tear erupted from the corner of the eyelid. The hand that came up from under the sheet was heavily bandaged.

"When you were kids, Liam. Before all this trouble. Before all this mess. Tell me about Mary then. The friends you had, Jammy Tierney and them. The things you liked to do."

CHAPTER 23

MINOGUE RUBBED AT HIS eyes again. They were burning. It was just gone nine o'clock. He'd slept four hours last night. He'd be destroyed by the middle of the day. Kathleen was still rummaging in her handbag. He looked down along by Stephen's Green at the bank of clouds. No mirage. Did they seem so white just because they were high?

"Yes, I have it," said Kathleen. She brandished the money purse. "I thought for a minute I'd left it at home. The head is gone on me."

She turned down the rearview mirror and examined her eyes. She pouted then and turned her head to one side. He yawned.

"You look smashing."

"Not overdressed now?"

"No. Just right."

"About half-ten then? Will that be time enough?"

"If I can find her by then, I'll bring her."

She opened the door.

"I'd go around to her place myself, you know, only she might eat the head off me."

He nodded and yawned again. She peered at him.

"Did you get any sleep at all?"

"A bit. Enough. Don't buy any of that stuff, do you hear me?"

"I'm just looking. It'd be good to have an idea of expense, wouldn't it?"

He edged back into the traffic and waved as he passed her. Home from the hospital just after one, couldn't sleep. Malone hadn't phoned. To hell with the time, he had decided — he needed to know what was going on. Malone had been out late, trying to find the brother. His mind was made up, he had told Minogue. Terry would be better off inside than on the street. He'd gone to bed wide awake at two o'clock, had read for awhile but still couldn't sleep. The odd thing was that he'd hardly thought about Iseult at all. It was some vague, airy feeling in his chest that had kept him awake. He still had a confused memory of sitting on the edge of the bed, looking out through the trees at the dawn.

Several times as he traversed the Coombe he found himself still searching for Liam Hickey's face on men he saw. He was last in for the briefing. He sat next to Kilmartin. Murtagh began detailing the timetables for Jack Mullen.

"Voh' Lay-bah's left us in the lurch again," Kilmartin whispered. "You and me are going to sit down and have a chat about this. Before this day is out too, pal."

"Later, James."

"Said he mightn't be able to make it in until Monday, if you please."

Minogue's turn came next. He found himself answering a query about Alan Kenny with the reply that he had not ruled out arresting Kenny on drug-trafficking charges. Kilmartin pressed him hard on Kenny's alibis. Minogue didn't argue: yes, he agreed with Murtagh, Kenny stunk. No, it wasn't too much of a risk to leave Kenny stew in the open. The surveillance on Kenny since his interview had shown nothing odd yet.

Presenting the business of Hickey knowing which tape had been stolen hadn't won Kilmartin over. It wasn't bulletproof, was it, was his attitude yet.

"Well, why the hell does this scut Hickey need all day to rest? Says who?"

"Says the doctor who examined him. A Doctor Monaghan."

"How bad of a hiding did he get?"

"He was up in a heap. Banged around the head, bruising all over. He was kicked unconscious."

"Huh. The poor little shite. I don't think. You don't think he was faking it?"

"Not that I could see."

Sheehy started into his lists next. In the laconic delivery, Minogue detected a weariness which told him that all the door-to-door officers were just about fed up. Kilmartin told him to get a second interview out of the barman who had put them on to Kenny. Sheehy nodded. Minogue waited until Murtagh began detailing from the photocopies of the final pathology report before nudging Kilmartin.

"Jim, I need to get away for a couple of hours. Personal."

Kilmartin kept reading.

"Back by dinnertime," Minogue added.

"First we have Molly falling by the wayside," Kilmartin declared. "Is this contagious or something? Or just because it's Saturday?"

For a reason that Minogue couldn't figure out even later as he sped down the quays, shaking his head with anger and embarrassment, he had told Kilmartin about Iseult. He turned onto Capel Street bridge, still squirming at the recollection of Kilmartin's wink. And Éilis giving him that look as he hurried out red-faced! Essex Street was chock-a-block. Reluctantly he paid a tenner deposit to the attendant at a new car park on the site of a recently demolished building.

Iseult needed ten minutes to finish planing a piece of wood for the installation. Minogue studied it and asked no questions. The horns were generic, he decided. He recognized a hoof farther back.

"So you and Ma were just meeting for a cup of coffee anyway," said Iseult. Minogue yawned.

"That's it. So you'll join us, will you?"

"And Ma didn't throw a fit?"

"Calm, cool, and collected. But she's hurt that you didn't tell her first, I think."

Iseult stopped planing and glanced over. Minogue looked back. She resumed planing.

"So will you?" he asked again.

"No lectures, no guilt trips?"

"I think your mother would like to hug you and hold you, Iseult."

She put down the plane and glared at him. He looked at his watch.

They turned onto Fleet Street. Bewley's was around the corner. He could smell the roasting beans over the diesel smoke from the buses.

"I make the decisions," she said over the noise of the traffic. She kept rubbing her hands with a rag she had brought from the studio. "No preaching, right?"

"Honor of God, Iseult, it sounds like the United Nations here or something. It's your mother and father you're meeting for a cup of coffee."

"Well, cranky, isn't it with you this morning, is it now!"

He debated telling her that this cup of coffee could cost him upward of five quid.

"I didn't sleep a whole lot last night."

"That's too bad. I had a great sleep. I think the morning thing might be over. Maybe now that everything's out in the open . . . Maybe it was just nerves."

"Well, you were never short of them."

"What?"

"You always had a nerve."

She flicked the rag at him before stuffing it into the back pocket of her jeans. Her pace slowed just after they turned onto Westmoreland Street. Minogue looked over at Iseult and then followed her gaze down through the crowd of pedestrians. Kathleen had been waiting outside the restaurant. She had spotted them. There was something about her broad smile and vigorous wave that made Minogue hesitate. At least she didn't have shopping bags under her arm, he thought, shopping bags full of baby clothes.

· · · · ·

"What the hell kind of a caper is this?" Kilmartin asked. "Still celebrating, are we? Ah no, man. Have to get back. Come on now."

The chief inspector belched.

"I mean, as if things weren't bad enough now with this . . ."

Minogue looked over at him.

"Oh, don't get me wrong! I didn't mean the good news, oh, no! Grandfather . . . Ha ha ha! Oops."

Minogue eyed his colleague. Kilmartin patted his stomach in an effort to tease out another belch.

"We have to move with the times now, Matt. If you're happy, I'm happy. And Kathleen is reconciled, isn't she? Sure, that's great! Great entirely, man, great!"

Reconciled, thought Minogue. He recalled Iseult and Kathleen embracing, crying both, and Bewley's clientele looking shyly on.

"What I actually meant," said Kilmartin in a voice laden with sarcasm, "was that bastard above in the hospital, Hickey, doing a bunk on us. Looks bad for us, very bad."

Minogue shrugged.

"My God, man, you don't sound too worried about this!" said Kilmartin.

"Ah, he'll turn up. He's off the list in my book, Jim. The tape thing was pretty solid."

"To hell with that! What did he run for, then? I'm going to tear the head off that bloody Guard —"

"Jim. I'd rather you let me do that. Really. It's my own fault, a bit of it."

"You don't know how to give people a proper bollocking! You told me he was in dog-rough shape there last night."

"He was, Jim —"

"Well, by Jesus, he was well able to leg it out of the bloody place at eleven o'clock this morning, wasn't he? There are no less than five cars looking for him. The bastard! And us like iijits, waiting for the go-ahead from a doctor checking on him every half hour. 'Sleeping,' my arse!"

Minogue waited for Kilmartin to subside.

"You asked me why he ran. He was scared we'd do him for robbing the stuff out of the car and the Egans would reach him in jail."

"Huh. Why don't you just phone them and tell them that you consider his alibi just grand, thank you very much. They'd appreciate that, I bet."

"Maybe the two pints wasn't enough to soften you up."

"Ho ho, cowboy! You won't get in my way when I have to tear strips off Malone. By Jesus! In our hour of need and all that. We all have to leave our personal lives at home now — well, I mean if it's bad news now, of course. Not your happy event."

Kilmartin suddenly sat forward.

"Here, turn around, will you! This is Dolphins Barn! Injun country, man! Turn around to hell out of this."

"We were in the vicinity, Jim. Why not tour around a bit now that we're here?"

"The vicinity? You're in the vicinity of getting us into a heap of trouble."

"When we were small," Minogue began. He was interrupted by another belch from Kilmartin. He held his breath for several seconds until he was sure the smell had wafted by him. He steered the Citroen by rows of flats, shops shuttered save for their doorways, walls alive with graffiti.

"You were never small," said Kilmartin. He turned and looked out the back window.

"My God, man. Did you see what road this is?"

"Tell me."

"The bloody Egans' place is down the way here, you gom!"

"Listen. I was saying. When we were small, we'd go into town. Ennistymon, say —"

"Where the hell is that? Look: turn this bloody car around."

"All right. Ennis —"

"Never heard of it. Let's get out of here. I know you're as frustrated with this hands-off thing on the Egans —"

"Galway city then, to get a suit of clothes —"

"Did they wear clothes back then? I thought ye'd be too busy fighting off the shagging dinosaurs to be looking in shop windows. Turn this car around, for the love of Jases!"

Minogue still felt dopey from the two lunchtime pints.

"If you don't turn the car around, I will!"

"We'd look in the shop windows," Minogue went on. "My mother'd say, 'Well, why not look. It doesn't cost to have a look, does it?'"

"It might cost you a puck in the snot, pal. Come on, let's get out of here!"

Minogue braked by the remains of a bus shelter.

"Look at the place," Kilmartin grumbled. "Beirut or something — look, there's the car. The blue Corolla. Look at them. Oh, Christ, they've spotted us."

"They'll log us in anyway, James. Let's mosey on over."

Minogue parked behind the detectives' car. Kilmartin stepped warily out onto the path after him.

·　　·　　·　　·　　·

"That's right," said Minogue. "First cousin on my mother's side."

Heffernan laughed. Macken, the other detective, smiled but did not take his gaze from the street. Heffernan drew on his cigarette again.

"That's the one, all right," he said. "Small world, isn't it?"

"Buried in Corofin," said Minogue. "I suppose we're third cousins then. Or is it second cousins once removed?"

"Thought you had to be dead for that," said Kilmartin.

"Hah," said Heffernan. "So you have a murder then. The Mullen girl?"

"And we have to be polite and take our turn with all of ye," said Minogue. Heffernan turned his head and winked at him.

"Being as we're cousins and all. Here, if you think you're put-upon here, wait 'til I tell you the kind of thing we have to swallow by the day here. Ever think you'd see the day when Special Branch officers —"

"Hardworking, conscientious Special Branch officers like the ones you are unofficially sitting with this very minute," added Macken.

"— would be ordered to line up behind civil servants from the Revenue Commissioners and Customs?"

"Never thought I'd see the day," said Minogue.

"It's an affront," said Heffernan.

"An affront," said Minogue. "Without a doubt."

Minogue took Kilmartin's silence to mean that the chief inspector was all too aware that these two Special Branch detectives had the disquieting freedom to say anything they wanted to them. They recognized that neither member of the Murder Squad wished to be officially present in their surveillance car.

"They'll fall between the cracks due some technicality," said Heffernan. "It's too complex to go right. That's what I think."

"Far too complex," said Minogue. "Won't go right."

Heffernan shifted in his seat, groaned, and looked down the street again. Rubble from a demolished building next to the Egans' shop had been there long enough to be almost completely taken over by huge-leafed weeds, cans, and plastic supermarket bags swollen with household rubbish. Why did the Egans keep a shop here, why did they not seem to care about the decay and squalor? Back up the street were buildings with blocked-in windows and doors. A pub, the Good Times. The Good Times? A bookies across the street was the only functioning building in a short block that seemed similarly slated for demolition. A gas company van was parked across the street behind a two-door Lancia that Heffernan told them belonged to Bobby Egan. The blocks of flats that had gained the area its notoriety were out of sight behind the street.

Traffic came in gluts, released by a traffic light two blocks back toward the city center. Little stopped or even slowed here on the street. Two young mothers wheeled their prams by, leaving their loud speech hanging in the air for Minogue to think about, to try to imagine what their lives were like. A trio of kids sauntered by and greeted the policemen with a combination of daring, humor, and hostility. The bad language didn't seem to have much effect on Heffernan.

"Say nothing now," said Macken. "But there's our Bobby. He's out."

Minogue's reaction was to be cautious, to look for cover. Heffernan seemed amused.

"There's only Eddsy and the other fella in there now," he said. "Don't be worrying. They know the most of us who've been on duty here."

"The state of him," Kilmartin murmured. "Walks like a gorilla. Look, the knuckles nearly running along the ground beside him."

And he does, thought Minogue. Bobby Egan had emerged from his brother's shop as he had entered — alone. He glanced up and down the street before settling on the unmarked Corolla and raising his eyebrows in greeting.

"Oh, here we go," said Heffernan. "See what kind of a humor the bold Bobby is in this morning."

"You mean he comes over to you?"

"'Course he does. For the chat, man. I mean to say, we're in the same business, aren't we? Almost. If we were social workers, he'd be our client, wouldn't he, Ger?"

"Our case, yes. Bobby's a case, all right. A head-case."

"Loves a dare," said Heffernan. "Smart the way only a header is smart. Bobby'd eat you alive for a joke. Know what I'm saying?"

Something in Heffernan's tone of bored wisdom pinged a bull's-eye in Minogue's mind.

"Oh, shit," said Macken. "Here we go now."

Bobby Egan ambled with a rolling gait to the car. He rubbed his hands and bent over, head next to the open window. Chewing gum slowly, heavy brows, a wide face under close-cropped hair. His eyes looked very blue. Was that a scar by his neck? Though Bobby Egan's face close up still retained a scuffed look, Minogue could see none of the malevolence he had expected. He was well turned-out. His polo shirt had a pricey logo on it, an alligator thing, and the trousers had a sharp fold. Minogue tried to read any inscriptions on the bracelet Egan fingered.

"'S'lads. How's it going."

The smile looked genuine, thought Minogue. He nodded back.

"How's Bobby," said Heffernan.

"Oh, topping. And four of yous? Of a Saturday? Oooh. Very heavy, lads. Here all night again, were yiz?"

Heffernan kept up his scrutiny of an approaching van.

"You know yourself, Bobby." Egan shrugged.

"Wouldn't want the marriage to go on the rocks on account of having to work nights now, would we? Who're the reinforcements in the back there?"

For an instant Minogue felt the urge to jump out of the car and go nose to nose with Bobby Egan. Was this fastidious thug the one who had slammed the senses out of Mary Mullen, slid her into the water to drown?

"CIA," said Macken. "But keep that to yourself. It's top secret."

"Ha ha! Such a panic yiz are. Fella here looks like a farmer."

Minogue stared back into Egan's eyes.

"Well, as long as yous're only cops, I don't mind."

Egan tapped on the roof and cleared his throat.

"All right so, lads. Keep it up. We all feel real safe here now, knowing that yous are around and all. Here — go in and support local enterprise here. Buy a packet of fags or something. The brother needs the money."

He hawked and spat across the roof.

"Be seeing yous. By the way, where's the other van, the telephone one? All the video and gear? Did one of the young lads around here rob it on you?"

Heffernan grinned and flicked his eyes skyward.

"Helicopter, Bobby," he said. "One of the new ones, a spy one from the States. Can't see it, can't hear it — but it's there all the time."

Egan glanced up and sniggered.

"Oh, you had me there! Yous are gas! Funnier every day."

Minogue watched Egan climb into the Lancia. He tooted the horn as he drove away.

"Bastard," said Kilmartin. "He doesn't know how close he is. I'd like to be there when the time comes."

"Now you're talking," said Minogue. Heffernan looked over.

"How close is he to getting his wings clipped anyway?" Minogue asked.

"Well, you'd need to be up on the, em . . ."

"'The Big Picture'?"

Heffernan's meaty hands tapped the steering wheel.

"That's the size of it," he said. "I know, I know. We heard ye wouldn't back down at all. But we've been after the Egans for years. We have to go for the whole thing, the whole racket, you understand? It's not just one, well . . ."

"Just one murder," said Minogue.

Heffernan pursed his lips and shrugged.

"Do you think it's fun and games for us?" asked Macken. He sat forward in the seat, his face not a foot from Minogue's. "See the names at the bottom of the sheet? Me and O'Hare? It's our surveillance work that puts Bobby in the clear for the night of that murder you're trying to sort out."

Minogue nodded.

"So don't be asking us what Tynan asked us here a few months back," Heffernan added.

"Tynan?" asked Kilmartin.

"The very X," said Heffernan. "Never in sixteen years did I hear of a Garda Commissioner sitting in on a surveillance unannounced. Drove up here one day on his own, didn't he, Ger?"

"An Alfa Romeo," said Macken. "Flag-red. Like a fire engine. Street threads."

"Oh, yes," said Heffernan. "Waltzes over to us. I'm having a stroke, I don't mind telling you —"

"Thought it was something he et," said Macken. "Seeing things, like?"

"'Mind if I sit in?' says Tynan. What am I going to say?"

"Ask him if he has a twin brother who's the Commissioner," said Macken, "and then tell him to shag off?"

Minogue smiled.

"So in he gets," said Heffernan. "Just like you sitting there. Sits there for about twenty minutes watching the comings and goings. Hardly says one word. Gets up then, goes across the street and into the shop. Comes out a few minutes later. Throws a few bags of crisps in the window —"

"Mars bar too."

"— Mars bar too. Don't know whether to laugh or what. 'Thanks,' says I."

"Cheese and Onion," said Macken. "The crisps, like."

"I mean, we all heard that Tynan's a real pit bull when he gets his teeth into something. Look out, et cetera. You could tell he was bulling when he came out of the shop. Livid, like. Face didn't change expression, of course."

"That a fact," said Kilmartin.

"Lips didn't move," said Heffernan, nodding. "Doesn't get back in the car. Just stands there, staring back at the shop. Like he's sizing it up for demolition. The fingers doing drum rolls on the roof. Says — and I'm sure he was talking to himself now — says, 'How is it that those reptiles are still abroad?' Didn't he, Ger?"

Macken nodded.

"Dead on," he said. "'Abroad,' I was thinking, you know? Thought he meant a holiday or something. Didn't twig, the way he said it."

"And that was when the big push started. Revenue woke up, Customs and Excise fellas started to attend the meetings. Branch Inspectors. Technicals. Task Force fellas who would step over your dead body in the hall in the normal run of things. Staff; equipment; overtime coming out our ears. Jam on the bread, the whole bit. I don't care what anyone says about Tynan. The Iceman; the Monsignor. Tell you this: he's the man to nail the Egans."

"Reptiles," said Kilmartin. He elbowed Minogue and nodded toward the Citroen.

Heffernan looked over at him.

"Are you going in to see Eddsy then?"

Eddy Egan, Eddsy, thought Minogue. A crippled reptile who commissioned pornographic pictures of girls trapped in poverty, in lousy jobs, desperate for a better life.

"I think we will."

Kilmartin's jaw was hanging but his eyes told Minogue enough. He put on his best blithe smile. Maybe he should have two pints of beer every lunchtime while the heat wave lasted. He stepped out onto the road and looked across the roof of the Toyota at Kilmartin.

"Are we right, Jim?"

Kilmartin caught up with Minogue before he reached the door of the shop.

"Right for what? What the hell are we up to? Wait a minute there!"

Chapter 24

Minogue stood to the side of the doorway as two teenagers stepped out of the shop. One was already tearing the cellophane from a packet of cigarettes. Recruits, he wondered. Start them with packets of fags, let them graduate to fencing stuff they robbed.

"I'm curious, Jim. Aren't you?"

"Curious? You're cracked, is what you are. What's here for us?"

"Remember the man you've been chopping at, the man unfortunate enough to be born in Dublin? The one —"

"Voh' Lay-bah? What's this got to do with him?"

"Terry, the brother, he's causing ructions since he got out of the 'Joy the other day."

"So? So?"

"Well, Tommy had to take time off —"

"I know, I know! Stop telling me things I know!"

"Bear with me now, James. Terry's in there right now. We can kill a few birds with the one stone now."

Kilmartin grabbed his arm.

"What are we up to here? Running messages? We have to keep to our own side of the bed with this mob, man!"

"Tommy was out looking for him and called in here. Nearly had a row."

"Why am I only hearing about this now? This is going to make a hames of the case if —"

"It's okay, Jim. I read him the Riot Act. I told him I'd have a word with the brother if I could. I, er, asked the lads to phone if they spotted Terry.

He's in there. That's why I've come by."

"Oh Christ! Now he tells me! First he buys me a dinner, then he tries to soften me up with a few pints! And I, poor iijit, thought we were celebrating something."

"And I want the Egans to know that we're out there too, about Mary."

"Back up there a minute. You want to come the heavy with Malone's brother here?"

Minogue was in the door now. The shop was small and cluttered and hot. It smelled of newsprint and tobacco and the trays of penny sweets. There was another smell mixed in, the inspector realized, a beery smell. A radio talk show was on, but not so loud that Minogue could hear more than snatches of the conversation about pollution. The elderly woman Minogue had seen enter the shop several minutes before was effusive.

"Ah, tanks, Eddsy! I knew I could depend on you, tanGod. You're a star! Jesus . . ."

She nodded at Minogue and shuffled toward the door. The man leaning against the wall held a cigarette down at his side. He brought it up slowly, rubbed his nose with his thumb and drew on the cigarette.

"Well, fuck me," he murmured. "Hey, Eddsy. Will you lookit these two?"

The face that Minogue found after several moments of baffled searching was at counter level. Eddsy Egan's face reminded him of a butcher's window display. Sausages, he thought: puffy, gray, and pink. The eyes were dull like a resting dog's and there was a cast of tired pain across his face. The face of a man beaten down with a migraine, he thought. Egan looked from him to Kilmartin.

"Oh, quite the resemblance," Minogue heard Kilmartin murmur.

"Oink, oink," said Terry Malone. "Sniff, sniff."

"Yeah?" said Egan.

"Just looking, thanks," said Minogue.

"You new? You don't look new."

"No, I'm not new."

"What about your pal there."

Minogue looked over at Kilmartin.

"Him? Oh, no. He's definitely not new."

"Oink, oink," said Malone.

"Something wrong with your mouth there?" asked Kilmartin.

"Me nose. I can't stand certain smells."

"Maybe someone could fix that for you. Finish off what your brother left standing."

Malone frowned and pushed off from the wall.

"What would you fucking know about that, pal?"

Eddsy Egan shook his head. The inspector saw a gleam on a patch of skin by Egan's ear, a graft or stitches, he thought. The radio-show host, a man Minogue fervently disliked because he so effortlessly patronized people, said something about a levy on polluters.

"What do you want," said Egan.

Stitched, stapled, and grafted together again, thought Minogue. Was he good at giving pain to others? He stood a foot or more shorter than the inspector.

"A couple of things. Start with pictures. Girls."

"Uh, uh. Who wants them? The weaselly guy, Macken? Or the big lad?"

Weaselly, thought Minogue. How did he know the name?

"Me."

"And?"

"My colleague here."

"For?"

"They'll lead me to who killed Mary."

Minogue followed Egan's gaze around the meticulously stocked shelves.

"Forecast said rain. Can you believe that though?"

"Eventually it will."

"What will?"

"Rain. I'm looking for someone in the photos."

"I don't mind rain. We need a bit."

"Same as yourself probably, right?"

"You can't have a garden without mud."

"Or maggots," said Kilmartin. Minogue took slow steps about the floor. He looked up and down the shelves.

"Is he a married man, I wonder. A friend of yours? Someone you trusted, maybe?"

"They sent the wrong guy," said Egan. "Tell them."

"How big is your collection?"

"Collection of what."

"Videos too?"

Egan grimaced as he shifted his weight onto his other foot.

"Doesn't make sense, does it," Minogue went on.

"What doesn't. You nattering on here?"

"What happened. How it happened. Who it happened to. How much did you lose?"

"The heat. Gets so it screws up your brain."

"I bet you're kicking yourself, aren't you."

"Haven't the time. I'm a busy man."

"Not like some people," said Malone. Minogue turned to him. Malone smiled. Kilmartin cleared his throat. He kept his eyes on Malone but his words were for Egan.

"You don't get to do the things you'd like to, Eddsy, do you?"

"I get by."

"Pictures? Videos even? Are they enough?"

"Tell me more. You don't meet so many comedians these days."

"I hear you like to know the faces. That's unusual, I was told. Revenge, maybe?"

"How much do you want?"

"How much of what?"

Terry Malone sniggered. Egan rubbed his thumb and fingers together.

"You want to get on the books here, don't you? That's what this is all about, isn't it, getting on the take? Like the other cops. How much?"

"That an offer now?"

"You're different anyway," said Egan. "About time I had a new one."

"If it's you, Eddsy, I'll have you," said Minogue. Egan's face seemed to have gone slack.

"So you came by to tell me that. A freebie."

Minogue nodded.

"What if I send the tape of this performance to your big chief, what's his name, Tynan."

Minogue glanced up into the corner. The video camera lens was small.

"As long as the color's good and the light's right, fire away."

"What's your job when you're working?"

"Point two, Eddsy. Your sidekick here. Terry Malone. Give him the sack."

Egan's face cracked into a smile. Malone laughed.

"A customer? You want me to put him out of the shop?"

"That's right."

"Where's the law? Show me the rule book on that one."

"Yeah," said Malone. He wasn't smiling now. "Just what kind of fucking harassment are yous trying to get up to now? Huh? You and this other fucking bogman here?"

"Long day before a gutty like you could do a day's work in a bog, pal," said Kilmartin.

"Take a running fucking jump at yourself," said Malone.

"Wreaking havoc on families is nothing new to you and your outfit," said Minogue. "But this one's off limits. You with me now?"

Egan's face grew suddenly flushed. His knuckles turned white on the counter.

"Is that so? You and this overgrown fucking chimp waltz in here to lecture me about family? After yous've been chipping away at friends of mine, trying to get them to lie about me?"

Minogue took a step toward Terry Malone. He studied the face, the bruises. Malone frowned back into the inspector's stare. His breath was coming faster. He bit his lip.

"You're high, aren't you?"

Malone was faster than Minogue had imagined he could be. He barely had his hands up when Malone's nose was inches from his own. Sour beery breath fanned over his face. Kilmartin's arm clamped around Malone's neck. All this Minogue took in with little surprise. He knew that Malone could have floored him. Malone's eyes were wide now but he was laughing. He had made no attempt to get out from Kilmartin's chokehold.

"Don't be a patsy for the Egans," said Minogue. "They'll throw you on the scrap heap." Kilmartin pushed Malone off. Egan seemed to be bored by the commotion.

"What's the name there, sheriff? Credits on the video, you know."

Minogue gestured to Kilmartin.

"I'll be seeing you, Eddsy."

"Suit yourself. I'll know the name of your dog even in a half hour."

. . . . .

"Christ, what a worm. A slimy, creeping Jesus of a worm."

"Kind of unnerving all right, Jim."

"Unnerving? Didn't I tell you it's in the genes, man? Twins. Ugghhh."

Minogue shrugged. Kilmartin gave him an elbow.

"Here," he said. "Does it occur to you there are regulations we have to adhere to?"

Minogue looked across the street. His Citroen was intact.

"You're the boss, Jim. Everybody knows that."

"Everybody except you. I should've let him give you that puck in the snot."

"I couldn't have stopped him, James."

"Well, I could have."

Minogue looked at Kilmartin as he stepped onto the road.

"I'll tell you how," Kilmartin went on. "I could have hit you myself before we ever came out to this kip! Saved him the bother. Jesus Christ, man, why didn't you tell me you were going to take that line?"

Minogue helloed at the detectives.

"Well?" said Heffernan.

"Nobody broke down and confessed," said Minogue. He leaned on the roof and looked back at the shop. "No. No glory here. It's back to just working for a living."

"Did you get what you came for, you know?"

Heffernan looked across the street at the shop and sighed.

"He thinks he's safe, you know. Eddsy. Bobby too. That we'll never nail them."

"Let him think what he wants. You file to who?"

"Serious Crimes."

"You wouldn't be sort of, well, be saving anything now? In a different file?"

Heffernan gave him a glazed look. A smile began to creep across his face.

"Oh, sure, we want him first. But no. There's too much depending on coordinating everything. Sure it's damn near political at this stage."

Minogue continued to give him the eye.

"No one slipped into the shop there this last while, while the lads in the van were changing tapes or the like?"

Heffernan spoke with a haughtiness that brought a smile to Minogue's face.

"God, no," he said. "Ah, no. Really. It's as boring now . . . This is symbolic half the time. Who'd go to Eddsy's shop for dirty work knowing we sit out here day in, day out?"

Minogue looked over at Kilmartin. The chief inspector was pacing up and down the footpath, smoking. J. Kilmartin would give him a right bollocking all the way back to the office, no doubt.

"Only me, apparently," he muttered under his breath.

The ache he had in his right arm flared every now and then. He'd had to stop several times when it had turned to pain. A hell of a lot of good it did for that bleeding doctor to be telling him that there was nothing broken. Shaking his head and looking down at him, with those X rays in his hand. Like he was looking down at a lower form of life.

The coin slipped in his fingers as he pressed it toward the slot on the phone. He heard it bounce off the ground but he couldn't turn fast enough. The pain in his side was too much now and he straightened up. Bruising — what had the doctor called it? Confusion? The doctor didn't look any older than himself; probably drove a BM — where the hell was the twenty pence?

He suddenly felt as if everything was draining down to his toes. He straightened up, steadied himself against the wall, and waited for the little starbursts to stop exploding around him. Rush hour, nearly. Maybe he shouldn't have had those few pints. To kill the pain, he had thought, to keep off the streets. They hadn't helped him think any clearer about the plan. He squinted and glanced up at the tops of the buildings. Christ, clouds for the first time in days. Weeks? A woman walking down the path eyed him and crossed the street. He watched her hurry along. He wanted to call out after her that even if he wanted to try and rob her bloody handbag he didn't have the energy. His mouth was still full of sticky spit.

He still had no appetite. He thought back to the hospital. Christ, he could get a job as an actor any day. And they thought they had him! That cop last night, the one he'd been on the phone to. Minogue. Playing good cop: let's have a chat there, Liam. Oh, yeah, your life story. Trying to come the heavy then with that crap about running out of friends or running out of places to hide. Daring him to prove he still had mates. But all the time he'd been planning. The questions he'd been asking, even. Christ, he'd learned a hell of a lot more from that cop talking than what the cop had learned from him! He hadn't been asking him about Jammy Tierney just to pass the time.

Lying there in the bed he hadn't been sure, but as soon as he'd made up his mind he knew he could do it. His clothes were a total mess. He looked like a knacker, probably smelled like one too. At least he didn't have to run down the street in a bloody hospital gown! That dopey cop

that was supposed to be guarding him, sneaking out to the jacks . . .
He'd be up the creek for that too. Great! The stars had gone but his
head still felt light. When he moved his neck it felt like it creaked. He
watched the traffic for several moments. Maybe it was a stupid place to
be, a place where he could be spotted too handy. A car braked next to
him. He was suddenly alert, ready to run, ready to try anyway. A man in
sunglasses climbed out of the passenger seat and ran into a shop. The
panic began to drain out of him. He stepped into a pub. There was a
phone inside the front door. He dialed and waited. The oul lad who ran
the place answered.

"Tell him Bobby. Bobby wants to talk to him."

He listened to the clack of balls as he waited. Someone called out,
"Who?" The phone was grabbed.

"Yeah? Who's this?" It was Jammy.

"Guess who."

"Is that you, Joe? Trigger? Don't mess, I'm in a game here!"

"How quickly we forget, Jammy. What's the story, man?"

A pause. Jammy's voice was different now.

"Is that you, Leonardo?"

He sniggered. His ribs hurt. He wasn't even angry now, that was the
weird thing.

"No, it's Bobby Egan."

"It's you, isn't it, Leonardo? Where are you, man?"

"Wouldn't you like to know. What's the story here? Did you think I
was just going to disappear? Outa sight, outa mind, huh?"

"Leonardo?"

It was the way he said it: that was worth everything. A way better buzz
than if he'd just started off sticking it to him. Tierney's voice was different now.

"I thought you were gone, you know? England maybe?"

"Gone, huh."

"Come on, man. You know what I mean."

"You're a lying bastard, Jammy!"

Now he felt angry. His face was hot again. He rubbed his hand over
the unfamiliar bumps, the soft, sticky scab already beginning to form
over his eyebrows.

"So you're in a game, are you now?"

"Well, yeah, I am."

"How much?"

"Twenty."

"Tell the guy you're out, Jammy."

"Are you serious, Leo —"

"Fucking *tell* him! And hey! Hold the phone up. I want to hear it."

"Jesus, Leonardo, I can't, man." The whisper excited him.

"Yes, you can. You tell him to fuck off too. I want to hear you say that."

"Leonardo, man . . . What's going on?"

He jumped with the fury now. The screech hurt his throat.

"Fucking *do* it! Or else!"

"Come on, Leonardo. What did you want? Where are you? I can help you out, you know. You sound like you're in a jam or something."

"'A jam'? You know why I'm phoning you! Don't fuck with me now, man!"

"I don't know what you mean! I thought you were long gone. The money and all? . . ."

"Oh, yeah, Jammy. Long gone, huh? What does that mean? This cop was talking to me last night, man. Yeah, I was in a bit of a jam last night. Like you'd never believe, man! This cop, he's asking all kinds of questions, isn't he? About you. He didn't give too much of a shit about me, did he. It's you he wanted to talk about."

Tierney said nothing.

"Hey, are you listening?"

"I don't get it. What's he want to talk to you about me for?"

"'I don't get it'! Like fuck, you don't! Now! Tell the guy! I want to hear it."

He listened to the click of more balls. He thought he could hear Tierney breathing but maybe it was his own breath or the sound of his own blood rushing around in his ears.

"Hey! I'm not going to stand here all day, man! I'm going to count to three and if I don't hear you say it, I'm dropping the phone! Then I'm going to make one more call, Jammy! That's all I need, man!"

"Are you here in town?"

Tierney sounded like he was trying not to show that he was in pain.

"None of your business. One . . . Two . . ."

"Hey, Anto . . ."

He stood still in the booth and pushed the receiver harder against his ear.

"Fuck off . . . Yeah . . . No . . ."

He kicked the wall under the phone. All his aches fled: he'd guessed right. That cop —

"There," said Tierney. "You heard that. That's twenty quid burned. Look, man, if I knew what you wanted —"

"Tell you what. Listen, just shut up and listen, okay? Now. Why don't you phone Bobby Egan and ask him. Say: 'Bobby, my good friend Leonardo — no, Liam — Liam said to phone you. He says you'd know what he wants.' Try that one. See what Bobby says."

"Jesus! I don't know what you want, Leonardo."

"How does it feel, Jammy? Do you like it?"

"Like it? Like what? Leonardo, I gave you the money, man. I got the word to you so's you could lie low and every —"

"Oh, yeah? What I want to know is this: how low?"

"I don't get it."

He kicked at the wall again.

"Better again," he hissed. "Just hang up the phone and forget I called. Save yourself the price of the phone. You can talk to Bobby when he comes looking for you."

He heard Tierney's swallow before the words came this time.

"Just tell me what you want, man. Are you stuck? Where are you?"

"Where am I. Listen to this and then give me a straight answer. What would the cops want with you? Why would that guy be asking me about you, about you and me and Mary from years ago? Huh?"

"I don't get it, honest, Leonardo —"

"It's Liam to you. Fucking *Liam!* Say it!"

"Liam."

"You don't know? Is that all you can come up with?"

"You know I was only trying to help you, Leonardo. The money —"

"It's Liam, you fucking bastard!"

"Liam . . ."

The warning pips sounded. He was ready with the coins waiting on top of the box.

"No, don't worry now, Jammy. I'm still here. And yeah, you can tell now, can't you. I'm in Dublin. Something went wrong for Mary, didn't it? And who would she phone, huh? She couldn't phone the Egans 'cause she was doing her own thing. Who would she phone then, Jammy? Who?"

"I don't know, man."

"Like hell you don't! Tell me I'm wrong, man! I fucking dare you!"

He wondered what Jammy Tierney looked like now. The sweat pouring out of him, standing there by the counter in the pool room.

"Here, Jammy, what's that guy doing, the guy you were playing? Is he still there?"

"Yeah, he is."

"Are you going to have a row on your hands? Are you?"

"Don't know. Don't think so."

"Are you going to just give him the money?"

"I suppose."

"What are you going to do then, Jammy?"

"I don't know."

"You want to talk about money some more?"

"What are you talking about? Is this the thanks I get for giving you a few bob?"

He laughed.

"I knew you'd say that! I did! The *exact* fucking words, man! Hey, I have to go. So. You know I'm in town, right?"

"Okay, yeah."

"You listen now, Jammy. Something's going on. I got my eyes open, man. That cop wasn't just talking about the weather, was he? All those questions about you."

"Like what?"

"Yeah, well, that's for me to know and for you to find out, isn't it? Or maybe for Bobby to find out! Listen, we're going to meet this evening. And you better change your tune."

"Jesus, man! How can you talk like this?"

"Just shut up a minute! You bring me in on this!"

"On what? I don't know —"

"Yeah, yeah, yeah! I been thinking about you, you know? You're just a bit too good to be true, aren't you? The perfect guy stuff. Yeah."

"You've got to be joking, man!"

"Oh, joking, am I? We'll soon see who's fucking joking! And don't get any ideas. I got this down in writing and I put it in a safe place, so I did."

He felt like he had run a mile flat-out. Had he gone too far? Jammy was talking.

"Look, Liam. I know you're under pressure. And when you're under pressure, the head can go on you, right? I mean, I felt bad me losing me rag at you the other day after finding out about Mary and all . . . Are you still there?"

"Ah, get off the fucking stage, will you? I could walk into Bobby Egan's and you'd be fucking history, man!"

"Liam, Liam — listen. Just let me ask you one thing. Do you really think I had something to do with Mary getting, you know?"

He studied the graffiti in the booth. What if he'd got it all wrong?

"Do you?" Tierney repeated.

"Meet me down next to the canal there by Portobello. The bridge? Seven o'clock."

"I can't make it, I've got to meet a guy —"

"Don't give me that crap, man! Eight, then."

Warning pips sounded again. He wasn't going to put in another coin.

"I can't! Later, maybe —"

"Nine, then! That's it! No more —"

The line was dead. He started at the little window on the phone. It'd be dark by nine. He should have made him stick to eight o'clock at the latest, the bastard. He placed the receiver back on the box. The pain in his side was coming back. He collected his coins off the top of the box. His arm hurt from just lifting it. He still didn't feel hungry. When had he eaten last anyway? He counted back. It had been around nine o'clock when he'd tried to score last night. The middle of the day when that other cop finally gets up, gives him the look-over close up, tiptoes out — boom, he's up and grabbing his clothes from the cupboard. No cop in the hall, hah! In the jacks, probably, having a smoke. Next thing he's down the stairs and out the back door. Right into the street.

Another pint or two wouldn't do him any harm. He had about four hours to kill. He stepped out of the telephone kiosk. He should make his way up toward the canal, get some smokes on the way. He should maybe try to get a snooze before that — no, he mightn't wake up in time. A sandwich or something, in case he got hungry later on. Find a spot near the canal and lie low there. The canal, yeah, that was using the head all right, the old psychology. He passed another pub. A couple stepped out of his way. He wasn't finished by a long shot. If it worked out tonight, maybe he was only starting. That cop, what the hell was his name again? Man . . . Minooley . . . Minogue. He stopped by the door of another pub and looked in. Half-full. One pint maybe.

CHAPTER 25

O KAY," SAID KILMARTIN. "Enough of that."

Minogue looked over.

"Kenny," said Kilmartin. "Round two with him. Now."

Minogue stretched. He eyed his watch as his arm slid by. God in heaven: seven.

"You want to pick him up?"

"Yes. No. Yes. Talk to me about him."

No Murtagh, Minogue realized. He had gone for his tea just after receiving a call from a Garda detective in Pearse Street: Jack Mullen had remembered that he had stopped into a shop while he was out of sight on the time log. The proprietor remembered him. The shop was in North Strand. It looked like Mullen was clear. Murtagh had merely thrown his biro across the squad room. Kilmartin, when he was told, had sworn for a count of ten.

"I've been reading and reading and reading. He's still off the map long enough to do it. And I'm not going to wait. I want him under pressure. So talk to me about him."

"Give us time to plant him for some of the gaps, James."

"No. He has everything. Motive — she was going to throw the Egans at him. I want to put him through hoops. What do you say?"

"You're just hungry. Look how late it is."

"That's your informed opinion?"

"When it is not necessary to make a decision, it is necessary not to make a decision."

"Christ, you're really contrary today. As for that frigging jaunt out to hell there with —"

"Scenery, James. Background. Context. Now we know whereof we speak."

Kilmartin sat on the edge of the desk and began scratching under his arm.

"And what was so goddamned edifying about meeting Molly's shagging brother? I mean, I hold with your good intentions and all that, but that brother's a head-case."

"So now you have a lot more sympathy for Tommy's plight then."

Minogue heard the rasp of Kilmartin's stubble as the chief inspector rubbed his jowls. Kilmartin turned to survey the boards again.

"Don't go getting ideas. I mean to say, look at us. Senior staff, seven o'clock in the evening. No Malone, no Murtagh. No firm road to follow yet. So why not squeeze Kenny?"

"Let him stew, Jim."

"Talking to the wall, I am," Kilmartin muttered. "How many left on the list John Murtagh finalized from the files?"

"Two that we haven't filled in. Both of them are making statements as we speak. One in Coolock, one's been interviewing since five over in Store Street. Nothing so far."

"Nothing," said Kilmartin. "Those thicks above in Serious Crimes! And us waiting around here like goms of the first order. You know what they're telling us, don't you."

"I think so."

"They're telling us that they'll get the statements, that they'll get the evidence, that they'll get the gouger we want for this case. 'It'll emerge' style of investigation. 'All in due course.' Like the Holy Ghost or something."

Minogue closed the folders. An image remained in his mind of the television schedule he had doodled on.

"Come on, Jim. Let's go."

"Go where?"

"Out. Away. It's the weekend, man. Buy me a sandwich."

The inspector pulled the phone out of the charger.

"Look at you," said Kilmartin. "Grabbing the toy there. You told me you consider that device I fought long and hard to get a ball and chain."

"Only sometimes."

"Oh, yes, run with the hare and chase with the hound. And I'm supposed to buy you a sandwich?"

"I'm expecting a call."

Kilmartin raised an eyebrow.

"'Expecting,' Matt?"

Minogue gave him a cool look. Kilmartin tried not to smile. Minogue locked the folders in his desk and walked out into the yard. Kilmartin wasn't long joining him.

"Do you know what I'm going to tell you, Matty boy?"

Kilmartin stopped by Minogue and looked up at the clouds.

"By God, now, there's something. Do you think?"

"What were you going to tell me?"

"Oh. Keane and his scouts in Serious Crimes would never have tried to pull a stunt like that in the past, let me tell you. Treating us like the country cousins. You know what it is? All this joint-op crap has become a fecking religion. Committees. Consultants. Civilians with Social Science degrees wandering the halls asking stupid questions. Paperwork. It's all a sham, man! All this 'cooperation' stuff makes me puke. Thicks and incompetents hide in committees. The real job's done well away from committees and bloody consultants and —"

"Yes, Jim. Okay."

The edges of the cloud were pink.

"Well, Keane and Co. in Serious Crimes know damn well I can't throw it back in their face like they deserve. And you know why, don't you? It's your butty Tynan is the witch doctor now. He's the one issuing edicts. 'Policing the Modern European State.' Did you read that? My Jases! I was halfway through the second page before I realized he meant Ireland!"

"He didn't write it. He commissioned it."

"Hah! Proves my point exactly!"

Minogue took a parting look at the massive cloud. Where had it come from so quickly?

· · · · ·

He drove the Kawasaki up onto the footpath and kicked out the stand, listened to it idle before switching it off. Then he took off his helmet and laid it on the tank. He looked across the canal. It was almost dark now. There had been no long sunset tonight. He unlocked the chain and put it through the front of his helmet before locking it to the back wheel. Leonardo must have been stoned, he'd decided. He'd take him for a few pints. Calm him down, loosen him up. No, someone might see them and remember them. He rapped the petrol tank with his knuckles hard enough to hurt.

He looked across at the canal. Lights shimmered on the water. He spotted the silhouette of a couple who had stopped to neck. They stayed at it for a few seconds and walked on. He stepped down off the road onto the bank and looked up at the wall by the bridge. Leonardo had ideas that were too big for his brain. Watching too many videos. Pills. He stared into the shadows by the bridge. No, no one. He let his eyes wander up and down the canal bank. A man carrying a bag was strolling along the far bank. He turned slowly, taking in the shadows and the parked cars, the office windows and the occasional figure walking by. What game was Leonardo up to?

He moved farther down the path. He stepped into the corner where the bridge met the wall and turned around. The noises of the city around him seemed to be coming down a pipe, mixed in with the splash of the water falling from the lock at the far side of the bridge. The water flowing fast from under the bridge lost its force not far into the canal. He kicked at a beer can, landing it in the weeds, stepped down the bank, and peered into the darkness under the bridge. Leonardo might even be watching him now, to make sure he was on his own. Leonardo Hickey, mastermind. Doper. He looked down at the dark waters. Out of his depth, the Great Leonardo. Where the hell was he?

A figure stepped down the bank, stopped, and stood facing him. A guy. Leonardo? Tight haircut, a bit heavyset. That wasn't Leonardo. He took a few steps back up along the wall but the face stayed in shadow. His heart began to beat faster. Leonardo playing games.

"Leonardo?"

The head moved from side to side. He stared into the shadows.

"Hey, Jammy!"

Something detonated in his chest and ran down his veins. Who was it? Had Leonardo sent him?

"Jammy! Come on out here. I know you're in there. Come on out and have a chat."

"Who is it?"

The answer came in a tired drawl.

"Santy Claus."

He'd heard the voice before but he couldn't put a face with it.

"Step out so's I can see you."

"Well, who are —"

"Don't be such a gobshite! Bobby sent me. Says howdo. Okay?"

"Well . . ."

"I'm coming in after you, Jammy, if you don't come out."

He took a few steps toward the figure. His hands began to tingle. He pushed his shoulders back and stepped on the balls of his feet. One guy, okay, but were there others?

"I don't know anything about this, man. Why did Bobby send someone —"

"Yeah, yeah, Jammy. Sure, sure — right over here, man. Don't be shy."

The fear tightened around his ribs now.

"Hey, look, I don't know anything about this, you know. I don't —"

"That's okay, man. It's okay. Come on out. Over here. Come on."

Stocky more than broad. It sure wasn't Lolly. Was this guy standing with his back to the streetlight on purpose? He stopped a dozen feet back from him. Still no others.

"What do you want, like? Bobby, I mean. What does he want from me?"

Was that a laugh? The man rubbed his nose and chuckled.

"'What does Bobby want?' Ah, come on up here. What does Bobby ever want? Who did you think you could piss on, Jammy?"

"I'm not trying to piss on anyone, man. I don't even know who I'm talking to."

The guy held out his arms and shrugged. Whoever he was, he enjoyed scaring the shit out of people. Was Leonardo watching all this? Like a knife sliding in between his ribs, it came to him that Hickey had fed something to the Egans, some story that'd get him a rep. The big prize for a moron like Leonardo, the price of an in with the Egans. Had they believed him?

"You know me, man. No? Ah, come on. When you used to go to the Club? No, you were never in the ring with me. Just as well for you too, ha ha. Come on, make a guess."

"Haven't a clue. There's a lot of fellas go to the Club —"

"Ah, come on! I'm a few years on, okay. Yeah, I've been sort of out of commission. Go on, make a guess — here, I'll even give you a clue. The Twins: okay, now you'll get it."

"Terry? Terry Malone?"

"Attaboy. Gone, but not forgotten, huh? You remember my ring name, don't you?"

"Well, yeah. Yeah, I do."

"But you don't know whether you should use it? 'Cause you're wondering to yourself, 'Jesus, Terry's a header and all. If I say anything he doesn't like, he'll go bananas.' Isn't that it?"

"Well . . ."

"You can say it. Go on, go ahead. Honest!"

"Terry the Bull."

Malone rubbed his hands together and chortled.

"Make my day, yeah! I like it! Say it again."

"Terry the Bull."

"Oh, yeah! How many times d'you see it?"

"Which, em . . ."

"De Niro, man! The film of the fucking century!"

"Oh, yeah. A few times. It was a great film, yeah."

"'Great'? Man, it was fucking *brilliant!* The slow motion . . . Did you see the sweat flying up with every dig, huh? Boom, boom . . . wham! I tell you, you could *feel* it, man. Right?"

His stomach had knotted up on him. Terry Malone sounded a bit pissed. Maybe he was out of his box on something.

"I thought you were inside, Terry. You know?"

"Well, I was, wasn't I?"

"How'd it go for you?"

Malone laughed.

"Poxy, that's how. Fucking p-o-x-y. Thanks for asking. But it's back to form, you know. Got me old job back. And I want to make up for what I lost, man. So Bobby knows that. He gives me this little number right off the bat. Call it a contract. And all this crap about unemployment, hah? You working, Jammy?"

"No. Rock-and-roll. A few nixers."

"Stuck for a few bob, are you?"

"No, not so much. The odd game too, you know. Snooker. Pool."

"Ah yeah. You used to be sharp. You still?"

"Yeah, well. I can still pot 'em."

"That's nice. . . . Wait a minute. I know. You'd a preferred that Bobby had sent Painless around here, right? Him and Lolly, the team. Laurel and fucking Hardy."

He thought about making a break for it.

"What's the matter, Jammy? Don't you want to hang around for a little chat?"

He could think of nothing to say. He shrugged.

"What are you scared of, Jammy? You know how to look after yourself, right? Come on up here, I want to talk to you, show you something. Come on, what's keeping you?"

He took a few halting steps into the space between them. Terry Malone's hand shot out. He sidestepped and moved down the bank a few feet. Malone gave a breathless laugh and let his hand hang in the air.

"You still got 'em, Jammy. You're quick. That's good. Now listen. You're a nice lad, Jammy. I mean it. Do you think I'm trying to get up your back?"

"No, I don't. No, Terry. It's just that, you know, I wasn't expecting . . ."

"Yeah, yeah . . . Your heart's in the right place. Eddsy told me that too. Believe me?"

"Yeah. Yes."

"That's good. You know how Eddsy is. Moody, right? Ha ha ha. But Eddsy's always rabbiting on about loyalty. You know what loyal is, Jammy?"

Terry Malone took a step toward him. The lamplight showed the bruises on his face.

"See them? That's about loyalty. You know what I mean?"

"No, Terry. I don't. Not really."

"Ah, some day I'll explain it all to you. When I got more time, like. I'll just tell you this much for now. I do me time in the 'Joy, walk out, look up and down the street. There's none of mine there at the gate to give me the big welcome or anything. Get the picture?"

"Sort of, Terry, but I'm not sure —"

"No, you don't," snapped Malone. "'Cause I fucking don't! How could you then?"

"I don't know, I mean."

He couldn't recall if he'd heard of Terry Malone doing drugs. Maybe he'd picked it up in the nick.

"Where was I? Oh, yeah. Loyalty. I had a few jars on me when I got in the door. Next thing I know is I have this two hundred percent dogfight with me brother, you know?"

"Ter — Tommy?"

"Tommy, yeah. Tommy the Pig. Call him that, I don't care. Really. Why should that bother me? So that's loyalty for you: I only get hammered at home. My own fucking brother. Isn't there some lesson in that or what?"

"I suppose, yeah. Yes."

"You were loyal to that fuck Hickey, weren't you? You felt sorry for him, right?"

Malone had calmed down a bit. He wondered if this was part of being high.

"Sort of. Well, I felt a bit sorry for him, I suppose."

"That so, now? Well, loyalty's a two-way street, Jammy. Eddsy thinks you can make people be loyal if you just scare the shite out of them. You think Hickey was loyal to you?"

He tried to swallow but his mouth was chalky. The stink from the canal seemed to have gotten suddenly worse.

"I don't know, Terry, like. I mean you never know with people, do you?"

Terry Malone had his hands in his pockets as he strolled toward him. The thick lip was twisted up weird because Malone was trying to smile. He smelled something from Malone's breath now, a sweet-sour tang in the air momentarily stronger than the stink off the water.

"'You never know,' huh." He shook his head. "Come here, will you. Walk down here a bit. I got something I want you to see. Somebody."

"Well, Terry, like, it's not like I don't want to talk to you. No, it's not that or anything."

Terry Malone laughed.

"Oh, yeah, man. I forgot. You think I'm here to do for you. Don't be worrying, man. It's just I get to talking and, well, the time just flies. You got to go? Go ahead."

Tierney shrugged.

"You're shitting bricks, aren't you, Jammy."

Tierney said nothing.

"Scared? Of Eddsy? You shouldn't be. If you were the job, you wouldn't be standing here talking, man. Okay? So take a walk here. Nobody else, man. You have my word."

Tierney took one step, then another up toward the footpath.

Why couldn't he breathe right? The night seemed to be tight over his face. Terry the Bull kept talking.

"So there's Eddsy himself waiting when I get out the door of the 'Joy. Right there in the car. Waves me in. Says he heard I was going to walk, thought I'd like to get back into the world, you know? And that feels good. Maybe not as good as if you'd a seen your own family there at the gate. Because, well, let's face it, I was no big thing to Eddsy, was I? Sure I did stuff with him and Bobby and Martin. But, hey — a welcome like that! Gives me a fistful of tenners. I had a half a bottle of champagne drunk before we hit town, man. Champagne! Tells me a place I can stay if things don't go over rosy at home. Eddsy knows more than I do about human nature, I'd have to say after that. Makes a point of being there himself, you see?"

He nodded. The fear was beginning to ebb a little.

"But I only cop on later why Eddsy's so interested in me. I don't get all the news inside, do I? It's Tommy the Pig. He's got himself a new job, hasn't he. And he's bent Eddsy's nose. To do with this girl getting done in. So Eddsy tells me about it. How she screwed up, how she tried to screw him out of merchandise. Know what I'm saying?"

"Well, I can kind of guess . . ."

"The brother's trying to break down a friend of Eddsy's. You know Lolly Lenehan?"

"Sort of."

"'Sort of'? Everybody knows Lolly. They put him in a corner, Tommy and the cops. Lolly's looking at five years. They want Lolly to help them nail Eddsy and the brothers, see? But Lolly's not saying anything. Lolly's bought into these speeches that Eddsy's always giving: loyalty. But Eddsy has this stupid thing, you know. It's personal with him now. He wants to hit back. Lolly and him were close, right? So I'm starting to get the idea. The car, the booze, the hits . . . Eddsy's got a job for me. See? Guess why I got the big parade and all?"

He shrugged.

"Ah, you're too polite, aren't you? Hey, Jammy! Polite can be a lot of things, man! Don't take me for a mug, okay? Polite can mean a sneak. Stoolie. It can mean thick, thick ideas you get because you didn't listen right! You know what I'm saying now?"

"Yeah, Terry."

"Okay. That's good. It's important we got off on the right foot. You don't want to waste time, you know? Time. Hey, do you know how you do time? How you get through? Loyalty. You don't rat on anyone. You don't stool. You stay loyal to the man you were before they took you off the street. You don't hang around with gobshites. You don't do favors and you don't ask favors. You don't ask stupid questions; you don't tell lies to your mates. You keep your self-respect. Under all conditions. Fella comes at you with a blade, you have to take him on. Whether you want to or not. Doesn't matter if you end up taking a rap for it either. You just do what you have to do. You might have to kill a man. That's how it is. There's no arguing. People will see that about you and they'll think, 'There's a guy; there's a guy to stick with.' You with me here?"

"Yeah, Terry."

"So here I am, man. Eddsy knows what I can do. But there's a price for everything, isn't there? All this crap Eddsy talks. Loyalty this and loyalty that. Let me tell you this: Eddsy has no loyalty. Did you hear that? None. Fuck-all. Eddsy, Bobby, Martin even — they're just fucking maniacs."

Malone nodded at the van.

"Surprise, surprise, huh? That's the price. Right over there. Eddsy tells me to find this Hickey. He wants me to bring him in. That proves my loyalty, see. See how everything comes around again? Now Eddsy's got something on me. I'm tied in. I get paid up — maybe even take over Lolly's job. See? Your fucking mate Hickey was my test. My loyalty test."

The suspicion came to him now as dread. Maybe Malone wasn't drunk after all.

"You're a sort of *decent* stupid, Jammy. A soft touch, aren't you?"

"I don't know what you mean, man — Terry."

"Cash to your old mate? Christ. You'd think he'd have used it to get well to hell out of here, wouldn't you? What a gobshite. What a total gobshite."

They know, he thought. Malone's face creased into a lopsided grin.

"Oh, he really rooked you, Jammy. Didn't he?"

He felt suddenly heavy, like in a dream he'd had over and over again when he was a kid. In some strange place, trying to avoid someone, trying to run before they caught him, but his feet wouldn't move. His mind couldn't put the bits together. They'd found Leonardo, or he'd found them.

"Don't you get it, Jammy?"

"I . . . Well . . ."

"Ah, you're thick, Jammy. Thick! But maybe it's being thick saves your neck now! Funny, isn't it? Someday I'll tell you just how close you came. With Eddsy, I mean. Eddsy . . . Jesus. Goes just fucking bananas . . . Totally out of it. He's a sadist, isn't he?"

He nodded.

"He wanted to hack Hickey's nuts off with a bread knife. What do you think of that?"

He took a breath and looked down at the path worn into the dry grass.

"Okay, I'll tell him you're speechless. 'No comment, Eddsy.' How does that sound?"

"Jesus, Terry. Why would Eddsy, you know? . . ."

"Weird, huh? But that's life. Listen to me. Things don't look good for you, do they?"

"Jesus, man, I don't know, you know?"

"Look. You could walk away from this. Or it's over for you. It's your choice. Hickey put on a good show before he pulled that stunt – Christ, that little bastard can run! For a minute, he nearly had me believing him. Maybe he could even have Eddsy believing him."

He was rooted to the ground now. Something was working its way up his spine toward his neck.

"So. You wanted to see Hickey, right? He called you. What for? For more jack?"

"Well, he didn't say really."

"Oh, come on, don't give me that shite, Jammy! Come on over here then."

Malone took a step away and stopped.

"Ah, I get it. You think I brought some lads here to get you, do you?"

He didn't answer. The smell from the canal was all through his head now.

"Don't be an even bigger gobshite than you were already, Jammy. Look at it this way: you came out to talk to a guy who would have pissed you down the fucking drain to save his own skin. I could have taken you myself if that was the job."

Malone reached under his denim jacket and opened his fist to show an automatic so small that at first he thought it was a cigarette lighter.

"Yeah, Jammy. It's all business tonight. The Boys Are Back in Town, you know? Boom-boom! You should have seen the bastard tearing off down the lane when he saw me!"

Buildings were sinking down toward him. It was like a hard punch, without the pain.

"What's the matter, Jammy? Lost your tongue? Come on, man!"

His legs began to move. He followed Malone up the path to the street.

"Oh, the other lads are long gone now, Jammy. Didn't want to hang around."

Malone was off his rocker because he'd done something terrible.

"Job's done, so they go home," Malone murmured. He turned and leered. "Have a bit of a wash-up before they sit down to their tea."

Malone stopped by the van. Already he had a piece of cloth in his hand. He turned the handle to open one side of the door. He looked up and down the street.

"Just don't touch anything. Unless you want to take the twenty-year trip. Ha ha."

The door squeaked at first. Something had crept into Malone's voice now.

"Hurry up! The van's robbed, so don't be worrying. I can do without any crowd."

The smell struck him as familiar. It was something that belonged with pressure, pain, fear. He held his breath. Malone tapped him in the arm.

"Take the torch. Quick."

The blood looked purple. He held his breath. It was all over the floor and the panels. They'd tied him up. Made a mess of his face. His hair to one side glistened with blood. His chest was rising and falling still. There was a hiss coming from somewhere by his face.

"He's alive. About ten percent though. Do you want to check him up close?"

He shook his head.

"He'd be a hell of a lot more alive if he hadn't pulled that stunt, I tell you. Did you ever chase a jackrabbit like him, a guy scared for his life, with a van? I mean to say, what am I going to do, me on me own? Go back to Bobby and tell him I had him, but I lost him? Hickey knew he was a goner. The half of him is still back on a steel door at the end of that lane."

He took a step back. The yellow light from the streetlamps made everything look sick, diseased. He turned with the bile rising in his throat and saw a hammer and a piece of pipe. The door slammed and Malone was beside him.

"Come on, man," he said. "I want to talk to you. Where's that bike of yours?"

He couldn't think. Malone's hand was on his arm, steering him across the street.

"You think he'll live long enough to talk to Eddsy?"

He swallowed. He didn't want to get sick.

"I wonder what he'd tell Eddsy. What do you think, huh?"

Tierney shook his head. His stomach was making these weird tics and he couldn't stop them. He'd heard that Terry the Bull was vicious in the ring, but this was way over the top.

"Nothing, huh?"

He looked up and nodded. They had reached the motorbike.

"Attaboy. Here, nice bike! What would you do? Bring him over to Eddsy while he's still with us, maybe? Get him to tell Eddsy what he told me?"

He looked into Malone's face.

"Yeah, well, I don't know either. I mean to say, you have to ask yourself: does it all add up? Hey. You're so quiet. Don't you want to know what he told me?"

"Leonardo could say anything, Terry! I mean, no one could believe him, you know?"

"Bobby could. What do you think? 'Hey, Eddsy. Leonardo Hickey told me Jammy Tierney had something to do with what happened that night at the canal.' 'Really?' Eddsy says. 'That's right. The cops are sniffing around about him, real sly, like.' 'Gee, I always thought that Jammy was straight. Why would I want to believe he was involved in that?' 'Well, Eddsy, Mary really screwed herself and she knew how you and the family would take what she'd tried to pull. The only place she could turn was Jammy. Yeah, Jammy'd do anything for her.' You think Eddsy believes in true love?"

"I don't know anything about it, man," he managed to say. "I swear to God."

"Yeah? So what are you here for then?"

"Leonardo sounded totally crazy on the phone, you know? I thought, well . . . I don't know. Terry, this is all so weird, man. You don't know how he can lie and stuff. Really."

"Jases, Jammy, maybe you're all right. It didn't really add up, what he was saying, did it. Maybe if he wakes up he'll make more sense, though. Maybe Eddsy'll understand."

"He lies — Leonardo, I mean. All the time! Eddsy knows that, right? You tell him —"

"I what?" Malone wagged his finger. "Big mistake there, Jammy. No matter how it happened, you know something. Eddsy'll find out that you gave Leonardo money to split. Yeah, he told me. So that makes you Leonardo's buddy, doesn't it? So if Leonardo did the job up there that night, then he would have told somebody. The only mate he had left was you. Jammy Tierney. Didn't you go around together when yous were young fellas?"

Tierney found no words. Terry Malone tapped his forehead.

"Let's go. There's a vanload of trouble I have to decide about. So, how about it?"

Tierney fell into step beside him.

"How about what, Terry?"

Malone threw an arm around his shoulder. He felt the arm tense. Still had the build, the strength. He must have kept up the training in the nick.

"Look, man, do I have to spell it out for you? Get this: I don't care who did what."

The arm around his shoulder had crept up to his neck.

"Get with it here, man! It's your one and only chance. It'll never come again. Hickey mightn't make a showing over at Eddsy's at all. I mean, a lot of things can happen on the way, can't they? So, does Eddsy or Martin need to listen to all of what Leonardo's going to be throwing around? I mean, would one of them get just that little bit suspicious? I don't know. It's a gamble, isn't it?"

"Wait a minute, wait. Terry . . ."

Even with the discolored eye, the mockery was plain on Terry Malone's face.

"Wait for what? Here — I'll spell it out, Jammy. Real slow. Number one: get the fucking money or whatever it is he took off her. Okay. Did you get that? Number two: give it to me. Tonight. No Eddsy, no Bobby. No Martin. No Leonardo. No problem. Number three: shut up. Now and forever. It's between you and me. You want to know why? I been inside too long, that's why. You can't buy time. There's no price you can pay. Eddsy Egan thinks I'm stupid. Didn't want to know me inside, but when I get out, they can use me. The movie-star treatment — yeah! But only so's I can do their dirty work!"

Tierney looked back at the van, the lights of the offices farther down the banks of the canal. The air was very still. There was a strange smell.

"And you know what pissed me off the most? It wasn't the rotting away in the nick even. And it wasn't Eddsy slapping me on the back the day I get out. It wasn't even them trying to use me to get at Tommy. No, what really got to me was them thinking they'd fooled me, that I bought into all this loyalty shite. 'We didn't forget about you, Terry. We'll look after you, man.' They took me for a gobshite!"

{ 322 }

He spat quickly down on the path and laughed.

"Stuck for words again, Jammy? You don't look too good there, man."

He laughed again.

"If Eddsy really thought you had tried to put something over on him, you'd be in the back of that van there with Hickey. Loyalty, huh. Eddsy talks about it because he doesn't have any. Outside of Martin and Bobby, I mean. He'd turn on anyone. But I done my time. I'm not going to shovel any shit for anyone. I'm going to get my own gig going. So you bring whatever you got. Whatever Leonardo left with you."

"Terry —"

Malone let go of his neck and pushed him away.

"Shut fucking up, Jammy! I've fucking had it here, man! What have I been talking about here the last five minutes? Look, she's dead. Leonardo's gonna be brown bread. So who cares? The rest, I don't want to fucking know!"

He stepped forward again and grasped Tierney's jacket.

"So, decide. Now! One hour, max."

Tierney shook his head. His arms came out from his side.

"Terry," he began but stopped to swallow.

"End of fucking story, Jammy! You know what I'm talking about. Pal Leonardo either gets to see Eddsy or he doesn't make it. Look. I'm going to be up in Phoenix Park with this van in an hour. That's where he was all the time, sleeping rough, did you know? You know the far end of the park, that lake with the island in it? The woods? One hour. I'm not going to sit on what's in the van for one minute longer. One hour."

CHAPTER 26

WHAT IF I WERE to tell you something?" said Kilmartin. Minogue studied his sandwich. "The Dublin crowd are all right."

"Am I hearing you right, Jim?"

The barman put two pints on the counter in front of them.

"Thanks, Seán," said Minogue. Kilmartin's hand was on his arm.

"No, no, no! Matt! Your money's no good now. My twist."

Minogue caught the barman's eye.

"Get the camera, Seán."

Kilmartin looked up from the bills he had in his hand.

"What was that?"

"Bag of crisps, please, Seán."

Kilmartin was maudlin and Minogue didn't know why. He looked at his watch again.

"What's the matter? Am I keeping you from your job or something?"

"No. You're all right. Go on."

"I'm serious," said Kilmartin. "What was I saying? Oh, yeah. The Dublin crowd. They're all right, you know. I mean to say, there's the perfect example in Kathleen. Always liked Kathleen. Always. The minute I laid . . ."

The chief inspector paused to take his change from the barman.

"You'd better finish that sentence, Jim."

"What? Oh, yes. Kathleen. The heart of the road. Do you know what I'm saying?"

"I do, I think."

"I'm happy that she's expecting now, you know?"

Minogue frowned. Kilmartin's grin was spreading.

"Expecting Iseult's fella to get a job! Ah, ha ha ha! Do you get it? Ah, ha ha ha!"

He punched Minogue in the arm. The chief inspector stopped and stared glassily at Minogue when the phone went. For a moment Minogue forgot where he had put it.

"Yes?" he said after the second trill. "Yes?"

He studied Kilmartin's face while he listened.

"Okay. Yes."

He put it back on standby. Kilmartin kept looking at him.

"I didn't know you could speak in Morse code there, pal."

"Nothing to concern yourself with there."

Kilmartin's gaze was broken by a sizable belch finding its way up through his esophagus. He bowed slightly, tapped himself on the chest, and barked.

"Ah, by God," he sighed. "If it's not one end, it's the other. Never been the same since that shagging surgeon got his hands on me."

He tapped Minogue with the back of his hand.

"You know you're gone fifty when things are either drying up or leaking, hah?"

The barman saved Minogue the need to feign a laugh.

"Hah, Seán? Seán knows what I'm talking about, don't you, Seán? Ha ha hah!"

Kilmartin's laugh turned to a cough. Minogue caught the barman's eye.

"So," said Kilmartin finally. "What do you think?"

"I'm betting on rain."

"The bloody case, man! Come tomorrow, I'm going to start a rehash. Right from the start. Fresh."

"Oh."

"Oh, yourself. Yes. And I'm going to sort out Keane and all the anti-racketeers we have over in shagging Harcourt Square in short order. Enough is enough: the hard tack and the iron discipline now, let me warn you. They can't be holding us back any more. They say they can produce for us — 'it's all grist for the mill' — but when do we actually get to sit down and talk hard to any of the Egans?"

"They're alibied, Jim. Did you forget that? The surveillance logs."

Kilmartin chopped at the countertop with the side of his hand.

"Oh, come on there, will you? I mean getting hold of other Egan cronies, putting them to the wall. Those bloody fellas haven't stayed out of jail for so long by being stupid now! There must be middlemen there between the Egans and selling stuff on the bloody streets, man. Have we been allowed into those files? We have not. Is that how we close cases? It is not. Is it good for morale? It is not. Will I put up with this much longer than dinnertime tomorrow —"

"You will not."

"Bloody right, I won't. Now you get the idea."

Minogue was staring into the mirror behind the counter. Dusk was on the windows behind him now. The customers in Ryan's seemed to be moving so slowly. Was the yellow tinge to everything his own tiredness? Even the laughter was muted.

The crash resonated in the windows and on the counter in front of him. An empty juggernaut hopping over a bad patch of road outside was his first thought. The barman stood up from emptying the dishwasher, the steam issuing up into his face. Kilmartin turned his head toward the open door of the pub.

"Name a Jases," he said. "I better cut down on the jar. That sounded too much like a bloody shotgun to me."

Kilmartin was about to take another swallow from his glass when the windows rattled again. This time the boom was unmistakable. Clients slid off stools and rose from chairs. The talk petered out. Minogue stepped over to the door. The air smelled odd now. He flinched when the thunder crashed again.

"My Jases," said a man next to him. "Will you get a load of that?"

The traffic had slowed. The air smells of vinegar, Minogue decided.

"My God, it's going to just lash." He looked back at the speaker. It was indeed an awed Kilmartin. "They told us about it but . . ."

The knot of patrons by the door grew larger. Someone laughed nervously.

"I'm for getting to hell out of here before we're drownded," Kilmartin declared. It was a five-minute walk to the squad room.

"Honest to God," he added. "I was just terrorized by thunder and lightning when I was a young lad. I used to hide under the bed. I thought it was the end of the world."

He went back to the counter to finish his drink. Minogue moved out onto the footpath. He tried hard to see the sky through the yellow streetlight. The few pedestrians were beginning to scurry now. He looked back up toward Phoenix Park and the zoo and thought of Iseult and the drive they had taken through the park the other day. The animals would be restless in their enclosures. Kilmartin emerged from the pub, wiping his mouth with the back of his hand.

"Come on there, Matt, or we'll be pissed on entirely!"

The two detectives hurried toward the bridge. The Liffey at Islandbridge was at full tide. Minogue strode on, his hand on the phone. He felt its vibration more than heard its chirp. Kilmartin stopped at the end of the bridge and looked back. His hands went up and flopped back down in exasperation. A lorry crossing the bridge stole some of the phone conversation on Minogue. He leaned away from the traffic, his finger in his ear, his eye on Kilmartin. Still he had trouble hearing. Kilmartin was coming back toward him.

"Okay," he said. "Yes."

He hung up and settled the switch on standby. Kilmartin was upon him.

"Well?"

Kilmartin saw the movement at the same time as Minogue. The two policemen ducked at the same time as the shapes rose up from the darkness below the bridge. Minogue heard the wings beat as they passed not ten feet overhead. He stood again and looked up as they disappeared over the buildings. Kilmartin's eyes were wide.

"As true as God," he began. "Did you ever in all your life? . . . That is the last time I go out for a shagging sandwich and a pint with you! Christ, man, for a minute there I didn't know what was going on!"

Minogue's heart was still thumping. He looked back at Kilmartin.

"Taking shelter, I suppose," he said. "They know what's coming."

"Jesus," exclaimed Kilmartin. "That gave me one hell of a fright, I don't mind telling you. I heard they had them up here all right. Didn't that famous fella, the doctor fella . . . that butty of Joyce donate some here?"

Minogue nodded.

"Gogarty," he said. "To thank the river god or something for saving his neck."

"Was that the Civil War when he nearly got his arse shot off hereabouts?"

"None other," said Minogue.

"And the size of them!" marveled Kilmartin. "But, sure, how could they survive with the place so builtup and rundown, and full of bowsies and gougers who would do them harm just for the hell of it?"

The thunder crashed overhead now. Minogue cowered. Kilmartin gave him a dig.

"What are we doing standing in the middle of a bridge like iijits? Come on now, for the love of God!"

The first flash showed as a flickering glow over the south suburbs. Kilmartin was breathing hard when they turned into the car park. Minogue drew his keys out.

"There!" Kilmartin called out. "That's the start of it. We were wise to run for it when we did, boyo."

Minogue clicked the remote.

"Hey, where are you off to?"

"Come in, Jim, before you get wet and mess up my nice upholstery."

"What the hell?"

"It's not often you get a night like this. Come on."

• • • • •

He looked back to where he had parked the Kawasaki. The trees merged into a continuous silhouette under the brassy glow of the city lights. In the darkness ahead lay the open fields. He listened. The Main Road was no more than a few hundred yards away, he figured, but the tunnel of light from the passing headlights seemed so far off. Over the distant hush of the traffic he heard the occasional squawk and groan. He listened harder. Night birds? He turned back to the grove surrounding the pond. Not even a breath of air to stir the leaves. Everything seemed to be just hanging there. He let his eyes move slowly across the grove. No van. He felt his back tightening up again and he shook his arms loose. He realized that he still hadn't decided anything. Since the phone call, the evening had gone by like a dream. Maybe that's what it was like being on drugs. Driving here, the night air hadn't refreshed him at all. He kept thinking about her. He thought back to the look on her face when he had told her. He'd known straight away that she'd read his face but still she had tried once. He'd felt nothing when he slapped her. He wondered when it would all become real, when feeling came back.

The ground dipped and rose again as he walked toward the trees. Maybe he should have tried driving in over the grass. The dry grasses lashed against his shoes, and he felt them rub, sometimes clutch at his feet. It was a longer walk than he had expected. The darkness had tricked him. He stared into the trees as they came closer. He couldn't even see the water. He stumbled over something with give in it, stopped, and felt around with his foot. The grass had been beaten down in a line. A few steps away he found the other track. A car had driven in here. A van? If he followed this track . . . Mad. They were all mad. Terry Malone was mad. He was mad to be here. He should turn back. Let everyone else sort out their own fucking problems. Problems they caused themselves, with their own stupidity and greed and . . . He should just turn back. The first flash had nearly caused him to drive right off the road. He'd braked hard and stopped right in the middle, barely keeping the bike upright. It had taken him a few seconds to realize that it had been lightning. There had been no thunder yet, only flashes like lights being turned on and off somewhere up in the sky. He had seen the massed clouds, blue and brown, lit up by the flashes. It's all a dream, was his first thought, the flashes and the strange smells all around him. If it turned to real lightning, he could get fried out here near the trees. He started walking again. This time the flash had him on his hunkers in a second. It had been his own voice he had heard as he had dropped down, he realized.

He stayed low and kept staring into the woods. They were even darker now that the lightning had robbed his night vision. Another flash, but shorter, and this time he was sure. It was the back of a van. He stood upright again and walked toward it. The sound of his own beating heart filled his head. He tried to get control of his breathing. It had to rain any minute, he thought. What if there was a screwup and he had to take off in a hurry? Would he lose his way running back to the bike? He'd tried again to make plans as he had turned into the park but his brain couldn't seem to stay with an idea. Fragments flew through his mind: drive with the lights off, park a long way off, sneak up on the place . . . The trees had come nearer to him now, the grass was not as high. He stopped. Was that straight line part of the van in there? If it started to lash rain now, maybe he could just take off. Blame it on the weather: it was too dangerous to drive, Terry, you know? Too dangerous. He held out his hand. Nothing yet.

His feet carried him forward in under the branches. Something light draped itself across his face. He turned and snatched it away. Cobwebs — Christ! He stumbled on a protruding root. A bird chattered overhead and fell silent. He laid his hand against a trunk. Old trees, twisted and huge, surrounded him. It seemed to grow even darker. He glanced up into the foliage. He could barely hear the traffic now. Where was the van? Blue light flared all around him. He froze, facing the van, and waited for his eyes to adjust again. The van had looked like it was floating in midair with the pond like silver behind it. His heart kept racing. Did he plan to ditch Hickey in the pond or something? The next thunder came as a murmur. He kept staring at the line that made up the roof of the van. It had been only fifty yards away.

"Hey!"

He spun around, already in a crouch.

"Terry? Terry? Is that you, man? I can't see a thing."

"Who're you expecting, Jammy?"

The voice was so close. He must be behind a tree or something. It felt like his eyes were sticking out of their sockets.

"Where are you, Terry?"

A black form passed in front of a tree trunk not fifty feet from him.

"Terry?"

"You don't sound too good there, Jammy. Lost in the woods, are you?"

"Terry? I thought you meant out there, out near the road."

He watched Malone's silhouette approach. Malone laughed.

"You're shivering, Jammy. What's the matter? It's boiling in here."

He saw the liquid glint of lights from the traffic in Malone's eyes. Definitely out of it.

"Well, it wouldn't have been the place I'd have picked, Terry, you know?"

"Oh. Well, who fucking asked you? Here — where's that fancy bike of yours?"

"Back out there."

"Why didn't you drive in like I done?"

"Well, I didn't know how the ground was and stuff, and —"

"Are you going to moan about the weather now or something? Here: if you're that worried about a bit of fucking rain, drive home in the van. Yeah. Try it, why don't you?"

He heard the liquid swill before he could make out the bottle that Malone put to his lips. Even Terry the Bull needed the booze to get by tonight.

"You want a little swig there, Jammy? Seeing as we're partners and all?"

"No. No, thanks, Terry."

Malone sniggered.

"You're not in the mood to celebrate? Christ, Jammy, you're no fun. Hey!"

He waited for Malone to down another gulp.

"You've had time to do a little thinking, haven't you, Jammy?"

"How do you mean?"

The hand was so quick that he felt the slap before he could move his head. Christ, how did he keep those reflexes while he was pissed?

"Speak fucking English, Jammy? Don't ask me what I mean! You saying I can't talk or something? I'm talking about you and your plans!"

He smelled the whiskey now, heard Malone's breath.

"You think I'm a gobshite too, Jammy? Don't tell me the thought didn't cross your mind that you might want to feed me to the Egans too. Like you could play it back on me the same as I could on you? Huh?"

"No, Terry! No way, man. I would never do a thing like that."

"That's right, you wouldn't! And you know why, don't you? 'Cause I'd fucking do for you, so I would!"

Malone took another swig from the bottle.

"So let's go. Partner."

Malone stumbled twice on the way to the van. Following, Tierney caught odd words from him as he walked.

"So don't even think about it, Jammy, you hear?"

The engine's oily smell mixed with the faint scent of heated rubber hung in the air around the van. Terry Malone turned.

"So gimme what you got, Jammy. Then it's a last look and bye-bye."

"Are you going to, you know, leave everything here, Terry?"

"You got a better idea? I spent ten minutes wiping the fucking seats and the wheel and God knows what's in there. I'm gone, man. You want to hang around, go ahead — but I was never here."

"Okay. I was just wondering and all —"

"Yeah, yeah, yeah. Gimme."

He took the envelope from the inside pocket of his denim jacket.

"What is it, Jammy? Powder, pills? Cash? What did he do her for?"

"Who — oh, Leonardo?"

"Who do you fucking think I'm talking about?"

"Cash."

Malone yanked at the side of the envelope.

"How much?"

"A thousand, Terry. Just short of a thousand."

"What if I find it was more and you kept stuff back?"

"That's all of it, Terry. I swear to God."

"Less the money Leonardo was talking about, huh? Some pal, man. Some pal. You wouldn't believe it, man. Some fucking pal."

"I don't get it, Terry. I know he wasn't straight-up about it all."

Malone stuffed the money into his pocket.

"Straight-up? Oh, Christ, what a gobshite you are! Right up to the end, man. There he was trying to sell you down the river, spinning some cock-and-bull about you — and you're the guy he stashes his take with! The only guy he could trust! Human nature, I'm telling you!"

Malone was shaking his head. The end, right up to the end. Was Leonardo dead?

"I tell you, if he hadn't tried to run for it — if I didn't have to throw a frigging van at him to stop him, he might have been singing a different story — Holy Jesus! Did you see that one?"

The color of the flashes seemed to have turned to green now. His mind was ready to burst. What the hell had happened between Leonardo and Malone? He looked back at the van.

"Let's go, man! It's been doing this for the last half hour. It's bound to start lashing sometime. Come on!"

He caught up with Malone, who tripped again, spilling a little from the bottle. He had to ask him.

". . . lift on the bike," he heard coming over Malone's shoulder. "Yeah! Should have come straight out and admitted it. Show a bit of self-respect, you know? Hey, where is this fucking bike of yours anyway?"

"Over that way. Terry —"

"He would have sold you down the fucking river for a tenner, man. Oh, stupid he wasn't — I mean, he knew that he better not have a heap of money on him, so he's smart enough to stash it. But, Jesus, Jammy, you were the right iijit to let him do that to you. Man! If Eddsy ever found out . . . Hey, what story did he tell you about where he got the money anyway? I never got that far with him. How did he get by you?"

"Well, it was like . . . well . . ."

Malone stopped. The grove was fifty yards behind them. The smell in the air had a sting to it now.

"Oh, I get it! You're too fucking embarrassed, aren't you?"

He watched Malone drain the bottle and reach back to fling it away. He stopped and turned around.

"Jases, that wouldn't be very smart, would it? Come on."

"Terry, what about him. You know. What's going to happen?"

"I'm going to get a lift down the quays off you. You're going to get five hundred quid — if there's really four and a half grand here. We're going to go on our merry fucking way."

"No. I mean the van and —"

"Shut up, would you? He's a goner, man: brown bread! Don't keep asking about him! Hey, I've got feelings too, you know. But fellas like him, they'd rob you blind. It'll square off okay with Eddsy. It's a message, right? I'm going to give Eddsy a thou and tell him that Hickey must've put the rest in his fucking arm. Hickey was a junkie, right? So a junkie'll go through big money in a few days. They get into a party, they lose the head — everyone bangs up — fuck, Eddsy'll be surprised there's anything left. Is that the road there? Come on!"

"But, Terry, what about the law? What did he tell you about the law? You said they were asking him stuff about me and everything —"

"Ah, give over, for Jases's sake! What have they on you, man? Have you got a record? Have you gotten picked up and given the treatment all day and all night? Don't be so fucking stupid! I can't believe it! You're a little bleeding angel, Jammy!"

"What?"

"Christ! Don't you get it yet? They never asked him anything about you! He was trying to buy time! He was lying through his teeth!"

Malone grabbed his forearm.

"Shit! Fuck it! Oh, man, here it comes. Did you feel that?"

He had felt it, he knew, but he had somehow ignored it. Another big drop landed on his head. Malone had let go his arm. He was swearing still, calling out to him as he hurried out toward the road. This time the thunder began with a snap. The noise seemed to roll across the sky.

CHAPTER 27

THE SAFEST PLACE TO BE, that's right," said Kilmartin. He leaned forward and pushed in the lighter. "Do you mind?"

"Long as you don't fart, I don't."

"Huh. Like I was saying. Safest of all. It's the rubber, you know."

Minogue turned the ignition key and pushed the window button. Lightning flared again.

"Listen, you've had your jaunt now. That's twice today I gave in to your, what'll I call it, your obsession, with this new motor of yours. Any excuse to go out for a drive, huh?"

"Maybe."

"Come on so. We've seen enough of nature at her finest. Let's get out of here. Never liked this kind of fireworks. Sort of puts me in mind of a Redemptorist sermon during Lent."

Minogue listened for the roll of thunder. It came from far off again, like a cardboard box falling down the stairs. Eleven seconds: eleven miles.

"Did you hear the screeching earlier on?" he asked Kilmartin.

"What? Where? Back up the other end of the park?"

"Yes. Just before the first bits of thunder."

"The zoo, man. Sure the poor beasts must be terrified. I mean to say. Even if they were born and reared in Ireland here — and there are many of 'em what are, I believe — they'd have their instincts. Yes. Fear. Arra Christ, I've had a headache hanging around all day. Like it was waiting to pounce on me. I held off with the bloody aspirin and now I don't have them with me. Typical, isn't it? If I wanted this class of tropical-type shagging weather, I would have taken a few bob out of the Getaway account and toddled off to somewhere you'd expect this class of typhoon. Know what I'm saying?"

"Of course I do, Jim."

He sensed Kilmartin's glare on him but he didn't turn. The lighter popped out.

"Just don't be using the ashtray, if you please."

Kilmartin stabbed a cigarette into his mouth and grunted. The car was full of smoke with his first pull. Minogue turned on the ignition and opened the window lower.

"I was checking the dollar the other day," said Kilmartin. "Always had it in mind for the young lad, you know? He sends money home every now and then. To Maura. For her to buy the odd thing for herself."

He laughed lightly.

"As if she actually needed it. But he's a decent boy."

Minogue wondered if Kilmartin was going to remain maudlin much longer. The Kilmartins' only child had emigrated to the States three years ago. He turned to his colleague.

"Well I know it, Jim. Always was, as I recall."

"Damn right, man. Didn't pick that up off the street either, so he didn't. Don't get me wrong now! Maura, I mean. I wasn't blowing me own trumpet now. Maura was reared to be helping everyone."

Minogue stared into the darkness where the trees were and listened to Kilmartin drawing on the cigarette again. Another flash of lightning lit up the park.

"Jesus, Mary, and Joseph!" said Kilmartin. He sat back slowly in the seat. "This was sport and games to us, of course. When we were kids, I mean. We'd be terrified, but we'd still want to see it all. The danger thing."

On to kids now, thought Minogue. Childhood. What next? Maybe the air pressure before a storm had altered the supply of blood to his friend's head and awakened dormant memories. Maybe Kilmartin was trying to draw him out, to see what Daithi did as regards remittances home from the States.

"They're never reared, are they?"

"Who?"

"Your kids."

"Mine are, Jim. They'd better be, is my attitude."

"Ah, don't be like that. You know what I mean."

Minogue turned and looked at his friend.

"Is there something you want to tell me? Is it that you're feeling sorry about Iseult or something?"

"Not at all, man."

"You are."

"I'd be less than candid —"

"Well, be less than candid, for God's sake."

"Huh. I think you're still in shock. That's why you aren't able to react. That's what I think."

That's what you think, thought Minogue. But he didn't feel irritated. Kilmartin had probably thought he was doing him a favor, humoring him by going to the pub, by going along with the jaunt.

"You never know what the boys will come up with," said Kilmartin. "I mean, you worry about girls, of course, but . . ."

Hasn't seen his own son since last year, Minogue had to remind himself. Maybe soon he could relay Kilmartin's hedging to Iseult, turn it into a laugh.

"What's the word from the States then?"

"Oh, good, good. Always good. He writes every few weeks, you know. As well as the phone calls, of course."

Cars continued to pass Minogue's parked Citroen. He and Kilmartin had cruised several roads in the park before stopping in the middle, by Áras an Úachtaran. He looked down in his lap again to be sure the low-battery light hadn't come on. The lightning flash was longer this time.

"By the divine hand a! . . . Will you look at that! Another one!"

Kilmartin nudged his colleague.

"Here, Matt, answer me this: who do you think organized this bloody show here tonight? Hah? All that stuff above there? We knew it was God when we were kids. What do you think it is?"

Minogue lifted the phone from his lap in the hopes it would ring.

"Who are you waiting for to get in touch there, Matt? The Man Himself? Ha, ha!"

Kilmartin threw his butt out onto the road. A tick on the window was followed by more.

"Okay," he said. "That's it. We're away. Now, about starting fresh tomorrow. Round two, like. Instead of Molly, I really want Fergal —"

The phone trilled in Minogue's hand. He jammed it against his ear.

"Now?" he asked. "Yes."

He started the car.

"What," said Kilmartin.

Minogue spun the tires as he accelerated away from the side of the road. Rain hit the glass like pebbles now. He brought the Citroen up to seventy before Kilmartin could finally take no more.

"Jases! Where are you taking us — to the shagging mortuary? Slow down, man!"

.   .   .   .   .

He put his head down as the drops hit harder and broke into a jog. Terry Malone could do what he bloody well wanted. He was pissed anyway. High too, probably. Thunderstorm or not, he was going to tear out of here on his bike. The rain began to beat the grass down and it snagged his feet as the drops landed. They drummed on his head and his sleeves. He pulled the collar of his jacket tighter under his neck and glanced back to see where Terry Malone was. He couldn't see him. He stopped and held his hand over his eyebrows. The raindrops stung the back of his hand now. Already he felt rainwater running down the back of his ears.

"Terry!"

Sheets of rain drifted like smoke across the city's yellow glow. To hell with him, he whispered. Maybe he'd gone back to get something from the van. He turned back toward the road and began walking. The water soaked in over his toes. He wiped the rain from his face but it kept flowing down his forehead. Was he headed the right way? The flash started as white but exploded into yellow. He dropped to his knees. He flinched and sank lower but kept his eyes open as another flash broke over him. His heart froze. For several seconds all he knew was the rainwater creeping along his spine, the drumming on his head, the tufts of wet grass between his fingers. Whoever they were, they had come out from behind the trees. The two cars beyond them couldn't have been there before.

.   .   .   .   .

"My Jesus," said Kilmartin. He sat forward in the seat and rubbed the glass with the heel of his hand. "What are you trying to prove? That this bloody car can float or something?"

Minogue had slowed to second gear. He sat over the wheel and changed the speed of the wipers every now and then. The rain drummed harder on the roof. Minogue checked the sunroof for the fifth time and squinted out through the flow on the windscreen.

{ 337 }

"Now that's a cloudburst," said Kilmartin. "And any man with any titter of wit would pull over to the side of the bloody road —"

"Be quiet, Jim. It's hard enough trying to see anything without you *ologóning*. We're nearly there."

"Nearly where? Christ, man, you're after driving us in the wrong direction!"

Kilmartin sat back and waved his hand toward the dash.

"What the hell use are all your feck-me-do buttons and switches now. Pull in off the road, man, or we'll be under the wheels of some big lorry here."

A flash showed the rain as needles but it was enough for Minogue to spot the cars.

"Now we're in business," he murmured.

"What business? What're all those cars there? They looked like unmarkeds . . . What are they doing in there off the road?"

Minogue pulled the lever next to the hand-brake and turned in over the grass. He heard Kilmartin's failing efforts to find words. He aimed the nose of the car toward the pair of dark-colored Corollas by the edge of the grove.

"The bloody car is after rising up!"

"It's supposed to, Jim. The suspension —"

"Shag this, man! You're up to serious messing now, I'm telling you. Stop this circus —"

"There it is."

"There's what?"

"His motorbike. It's parked just off the road."

The Citroen wallowed but came out of the depression without bottoming out.

"You knew there was something on here. You —"

Kilmartin stopped talking when the beams went on. Two sets at the same time, then more, some moving until he gave up trying to decide how many cars there were. Minogue stopped the Citroen.

"Come on out," said Minogue. "We can fill a space somewhere." Kilmartin was staring at the headlights.

"Those are Guards out there," he said. "Am I right?"

Minogue nodded.

"That's him," he added. "And there are patrol bikes in or around here if he tries to leg it over the fields."

"Who? Who, for the love of God?"

He rose up slowly. He wasn't sure if his knees would hold him. The words and hoarse pants he had been hearing were his own. The trees, he thought. They've staked the motorbike, so head into the trees. Headlights came on as he began his run. Two sets ahead caught him immediately. He stopped and turned. Others came on. The lights that aimed away began to turn toward him. They were all around. Something began to give way in his stomach. Would Bobby Egan have all this stuff? Where was Terry Malone? The bastard. A single light detached itself from the others and began weaving its way toward him. Still he stood, frozen, his lips moving, his breath coming in huge gulps. It was a motorbike. Mesmerized, he followed its passage over rises and bumps. It stopped fifty yards from him. Over the rain he heard engines now. He turned and tried to see where the gaps were. He could take a run toward —

The tinny screech stopped his thoughts. A loudspeaker? It had said his name. The rain was streaming over his eyes now. What, he called out. He heard "Gardai" before the flash. Ducking, he saw the white helmet of the cop on the bike as he too flinched. He sank to his knees in the grass. The rain hit his neck harder. He didn't lift his head even when he heard them telling him to lie down. They told him again. He sat back on his heels. The motorbike put on blue flashing lights as it approached. Two cars came in. He heard doors being slammed shut and he looked out into the glare. The lights were on the move again, coming closer. The cops walked in front of the beams. Voices shouting at him now, using his name. Lie down. He wasn't going to lie down. They had been tailing Terry Malone since he got out, that's what did it. The rain was made up of solid lines all the way back to the clouds, he thought. Like waves across the headlights. He was staring at the rain by his knees when he felt them push him over. The bands on his wrists were pulled tight. They pulled him up. He looked into their faces and saw that they looked kind of scared. More cops walked in out of the glare. A tall one with his hair plastered down over his eyebrows came up. He waved something at him. It caught the lights once before he put it away. Another big cop came up behind him.

"James Tierney," said the dark-haired one. "I'm Inspector Minogue. I'm arresting you for the murder of Mary Mullen . . ."

He looked beyond the tall cop to the others. Two of them were already going through the grass with flashlights looking for anything he had dropped. It's all true, he thought.

". . . to remain silent . . ."

His gaze stayed on the silhouette of one of the cops standing to the side.

"You have the right to consult counsel . . ."

Why was he on his own?

"Terry?"

". . . you will be brought before . . ."

"Terry!"

"Shut up there," said the cop next to the one reading him his rights.

"Terry! Over here, man!"

The man turned away. So did the cop who had told him to shut up.

"Do you understand what I have told you?"

"What?"

"Do you understand your rights as I have told them to you?"

The grip tightened on his arms when he tried to see around this tall cop with the eyes boring into him.

"Terry! You bastard! You stoolie bastard!"

"Okay, Fergal," the cop said. Still he tried to stop them pulling him away.

"Don't pay that bastard! Yous're all wrong! He lied! It's a fix!"

"Out of here, Fergal," the tall cop was saying. "Before we're toasted by lightning."

·   ·   ·   ·   ·

Kilmartin's hair reminded Minogue of a villainous professor from a silent film. As though privy to his colleague's thoughts, the chief inspector ran his hands over the wet strands, patting them back over his head.

"You," he said in a pensive tone, "are getting worse."

Minogue glanced up at the deserted offices of the Financial Centre as the Citroen glided through the orange light and onto the North Wall. He checked the mirror to make sure the other car had made it through. The Citroen crashed over a puddle.

"You told me that quite a number of years ago."

"I know I did. I meant it then and I mean it now. Me head's still spinning with all this. Why didn't you tell me you had moved on this?"

Minogue looked down at the clock. Half past nine. He felt keen, alert.

"I wanted it to be a surprise. You trust me, don't you?"

{ 340 }

Kilmartin stopped patting his crown.

"I trust you for the next ten minutes. Then your time is up. I want to know everything. That's the deal."

"Yes, James."

"How Tierney got to be there. Where you got the giveaway. When. With who —"

"Whom."

"What?"

"No. With whom."

"Bugger off trying to show me up! Ten minutes, and counting!"

"Yes, James."

"This stinks. Worse and worse as the minutes go by."

"I understand how you feel."

"The hell you do! Don't play social worker on me, pal. Who was it decided that I was to have spectator status on this caper?"

"Me. You have Keane and Co. to answer to. All the courtiers. I have to do what I can to make a living."

"Sweet suffering hand of the divine crucified Je —"

"We're almost finished, Jim. The world will unfold as it should."

Kilmartin let out a breath and looked out the side window.

"You bloody well better not be teaching this type of procedure, you know," he said.

You're right. Absolutely."

"Couldn't stand up at all if the case gets thrown upstairs at HQ."

"Well, there's not much you can do with one arm tied behind your back, is there?"

"Tell that to Serious Crimes and their European pals! Listen. One word I never want to hear about this — are you listening? Not a whisper do I want to hear of it: entrapment. Now or ever. Are you with me?"

Minogue looked across the Liffey as they coasted along, the broken surface of the roadway registering only as a flapping sound over the hiss from the rain.

"All water under the bridge, James."

"What is? Your trick-acting?"

Minogue turned the wheel sharply just to see how the car would take abrupt driving. Smooth as silk.

"Nice car all the same, don't you think?"

Kilmartin grunted and looked down at the lights on the dashboard.

"Wake me up when we hit Mars. Where's the button for making the breakfast?"

Minogue saw the Toyota behind lean hard as it turned in behind. It threw up a wave to the side as it crossed the gutter.

"They have no complaint," he said. "Have we jeopardized any of their operations?"

"How the hell would I know? They never gave details! Then you decide to keep me in the dark too!"

Minogue looked over and gave a wan smile.

"For your own good, Jim."

"Oh, my God! Anyway. The father will be trouble."

"All right. You take her then. There's me and John Murtagh if Plateglass doesn't feel up to it. Aw'royh' loike, Jimmo?"

"Jesus, the gurrier lingo out of you. You're hanging around Molly too much. I have a few choice things to tell that fella whenever he sorts out his personal life."

"His brother's personal life, loike."

"'Loike' yourself! Will you never learn? Genes! Science! Hard facts! Didn't you get just one little twinge when we ran into the brother over at Egans' shop the other day?"

"I don't get little twinges, Jim. Probably an age thing."

"Come on! When you saw the brother, didn't you really think — even for a minute? They look identical, they act identical —"

"Can't prove it."

"*Science* proves it, man! That's why we have bloody science! Walks like a duck, talks like a duck —"

"Ever heard of free will?"

"Oh, Christ! And you're the one always pulling on me about the layabouts in fecking Finglas and the flats and wherever: 'Ah, Jim, they can't help it, it's the environment —'"

"You're way to hell and back offside with that. Context, Jim, context."

"Spell it out for me then. Context, my arse! Human nature, bucko — since Adam was a boy! Open your eyes, man. We'll be well rid of fecking Molly."

"He'd be well rid of us, the way you're talking."

"Read a thing in the *Reader's Digest* about long-lost twins, so I did. Grew up on either side of the bloody States, farmed out to different families — and what happens?"

"You fell asleep."

"Hah. They turn out to be the same."

"A miracle."

"The same clothes. Favorite drinks. Cars. Each had three kids. Petite wives —"

"What's petite?"

Kilmartin folded his arms and looked away.

"You just don't want to find out I'm right, that's your problem."

Minogue yanked the wheel to take the turn. He released it quickly. The Citroen righted itself immediately. Great stuff. He slowed for the Toyota to close the gap. Ahead of him he saw the Garda van parked. There was no traffic. He pulled into the curb and switched off the engine.

"Asked for a van, did you?"

"Wild West here sometimes, Jim. You never know."

"'Sometimes'? Christ. Understatement of the year. Okay. Are we right?"

"Yep. Let them go in first."

"I thought —"

"I don't want the glory, Jim. I just want the arrest."

Kilmartin rubbed the passenger-side window as the three figures passed along the footpath. Minogue saw the passenger door of the van open, a uniformed Guard step out.

"Oi! Who's number three of ours there? Christ! Where's the bloody winder for the window?"

"The ignition has to be on. It's electric."

"Let me out of this bloody box! Where's the door thing? Jesus Christ! What kind of a shitbox am I stuck in here? Bloody Frenchmen! They shouldn't be let near anything to do with cars!"

He turned angrily to Minogue. The inspector ignored him. He switched on the ignition and pushed the wipers. Two detectives were at the door already. Fergal Sheehy was the backdoor man.

"Open the frigging door, for Christ's sake! They're nearly in the house already."

"Sorry, Jim. It's that sideways-looking thing there. Yes. Don't break it off now . . ."

Kilmartin was out. He slammed the door hard and took off at a trot down the gleaming footpath. Minogue winced before completing his sentence.

". . . you clumsy bullock."

The hall door was opened. One of the figures stepped in smartly. Someone tried to close the door but Murtagh had already put his shoulder to it. Minogue heard a shout. Kilmartin was almost there now. A second Guard had emerged from the van. A scream now, a woman's. Minogue stepped out of the car. It was Patricia Fahy's da all right. The door was being pushed and pulled. Kilmartin skipped in and pushed at the door alongside Murtagh. The Guard in uniform stepped around them. He reappeared almost immediately and came out the door backward, his arms tight around Fahy's neck. Kilmartin followed them out onto the terrace. Murtagh slipped into the house. Kilmartin slid a leg behind Fahy's knees and the Guard turned Fahy as he fell. The second Guard stepped around Minogue, bent down, and yanked up Fahy's arm. Kilmartin stepped away. Minogue asked the Guard with the knee in Fahy's back if he wanted help with the restraints. Fahy stopped groaning and began shouting.

"Shut up," said Kilmartin. "You're in enough trouble."

"Don't you fucking touch her! Yous don't know anything about what goes on out here, you bastards! Useless, yiz are! The crimes is going on all around and yous are blind!"

"You're under arrest too, Mister Hard-chaw. Is your daughter inside?"

"None a your fucking business! Why aren't yous tearing into the Egans and their like?"

The two Guards lifted Fahy to his knees and pulled him upright. A shriek erupted from the top floor of the house. Minogue looked up and down the street. The rain had lightened to a patter on his crown. He caught one Guard's eye and nodded.

"We all right inside then?" said Kilmartin.

"'Course we are. Come on in and we'll see."

More shrieks from upstairs. A woman screamed No. Kilmartin looked into all the rooms. Minogue stepped into the kitchen and made for the back door to let Sheehy in.

"Action's all upstairs, Matt."

"I'll follow you up, I just want to get Fergal in."

Minogue watched Kilmartin lumber up the narrow staircase. Patterned socks again today, he thought. Over the lumpen tread of the chief inspector's leather-soled shoes, Minogue could hear the crying still. The detectives' voices came to him in tones only. Kilmartin reached the top of the stairs. Minogue looked up at the ceiling and tried to follow Kilmartin's passage through the bedrooms. Another shriek. Patricia Fahy's mother called out. Something heavy clumped on the floor. Minogue studied his own face in the hall mirror. It looked jowly, different. Fergal Sheehy appeared at the top of the stairs. He descended sideways, his hand on Patricia Fahy's elbow. No cuffs, thought Minogue. Mrs. Fahy told someone to get out of her fucking way. An answering growl came from Kilmartin.

Patricia Fahy's hair looked like it was glowing. Her head bobbed at each step. Behind her came Malone, each step almost grudging. He caught Minogue's eye but did not smile. The mother was shouting now. Minogue leaned around the banister and looked up to catch a glimpse of Kilmartin's back pressed against the banisters on the landing. That'd keep him busy for awhile. Patricia Fahy didn't look at him as she passed. He said her name again. She told him to fuck off. A handful of neighbors had gathered on the path outside. Two Guards in uniform were standing in front of them. Let me down the fucking stairs in me own fucking home, Mrs. Fahy was shouting at Kilmartin now.

Malone looked like he had fallen into the sea. Minogue followed him outside and watched Sheehy lead Patricia Fahy to the Toyota. Patricia Fahy's father was shouting inside the van. He began kicking the panels as it pulled away. Another unmarked car drew into the curb across the street, splashing a puddle across the full width of the path. Three Guards stepped out. Minogue heard the footsteps clattering down the stairs fast. He turned to see Kilmartin coming out the hall door. The chief inspector had his head down and his arms were out from his side, the hands clawing at the air.

"Get in there to hell and put that woman in order!" he barked at one of the Guards. "She's off the deep end."

Kilmartin had stopped to talk to the Guard. He stayed put, his hands still working, glaring at Minogue. Malone came up the path behind Minogue and stood next to him. Minogue saw Kilmartin's chest heaving. Kilmartin began to walk slowly toward them.

"This . . . is . . . fucking . . . serious . . . messing," Minogue heard him say. Kilmartin stopped abruptly in front of Malone.

"Molly. What the hell are you doing here?"

From the tone, Minogue knew that Kilmartin was still off-balance.

"Helping to arrest the person who murdered Mary Mullen."

Kilmartin's jaws opened for several seconds and then closed. Two teenaged boys on bikes, soaked and euphoric from cavorting around in the cloudburst, Minogue guessed, stopped their bikes next to them.

"What's going on?" one of them asked.

"Bugger off," said Kilmartin. He hadn't taken his eyes from Malone's face. He took a step closer to Malone. His voice was a monotone now.

"What are you doing here then, Molly? You're supposed to be sick or something."

"Oh, right. Yeah. Well, I'm feeling better now, like. Thanks. Yeah."

Loike, thought Minogue. *Betther.* He smiled.

Kilmartin blinked and looked from Malone to Minogue. His hands fell limp by his sides now. Patricia Fahy's mother was shouting again. Kilmartin pivoted to have a look at the doorway and turned back with a look of distaste. The chief inspector had put his hands in his pockets now too. He leaned toward Malone as he spoke.

"You . . ." he began. He stopped and shook his head. "You got beat up, did you?"

"Yeah. But you should see the other fella."

Minogue turned away.

"What other fella?"

"The brother."

"The brother," said Kilmartin. "The brother? Tell me something, Molly. Where is that brother of yours right now?"

Malone stuffed his hands in his pockets and looked down at his sodden shoes.

"Terry?"

"Terry. The fella with your face."

Malone looked up with a frown.

"Terry's in the nick."

Kilmartin glanced at Minogue.

"Your brother got out of the nick was what I heard."

"Oh, he got out all right. Yeah. But he got back in again."

"He got back in again."

"Yeah. It's a different nick, though. It's a treatment facility with a lockup. The new one up by Clanbrassil Street. Drugs and all, you know?"

Kilmartin cleared his throat. Minogue studied faces in the knot of people on the path.

"That's, er, good, Molly," said Kilmartin. "You did the right thing there. He was after falling into the hands of the Egans, I believe."

Kilmartin nodded at Minogue to indicate the source of his intelligence.

"Oh, you heard."

"Matter of fact, himself and myself bumped into him there in a shop belonging to one of the brothers. Looked like he was in a bad state, I don't mind telling you. Right, Matt?"

Minogue nodded. Malone frowned, took his hand out of his pocket and began scratching at his scalp.

"You met Terry?"

"Your man here decided to do a bit of crusading there. Let them know who's boss and all the rest of it. He sort of told me that, well, the Egans wanted to use your brother to get at you. To get at us, I mean. The Guards in general, like."

Malone nodded.

"Well, yeah. They were up to that, all right. Tell me, when were yous up there?"

Kilmartin looked at Minogue.

"Earlier on today," said the Inspector.

"Today? No. You must have gotten your days mixed up. Couldn't have been today."

Minogue shrugged.

"It was today," said Kilmartin. "And well I remember it. Brother of yours is hardly civil to the Guards, is he? He gave us — well, he tried to give us — a bit of a bollocking there."

"Today?"

Kilmartin cleared his throat and took out his cigarettes. Malone looked him in the eye.

"What's the story there, Molly? What are you looking at me like that for? You're the one should be answering the bloody questions here. As a matter of fact, now that I have the both of you here . . ."

Kilmartin's words trailed off. Minogue and Malone both studied the smoke flowing out of Kilmartin's open mouth.

"What?" Kilmartin murmured.

"I got Terry committed yesterday," said Malone. He nodded at Minogue. "His idea. Gets him off the streets. It was either treatment or arrest for assault, right?"

"Right," said Minogue.

"No, no, no," said Kilmartin. "I — wait a minute — Matt, you were there with me . . ."

This time Minogue saw that Kilmartin knew. His eyes opened wide and he leaned in toward the two policemen.

"That wasn't Terry up at the shop, like," said Malone. "That was me."

CHAPTER 28

MINOGUE WIPED AT the smudge again but got nowhere. It had to be from the photocopier. He and Malone had taken her statement, had her charged, and had signed over just before one o'clock. He let the copy of Patricia Fahy's statement drop onto his desk, leaned back until the chair bit into his back, and stretched. Éilis wandered over and dropped a yellow phone-message sheet on the desk.

"Waterford city," she said. "They're far from sure. He was missing for two days. Someone spotted the car under the water yesterday evening and they walking by. The rain delayed them getting it out."

He searched over the note.

"Lost his job, they said . . . . Who reported him missing again?"

"Oh, I forgot to write it in. Sorry, I'm half asleep, so I am. Will I phone them back?"

Minogue shook his head.

"No, I'll do it."

Kilmartin sauntered in from the car park. He had draped a double-breasted jacket over his shoulders. The debonair air puzzled Minogue. Kilmartin looked like a cross between Maurice Chevalier and a bouncer. He surveyed the squad room as though visiting it for the first time.

"Oh, oh," Minogue heard Éilis murmur before she walked off.

Kilmartin seemed to be examining the surfaces of the desks now. He turned to the notice boards and studied them with the respectful interest of a visiting civilian. Minogue decided to test the waters.

"How's Jim this fine morning?"

Kilmartin's brow shot up. He looked over with a smile.

"Oh, fine, thanks, Matt. And how's yourself? Family well?"

"Topping, thanks. Nice jacket there."

Kilmartin looked down at his shoulder.

"Do you like it?"

"I certainly do. Well wear to you."

Kilmartin smiled faintly and returned to his survey of the squad room.

"Nice to have the change of weather, isn't it?"

Like a tourist in the National Gallery, Minogue thought. Should he wait until Kilmartin brought it up before asking how the summit with Serious Crimes and Co. had gone?

"Couldn't be better, Jim. Couldn't be better."

Kilmartin smiled again and squinted close up at a photocopy of Leonardo Hickey's mug shot. His tone was warm and inviting when he spoke.

"Any sign of that trick-acting bastard?"

"He's getting better. He's taking counseling already. Wants to go into acting now, he says, after his taste of the big time lying in that van. He's even willing to take the rap for doing that car. Says those few days changed his life."

Minogue stopped and watched as Kilmartin gently tore down the photo of Leonardo Hickey and crumpled it in his hand.

"It wasn't that Hickey character I was referring to," said Kilmartin.

He began to scrunch up other papers on the notice board.

"Oh, em, Tierney? He's appeared and got remanded —"

"No, no, no. Not him either. No, I saw his statement this morning before I went off to Keane. No, no. His goose is cooked. So's the Fahy one, for that matter."

Was he to expect a compliment from Kilmartin?

"Er, who then, Jim?"

"Your sidekick. Molly. Al Capone. Voh' Lay-bah. The Play Actor."

"I told him to go home and see about his family. He's to phone in before twelve."

Kilmartin seemed to suddenly tire of his task. He looked across at Minogue, the vaguely satisfied smile still playing about his face.

"How'd it go, Jim? The meeting with the task force — Keane and the rest of them?"

Kilmartin opened his eyes wide again. No wonder Éilis had headed for the sanctuary of the ladies' toilet, Minogue thought. Perhaps he should join her.

"Grand thanks. Grand. No problem."

"No, em, questions you couldn't answer?"

"Man dear, there are no questions that I couldn't answer."

"Virgin Birth, then. Start with that one. How'd they do it?"

Minogue's taunt had no noticeable effect. Instead of provoking Kilmartin into wrath, his colleague merely looked down at the floor and shook his head.

"Ah, Matt, Matt. Will you never get sense? Always the wag. Always the tart quips. That's attention seeking, you know. No. Keane and Co. were intrigued, I'll tell you that. Very intrigued. Of course, I was well briefed. I had nothing to worry about, did I?"

Minogue ran his tongue around his upper teeth while he gave Kilmartin the eye.

"Oh, yes," Kilmartin went on. "Got the signal very early on. I knew things were going to go smooth."

"Ah."

"'Ah' yourself. Did you phone him?"

"Phone who?"

"The Iceman. He was sitting up there at the head of the table. Looking very pleased with himself."

"John Tynan?"

"Did you phone him?"

"Yes."

Kilmartin slowly nodded.

"Well, now. I sort of thought so. As I was saying. Tynan set the mood. Do you want to know what happened? Of course you do. Yes, Tynan backed us up to the hilt. What's this he said again? Something about orthodoxy for its own sake . . . Very smart, I remember thinking . . . Ah, I forget. Anyway. It's Keane's stuff now. He thinks he can use the bit in Tierney's statement more than Kenny's. About the source of the drugs, I mean. It's a bit better than hearsay so he might just stuff a warrant with it when they pounce. Says it'll be a handy option for when they put the drop on the Egans."

"The bit about what Mary said on the phone to Tierney?"

"Yup. How she was out of her mind worrying that Eddsy'd come after her if she couldn't come up with the money. Odd she never mentioned Kenny to anyone, says Keane to me later. Who cares, says I."

"Kenny was her own job, I think. She didn't even mention Tierney's name to Kenny when she threatened him with the same Tierney either. She'd learned to keep things in different compartments."

"Um. I think you have it there all right, old bean. Yes. Keane wanted to talk to me all day about the whole thing. So did Daly, the other fella . . . Oh, yes. Well, I left them shaking their heads, so I did. You know the style."

Indeed Minogue did. Few things pleased James Kilmartin more than seeing other Guards slack-jawed about how the Murder Squad closed a case. Keep 'em guessing was so often Kilmartin's byword.

"What a dummy though," said Kilmartin. "Tierney, I mean. Right thick. A sucker."

Minogue sat back and looked out the window. Kilmartin's mood seemed to be holding.

"She turned to him in her hour of need and all that," added Kilmartin.

Minogue's mind went to the canal that night, to Mary Mullen's panicked vigil by the bridge. The minutes must have crawled by for her, worse as each passed. Everything was crumbling about her, slipping away, falling back into the world of fear and violence that she had grown into and struggled to shake free of. Kenny's expression when he had talked about her that night: where did she get the ideas she had about how money was made, from the television or something? She had tried to cross the line but Kenny had left her out there in the night.

"Whatever about Tierney, that Kenny fella should swing for some of this," said Minogue. "I'm going to look it over again and get some advice toward a file."

Kilmartin nodded. Minogue fell back to wondering. And who else could Mary Mullen have turned to? She had learned too well how to shut others out, to keep her secrets and her ambitions free within herself alone. That was what had gotten to Patricia Fahy, that reserve of Mary's, her refusal to admit another into her life. Her determination to win out, to make it.

"Only Tierney," murmured Minogue.

"What?"

"She phoned Tierney because she knew he couldn't turn her down."

"And that's where it went wrong, you know," said Kilmartin. "That's what I decided on the way here in the car. She might have been able to work it out with the Egans. Sure we'll never know. The main thing is the bullet-proof statement from her nibs, Fahy."

Minogue remembered when he too had concluded that Patricia Fahy's statement was what would send her away for murdering her flatmate. It was when Malone had paused during the reading aloud of the statement she had signed, that he, Minogue, had felt eyes on him. They had belonged to Patricia Fahy's lawyer and, for that moment, they had a resigned cast to them.

"So," said Kilmartin. "Any forensic on her helmet yet?"

"No word yet. Maybe I should phone Eimear again."

Kilmartin waved the suggestion away.

"I tell you, Matt, I believe Tierney when he says he didn't know until they got home. I do."

"I sort of believe him myself."

Kilmartin lit a cigarello.

"Sure, how was he to know he'd started the whole thing just by telling the girlfriend, the Fahy one? I mean, he probably thought it was for the best. Let her have a chat with Mary, see if the two women could sort it out. Calm her down a bit maybe."

Minogue nodded his agreement.

"And then he lets her have her way," Kilmartin went on. "Letting her go down to the bridge to talk to Mary first. But did he really think that the Fahy one could sort it out or something? I say he was too scared to go down and talk to her himself."

Minogue looked over at the thoughtful face of his colleague.

"He thought Patricia Fahy could help out. She admits to suggesting it."

Kilmartin blew out a cloud of smoke.

"When she takes off the helmet and Mary sees who it is, that's when the shouting and roaring starts. Patricia Fahy loses her cool and lashes out with the helmet. Bang! And that's that. Some rap off one of those if you're swinging it, man. Ow."

Kilmartin slid his jacket off his shoulder and sat back farther on the desktop. He planted his cigarello between his lips. Minogue looked down at his job list. Éilis returned from the bathroom, nodded at Kilmartin, and threw a quick glance at Minogue.

"How's himself," she said.

"Steady enough, Éilis. For the day that's in it. Count us off operational with the Mary Mullen case now, will you. We'll start back with the hit-and-run John Murtagh has tagged there, rake through the —"

Minogue was closest to the phone. He continued to study Kilmartin's jacket while Iseult talked. A summer-weight wool, he guessed. That'd be two hundred quid's worth.

"Did you hear me?"

"Sorry," he said. "I was distracted. Half-twelve, you said."

"And we'll bring the stuff. The rolls and things. You like red, right?"

"With soda water, yes."

"And we'll bring something waterproof for the grass."

"Good."

"You know where I mean now? You won't get lost?"

"Yes. No. By the trees, back from the fence near the camels."

"And we'll pick up Ma, don't you worry."

They had a car, he had nearly forgotten.

"I won't worry."

He watched Kilmartin's slow, reflective movements with his cigarello, his gaze set on the window. The chief inspector was certainly keeping him guessing as to his real mood.

"It's just a picnic, okay?"

"That's what you told me."

"No questions. If he wants to say something, then that's okay. Right?"

"Right."

"Don't take sides."

"Any further orders?"

"I want everybody to have a good time, Da. That's all."

"Are we there to praise Pat or to bury Pat?"

"Stop it! I'm calling it off if you're in one of those humors!"

"Okay, okay. So I know how you are anyway. Now tell me, how's Pat?"

"He's better."

"Was he sick or something?"

"Very funny. I'll tell you one thing, he's tired."

"Sick and tired?"

"No, silly! He couldn't sleep the last week. He was waiting outside the door all night. I got up and there he was. Sitting in the car. I nearly fainted."

"That's nice."

"He actually looks really wrecked. Don't say it to him though, do you hear?"

"'Pat, I was told not to comment on the fact that you look wrecked.'"

"Don't get mad at him, Da! He's worn out from worrying and everything. Honestly! You can be very cutting sometimes."

Minogue closed his eyes for several seconds.

"Are you the same woman who was offering to drop-kick Pat into Dublin Bay?"

"Ah, people say things!"

Minogue held out the receiver and looked at it for a moment.

"What's the verdict on Pat then? A stay of execution or what?"

"It won't be fancy wine now. We're on a budget, so don't expect a garden party."

We're on a budget, he thought. He let the receiver slide down his hand and caught it. He lifted it to his ear again. Kilmartin still wore that same smile. He pushed three of the buttons for Kathleen's work number and stopped. Kilmartin raised his eyebrows and let out the smoke in balls. Minogue put down the receiver.

"Well," said Kilmartin.

"Well," said Minogue. "The phrase 'we're on a budget' was used. What do you think?"

Kilmartin rubbed his lower lip with his thumbnail.

"Sounds serious. She back with her fella?"

"Yes."

"You still like him?"

"Yes, I do."

Kilmartin looked away from the window. He winked at Minogue.

"That's it then. Case adjourned, man."

Minogue supposed that James Kilmartin was right. He did not tell him that. He looked out the window himself then until his eyes lost their focus. Some time later he was vaguely aware of Kilmartin awakening to his normal mien. The chief inspector stood and stretched.

"Christ," said Kilmartin in mid-groan. "I must be coming down with something. Staring out the bloody window half the day. Getting as bad as you, nearly. Mooning about the place. Come on, let's tidy up on Mary Mullen."

"Yes, Jim."

Kilmartin looked down at Minogue.

"One thing," he said. Minogue broke his gaze on the view outside. He had been imagining a baby. He looked up at Kilmartin. There was a strange light in his eyes.

"When you talk to Molly or when you see Molly, give him a message for me?"

"To be sure I will. After I hear what it is, Jim."

"I don't want to talk to him for awhile. And don't get the idea that I'm still sore after that stunt. I'm not pushed about that. The message is this: one word."

"Does it start with an F?"

Kilmartin's lips twitched a little.

"Not that one. Not this time at any rate. No. A very simple word. They even use it in Dublin. Your job is to make sure that Molly has the wit to fully grasp what this one simple word means, all it entails. It'll have a bad effect on his health and well-being if he does not hear and act accordingly. Are you with me?"

Minogue nodded. He threw a glance at Éilis. She sat stone-faced, pretending not to listen. Small creases appeared by Kilmartin's eyes.

"Tell that Dublin bowsie this: Quits."